ALSO BY TASHA ALEXANDER

In the Shadow of Vesuvius

Uneasy Lies the Crown

Death in St. Petersburg

A Terrible Beauty

The Adventuress

The Counterfeit Heiress

Behind the Shattered Glass

Death in the Floating City

A Crimson Warning

Dangerous to Know

Tears of Pearl

A Fatal Waltz

A Poisoned Season

And Only to Deceive

Elizabeth: The Golden Age

THE DARK HEART OF FLORENCE

THE DARK HEART OF FLORENCE

Tasha Alexander

MINOTAUR BOOKS
NEW YORK

This is a work of fiction. All of the characters, organizations, and events portrayed in this novel are either products of the author's imagination or are used fictitiously.

First published in the United States by Minotaur Books, an imprint of St. Martin's Publishing Group

www.minotaurbooks.com

Designed by Omar Chapa.

Library of Congress Cataloging-in-Publication Data

Names: Alexander, Tasha, 1969– author.
Title: The dark heart of Florence / Tasha Alexander.
Description: First Edition. | New York : Minotaur Books, 2021. | Series: Lady Emily mysteries ; 15
Identifiers: LCCN 2020053685 | ISBN 9781250622068 (hardcover) | ISBN 9781250622075 (ebook)
Subjects: GSAFD: Mystery fiction.
Classification: LCC PS3601.L3565 D37 2021 | DDC 813/.6—dc23
LC record available at https://lccn.loc.gov/2020053685

Our books may be purchased in bulk for promotional, educational, or business use. Please contact your local bookseller or the Macmillan Corporate and Premium Sales Department at 1-800-221-7945, extension 5442, or by email at MacmillanSpecialMarkets@macmillan.com.

First Edition: 2021

10 9 8 7 6 5 4 3 2 1

For Alexander, whose work on Lucretius was essential to this book. Someday we will visit Florence together.

The deceiver is at the mercy of the one he deceives.

—GIOVANNI BOCCACCIO, *The Decameron*

London,
1903

1

Before plunging into my narrative, I must first state categorically that no reasonable person could have anticipated a murdered corpse turning up in my stepdaughter's bed. I reject all charges of insensitivity lobbed at me following those chaotic and desperate days in Florence. It should also be noted that Kat was not in her room, let alone her bed, during the moment in question, a detail that surely must mitigate the situation.

It all began on a seemingly mundane Tuesday. As a rule, I do not take naps. Much though I appreciate the wisdom of a siesta in hot, southern climates, it can hardly be justified on our sceptered isle. Our rocky shore may beat back the envious siege, but given our geography, we're more likely to be plagued with cold rain than a lethargy-inducing heat wave. On that day, however, I did succumb to slumber, and I lay the blame entirely on my dear friend Cécile du Lac. A relentlessly elegant Parisian of a certain age who, after more than a dozen years of friendship still hides from me her family's involvement in the French Revolution, Cécile had long harbored a passion for bohemian sensibilities. The latest manifestation of this leaning was her decision to embrace the designs of a Belgian architect, Henry van de Velde. Not the designs of his buildings but of ladies' dresses. For reasons incomprehensible to me, he turned part of his attention to fashioning gowns in a reform sort of style, not requiring a corset. Granted, no one who has spent decades encased in such undergarments would mourn their demise, at least not entirely, yet one might also hope for something rather less frumpy than Mr. van de Velde's creations.

Cécile, a fellow devotee of the cosmopolitan House of Worth, sent a van de Velde original cut to my measurements and implored me to give myself the gift of comfort at least once before condemning the dress to flames. And so, that morning, Meg, my maid, lowered it over my head, frowning the entire time. Fitted only through the bosom, its fabric—dark red velvet—flowed freely to the floor, enabling the wearer to both breathe freely and slouch. Attractive it might not be, but what did it matter when I planned to spend the day in my library, reading?

I went downstairs intent on doing just that, only to find that for me, certain books might indeed require a corset. Relishing the freedom of movement Mr. van de Velde's gown allowed, I stretched out on a long chesterfield sofa and fell asleep before I'd got through a dozen pages. Sometime later, a voice I did not recognize woke me.

"The world can change in an instant. It falls on gentlemen like us to determine the course of that change. What you have done, Hargreaves, is nothing short of saving the empire. His Majesty is beyond grateful."

I was about to sit up and announce myself when my husband's reply stopped me cold.

"I fear it may not be enough," Colin said. "The danger is alleviated but not eliminated."

I do not condone eavesdropping. It is underhanded; dishonorable; and something a lady should never, ever do. It is also undeniably useful. Furthermore, when one is thrust accidentally into a theoretically private conversation, as was the case that October afternoon, it is less morally dubious. I lay perfectly still, not allowing myself even to blink.

"Alleviated enough that you are free to deal with the situation in Florence. Once that's in hand, you can return your focus to this other business. But while you're away, the prescribed methods to contact me, yes? This is not the time for open communication."

"Quite. I'll spend as little time as possible abroad, sir. This won't prove a distraction."

"I'd choose a different tack, Hargreaves. Bring your wife and give every appearance of this being a holiday. Gaze on Michelangelo's masterpieces and climb the steps to the lantern of Brunelleschi's dome."

"You believe there's a connection between this and the other?" Colin asked.

"We cannot afford to dismiss the possibility. Your daughter is safely at Oxford, is she not?" My husband must have nodded; the other man continued. "I'll put two on to watch her. She'll be in no danger while you're away."

"Thank you, sir." Colin's clipped tone told me he was not wholly convinced.

"Three, if you'll feel better. And make use of Benton-Smith. He's at Lake Garda, but could get to Florence easily enough."

"I shall get in touch with him at once."

The conversation descended into social niceties as they parted ways. Only when I heard their footsteps trail through the library and out into the corridor did I sit up and lift the book resting on my chest. I have never hidden my love for sensational literature and have long counted Mary Elizabeth Braddon's novels among my favorite diversions. Today, however, I had turned to William Le Queux, not one of his myriad detective stories but the breathless tales of Duckworth Drew, "chief confidential agent of the British Government, and next to Her Majesty's Secretary of State, one of the most powerful and important pillars of England's supremacy." They were not quite so engaging as I had hoped—as evidenced by my having fallen asleep reading them—but I could not help notice the similarities between Mr. Drew's work for his country and that of my husband's.

From almost the moment he completed his studies at Cambridge—Trinity College—Colin had served as one of Queen Victoria's most trusted agents, charged with assisting the Crown in matters requiring a modicum of discretion. Or so I had understood early in our relationship. As the years passed, it became clear his work entailed more than helping aristocrats out of embarrassing situations; and since the succession of Edward VII to the throne, official demands on his time had increased steadily. Naturally, he was not at liberty to discuss any of this with me, and naturally that only heightened my curiosity. As there existed no legitimate method for me to satisfy this curiosity, I indulged my imagination and turned to Le Queux.

I closed the book, rose from the chesterfield, and crossed the room to my desk, where I was standing when my husband entered.

"Hello, where did you come from?" he asked, drawing a hand through his tousled dark curls, his manner breezy and casual. "I thought you were upstairs."

"I've just come down." As the words came out of my mouth I wondered why I had decided to lie. "Have we had a visitor? I thought I heard the door."

"Sir John Burman proffering an invitation to a shooting party. I declined for a multitude of reasons. He sends you his regards." His own falsehood rendered mine more palatable.

More than a year had passed since Katharina von Lang, Colin's hitherto-unknown grown daughter, had disrupted our bucolic family life. My initial acquaintance with her proved challenging to us both, but I had done my best to welcome her into our household. Although the specter of her late mother, whom Colin had loved long before we met, still haunted me, I found Kat's quick wit and intelligence endearing, at least when she resisted the urge to sermonize about wicked stepmothers. The situation called for understanding. She had lost a mother she'd hardly known; that she would not immediately embrace me came as no shock.

Introducing her to our three sons, Henry, Richard, and Tom (currently all at Anglemore Park, our country estate in Derbyshire; I had come to London alone to meet my husband upon his return from weeks abroad), had proved shockingly easy. At seven years old (technically our ward, Tom, was a few months older than his brothers), none of them had much interest in a girl of any age. They dismissed her as a boring grown-up until Henry realized her potential as a useful ally. In possession of a fortune of her own (albeit one her mother's solicitor would control until she turned twenty-five), she could buy sweets without begging for spending money. They accepted her without reservation. Less simple was introducing her to my mother.

Lady Catherine Bromley could be accurately described neither as understanding nor accepting, particularly when it came to matters that might prove socially embarrassing, a camp into which illegitimate children unquestionably fall. Colin and I broke the news to her at my parents' home in Kent. She fainted and refused to be brought around for forty-five minutes; the deep frown frozen on her face the entire time told me she was not, in fact, unconscious. My father, accustomed to her dramatics, was unmoved. He called for his newspaper and read it without giving her so much as a passing glance until she made a great display of coming round, at which point she insisted we bring Kat to her the next day. Their meeting did not go quite as I had expected.

"No, no, my dear, you must not adopt so coarse a nickname. Katharina is much more elegant, suitable for the daughter of a countess," my mother had said.

"I shall rely on you, Lady Bromley, to guide me through society. London is so different from a convent school."

Kat's effort to torment me by manufacturing a closeness to my own mother could not have been more misguided. She tried, though, and spent several months under a most unpleasant tutelage before recognizing her error and decamping to St. Hilda's, Oxford. This suited me well, as my friend Margaret Michaels, wife of an Oxford don, had recently given birth to an adorable baby boy. This having led to *inconceivably tragic boredom* (her words), she welcomed Kat into her household, delighted at having someone new to converse with, even if Kat's interests did not intersect with Margaret's passion for Latin.

"I do wish I hadn't missed Sir John," I said to my husband, turning my thoughts back to the present. "Such an amusing gentleman."

Colin's eyebrows shot nearly to his hairline. "I'm afraid I see rather less of his humor than of his devotion to king and country."

I fluttered my eyes. "Surely you don't expect a silly girl like me to be more concerned with work than amusement?"

"You're dreadful, Emily." He took my hand and raised it to his lips, his dark eyes intense. "You know I would tell you more about my work if it were possible. That I can't is in no way a comment on either your intelligence or your gender."

"I know, I know, it's not me. You can't take anyone into your confidence."

He shifted uneasily and sighed. "It's a matter of—"

I put my palm on his cheek. "I'm only teasing you. I know how important your work is." I felt guilty for having overheard his conversation. "Surely Sir John wouldn't object to you taking a little holiday after all the weeks you've just spent doing heaven only knows what while I waited, not asking a single question."

"My dear, in all the years that I have known you, you've never gone more than two hours together without asking impertinent questions about my work."

"I had rather hoped you find it endearing," I said.

"I do." He pulled me close and kissed me. "As things stand, Sir John himself made the same suggestion of a holiday. What would you say to Florence?"

"A busman's holiday, then, that involves determining who broke into Kat's house there?"

"How do you know about that?" he asked.

"Davis knows better than to hide burglaries from me." My incomparable butler had been with me longer than Colin, and while he objected to some—many—of my unconventional habits, I never doubted his stalwart devotion. My husband raised his eyebrows again, and now it was my turn to sigh. "I can't wrongly impugn Davis. He didn't tell me. I knew you'd received a telegram. When you didn't mention it, I read it for myself."

"When? It was in my study—"

"On your desk, where I perched while watching you solve a particularly egregious chess problem. You were too focused to notice me pick it up."

"I'm ashamed it was chess, not you, that distracted me so," he said, pulling me even closer.

"I wouldn't be so underhanded as to use my wiles to distract you," I said. "That would be unfair."

"No secret of the realm could remain safe."

"I shall bear that in mind. Now, tell me everything."

Along with a substantial fortune, Kat's mother had left her daughter a palazzo in Florence not far from the Uffizi Gallery. Kat had planned to live there, but upon learning the identity of her father the previous year, decided to locate him first. Needless to say, Colin objected to the idea of his newly found offspring living abroad, alone and unprotected. He persuaded her to come to England with us and was confident her studies at Oxford would keep her from returning to the Continent. At least for now.

"If you read the telegram, you know as much as I," he said. "The house has been broken into twice, but so far as anyone can tell, nothing was stolen either time."

"Which suggests something other than an ordinary burglar."

"It might be nothing more than an incompetent thief who is easily scared off. I'd feel better looking into it myself, and it gives us an excuse to explore Florence," he said. "You ought to invite Cécile to accompany us. It's been too long since we've seen her."

I kept every muscle in my face as still as a statue. Cécile had not only spent New Year with us but had hosted us for a fortnight in Paris not two months ago. That Colin wanted her to join us told me in no uncertain terms that there was more to this break-in than he was letting on; he wanted me to have a friend to keep me occupied while he worked. I once again resorted to fluttering my eyelashes and then cooed over his suggestion, leaving him in no doubt that I was onto him. He said nothing, only leaned forward as if to kiss me, before changing course and sweeping me into his arms so that he could carry me upstairs to our room.

It was an excellent attempt at a distraction, one that worked almost flawlessly. He forgot, however, that despite his talent as a cricketer, I could play the long game better than he. After he'd drifted into a blissful sleep, I remained awake, already plotting my strategy for Florence.

Florence, 1480

2

Any discussion of Florence in those already fabled days must begin with the acknowledgment of it as the most glorious city in the world. Here, learned men debated Neoplatonism while the most sublime artists in history brought their work to ever-greater heights. There was no better time—or place—to be alive. Only a year or so ago, our leader, Lorenzo de' Medici, il Magnifico, upon learning that King Ferrante of Naples was scheming to assassinate him, rushed straight to the citadel of his enemy to demand an explanation. Not only did he survive the encounter, he emerged with the king as an ally. This is the sort of character necessary to impress us Florentines.

These were days when anything seemed possible. We did not feel bound by the rules that governed the world's more mundane places; we took for granted our exceptionalism. Our building materials came from our city, the sandstone of our houses quarried within the town's medieval walls and held together with mortar formed with sand from the Arno. Those golden-brown façades hid the monstrous arrogance behind the quest for our cathedral's magnificent dome, designed before anyone knew how it might be built. Yes, the Duomo glorified God, but one could not separate the achievement from the genius of the men behind it. We all marveled at Brunelleschi's creation, never balking at his background as a goldsmith and clockmaker. We were not trapped by our pasts. At least our men weren't.

For most girls, the city was less vibrant. They stayed inside, where they would not risk bringing dishonor to their families, waiting to be told who they would marry, warned against even being seen looking out the windows of the palazzi in which they dwelled. But I, Mina Portinari, had grown up with a freedom shared by few of my peers, thanks to my unconventional grandfather Teo Portinari, an extraordinarily learned man who, after serving the pope, embarked on a quest to help Cosimo de' Medici and his heirs find books lost since the days of antiquity. When he returned to his native city, the upper echelons of society embraced him. While my friends learned how to run complicated households, my grandfather taught me to read Latin and Greek and took me to il Magnifico's villa to visit his giraffe. I fed it an apple, delighted at the feeling of the beast's impossibly long tongue against my hand. Nonno let me dine at his table with artists and great thinkers, my parents too busy with their own lives to take much notice. His guests called me charming and complimented my bright blond hair, competing to see who could bring forth my eager laughter. Until I grew old enough to stir in them other longings.

That was when my mother interfered. Which explains why I have no more intellectual evenings. Instead, I help her balance household accounts, manage servants and slaves, and am only allowed out of our palazzo to go to church or, accompanied by my mother, to visit friends. When I complained to my compatriots, they teased me mercilessly. I was living the way they had always done, and they had no sympathy for my plight, leaving me to wonder if never having known the delights of academic conversation would be preferable to missing them so keenly.

Almost by accident, I started spending more time in the confessional, an action that bore no relation to the sin, or lack thereof, in my life. I was not always kind to my brothers. I sometimes disobeyed my mother. I often fell asleep while at my prayers. But, fundamentally, I considered myself a virtuous person. I feared God and obeyed His commandments. Yet I found I was saying more in confession than I intended. Not that I had been hiding sins. Rather, I had settled into a habit of giving arduous explanations for my misdeeds, to the point that Father Cambio, a priest at Santa Trinita, the church where my family heard Mass, started to laugh.

"How old are you, Mina?" he asked.

"Sixteen last month. How old are you?"

"Thirty-two."

"So ancient! I would not have guessed."

He did not balk at my impertinence. "You're old enough to be married. Has your mother spoken to you about this?"

"More than I would like."

"What would you prefer?"

"I'd prefer she let me return to dining with my grandfather and his humanist friends. Is that a sin?"

He laughed again. "No, in and of itself, it is not a sin. But you ought to be careful about the company you keep, lest you be led astray."

"So far as I can surmise, the only imminent danger I face is succumbing to boredom after repeated exposure to the minutiae of household management."

"When you marry, your husband will rely on you to handle all such matters. It is a critical responsibility. We are not all so fortunate as your grandfather when it comes to our daily lives. Most of us will never comb the libraries of German monasteries in search of ancient manuscripts."

"I never dared hope for a life half so interesting."

He studied my face, his eyes full of sympathy. "I have an idea that might help. When I see you next for confession, I will have a book for you, something we can read and discuss."

I felt a thrill of emotion as I walked up the church steps the following week. Books had always held an important place in my life, and there had never been a shortage of them in our home. My father, a wealthy wool merchant, considered them essential household objects but more out of a desire to appear cosmopolitan and educated than because they stirred his intellect. Like all successful businessmen in Florence, he cared very much about enhancing his family's reputation, and our city valued a classical education almost as much as it did money. For me, though, books spoke to my soul. I needed them more than food or water. Or so I believed at the time. But when I saw the title of the slim volume Father Cambio pressed into my hand, I felt only disappointment.

"You do not like it?" he asked.

"It's not that," I said. Petrarch's *De vita solitaria—On the Life of Solitude*—was not what I had expected. "Petrarch . . ."

"You wanted his poetry." Father Cambio smiled. Despite his age, he was an attractive man, with dark hair and green eyes, built more like a knight than a priest. A bit of a waste, I thought. "I could hardly be the one to encourage you to drink in his adulation of the fair-haired Laura, whose own locks couldn't have been brighter than yours."

My face flamed. "No, it's only—"

"We neither of us is here for poetry. Come, I shall hear your confession."

That day, I did not speak so long to him as had become my habit, nor did I feel lighter after he granted me absolution. This left me with a lingering confusion. Back at home, I opened the book. *I believe that a noble spirit will never find repose save in God, in whom is our end, or in himself and his private thoughts, or in some intellect united by a close sympathy with his own.* Petrarch suggested that leaving a crowded city was an excellent idea for one seeking repose in God, no doubt a view influenced by his own family's exile from Florence. But how did this pertain to my life? I could no more leave Florence than I could choose my own husband; what was the point to contemplating either? Furthermore, the concept of finding repose in God sounded tedious to me. I did not much care for solitude in those days. Then, the poet suggested that solitude did not preclude friendship, and as I continued to read, his prose offered a welcome balm for my turbulent emotions. *It will never be my view that solitude is disturbed by the presence of a friend, but that it is enriched. If I had the choice of doing without one or the other, I should prefer to be deprived of solitude rather than of my friend.*

These sentences grabbed me, opening my mind to the idea that two seemingly contradictory positions might be reconciled in a most satisfactory manner. I longed to speak to someone about this, longed for the company of my grandfather and his friends, but had no one but my brothers to whom I could turn.

Until I went back to confession, where Father Cambio awaited me, ready to discuss more than my as yet underwhelming sins.

Florence, 1903

3

Despite the multitudinous descriptions penned in both poetry and prose, no account of Florence can adequately capture the serene essence of the place. It possesses none of the outlandish beauty for which Venice is famous, instead sits elegantly awash in soft gold on the banks of the Arno River, its backdrop the blue peaks of the Chianti Mountains. The Piazzale Michelangelo—built above the city on a hill in 1869, when Florence was the capital of the newly unified Italy—provides an incomparable view and is where one ought to begin every visit, letting the home of Dante and Michelangelo, Botticelli and Leonardo da Vinci, sink into one's soul. For that is what Florence does, undulating gently through one's body, taking possession of everything it touches, satisfied only once it has reached the core. Venice grabs one in an instant; Florence seduces more slowly.

Yet even upon first arriving, one understands, in some fundamental, almost primal, way that this is a city of bankers, bankers and merchants who held most of the wealth in the Renaissance world. Perhaps this is why its beauty is more reserved than that of Venice. At least on the exterior.

Colin and I had broken our journey in Paris, where we collected Cécile (along with her two tiny dogs, Caesar and Brutus). We arrived in Florence at the Stazione Centrale Santa Maria Novella in the midst of a downpour—not the time to take in the view from the Piazzale

Michelangelo—so I ordered our carriage straight to Kat's house, a mile away in the Via Porta Rossa. Its imposing medieval sandstone façade towered above as we ducked through large arched doors into a vaulted loggia where a serious-looking middle-aged woman, as wide as she was tall, and a willowy young maid welcomed us. The latter grinned and nodded a greeting; the former frowned at my husband.

"Signore Hargreaves, it has been many years. This is your wife, I presume?" Her withering glare left no doubt as to her opinion of me.

Colin kissed her on both cheeks. "Yes, Signora Orlandi, and there's no need to be severe. If you can't behave, I'll book us rooms at the Grand Hotel Continental and never see you again."

The signora flitted her hand in a quick, dismissive gesture. "You men are even worse about deciding who to love than we women. Who am I to judge? It has been many, many years since we lost the contessa." She gestured to the girl next to her. "This is Tessa. She is learning English, but only knows a bit so you will have to be patient with her."

"A very little *inglese*," the girl said, smiling. Her golden hair and slim figure brought to mind Botticelli's depiction of Venus in his *Primavera*. I extended my hand to her and introduced myself in Italian, which prompted an excited response from her, only half of which I could understand.

"Tessa grew up in a small village near Pisa. She speaks the *dialetto toscano*—the Tuscan dialect," Signora Orlandi said. "Your Italian is good, Lady Emily. You will have no trouble picking it up. It is not so different from what you already know." There was a begrudging admiration in her tone.

"I've long admired your nation for adopting Dante's vernacular as its own," I said. "I will always prefer the sound of Tuscan to that of Neapolitan."

She squinted her dark, almost black, eyes. *"Il diavolo non è nero come si dipigne."* The devil is not as black as he is painted.

"That's a proverb, Signora Orlandi, not Dante," Colin said. *"Ella è quanto de ben pò far natura; per essemplo di lei bieltà si prova."* She is the sum of nature's universe. / To her perfection all of beauty tends.

She threw back her head and laughed. "I will never argue with a man so much in love. It is good to have you back, signore, especially after these dreadful break-ins. Come inside before you catch a chill in this damp. Signora du Lac, your champagne arrived yesterday. I have a bottle ready for you."

Cécile, who on principle refused to drink anything but champagne (except first thing in the morning), sent her preferred vintage ahead whenever she traveled. She nodded appreciatively at the housekeeper. "I find myself already *innamorato* with Firenze." Caesar barked, as if agreeing with his mistress. Brutus showed no sign of interest.

The housekeeper led us out of the loggia and into a courtyard, where we mounted a staircase and climbed up one flight. At the top, a covered gallery landing skirted the perimeter of the house's interior. Each floor above was arranged identically.

"The Sala dei Pappagalli—the room of parrots—is the warmest in the house at the moment," Signora Orlandi said, ushering us inside, where a large stone fireplace boasted a most welcome roaring blaze. "Tomorrow the sun will come out and all will be better. October is not usually so cold." The ceiling loomed high above us, its heavy beams and painted trusses complementing the walls, which were decorated in red and blue geometric shapes that would have felt familiar to any fourteenth-century resident of the city. Above the pattern, the artist had painted a lush band of trees with parrots in them.

I dropped onto one of the leather chairs in front of the fire while Colin opened the bottle of champagne chilling on a table in the middle of the room and poured a glass for Cécile.

"You would prefer something warm?" Signora Orlandi asked me. I thanked her and requested tea. She and Tessa set off for the kitchen just as the third member of the household staff, a young man called Fredo, entered. He explained that he was responsible for all work requiring a masculine touch and that he was the only person to have nearly seen the person who had twice broken into the house.

"There is little to tell that you do not already know from my telegram, signore. I only noticed the first incident because the intruder knocked over a stack of pots in the kitchen. The noise woke me and I made chase, but he had already fled downstairs and out the front door."

"Is the kitchen not downstairs?" I asked.

"No, Lady Emily, it is on the third floor."

"How curious you Italians are," Cécile said, taking stock of the young man. His age precluded him from being of much interest to her—she believed strongly that no man was worth anything before the age of forty—but that would not stop her from enjoying his swarthy good looks. Fredo met her appreciative gaze without hesitation and grinned.

"After the second time he came in, I took to sleeping in the loggia," he said. "That way I could hear anyone who tried to get in."

"Assuming they entered through the front door," Colin said.

"There's no other point of entry. There are no windows on the ground floor except in the loggia."

"What about a door from the alley?" Colin asked. "Is there no servants' entrance?"

"The Contessa von Lang did not want anyone to enter the house except from the front. She had every other door bricked up."

Kat's mother, the countess in question, had met Colin in the course of her work as an agent of the Austrian government. The house in Florence was the place to which she could escape, unnoticed, when she wanted respite and privacy. Possessing a sharp intelligence and fully aware of the dangers of her work—she was eventually killed in the line of duty—she would never have tolerated an unsecure residence.

Signora Orlandi returned, but not with my tea. "Signore Hargreaves, there is a gentleman here to see you." She handed Colin a card, which he glanced at and nodded.

"Excellent. Send him in at once." He turned to Fredo, dismissing him. "We will speak again. Thank you."

"Were you expecting someone?" I asked.

"Yes, a colleague, Darius Benton-Smith. He was at school and then Cambridge, but before me. He's quite possibly the most charming gentleman on earth. You'll adore him, Cécile."

"How old is he?" she asked.

"Old enough," Colin said, knowing her proclivities.

"I do believe, Monsieur Hargreaves, that you, too, are finally now old enough. I had not realized that until this moment. How very interesting."

The door swung open and Mr. Benton-Smith stepped into the room, pausing to bow the moment he saw Cécile and me. "Good heavens, Hargreaves, you should have warned me you'd brought ladies with you. I was not prepared for such an onslaught of loveliness."

My husband made introductions, while the newcomer kissed our hands and bestowed upon my friend and me a barrage of earnest compliments. He was ever so slightly taller than Colin, with dark blond hair and green eyes that flashed with flecks of amber. His features could be lauded as a study of English handsomeness.

"I'm more than sorry to arrive and disrupt this enchanting party. Can you ladies ever forgive me?"

"Has a woman yet been born who could answer that question in the negative when posed by you, Monsieur Benton-Smith?" Caesar and Brutus, seeing their mistress's attention so thoroughly fixed on someone other than themselves, rushed for Mr. Benton-Smith's ankles and nipped at them furiously. He crouched down and spoke to the little dogs in a voice that would have soothed even an enraged lion. Caesar succumbed to him at once, Brutus following half a heartbeat later, neither objecting when he scooped them up and lifted them to his face, accepting their enthusiastic kisses. "You need do nothing more to prove your worthiness to me, monsieur," Cécile said. "They do not usually welcome newcomers with such eager passion."

"You must call me Darius."

"I wouldn't hold out much hope," Colin said. "I've known her for more than a dozen years and she still won't call me by my Christian name."

Mr. Benton-Smith returned the dogs to the floor. "Hargreaves, is there somewhere we speak privately? I'm afraid work is rearing its unfortunate head."

"There's no need," Cécile said. "Kallista and I will make a little exploration of the house and leave you to your work." Almost the moment she met me, Cécile adopted the nickname bestowed on me by my late first husband and since had never called me Emily.

"That's very kind of you," Colin said. "I shall have your tea brought to wherever you wind up."

"Monsieur Hargreaves, I would deny you very little, but must ask, in return, that you never, ever suggest I would drink tea." Cécile took her empty glass and the bottle of champagne, smiling at Mr. Benton-Smith as she glided out of the room. I came behind, raising an eyebrow at my husband before closing the door behind us.

Tessa, tea tray in hand, was upon us almost at once, so we postponed our exploration for the moment and followed her up two flights of stairs, across the gallery landing, and past the kitchen to a narrow and brightly painted corridor that led to a cozy room. Like the one in which we'd left the gentlemen, its walls were covered in elaborate painted designs. Wooden shutters in the wall near the stone fireplace stood open to reveal a niche that held a statue of the Virgin Mary holding the baby Jesus. A single chandelier hung between painted beams on the ceiling, glowing gold, but not providing a great deal of light. After depositing her tray on a convenient table, Tessa stoked the fire and then left us alone.

"Kallista, Kallista. We live in such interesting times, do we not?" She took away the tea I had poured, picked up the remaining cup from the tray, and filled it with champagne before passing it to me. "The addition of Monsieur Benton-Smith to our party is a welcome one. I did not suspect your husband's interest in coming here had to do with his work, but that is now undeniable. I assume you know more. What's going on?"

"My knowledge of the situation is limited in the extreme." I recounted for her the conversation I'd overhead between Colin and Sir John.

"Ah, as if Monsieur Hargreaves, who is already impossibly handsome, needed something to make him even more intriguing. We've known all along his work was both secret and important, but are you telling me he holds the fate of his beloved British Empire in his hands?"

"I wouldn't go quite that far, Cécile, but these break-ins are more significant than we're being led to believe."

"*Bien sûr,* particularly if they require the services of two agents of the Crown. I must say, Kallista, I had never expected to be faced with a pair of such handsome spies. Are they spies, do you think?"

"I don't know that I'd go that far," I said, "although I have been reading a book that is starting to make me think otherwise—"

A piercing scream interrupted, startling me so that I dropped my champagne-filled teacup. I raced out of the room and looked down to the courtyard below. There, sprawled at impossible angles, lay a dark-haired man, his eyes open but vacant, staring but not seeing, a frayed rope tied around his torso.

Florence, 1480

4

Confession must ordinarily be the least-enjoyed sacrament—other than, I suppose, last rites—but over the subsequent weeks, I began to look forward to it with increasing anticipation, until I had to admit I was not using the ritual as intended, more interested in asking questions about Petrarch than on my own mundane sins. But as I thought about it, I started to worry that they were no longer so mundane, and found myself unable to sleep, wondering if I were on the cusp of imperiling my immortal soul. The time had come to confront Father Cambio, who, when I next came to him, listened to my concerns, then spoke in a tone of quiet reassurance.

"You are not making bad confessions, Mina, but you are right that we should separate our discussion of books from the sacrament. Here is what I propose: after we are finished here and you've made your Act of Contrition, we will take a turn around the church and discuss Petrarch."

We adopted this practice, and after a few weeks had finished with *De vita solitaria*. Father Cambio lent me his copy of Cicero's speeches. I found his powerful rhetoric deeply moving. After that, we moved to Plato, then Aristotle. Both fed my infinite curiosity. From there, I suggested *The Decameron*, which caused the good father to furrow his brow and shake his head.

"There is no denying the satisfaction that comes from reading a good story, and Boccaccio gives us many, but they are not something I would consider appropriate for a young lady." His reaction did not surprise me—I had read enough of my oldest brother's copy to know it contained more than a few ribald bits—but I blushed nonetheless, suddenly aware of a warm and not altogether unpleasant sensation coursing through me. Father Cambio made no mention of my crimson cheeks, but set me to reading excerpts from St. Augustine's *Confessions,* starting with the story of the pears.

Augustine, before possessing any interest in becoming saintly, ran with a group of friends that reminded me very much of the unruly gangs that had marauded through Florence until the city's merchants convinced the government that unchecked violence was bad for business. For whatever reason, despite having no interest in eating them, Augustine and his friends decided to steal pears from a tree and then fling them to some nearby hogs.

"Did you give me Augustine as a rebuke for my having wanted to read *The Decameron*?" I asked the following week.

"No," Father Cambio said, "but it is worth giving consideration to how you occupy your mind."

"If you force me to keep reading Augustine, you may find you're pushing me into Satan's waiting arms. Has there ever been a more smug saint? I find him repellent. What right has he to ask us to be holy from the beginning when he had all those years of fun?"

"We are not supposed to enjoy sin, Mina."

"Perhaps, but it's naïve to believe people don't."

"Augustine didn't want the pears," he said. "He knew stealing them was wrong. I would argue he didn't enjoy any of it a bit."

"Maybe if he'd done something more interesting than taking pears for which he had no desire, he would have found pleasure in it."

"I'm afraid this conversation is taking a dangerous turn. Next week, let's turn to Thomas Aquinas, his commentaries on Aristotle's ethics."

I muddled through Aquinas for more than a month. It did not speak to my soul. Even so, the discussion it catalyzed awakened something in me, something that had budded with my contempt for Augustine and now began to blossom. Father Cambio did not tolerate nonrigorous argument, holding me to the highest standards of both logic and rhetoric as he taught me the art of expression. He made me explain why I despised Augustine and then insisted that I defend my position, pushing me to revise and polish it until no obvious weaknesses remained. The exercise stimulated my mind like nothing before. I so enjoyed the art of persuasion that I no longer viewed Augustine as irritating, but rather a much-welcome starting point for biting criticism. No matter what we read, I could find within it either a position to defend or one to savage, and I was good at it. So very, very good at it.

My newly honed skills proved beneficial at home. My brothers were no longer able to trick me into taking their sides in arguments. I could persuade my parents to allow me to do more of what I wanted. And, most significantly, I convinced my slave, Alfia, to stop reporting my behavior to my mother. She now believed that I was a better judge of what was acceptable than the mistress of the house.

And what was the result of my newfound freedom? Did it lead to personal and moral disaster? In fact, it did. In ways I could never have imagined.

Florence,
1903

5

The screaming continued. I gripped the landing's stone railing, leaned over, and saw Tessa two floors below, her high soprano reaching a pitch I feared might shatter glass. Colin and his colleague, having reacted more quickly than Cécile and I, were already most of the way down the stairs. Soon the entire household was in the courtyard, or, at least, sheltered in the gallery rimming it. Braving the rain, I joined my husband, who was crouched next to the body.

"What a hideous way to die," I said.

"The fall didn't kill him," Colin said. "The back of his skull is shattered, but there's no bleeding. He's been dead more than a day."

"At least." Mr. Benton-Smith scowled. "Burman was right to be concerned. I only wish we had come to Florence sooner. Poor Spichio."

"You know him?" I asked.

"Yes, he was a font of useful information, although that makes it sound as if his contributions—" He stopped and swallowed hard, a pained expression on his face. "I would not want to minimize the importance of the work he did for us."

Colin clapped his hand on Mr. Benton-Smith's shoulder. "No one would ever accuse you of that. It was you who ensured his safety, again and again. This just proves the impossibility of perfect security."

"Who is he and why did he need to be kept safe?" I asked.

"I'm afraid I can't disclose the details," Mr. Benton-Smith said. "His work can never be lauded, not publicly, despite the profound impact it had—and will continue to have—on us all."

"I'll make arrangements for the body," Colin said.

"What about the police?" I asked.

"No police." The gentlemen answered in near unison.

"I agree they're often useless, but he's clearly been murdered. It will have to be investigated," I said.

"Cases like this are not handled by local authorities, my dear," Colin said. "No one can know what has happened. His death will be recorded as an accident."

I balked and looked at my husband in disbelief. "Oh, yes, an accident. One cannot walk half a mile without encountering a corpse who has flung himself off a roof these days. I have as little faith in the police as you do, but to suggest that a murder should not be investigated—"

"I never said that. Darius and I will handle it."

"What about his family?" I asked. "What are they to think?"

"They, like everyone else, will believe he suffered a tragic accident."

"That's outrageous!"

"It's part and parcel of the work," Colin said.

I crossed my arms and scowled. "So if you were to die in the line of duty, what would I be told?" I knew his answer before he gave it, and while I could not object in principle, my emotions were another thing entirely. Every atom in my body felt as if it were being torn apart.

"Whatever would cause the least harm to the empire."

"I'd rather know the truth."

"Sometimes that is not possible." He pressed his lips into a firm line as he met my eyes.

"I can be discreet."

"I don't doubt that. Most people believe themselves to be discreet, but it cannot be relied upon. You're soaking wet, Emily. Go inside before you catch a chill. I won't have you missing out on the delights of Florence."

I opened my mouth but found I could not form words until he took me by the arm and led me toward Cécile. "Stop, right now. If you're suggesting that I should play holidaymaker when a murdered man has turned up in your daughter's house—"

"It wasn't a suggestion." He turned to my friend. "Will you please take her inside, Cécile?"

"*Oui, bien sûr,* Monsieur Hargreaves, but—"

"Please, Cécile. This is not the time for questions."

Signora Orlandi stepped forward and ushered us toward the stairs, Tessa following. Fredo stayed behind with the gentlemen.

"Your luggage is in your room, signora," the housekeeper said, "although Tessa has not quite finished unpacking. You will want a warm bath, yes? We will get the water ready as quickly as possible and in the meantime bring you tea."

Recognizing that I would not get anywhere trying to change my husband's mind at the moment and no longer able to ignore the fact that I was shivering with cold, I had to admit a bath was an excellent idea. The chamber on the second floor assigned to Colin and me contained an en suite bathroom, a pleasant surprise, as medieval buildings do not lend themselves to modern plumbing. The facilities were small but more than adequate, even if the copper tub had to be filled by hand, a task handled ably by Tessa, whose lithe figure disguised her strength.

Warm and dry after my ablutions, I was grateful for the girl's assistance with my hair, which, if left to me, would never be controlled. She attacked the task with evident skill and steady hands, but I could see from her pale face that she was upset.

"It's a dreadful thing to see so violent a death." I spoke to her in Italian. "I'm more than sorry you had to face it."

She answered in English. "This house is supposed to be a place of safety. How could this happen here?"

"Your English is flawless. Why did you pretend otherwise?"

"It is bad of me, I know, but I find it useful to let people think I cannot understand them."

"Yet you've shared your secret with me."

"I like you, Lady Emily. I knew immediately I could trust you. This is a place where I must be careful. Secrets abound."

"Florence?" I asked.

"This house. Do you know much about it?"

"Nothing at all."

"You're lucky," she said.

"What did you mean by saying this is supposed to be a safe place?" She was too young to have worked for the countess. I wondered if the palazzo was more than my stepdaughter's would-be home. Did it serve an official purpose? One made use of by my husband and his colleagues?

"Only that the mother of Signorina Katharina is said to have made it so. To keep her daughter safe. It is not wise to let a young lady live alone somewhere that is easy to violate."

Most would argue it was not wise to let a young lady live alone in any circumstances. Regardless, whatever measures the countess had taken, they could not be explained by concern for a daughter whom, at the time, had almost no connection to her mother and certainly had no plans to live in Florence. "Did you recognize the man who fell? Signore Spichio?"

She shook her head. "No. I've never seen him before. He must have slipped, but why was he there? How could he get on the roof?"

I didn't tell her what Colin had said about the poor man being dead before the fall. I had liked her from the first, but didn't entirely believe her explanation as to why she thought the house was safe. And what did it matter if we knew she could speak English? Were her colleagues aware of her fluency? "I haven't the slightest idea, but the gentlemen will figure it all out."

She snorted. "You English are no different from us Italians. The men always keep the fun to themselves."

I could not help but smile. Perhaps she did deserve my trust, at least provisionally. "Then it is down to us to change that. Do you think you could find out anything about Signore Spichio? His profession? Who his family is?"

"I can certainly try. Florence is a small place. But this house . . ."

I waited, but she did not continue. "Yes? What about it?"

"This house holds its secrets. It always has. If the signore's death is part of that, we will never learn anything."

"I'm not sure I understand."

"It started in the days of Savonarola, the monk who preached against the Medici four hundred years ago. I cannot say more now, as I must get back to work, but we will speak again and I will tell you everything I know. Signora du Lac is in the room where you earlier took tea. She will be waiting for you." She made a little curtsy and left the room. I went to Cécile and recounted for her my conversation with the maid.

"What are you saying, Kallista? That this wisp of a girl is a spy?" My friend was feeding bits of sandwiches to her dogs, Caesar getting three for every one given to Brutus. Although she loved both little creatures and would never allow harm to come to either, on occasion she doled out what she believed to be a small measure of justice against Brutus's namesake. The dog accepted this with equanimity.

"I'm not sure I'd go that far, but she's awfully well educated for a maid."

"It's not unusual for servants on the Continent to speak good English, and a city like Florence is full of British travelers."

"I think it's more than that," I said. "We are told the countess secured the house. Would she not also have installed a staff suited to the requirements of her work for Austria?"

"Such measures would be sensible, *oui,* but she has been dead for more than ten years. Signora Orlandi was in her employ, but not Tessa nor Fredo. They are both too young. And given that Katharina only recently learned of her mother's work, she would not have had cause to screen her servants accordingly."

"We don't know who hired them."

"Could Monsieur Hargreaves enlighten us?"

"I wouldn't expect him to be sharing any information for the foreseeable future," I said. "He'd like us to explore Florence as if nothing has happened."

"He knows you too well to expect any such thing."

"Quite, but I must accept that the nature of his work requires my exclusion. That does not, however, mean we must content ourselves with doing nothing. We shall find out whatever we can about Signore Spichio, employing every ounce of discretion we possess. So far as the gentlemen are concerned, we will be carefree holidaymakers. Should we stumble upon something that might help their own investigation, we can then offer our services."

"I've never known you to stumble, at least not accidentally," Cécile said. "And what about Tessa?"

"I'm confident she will prove an able assistant, although we must proceed with caution. We don't know how far we can trust her."

"Does she speak languages beyond Italian and English?" Cécile asked.

"I haven't the slightest idea. I never would have suspected her to mention Savonarola and the Medici. She's better informed than one would expect. I'd like to know why."

"I shall make it my business to learn everything I can about her. No one is better able than I to uncover the truth about servants. It is why I have so little turnover among my own staff."

"Because they're terrified you'll reveal their secrets?"

"*Pas de tout.* That would be gauche. They know I respect them, and that my respect comes from knowing even their secrets. That, Kallista, breeds loyalty." Brutus howled. She bent down and patted his head. "Yes, you poor beast, anyone with your name must lament every mention of loyalty."

"I'm curious as to her comments about the house keeping secrets. I wonder if there's any record of its history."

"Better still, a diary with a complete account of its mysterious past, written in turn by each of its owners. Volume after volume, a new one started the moment the previous was filled."

"Things like that, Cécile, only appear in conveniently plotted novels. I'm afraid we'll have to rely on drier documents."

She shrugged. "I've never been one to abandon hope."

Cécile's optimism had no impact on reality. I summoned Signora Orlandi—who took the appearance of the corpse in the courtyard in such easy stride that I was convinced she had been more colleague than servant to her original employer—and asked for her assistance. Household records, she explained, were kept in the ground floor storerooms. She took us downstairs and directed us to two enormous dusty volumes filled with rows of figures and half a dozen boxes stuffed with old papers, none of which could be described as useful to our purpose.

"Do you know anything about the family who originally lived here?" I asked.

"Their name was Vieri and I believe they were connected to the Medici in some way. You could go to the Laurentian Library and ask there. There may be mentions in the old histories of the city."

"That's an excellent suggestion. Thank you." She left and Cécile and I decided to search the palazzo, in as inconspicuous a manner as possible, letting Colin and Mr. Benton-Smith think we were doing nothing more than exploring our accommodations. They were still outside in the courtyard with the body—a sheet now draped over it—hardly noticing us as we passed them on our way to the stairs. We climbed to the roof terrace that on a clear day would have provided a stunning view over the city, but could not have made a useful point of entry for whoever had flung the corpse into the courtyard. The eaves hung too far over the railing. On the opposite side of the landing from the terrace was Fredo's room.

The three floors below all shared the same basic layout: one large hall that ran the width of the front of the house, one good-sized rectangular room perpendicular to the hall, with a *studiolo* coming off the opposite end, and one trapezoidal bedroom jutting from the back corner. Each of the halls had at least one attached annex. On the ground floor, the storerooms—two of them—and the loggia could be accessed from the courtyard.

Cécile and I methodically made our way through each of the spaces in the palazzo. The house was a glorious example of medieval architecture, and I'd half hoped for a secret compartment in the walls or a hidden door leading into an unknown chamber, but we found no such things. Nor did any of the objects in the rooms, furniture or otherwise, prove revealing. Finished, we trudged back up the stairs to the first floor. There, I slumped against the half wall of the gallery landing and sighed.

"I ought not feel this frustrated," I said. "It's absurd to believe a house holds secrets. I let Tessa's ideas influence me too much."

"Don't your investigations generally include early failure? If not, they would end almost the moment they started," Cécile said. "One must begin somewhere, and at this moment, we have very little to go on."

She kept talking, but I was no longer listening. I had not noticed it before, but graffiti was scrawled on the wall across from me. There was something that looked like a date, *8 di zuge 1509*—I did not recognize *zuge* as an Italian word, but perhaps it was old dialect—then *vene le nuove di Pisa a ore 18½*. Something about the city of Pisa, presumably. Below that, the name *Tomaso Pasera,* under which *1509* was repeated. Scrawled at the bottom was *Non de ponte.*

"Not the bridge . . ." I spoke the words as I contemplated what they might mean.

"Bridge?" Cécile asked. I pointed her to the graffiti. She stepped close to read. "*Mais oui,* eighth of June 1509, during the Italian Wars, when Pisa surrendered to Florence to avoid continued starvation after a long siege."

I looked at her with amazement. "How do you know that?"

"I was briefly entangled with a gentleman called Riccardo who was a scholar of Renaissance history. We spent a fortnight in Pisa. The city's tower may lean, but nothing of Riccardo's ever did."

"Cécile!" I could feel my cheeks color.

"Don't pretend to be shocked, Kallista. It demeans you." She brushed the graffiti lightly with her fingers. "I cannot understand why anyone would allow writing on the wall of his house."

"The Romans did. This could be the natural extension of that." The letters had faded over the centuries, but it was not too difficult to make out. Closer examination revealed much more of it along the length of the wall: dates, names, and the occasional phrase. Some had been rubbed almost clean, others were easier to read. One stood out, partly because the handwriting was neat and elegant, reminiscent of the fonts developed by the humanists of the fifteenth century. More striking was that the language was Latin, not Italian—or, rather, *dialetto toscano*—like the rest.

"'*Quod nequeunt oculis rerum primordia cerni.*'" While I had a decent mastery of ancient Greek, my knowledge of Latin was limited. Or, as Margaret insisted, an absolute disgrace. Fortunately, I knew at least enough to translate this sentence. "The first beginnings of things cannot be distinguished by the eye."

"Prescient?" Cécile asked.

"Let's hope so."

Florence, 1480

6

What felt like an eternity passed from the time Father Cambio told me to read Augustine before, at last, he gave into my pleas for poetry. He rejected both Petrarch and Boccaccio but agreed to Dante.

"Only *Paradiso,*" he said. "I fear you will find hell too appealing. Better that you learn to admire Beatrice, a model of feminine purity and goodness."

I laughed. "If, upon finishing *Paradiso,* I emulate her for two weeks together, can we then read *Inferno*?"

"Hell, Mina, is never a reward."

"We should read the *Commedia* in the order the poet intended so the progression leads us to heaven, not hell. Is that not where the faithful ought to end? Unless you think me so corrupt that I'd prefer the devil to Our Lord."

"You should not speak like that, even in jest. I notice you make no mention of *Purgatorio.*"

"I shall spend enough time there myself," I said. "Or so I assume, given your judgment of me."

"I do not judge you, Mina. That is God's task alone." He stood close to me and stared into my eyes. I could not decide if it was exciting or unnerving. "It is critical to remember that. You and I, we are not divine, only flawed humans."

"I'm more flawed than you."

"I cannot agree."

I looked down, uncomfortable—pleasantly so, if such a thing is possible—at the intensity I saw in him. "I ought not have asked to read *Inferno*."

"I ought not have had the audacity to suggest you are too weak to read all of the *Commedia*. The poem does not romanticize damnation but leads the reader to long for Paradise. We will start at the beginning. I apologize for having so insulted you."

"I feel no insult. You have always cared more about the fate of my soul than I have myself. I should be ashamed, but to claim I am would be a lie. A sin."

"You are young, Mina, and youth, by nature, compels us to feel in possession of a sort of immortality, even though we know this to be impossible. Death resides far away, far enough that it does not trouble us. But it will come, and when it does, it will be too late to change course. Even the Holy Father will be held accountable for his sins."

"I'm certain my own life has proved far less interesting than that of many popes."

Father Cambio frowned and shook his head. "This sort of observation, Mina, is precisely what worries me about you."

"I meant no disrespect."

"You must learn to speak only after giving due consideration to what you plan to say. Unguarded words often prove dangerous."

Now it was my turn to frown. I understood his advice, but must I adopt a manner dictated by restraint? I found very little to admire in caution. I wanted to live with abandon, not to become circumspect and wary. New ideas all but defined Florence in those days, and I had no intention of ignoring any of them, so hungry was I for learning. "I shall do my best."

"It would behoove you to take my warnings more seriously. You don't want to face the difficulties posed by finding oneself on a perilous path. Let me guide you, Mina."

His face had settled into such a grave expression that I could not help but laugh. And then, as the sound echoed through the church, I saw something in his eyes—buried deep but there—that told me he understood, despite his misgivings. Could it be there was a man there, somewhere, hidden beneath his cassock?

Florence, 1903

7

"It's Lucretius," Colin said. "From his only work, *De Rerum Natura—On the Nature of Things*—a poetic explanation of Epicurean philosophy and physics. Written in hexameter. If I recall correctly, the passage has to do with the idea that objects cannot be created from nothing. *The first beginnings of things cannot be distinguished by the eye.* You will not be able to see the material that makes them up, but it existed long before the things in question. He also believed that there is no afterlife, and hence, no need to fear death."

We had dined late, not sitting down until after Colin and Mr. Benton-Smith had removed—to where, I had no idea—Signore Spichio's body from the courtyard. The subject was entirely avoided at the table, not out of respect for decorum but because Cécile and I were meant to take no part in any discussion of the man's death. Apparently, they hoped this would persuade us to pretend that nothing unusual had happened; and for the moment, at least, I was content to let the conversation drift from Botticelli to Lorenzo the Magnificent to Michelangelo.

When we'd finished eating, Colin produced a bottle of port brought from our cellar in London and passed it around the table. I saw it for what it was: an apology for cutting me out of his investigation. It was well played, a nod to his acceptance of my habit of drinking a beverage reserved by polite society for men alone, a reminder that he considered me an equal. The fortified wine took the edge off my irritation, just as he knew it would. A box of fine cigars provided additional balm.

"Dangerous ideas," Mr. Benton-Smith said, puffing as he lit one for himself, only after first having assisted me with my own. "How is the church to control its flock without the threat of hell?"

"Or the promise of heaven," I said. "I've not read Lucretius. Tomorrow, Cécile, we will look for a bookshop."

"You're unlikely to find it here in English. I can have Hatchards send it if you'd like." My husband's tone was congenial, his deep voice full of warmth. I appreciated the effort, even as I resented its cause. No amount of kindness could make me forget about Signore Spichio's murder.

"That would be lovely, Colin, thank you," I said. "I'm not sure how much time I'll have for it, as I've decided to embark on a new project. I found the Lucretius quotation among graffiti on the landing walls. Further exploration revealed more writing in the kitchen, the lavatories, and other spots in the house. I want to record all of it and translate it into English."

"What a marvelous idea, Lady Emily," Mr. Benton-Smith said.

"You need not be so formal," I said. "Please call me by my Christian name."

"Only if you address me as Darius."

"With pleasure. Dare I hope you're named for the Persian king?"

"My father dabbled in archaeology as a young man. He was particularly keen on Persia and spent time at the site of Persepolis. Which is a terribly roundabout way of saying, yes, I'm named for Darius the Great. Not an entirely happy situation. Whenever I was caught doing something naughty, dear old Pater was wont to remind me that the name means *he who holds firm to good*. Quite the burden for a young boy."

"At least he didn't call you Xerxes," I said. "It would be even harder to live up to being a ruler of heroes, in this day and age."

"Your husband did not exaggerate when he lauded your knowledge of history. I'm impressed, Emily."

"You needn't bother with flattery. It doesn't ease the sting of knowing nothing about the murdered corpse in the courtyard."

Darius glanced across the table to Colin, who shrugged. "She's not easily put off."

"No, I'm not," I said, "but I promise I shan't give either of you a hard time. I do understand the need for discretion and that the decision to keep your work to yourselves is not yours alone to make. Forgive me if I reacted badly. Seeing the body was a shock. It's not my first brush with violent death, but I never quite manage to take it in stride."

"As you shouldn't," Darius said. "I'm well aware of the laudable role you've played in bringing murderers to justice. Lose the horror at seeing a body and you lose a piece of your humanity, a piece I consider essential to solving a crime. If one does not care, one cannot succeed."

"What a morbid topic," Cécile said. "If Kallista and I are to have no part of your investigation, would it be too much to beg that you not torment us with reminders of it?"

"It would be best if we refrained from mentioning poor Signore Spichio," I said. "It's all I can do to resist digging in and looking for clues. If that's forbidden, I shall have to try to pretend the two of you gentlemen aren't doing exactly that."

"We do appreciate the difficulty of the situation, my dear," Colin said. "Thank you for your understanding." I noted the very slightest hint of sarcasm buried in his tone. He would never believe I would be easily persuaded to step aside.

"*Bien.*" Cécile rose from the table. "Let us retire to the Sala dei Pappagalli and turn our attention to entirely different matters. Monsieur Benton-Smith, I am eager to learn more about you. Escort me downstairs and tell me all the shocking stories of your misspent youth."

"I'm afraid there's very little to tell," he said, rising and offering her his arm. "At least in polite company."

"I am many things, monsieur. Polite is not one of them."

Colin and I retreated to our bedroom at the first opportunity, once he was convinced we weren't insulting Cécile by abandoning her and I was reasonably certain that Darius was safe alone with her. Our room, on the second floor, was painted with scenes from a tragic thirteenth-century chivalric romance, *La Chastelaine de Vergi*. The chatelaine, in love with one of the knights in her uncle's retinue, insisted that their relationship be kept secret from everyone. They used a little dog—trustworthy as he could not speak and reveal their relationship—as a signal to indicate when it was safe to meet. But the chatelaine was not the only lady to take notice of the knight. Her uncle's wife, the duchess, yearned for his attention, too. When the loyal man rejected her, she accused him of treason. What followed was a mess of manipulation, treachery, and death. No one got a happy ending. The beauty of the paintings could not be denied—the little dog, in particular, was charming—but I wondered who had made the decision to commission the work. I would not have chosen scenes from it to decorate a bedroom. Had it, perhaps, commemorated the occasion of the arranged marriage of a bride whose heart longed for a different groom? I was sitting on a chaise longue contemplating the question when Colin emerged from the bathroom, ready for bed, dressed in nothing but a pair of loose silk pajama trousers.

"Are you truly content to leave me to my work?" Colin asked, brushing damp curls back from his forehead. Ordinarily, he would have approached the question more obliquely and prefaced it with his most distracting kiss, especially given his knowledge of the effect his current attire had on me. Tonight, though, he stood far away, in front of the fireplace, arms crossed over his bare chest.

"I can't claim to be delighted by it, but there's nothing else to be said. I have no choice in the matter."

"I'm sorry. I prefer when we can work together."

"It's easier to tolerate being excluded when you're off in parts unknown and I haven't the slightest idea what you're doing. Being here, knowing that I could help, is immensely frustrating."

"Would you prefer to return home?"

"Would you prefer that I did?"

He came to the chaise and sat beside me. "No. I knew before coming here that I would have to work. I should have told you that from the first. You've no doubt ascertained that the break-ins are tied to something of larger significance to Britain. I wish I could say more, but I can't.

Despite knowing that, I wanted you with me. Not only because I hate us being apart but also because I value the contributions you make when we work together. Darius and I have faced countless difficult situations and always achieved what needed to be achieved; but I have seen, time and again, that your insights neatly complement what I do. You would be an asset to us."

"Yet you are not allowed to make use of me."

"No."

"I've already set in motion a plan to learn whatever I can about Signore Spichio."

"It would be dangerous for you to expose any of the work he did for us."

"I wouldn't do that, but might it not be useful to know other, broader things about him? What if his work did not lead to his death, but a bungled love affair or a dispute over money?"

"It's unlikely in the extreme."

"Whoever killed him could have covered his tracks by making use of some sort of ordinary problem he had. I may be able to learn things that could assist you in unearthing the truth. If you and Darius are nosing around his family and friends, you risk exposing your own roles. Don't tell me you know how to be subtle. A wise gentleman informed me that everyone believes himself to be discreet."

"I cannot deny that your assistance could prove useful, nor can I deny that I've known from the instant Tessa screamed that you would not be kept away from investigating." He took my hands and squeezed them, hard. "I trust you absolutely, in ways that I could never make Darius understand or accept. I trust Cécile, but it's not the same thing. If you choose to proceed—which I know you will—I need you to convince her that I know nothing of it. That way, she'll be less likely to slip in front of Darius."

"Of course."

"Don't answer so easily, Emily. It is an unwelcome slope you approach, deceiving a friend, a slope that can't ever be climbed after you start your descent." He closed his eyes and drew a deep breath. "It will plague you, every single day, even when you're not being deliberately disingenuous, even when your conversation has nothing to do with the work at hand. You will have to learn to become comfortable with lies, so comfortable that you turn to them even when it appears unnecessary. You will learn that it is, in fact, always necessary, because the truth must be treated as a potential danger."

"Do you lie to me?"

"Yes." His voice was barely audible. "Not about things that matter, not between us. Only regarding my work, and then—in order to justify it to myself—only by omission, as if that mitigates the sin."

"I've always known that," I said. "I am confident that if it did matter, you would tell me, regardless of the consequence. I trust you to keep only the right secrets."

He dropped his head to his chest. "Deceptions, even worthy ones, take their toll. I want to beg your forgiveness but am not hypocrite enough to do so. I've never doubted the necessity of keeping my work separate from you."

"And I want to admonish you for hiding things from me, even as I've never doubted the necessity of your doing it." I tilted my head and half grinned. He rarely allowed anyone, myself included, to see even the slightest chink in his emotional armor. I would not make it harder for him than I knew it already was. Eventually, I would acknowledge the effort it must have taken for him to confide these thoughts, but now he needed something else. "Well. Not *never* doubted the necessity. Accepted it, yes. Begrudgingly. Reluctantly. Wandsomely. With ill humor. Against my will. Without patience. Shall I continue?" I placed one hand on the back of his neck, the other on his chest, feeling his firm muscle beneath my palm.

"I'd prefer you didn't, at least not your reproof." He looked into my eyes with such intensity I found it difficult to breathe. "Before we turn our attentions to things more pleasant, we ought to establish some ground rules. For our work."

"I shan't let Cécile know I'm telling you anything," I said.

"I will ensure Darius is equally unaware, but that will be simpler than keeping Cécile ignorant. She knows you well. Darius does not. It would be helpful if you could somehow persuade him you've lost interest in what we're doing."

"I can try, but he does know my history with investigations. As for Cécile, she and I have already planned to investigate quietly, without letting you know what we've learned until absolutely necessary. Can you tell me anything harmless about Signore Spichio? His full name, perhaps?"

"I can't, Emily. To reveal information about a confidential source would be a serious breach. Darius shouldn't have let his surname slip when he saw the body," he said. "We ought to agree on a way to communicate what you learn without either of our friends suspecting what we're doing."

"We share a bed, Colin," I said. "How difficult can it be?"

"There may be nights I don't return to the house, or times when something is too urgent to wait until evening. We can't do what Darius and I do—beg to be excused so that we can discuss something sensitive. We shall have to be more creative. An amorous signal might do."

"Amorous?"

"Yes. Florence is a romantic place. You may be swept away by its charms. You may require the attentions of your husband more frequently and less discreetly than usual."

"I am not about to make it obvious that—"

"Of course not. But a not-quite-subtle longing glance can go a long way, my dear. Darius will notice and never, ever question."

"Cécile will notice and have many questions."

"I'll leave it to you to decide how much you'd like to tell her. About the amorous details, not the rest."

"It's awfully convenient, Colin, deciding that your work now requires frequent amorous encounters."

"I would never insist we act upon said longing glances once we're alone. They needn't be more than pretext for an exchange of information, if that's what you'd prefer."

"You're an evil, evil man," I said.

"Of course, if you'd rather I bring the promises of those glances to fruition, I would never object." He traced a finger along the neckband of my nightgown.

"I'm beginning to see a benefit to the discretion required by your work. Secrets, in the right circumstances, can be most invigorating—" I stopped speaking, only able to gasp given what he did next. I gave no further consideration to secrets or anything else for a long, long time. This new arrangement of ours looked to be quite promising.

Florence,
1480

8

The moment I returned from church that day, I pulled down from a bookshelf our family's copy of Dante's *Commedia,* eager to read. The house was unusually quiet, my father still at work downstairs in the loggia, my brothers out with their friends, and my mother nowhere to be found. I climbed the stairs to my bedroom on the third floor of the house, near the kitchen, where I stopped to persuade our cook to give me a small dish of walnuts spiced with ginger, cinnamon, and honey.

After flinging open the wooden shutters in my room to let in what light a February afternoon could offer, I lit a lamp and settled into my favorite chair, immediately lost in Dante's exquisite verse. I had not finished with even the first canto of *Inferno* when Alfia burst through the door and shattered my tranquility.

"Your grandfather is downstairs, signorina, inviting you to dine with him this evening at the Palazzo Medici," she said. "He is with your father now, and you will leave from here together when it is time. We must start to dress you now or you'll be late. You will wear the azure silk overgown, yes? The blue sets off your golden hair. And flowered sleeves?"

I heard almost nothing she said after *Medici.* It had been so long since my grandfather had taken me anywhere. My mother had forbidden his outings once the changes to my body that deemed me marriageable had occurred. No doubt my father agreed only because he hoped I might be noticed by a wealthy bachelor at the Medici table, but on this count

I knew better, as would have my mother, but she was not home. Nonno did not socialize with the Medici in a way useful for social climbing. He and il Magnifico were close, friends even, but theirs was an intellectual relationship that stemmed from Nonno's work as a book hunter. He and Lorenzo discussed the ideas found in those manuscripts, sometimes staying up most of the night engrossed in conversation. His patron included him in small gatherings of artists, humanists, and scholars, not events intended to cement the family's superiority over other members of the ruling class.

Which was precisely why I was so excited at the prospect of going. At long last, an evening of intellectual stimulation! I let Alfia dress me in a fine gown—the blue, as she desired—and did not complain as she coaxed my long hair into perfect loose curls. She oiled my eyelashes to make them appear darker and barked at me to bite my lips to give them color. I did as she asked, knowing no one I encountered that evening would take the slightest interest in my appearance.

The Palazzo Medici was only a ten-minute walk from our house, so I slipped wooden clogs over my cloth shoes and set off on Nonno's arm. As I expected, we were not shown into the Medici's formal dining room but rather a smaller chamber Lorenzo used for more intimate gatherings. Its arched ceiling made the room feel bigger than it was, and we gathered immediately around a heavy square table, making no nod to the ordinary rituals of society. One servant filled our cups with wine while another served soup with large chunks of meat seasoned with cinnamon.

We were not a large group. Aside from Nonno and me, il Magnifico had invited Marsilio Ficino, who headed the Platonic Academy in Florence and had become a priest; Giuliano da Sangallo, an architect and sculptor; and the artist Sandro Botticelli, whom Lorenzo's mother had brought into the Medici household when her sons were young. I had met all of them many times before, but had not seen them in more than a year, and felt a prickle of nerves, wondering if I would be able to converse effortlessly with them as I used to.

"How you have grown," Lorenzo said. "I fondly remember you as a ten-year-old, proud of your knowledge of Latin, reciting excerpts from one of Cicero's speeches. Your grandfather taught you well."

My education benefited greatly from Nonno. My parents, neither of them particularly interested in the details, were happy to let him arrange tutors for my brothers, and he insisted that I study with them as well. Time proved me to be the only sibling who showed either aptitude or interest for scholarship. Nonno began bringing me books to supplement my studies. He also worked with me himself, teaching me penmanship, so that my handwriting was nearly as beautiful as his own.

"You are very kind, sir," I said, as the servants cleared our soup bowls.

"And now you are old enough that we rarely see you." He shook his head. "It's time you focus on other things."

"Marriage and motherhood," Signore Botticelli said. "Underwhelming and disappointing."

"Not necessarily," Lorenzo replied. "Don't discourage her."

"There's no need to. Life will take care of that itself." The artist swigged his wine and leaned back from the table so it was easier for the footman, who was serving the next course, to place a plate laden with pork in a pepper sauce in front of him.

"What are you reading now, child?" Father Ficino asked.

"I've studied Augustine and Aquinas and am now turning to Dante."

"What a relief," Botticelli said.

"I couldn't agree more," I said, my confidence returning. "I found Augustine and his pears infuriating."

"The great Dante knew we are drawn to religion," Father Ficino said. "Augustine may irritate you, but his ideas should not be dismissed. Better that you consider them, internalize them, and come up with your own way of expressing the saint's thoughts. It might prove a useful exercise."

"Let her indulge in Dante, Marsilio," Signore da Sangallo said. "She can rewrite Augustine when her grandchildren are old enough to marry."

A look of horror crossed my face. "I cannot contemplate reaching so advanced an age. What would it be? Nearly fifty?" The men laughed.

"I'm fast approaching just that," Father Ficino said. "You will find,

Mina, that age does not change you so much as you might expect. I feel no different now than I did as a youth of twenty."

"I'm not sure whether that's encouraging or terrifying," I said.

The conversation continued as we ate, moving to the Platonic idea of love bringing us closer to God by enabling us to recognize divinity in each other's souls and then to the difficulties posed by free will and then to more mundane things. Signore Botticelli asked for paper and pencil. I did not know what he was drawing until the party broke up and we stood to leave the room. As I walked through the door, he touched my arm and showed me his work. He had sketched my face.

"Someday," he said, "I will use you as a model for one of the Three Graces. I have only to decide which you embody: Aglaea, Euphrosyne, or Thalia. I'm inclined to Aglaea, as no one who sees you could doubt that you shine."

"Splendor and beauty, quite fitting," Signore da Sangallo said, winking at me. We made our way down to the ground floor and entered Michelozzo's Corinthian-column-lined cortile. I was feeling quite pleased with myself. Their attention was flattering, and I wanted to believe it sincere, even if I suspected it had to do more with pleasant memories of me as a child than it did my current appearance.

A man stood on the far side of the courtyard, near the palazzo's main door, his hands clasped in front of his waist. Seeing Lorenzo, he straightened himself as we approached, but il Magnifico did not hail him. Instead, he stopped walking and turned to my grandfather.

"I have something for you, Teo," he said, holding out a small velvet bag. "A mark of appreciation for all you've done for me. You have a keen eye when it comes to ancient beauty; it is a trait we share. When I found this, I knew you would hold it in the same esteem as I."

"This is unexpected," Nonno said. He gently removed an object from the bag. Lorenzo, whose collection of cameos was the envy of wealthy princes all over Italy, adored these pieces, even accepting some from Pope Paul II to offset Vatican debts to the Medici bank. This one, made of sardonyx and showing Minerva in profile, her hair flowing from beneath her helmet, was a spectacular example. "It's extraordinary. I shall treasure it. Thank you."

"It's my pleasure," Lorenzo said as clapped him on the shoulder. He called out to the man waiting near the door. "Agnolo! I'm glad you had no objection to meeting on such short notice. Let me see off my guests and we shall retire to my study."

I felt the stranger's eyes on me as we passed, but they were more critical than appreciative, and the boost of confidence the evening had given me faded in an instant. He was sneering at me. I would be glad to return to the quiet comfort of home and Dante's *Commedia.*

Florence, 1903

9

I woke up the next morning utterly disoriented, only half remembering where I was. The bedroom was dark except for a crack of light coming in where one of the shutters had pulled slightly open. I slid out of bed and padded toward it, cringing when I stepped off the soft carpet and onto cold tiles, and then flung back the shutter and its mate, revealing the splendors of Florence. Terra-cotta roofs glowed golden red in the sun, and the distinct sound of Italian church bells echoed against stone walls.

I opened the rest of the shutters and light filled the room, or at least made a valiant effort to do so. There were only three windows and the narrow streets below did not leave space for much sunlight to pour in, but the chamber wasn't gloomy. Outside, yesterday's rain had stopped, and I was filled with a rush of enthusiasm. I allowed myself to delay thinking about the murdered Signore Spichio long enough to silently murmur a prayer of thanks for finding myself in such a beautiful place.

Colin had left a note on the bedside table. He and Darius would be gone all day and did not expect to return in time for dinner, which meant there was no need for me to dress before seeking out Cécile, whom I found in the Sale Madornale on the first floor. This, and its counterparts on the floors above, had five enormous windows on the front wall, and, hence, more natural light than was found in the rest of the house. There was no view, however, as the windows were fashioned from lead-rimmed bottle glass. The furnishings looked medieval, though I assumed them to be reproductions; the hulking oak table in the middle of the room was in far too pristine condition to have weathered centuries. The walls were whitewashed, with tapestries hanging on them. Three Persian rugs covered parts of the floor's octagonal terra-cotta tiles. All in all, it was a pleasant space, although I preferred the riot of color in the Sala dei Pappagalli.

Cécile was sitting near the fireplace with a book on her lap. Caesar and Brutus were nowhere to be seen, so I inquired after them.

"Fredo has taken them for a walk. I wanted to bring them to the Boboli Gardens at Palazzo Pitti, but your Baedeker's tells me it does not open until noon. They could not wait so long. You slept late. Was that due to the attentions of your diabolically handsome husband?"

I raised an eyebrow and smiled, no longer shocked, but amused, when she asked such inappropriate questions. "I do hope Darius didn't keep you up."

"He is charming, but not interesting enough for that," she said. "He returned to his lodgings soon after you retired. I do not consider it a disappointment. Other than your own Monsieur Hargreaves, English gentlemen are not universally appealing. They are too proper. The Italians are a more passionate people."

"The appearance of being proper might be nothing more than a front, you know," I said. "Did you breakfast?"

"Hours ago. Monsieur Benton-Smith arrived early and ate with your husband." Darius had elected not to stay with us, explaining that he had rooms across the Arno, not far from the Palazzo Pitti, in the building the Brownings had once called home. His family had a villa on Lake Garda, to the north, and, when there, he made frequent trips to Florence in order to spend time in the city's myriad museums. I did not altogether doubt his motivation, but Colin had made a few comments that led me to suspect his friend was more interested in privacy than art. There was, it seems, a lady. "They left before eight o'clock. The Laurentian Library opened at ten, if you're still inclined to visit it today."

I rang for tea and toast, ate it quickly, and then had Tessa help me dress. As she pulled my corset strings, I almost longed for one of Mr. van de Velde's loose-fitting gowns, but it never could have matched the elegance of my navy silk Worth walking dress. The current craze for S-shaped silhouettes was not my favorite, but I found that a modestly puffed bodice could make the waist appear tiny without causing one to look like a pigeon. Why anyone would model fashion on a wholly unattractive bird was inconceivable to me.

The walk to the library was a pleasant one, taking us through the Piazza Vittorio Emanuele II. The square, which for centuries had served as a public market—the Mercato Vecchio—had been renovated in the nineteenth century, following the unification of Italy. Gone was the Colonna della Dovizia—the Column of Abundance—that since 1431 had marked the location of the ancient Roman forum. A bronze equestrian statue of Victor Emmanuel II, united Italy's first king, now stood in its place. Words carved on a new arch, built to look like a Renaissance rendering of something Roman, read *L'antico centro della città da secolare squallore a vita nuova restituito*—The ancient center of the city restored from age-old squalor to new life—but many Florentines considered the changes to the ancient space ruinous. I wished I had seen its previous incarnation.

We continued on, past the Duomo and north to the monumental complex of San Lorenzo, the Medici family church. The library within held more than ten thousand priceless ancient manuscripts (among them the codex of Virgil); an extensive collection of books that had been owned by the Medici family; and countless historical documents, including Dante's letters.

We introduced ourselves to a librarian called Renzo Tazzera, who stepped forward to assist us. He recognized the Vieri family name as soon as I mentioned it. "You are living in their palazzo? Marvelous," he said, his English flawless, his lilting accent mesmerizing. "It is, to my mind, the finest example of medieval architecture in the city. I prefer the innovations of the Renaissance, but one must have a firm understanding of what came before to understand the accomplishments of men like Brunelleschi and Alberti."

"You are quite right, monsieur," Cécile said. "Brunelleschi would be the first to acknowledge it was the study of ancient buildings that made his own designs possible. Did he not visit the Pantheon in Rome before constructing the dome of the cathedral?"

"He did indeed. I should like to speak with you more about this, signora, but first, please, make yourselves comfortable. I will bring you all the records we have pertaining to both the family and the structure. Then, perhaps we may return to discussing architecture."

The Reading Room was a glorious space, with sunlight streaming in from windows on both sides and an inlaid marble aisle dividing rows of carved walnut benches and lecterns. Cécile and I sat down and I pulled a notebook and pencil from my handbag.

"He is most attractive, this Monsieur Tazzera, is he not?" Cécile asked. "Far more interesting than that colleague of Colin's. And his voice. A perfect tenor. There can be no doubt he sings. All Italians do. How else are they to effectively express their ardent natures? I should like to know him better."

Judging from the way the librarian looked at Cécile when he brought our materials, it was obvious the attraction was mutual.

"If it is not too forward of me to make such a request, it would be my greatest honor to take you on a tour of the library, Signora du Lac," he said. "Michelangelo designed it, you know, and it is arguably one of the most important examples of Renaissance architecture. Your earlier comments led me to believe this is a subject of interest to you."

"I have a great passion for it," Cécile said.

"If your friend would not object—"

She interrupted him. "Kallista would never be so tactless as to stand in the way of me continuing my studies."

Continuing her studies? I might have rolled my eyes if anyone else had behaved in such a way, but not Cécile. She would never feign interest in a subject to gain the attention of a man, no matter how attractive he was. That heretofore I was unaware of her fascination with Renaissance architecture was irrelevant. I couldn't claim to know everything about her.

"You are very kind, Lady Emily," he said. "I do hope your research will not suffer without Signora du Lac's assistance."

"I shall do my best to soldier on without her," I said.

"I am most grateful," he said and then turned to Cécile. "Signora, if you will come with me, we will start at the staircase you climbed to reach this room. Michelangelo's plans for it caused quite a stir. After we examine it, I will show you his original drawings."

"Monsieur Tazzera, I am at your disposal." She slid to the edge of the bench, offered her hand to him, and took her leave from me, a wicked grin on her face. Cécile never shied away from admiring a handsome man, but only those whose intellectual or artistic leanings interested her had a chance of becoming, shall we say, *close* to her. The librarian was well on his way to making a most favorable impression.

I turned to my books, starting with an overview of Florentine palazzos that gave the date of construction of Kat's house as sometime in the mid-fourteenth century. The Vieris, wealthy merchants, built it, conducting business from the ground floor loggia. It stayed in their hands until 1838, when Bartolomeo di Vieri, the last member of the family, died without an heir, and it sat empty until the middle of the century, when a banker bought it and started renovations. The project fell to the wayside after he lost his fortune. There was no mention of what happened next, but I knew from the legal documents now in Kat's possession that her mother had purchased it in 1886.

The next volume in my stack was a history of Florence written in the sixteenth century. In it, I found a reference to Agnolo di Vieri, a spectacularly wealthy silk merchant who was a confidante of Lorenzo the Magnificent. In a time when other rich Florentines were building new and bigger palazzi, Agnolo chose to stay in his family home. The author offered no explanation for this decision, but another work, written more than a hundred years later, mentioned a priceless treasure—still unfound at the time—hidden in its walls. Had Agnolo remained, searching in vain for it?

I came across one other mention of the treasure, in a letter written by Bartolomeo di Vieri two years before his death. It was the only pertinent piece of information in the large archival box of family correspondence Signore Tazzera had brought me; and while it was intriguing, even I could not argue it shed any light on Signore Spichio's murder. Regardless of the secrets to which Tessa had referred, I had found nothing to suggest the palazzo had a nefarious history.

A quick glance at my watch told me I'd been buried in research for more than three hours, yet Cécile had not returned, and despite searching the public spaces of the library, I could not locate her. Perturbed, I went back to the main desk, where a librarian greeted me by name.

"Lady Emily Hargreaves?"

I nodded.

"Your friend has left a message for you. She will be indisposed for the rest of the afternoon and says she will see you for dinner this evening."

"Thank you," I said. "I've a rather large stack of materials Signore Tazzera fetched for me. Shall I bring them back to him?"

"Signore Tazzera has left for the day—he fell suddenly ill—but you can leave it to me. I'll return them to the stacks. I do hope you found what you were looking for."

I may have made a small bit of progress, but it was clear that Cécile had found exactly what she sought. I didn't begrudge her the distraction. Signore Tazzera was rather handsome, not to mention an educated, interesting man. Beyond that, he had to be at least forty-five, so well within the bounds of potentially fascinating. I didn't believe for a second that he was ill.

I exited the library and returned to the palazzo, heading straight to the room on the third floor near the kitchen, which I'd decided to use as my study. I asked Tessa to bring tea there for us both. She had coffee instead, into which she dipped a long, hard biscuit.

"I have not learned much, Lady Emily," she said, "but I hope what I tell you proves to be of some use. Marzo Spichio lived with his parents and brother near the church of Santa Croce. I can direct you to the house. He was thirty-two years old, not married but engaged, and had a reputation for having a short temper. He worked doing repairs to buildings."

She'd abandoned all pretense of not being fluent. If anything, her English was even better than the last time I'd talked to her. "How did you find this out?"

"I went to the Mercato Nuovo. Do you know it? It is the market very near this house. I know many of the merchants who sell their wares there, and two in particular are always acquainted with the latest gossip. They both knew that a man plummeted to his death from your roof, and one knew his family."

"How had they heard anything about it?" I asked.

"This morning, your husband notified Signora Spichio of her son's death. The unusual nature of the circumstances made the story spread like fire." That Colin couldn't share with me these details infuriated me. It was so inefficient, my having to have a maid poke around for half a day to learn something he could have told me in an instant.

"Do you know the family?" I asked.

"I do not," she replied and then stopped speaking, glancing at the door. A moment later it opened, and Signora Orlandi entered.

"Tessa, you must get back to work."

"I'm afraid I must keep her for a bit longer," I said. "Her English is much better than you led me to believe."

"We all have our secrets," she said. "Please don't keep her too long, Lady Emily."

When she'd retreated, I turned back to the maid. "I will visit the family tomorrow. Before you go, I wanted to ask you about the secrets you mentioned yesterday. Those hidden by the house. You promised to explain."

"There are many stories about this palazzo. It is older than most in Florence, and hence full of ghosts."

"Ghosts?" I like a good ghost story as much as the next person, but had hoped for something more concrete than ethereal spirits unlikely to have murdered a man.

"Not the souls of the dead, but the memory of what has happened here. Do you know about the little friar, Savonarola?"

"Some, though I cannot claim extensive knowledge," I said.

"He hated the excessive luxury of the Florentine people and preached doom and judgment, claiming that Florence was to be the next Jerusalem and that Our Lord Jesus Christ would soon return to earth. Within two years of Lorenzo il Magnifico's death, Savonarola controlled the government. The Medici fled, and the city once again became a republic. The details are unimportant. As is so often the case, what is critical in one moment is irrelevant later."

"What has Savonarola to do with this house?"

"The family who lived here opposed him. There are stories that they were tormented by his Bands of Hope—boys who roamed the streets in search of people ignoring the friar's newly imposed rules. They stripped women who dressed in luxurious fashion, confiscated items they deemed to be sinful possessions, and generally caused trouble. They were thugs. Violent thugs."

"How did that lead to this house keeping secrets?"

"Many things happened here that shouldn't have, but no one, not even Savonarola himself could prove any of it," she said.

"What sort of things?"

"That I do not know. It was many centuries ago. My great-grandmother also worked here, for the last surviving member of the family who built the house. She told me that her master was plagued by trying to uncover something hidden in the palazzo. Every time he came close to finding it, something happened to stop him. A shutter fell off its hinges and nearly killed him when it hit his head. The well flooded. A fire broke out in his bedroom. It nearly drove him to madness."

"For what was he searching?"

"That I cannot say."

She might not say, but neither did she deny knowing. "What did Signore di Vieri think caused all of this?"

"You know his name?" she asked.

"Was it meant to be a secret?" She obviously knew it.

"No, of course not. You just surprised me, that's all. To answer your question, Signore di Vieri said the house caused all of his ills. Not a ghost, the house."

"Do you believe that?" I asked.

"No, signora, I do not. A house is not alive. But Signora Orlandi told me a story about the countess who lived here. She, too, believed the house protected its secrets. That is why she wanted it for her daughter. I must go now and help Cook with your dinner. We will talk more later."

Grateful though I was for the information she provided about Signore Spichio, the rest of what she said was decidedly odd, as if she'd constructed it deliberately to mislead me. On the surface, it was innocuous enough. What did it matter if I—or anyone—believed superstitions about the house? Yet my instinct told me there was some thread of truth in her story. The sources in the library confirmed that something had been hidden here, something I suspected Tessa did not want me to find. I would tread carefully, knowing I could play the game of misdirection just as well, if not better, than she.

Florence, 1480

10

My mother was furious Nonno had taken me to the Palazzo Medici. "It is wholly inappropriate for her to dine in such circumstances." She would never have dared say such things to my grandfather and spent the next morning railing at my father instead. "Yes, she should—must—associate with the finest families in Florence. But to do so when there are no other ladies present and at a gathering with individuals of dubious merit—"

"Now, now," my father said. "No one would consider any of them less than meritorious. You would criticize Botticelli?"

"No, of course not." She had been pacing, agitated, but now calmed down and sat across from my father at the dining table. The change in her attitude emboldened me to speak.

"Signore Botticelli sketched me," I said. "He plans to use the drawing as a model for one of the Three Graces in a painting."

"Did he?" Now she looked almost cheerful. "Who commissioned the painting?"

"I don't know," I admitted. "But—"

Her countenance darkened. "Mina, you are woefully naïve. I doubt he has any plans for the drawing."

"Leave the child be," my father said. "No harm has been done." He had a tendency to indulge my brothers and me, not to the point that we were spoiled but enough that my mother frequently felt the need to rein him in.

"Far better that she attend social functions that include eligible bachelors than one with a priest and a handful of married men," she said.

"I understand your concerns, but for her to have such ready access to Lorenzo de' Medici can never be a liability."

"It is not she, but your father, who has the access."

"Which should make the events of last night all the more palatable to you," he said. "No one would suspect impropriety at any function he attended. His reputation is spotless. As, I may add, is Mina's."

My mother frowned. "She is at a vulnerable age."

"I shall leave so you can speak about me more freely," I said, knowing all too well where the conversation was heading. Marriage. "I mean to go to confession this morning and ought not tarry any longer."

"Go, go," my father said. "You might inquire if any of your brothers want to join you. There's no question they would all benefit from the sacrament."

Less concerned about my brothers' immortal souls than I perhaps ought to have been, I scurried off with no intention of inviting them to accompany me. Alfia was an adequate chaperone and would never comment on the conversations Father Cambio and I had after I'd made my confession. My brothers, on the other hand, would tease me mercilessly and threaten to have Father send me to a convent, which is where they believed all women who spent too much time gabbing about religion belonged. It would never occur to them that we might be discussing something else.

Although, today, I had little heart for any sort of conversation. The look of contempt Lorenzo de' Medici's friend had given me when I was leaving the previous night was still troubling me. I could not get the image of his sneer out of my mind. He had no cause to dislike me; we'd never met. Yet somehow he'd managed to disturb some insecurity lurking deep inside me, leaving me less confident than normal. Father Cambio did not seem to notice, at least not while I made my confession. But as we started to take our usual turn around the nave of the church, my dispirited manner could not be denied.

"You are not yourself today, Mina," he said. "Did the sacrament fail to soothe your soul?"

"I did not hold back anything, Father."

"That's not what I meant. Not all troubles are of a spiritual nature." There was a reassuring kindness in his face I had not previously noticed. He was younger than my father, but older than my brothers, and I started to wonder what his own family was like. I'd never considered priests as men, just accepted them as vessels of the Church. "I do remember life before I was a priest."

It was as if he could read my thoughts. I blushed, embarrassed. "I—I—"

"Give me your hand." I did as he asked. He took it in his own, which was warm and soft, large. We had stopped walking and stood beneath a sculpture of the Virgin Mary and the infant Jesus. "Our Lord understood the troubles of the ordinary man. Look only to his miracles to know that. He changed water to wine at a wedding, satisfying a very human desire. Now, tell me, what happened to take the light out of you?"

I told him about the dinner and about the man at the Medici's door. "I don't know why it hurt me so. He is nothing to me. I don't even know his name."

"You were coming from a gathering where you were a vital part of a stimulating intellectual exchange, where you were noticed and respected. But as you exited the house, you returned to the world you inhabit nearly all of the time, one where your mind is not appreciated, where your value lies in your physical appearance and reputation. You have reached the age where you will soon be married. This stranger represents the sort of person you will take as a husband. It is understandable that you would have doubts and fears about this. Will your parents find for you a man who wants more than someone to bear children and run his household? Will you be allowed to read? Will you—"

"It never occurred to me that a husband might forbid his wife to read."

"I do not suggest it is a common practice. The Bible teaches us that a husband should love his wife as Jesus does the Church. It also tells us that a wife of noble character is her husband's crown, while a disgraceful wife is like decay in his bones. A husband cannot leave his wife to do whatever she wishes. There may be times when he must guide her behavior."

"By not letting her read Dante?" I asked, feeling myself growing angry.

"I would not say so, but I shall never be a husband."

"I wish I would never be a wife."

"There are other choices, if you feel a spiritual calling."

"No, I can't say I do. I just wish . . ."

"What?"

I did not reply.

"What do you wish, Mina? That you could marry a man you love?"

This made me laugh. "I am young, Father, but not that naïve. I'd like to marry a man who doesn't repulse me and one who doesn't stop me reading. Is that not sadly little to ask? If I had a wish, it would for a life that allows for the possibility of higher expectations."

He raised his hand to my cheek, resting it lightly against my skin. "It is sadly little to ask and it should be reasonable to want more. You deserve more." My eyes grew hot with tears. "Don't cry, Mina. It is not all bleak."

"Forgive me, I am overcome," I said.

"Let us abandon this depressing course and talk about Dante."

I blinked, but could not stop the tears from falling. "I haven't the heart for it today."

"Come back tomorrow, then. Not for confession. I can't imagine you'll need that after only one day. Morning Mass and then we shall go for a walk and discuss poetry."

Florence, 1903

11

In the time between my arrival home from the library and Cécile's from wherever she'd gone with Signore Tazzera, I wrote letters to the boys and Margaret, read half a novel, and dressed for dinner. When Cécile did return—half an hour before we'd planned to dine—she was glowing. "Will you object if I don't change my gown?" she asked. "I'm famished and would prefer to eat without delay."

"I shan't object so long as you tell me where you've been all afternoon," I said. "Although my mother would be horrified and present this as yet another example of standards slipping to unacceptable lows. If we don't dress for dinner, how will anyone recognize us as civilized?"

"*Alors,* there are times the uncivilized proves much more satisfying. And that, Kallista, is all you need know about my afternoon."

"I take it you will see Signore Tazzera again?"

"I've invited him to dine with us tomorrow evening."

I rang for Tessa, told her we were eager to eat whenever Cook was ready, and asked her to bring us a bottle of Cécile's champagne as an aperitif.

"*Non,* Tessa, there was a case of prosecco delivered earlier today," my friend said. "Bring us a bottle of that instead."

Would that it were possible for me to adequately describe the shock I felt. Imagine London destroyed by vicious butterflies. Or the Parthenon of Athens felled by a child's kite. I would have sworn either more likely than my ever hearing what Cécile had just said. "You are knowingly and willingly eschewing champagne in favor of prosecco? Who are you?"

She shrugged with the elegance only a Parisian can possess. "Renzo sent the wine and made me promise to try it. In the circumstances, I could hardly refuse. He had me at an extreme disadvantage."

"I dare not ask for further explanation."

Tessa returned with the prosecco as I finished updating Cécile on my progress, such as it was. We fell silent as the maid opened and poured the wine, our conversation not resuming until she'd left the room and I pulled the door open enough to make sure she had well and truly gone.

"You do not trust her?" Cécile asked.

"I don't think she's a villainess, but we ought to be careful what we say in front of her."

"Perhaps you are correct in believing that she is an agent of some sort. If that is the case, surely it is Monsieur Hargreaves who would have hired her."

"I will press him for information, but don't expect to learn much."

"Let us talk more about this hidden treasure." She eyed the glass of prosecco sitting on the table next to her chair, sighed, lifted it, and put it to her lips. "It's not so dreadful as it might be."

"I think it's lovely."

"It is not champagne."

"It's not meant to be."

"An unforgivable failing. Now, tell me about the treasure."

"You know everything I do. I don't consider Tessa's story from her great-grandmother wholly credible. The house is an inanimate object and as such was not stopping Signore di Vieri from searching for a treasure or anything else."

"*Bien sûr,* but it is possible he believed it to be. Someone could have exploited his fear in order to get whatever it is that's hidden."

"We don't know whether it was ever found," I said, "or even what it was. It may be an old story dredged back up to distract us."

"I have no doubt that two ladies so capable as we have the capacity to simultaneously investigate a dead man and search for hidden Renaissance treasure," she said. "We ought to welcome the challenge."

I fell asleep that night before Colin returned and did not hear him creep into our room. When I awoke the next morning, I shook him gently, but he did not stir. A bruise was blooming across his cheek, so I let him rest, despite desperately wanting to know what had caused it. Not wanting to disturb him, I slid out of bed silently, went into our bathroom, washed up as best I could without summoning Tessa for more water, and pulled on a tea gown.

Downstairs, I found Cécile and Darius in the dining room, steaming cups of coffee on the table in front of each of them. Darius bore no visible marks of violence, but when he stood to refill his plate at the sideboard, he was limping.

"I see you are in no better shape than my husband," I said, pouring myself a cup of tea.

"Hargreaves saved me from what might have been a very bad outcome."

"What happened?" Cécile asked.

"I shouldn't bother to inquire," I said. "Gentlemen are most unwilling to share the details of their exploits with us ladies. I suppose we should be grateful neither of them was flung off someone's roof. Please tell me no one witnessed whatever transpired. It's embarrassing enough without wondering if every Brit in Florence already knows about it."

"It was nothing, really. Mortifying though it is, I admit to having taken more drink than I could handle last night, in a vain attempt to dampen the blow of losing Spichio. Your husband tried to stop me, but I was rather pigheaded about the whole thing and staggered off back toward my rooms without waiting for him to leave the tavern, which was the scene of my disgrace. I assure you it is not a place frequented by tourists. I hadn't gone more than a block before thieves set on me. No doubt they could sense my vulnerability the moment they laid eyes on me. I was in a disgraceful state. Fortunately, Colin had followed me and fought them off before they could cause any serious injury. He even managed to retrieve my watch, which they'd taken. It was a gift from my grandfather when I received my degree at Cambridge. I would have hated to lose it."

"Am I correct in assuming that Monsieur Hargreaves was harmed in the struggle?" Cécile asked.

"I'm afraid so, although his injury looks worse than it is."

"*Mon dieu,* not his face?"

"No permanent damage done," I said, returning my teacup to its saucer. "I do appreciate your candor, Mr. Benton-Smith, and can only admonish you to, please, try not to entangle my husband in any further such incidents."

"That you do not use my Christian name wounds me," he said. "I hope I have not lost your friendship."

I gave him a wry smile. "Of course not, but you must have expected I wouldn't be pleased at hearing such a story. I know how it is with gentlemen. You all do things of which we ladies disapprove. Do try to avoid us learning about them." Cécile shot me a confused glance.

"I promise to do that and, further, shall worm my way back into your good graces," Darius said. "I assure you this was not the sort of behavior in which I ordinarily indulge."

"I should hope not," I said. "I think you ought to let Colin have a lie-in, so whatever the two of you have planned for the day, delay it."

"I quite agree, Lady Emily. Where are you off to?"

"The church at Santa Croce, to see Michelangelo's grave," Cécile said.

"Machiavelli is buried there as well." I folded my napkin and put it on the table as I rose from my seat. "I thought I might leave flowers for him."

"Machiavelli?" Darius squinted, looking at me with disbelief.

"I'm a great admirer of his work," I said. "*Everyone sees what you appear to be, few experience what you really are.* It pays to heed his words."

"I shall never underestimate you, Lady Emily."

I bestowed on him my most charming smile, took Cécile by the arm, and steered her out of the room.

"What is going on, Kallista?" Cécile asked as we stepped into the crowded street in front of the house. "I do not believe Monsieur Benton-Smith was attacked by petty criminals."

"Nor do I."

"Monsieur Hargreaves is not seriously injured, I hope?"

"Not so far as I could tell, but I thought it better to let him sleep than to conduct a thorough examination. The sooner we can figure out who killed Signore Spichio, the sooner Colin and Darius will be out of danger."

"And this, I assume, is why you are leading Monsieur Benton-Smith to believe you're an ordinary concerned wife?"

"Yes. It's best that we don't give him any reason to suspect we're investigating on our own. Let him think I'm nothing more than an uninterested society wife."

"Then it might not be advantageous to quote Machiavelli, Kallista. Hardly the thing for an uninterested society wife."

"I said uninterested, not uninteresting."

Tessa had written out directions to the Spichio home, which was only a few blocks from the church of Santa Croce, where I'd told Darius we were going. When being deceptive about my plans, I stay as close to the truth as possible. To do otherwise risks inadvertently making a mistake when later recounting what one has done. Cécile and I would visit the church, but only after first talking to the dead man's family.

The Spichios lived a little more than a mile from Kat's palazzo, a short walk on a day that was fine, sunny, and bright, more like summer than autumn. Much as I welcomed the feeling of setting off with purpose, when we reached their building, I paused, uneasy at disturbing them in their grief. When I could delay no longer, I rang the bell. A few moments later, a man in his mid-twenties opened the door. I asked him—in Italian—to direct us to the Spichios' apartment.

He frowned. "I am afraid this is not a good time. My family is in mourning."

"I'm so sorry for your loss," I said. "Marzo was a friend of mine. We are here to offer our condolences."

"A friend?" He looked incredulous, but motioned for us to follow him. We climbed four flights of stairs to a shabby doorway. A long, dark corridor led to a modest parlor, where a middle-aged woman, swathed in black, sat on a settee. She was flanked on one side by a shrunken elderly grandmother and on the other by a young girl of astonishing beauty with red lips like a Cupid's bow, flawless skin, and thick dark hair.

"Signora Spichio, I am Lady Emily Hargreaves, and this is my friend Cécile du Lac. I knew your son and wanted to offer my condolences in person."

She dabbed at her eyes with a handkerchief and looked up at us, but did not offer us a seat. "You knew my Marzo?"

"Not so well as I would have liked, signora," I said.

"You told me he was a friend," the young man who answered the door said. "Did you know my brother or not?"

"I considered him a friend because he went out of his way to be kind to me." It was not much, but I knew almost nothing about the man and had to be vague.

"Your name is Hargreaves," Signora Spichio said. "Your husband must be the one who told us of Marzo's accident. He was working to fix the roof of your house, yes?"

Now, at least, I knew Colin's cover story. "Yes. What happened is terrible. If there is anything at all I can do to help you or your family, please let me know."

The striking young girl narrowed her eyes. "Marzo and I were to be wed and nothing will ever bring back the happiness I have lost. He should never have been on that roof, but he would take any job, so desperate was he to save enough money that we could finally start our life together."

"He wouldn't have been desperate if you hadn't put on airs and insisted on living in a home far above his means." The dead man's brother spat the words. "He belonged here, with his family, like a good son. But, no, Lena had to have a house of her own, even if it meant leaving Florence."

"You always hated me, Ridolfo, but remember I know the reason why." The girl's voice was barely above a whisper but her venom unmistakable.

Ridolfo raised his hand and stepped toward her, stopping when the older woman next to his mother rose from the settee, balancing herself with a cane. "Enough!"

After that single word followed a stream of rapid-fire invective my Italian was insufficient to comprehend. I folded my hands in front of my waist and stared at the floor until she had finished. The subsequent silence lasted approximately thirty seconds and was broken simultaneously by Lena and Ridolfo, each screaming over the other.

Cécile leaned closer to me. "Perhaps we should leave them to their grief."

Signora Spichio stood up and slapped her son, then Lena. This time, it seemed, they were well and truly silenced. Ridolfo slunk out of the room. Lena sank back onto the settee, buried her head in her hands, and shook as she wept without making a sound.

Signora Spichio took my arm and pulled me into the kitchen, just off the parlor. "Could you please take Lena home? She and Ridolfo . . . I cannot deal with them now. Her family lives across the river. She can tell you the way. There is nothing for her here anymore."

"Of course. If you need anything else, don't hesitate to contact me at the Palazzo di Vieri."

"I know the house. It is not somewhere I would ever go." Her voice trembled.

"You can send a message and I will come to you here," I said, wondering if I was imagining fear in her words.

"Now that Marzo is away from that place, nothing else bad will happen to us."

Apparently, I was not imagining her fear. "Even so, I am here for you, signora. No mother should lose a child. I can only imagine your pain."

"If you mean what you say, pray for me. That is the only thing that can save any of us." She turned away and walked back to the other room, barking a command at Ridolfo, wherever he was, and then pulling Lena to her feet. "You will be at the funeral, but it is unlikely we will see each other again after that. I will remember what you did to and for my son, both the good and the bad. I thank you for the first. The second, I will never forgive."

Florence, 1480

12

I did not return to Santa Trinita for Mass the next day, nor the day after that. More than a week passed before I saw Father Cambio again for confession. I was upset, and at sixteen, that meant I wallowed, shamefully indulging myself. Soon, though, I grew bored, and turned back to Dante. It did not take long for the poet to distract me from my woes, which was not surprising, given how trivial they were compared to the trials faced by the damned in *Inferno*.

When I began reading, I immediately empathized with the inhabitants of limbo, who spent eternity unpunished but unhappy. The young see themselves in everything, and I was foolish enough to believe this first circle of hell very like my place on earth. My life was too comfortable to merit complaint, but I had no joy. I rushed through reading about the second circle, populated by those who had been ruined by lust. I could not muster up much interest in something wholly foreign to my world. Desire seemed so unworthy a sin. If I were to be damned, it would be for something serious, like murder or treason, not an ill-conceived romance.

The third circle punished gluttony, which I never before had contemplated, probably because my family's wealth ensured that I never wanted for anything. I always had enough. As a result, it never occurred to me to take more than I needed, although as I thought about it, I realized that this was not a logical conclusion. All around me were examples of people who hoarded far more than they needed. Was not excess the goal of us Florentines, wrapped in our luxurious trappings? This observation made me uncomfortable, as did Dante's description of the punishment suffered by gluttons.

Gluttony and abundance go hand and hand. The damned, mired in filthy muck, cry out in vain as an abundance of cold rain and icy hail ceaselessly fall on them. But that is not enough. Cerberus, the three-headed hound of classical mythology, attacks their flesh, the wounds not healing before he bites again and again and again. The misery is unrelenting.

When I think back on that first reading of *Inferno,* my youthful naïveté embarrasses me. There was no denying the hideous nature of the punishments Dante meted out to sinners. But rather than feeling scared or horrified, I took pleasure in reading about them, safe as I was in my comfortable room. The poem's torments illuminated the sublime contentedness that comes from knowing one is not suffering. That, however, was an idea I was not yet ready to contemplate.

As I reached the final canto of *Inferno,* I was wholly consumed by Dante's epic and stayed awake two nights in a row to finish that first volume. Exhausted yet exhilarated, I collapsed into bed and slept so long that my mother feared I had fallen ill. I forbade Alfia from telling her the truth, afraid she might take away the book.

Only after I'd finished did my thoughts return to the mortal world I occupied. I needed to go to confession, but at the time, I cared more about discussing the poem with Father Cambio than the status of my immortal soul. That alone should have concerned me.

When I reached Santa Trinita, Alfia trailing behind me, my excitement surged as I approached the door. Inside the confessional, I lost my balance when I heard an unrecognizable voice coming from the other side of the grill. Righting myself and returning to my knees, I rushed through the list of my sins, hardly hearing what the unfamiliar priest gave me to atone for them. I went into the nave and prayed, murmuring what I hoped were the correct number of Hail Marys to earn absolution, focusing not on the words but instead, searching for any sign of Father Cambio. He was nowhere to be found.

Finished, I looked for excuses to stay in the church, but nothing would persuade Alfia that I was unaccountably captivated by Lorenzo Monaco's painting of the Annunciation—a sure sign that I was not thinking clearly, as I ought to have been able to argue my way around her, no matter the situation. She insisted we go home before my mother despaired of us.

The emotions that consumed me, starting in the confessional and following me home, gripped me like nothing I'd ever before experienced. I could not identify them, let alone begin to understand them. There was a measure that felt like abandonment, another like despair. But none of it could be described as either rational or justified. I had no control of my racing thoughts. There was nothing to do but give into them, and as I did that, I started to find clarity, clarity that terrified me.

My mind could focus on nothing but Father Cambio. At first, I credited this to my passion for Dante's poem, but as the days passed, I had to admit that it went beyond that. I was angry at not having seen him, hurt by feeling ignored. Desperate to know if I'd somehow brought this on myself, I longed for someone with whom I could discuss my troubles, but even in the throes of my misery, I knew I could not unburden myself to anyone.

I saw him at Mass on Sunday, but did not interact with him beyond taking Communion. The following Wednesday, I returned to Santa Trinita and stepped into the confessional, rejoicing when I heard Father Cambio's voice. The list of my sins tumbled from my lips and my heart raced. Once he'd granted me absolution and I'd said my prayers, we started our usual turn around the nave. I wondered how I could have let myself get so caught up in a tumult of emotion.

"I was sad not to see you last week," I said. "It affected me more than I expected."

"How so, Mina?"

"I can't say I fully understand. I desperately wanted to discuss *Inferno,* of course, and when you weren't here, it forced me to acknowledge that there is no one else in my life I can really talk to, not in any meaningful way."

"I'm sorry you were upset," he said. "Our friendship is important to me, too, but you must know that I am first and foremost your priest. It would not be appropriate for anything else to eclipse the nature of that relationship."

"Of course not," I said. "I wouldn't want it to."

"Good. Then we can continue."

Something about the way he spoke tugged at me. *Then* we can continue? "Did you deliberately distance yourself from me?" I asked.

"I did."

"Because of something I did?"

"No, Mina. Because I could sense that you were being pulled in a dangerous direction. Think not on it anymore. We've addressed it and can put it behind us. For now, though, it would be best if you go home. Next week, you will be in the proper frame of mind to consider Dante."

It gutted me to be pushed away from him without any real conversation, and left me longing all the more for it. It was the first experience of my life that began to teach me that we humans want things most when we're told we can't have them. An obvious point, but a powerful one.

Florence, 1903

13

Lena was quiet, keeping her head bowed as we exited the Spichio apartment. I waited to break the silence until after we'd stepped into the sunshine on the street outside. "We walked here, but I can hire a cab if you'd prefer," I said. "There are plenty in the Piazza Santa Croce."

"I would like to speak to you before you do Signora Spichio's bidding and force me to go home," the girl said. Her eyes were still red and swollen, but her voice was stronger now. "Can we find somewhere quiet?"

We walked to the piazza, past the nineteenth-century statue of Dante erected in its center to honor the six-hundredth anniversary of the poet's birth, and climbed the steps to the entrance of the church. Given that Santa Croce was more or less the Italian equivalent of Westminster Abbey, with monuments and memorials to Galileo, Michelangelo, Dante, Machiavelli, Rossini, and more, it was unsurprising to see it filled with tourists. We headed toward the cloisters, ducked through an atrium supported by Corinthian columns, and stepped into a perfect domed chapel—empty, aside from us—designed by Brunelleschi for the Pazzi family. As they had led the fifteenth-century conspiracy against the Medici that ended with a dramatic assassination in the Duomo, it seemed an appropriate place for our own collusion, even if poor Lena had no idea we were hiding the truth about her fiancé. She believed him to have died in an accident, not at the hand of some yet-unknown villain. Or so I thought.

"Marzo's fall was no accident," she said, pulling Cécile and me close, her voice hushed.

"What makes you say that?" I asked.

"Ridolfo knew his brother was dead before your husband told the family yesterday. Just after lunch the day before Signore Hargreaves came, I was in the apartment with Signora Spichio, making pappardelle while her ragù al cinghiale—wild boar ragù—simmered. She told me she wouldn't share her recipe for that until after the wedding but was more than happy for me to help with the pasta. Ridolfo came in, when he should have been at work, a crazed expression on his face, and told us Marzo would not be home for dinner."

I waited, assuming there was more to her story, but nothing came. "Did he say anything else?"

"There was no need to," she said.

"His suggestion that Marzo would not dine with his family that evening was enough to make you believe your fiancé was dead?"

"Oh, no, not that," she said. "Obviously, Marzo never did come home; and later in the evening, when Signora Spichio commented that she would save some of the ragù for him, Ridolfo said not to bother, that he was the elder son now. At the time, I thought it was just a nod to their usual rivalry, but now I see it was more. Ridolfo already knew Marzo was dead."

"They did not get along?" Cécile asked.

"Not since Marzo and I agreed to marry. You see, I used to walk out with Ridolfo, when we were young, but he is a man with no ambition, and once I became old enough to recognize that, I stopped seeing him. Ridolfo was furious when he learned I was with Marzo, even though years had passed since we had been together."

"Do you think Ridolfo killed his brother?" Cécile asked.

"No, there's no chance of that. Marzo was working on your roof. Ridolfo is far too lazy to have ever climbed up so high. And he is not a man to see to dirty deeds of that sort."

"Would he have hired someone else to do it for him?" I asked.

"There was much bitterness between them, but neither would murder the other. As for paying, Ridolfo would never be able to afford that. I suspect, though, that he was aware of another person who felt hatred for Marzo."

"Who?" I asked.

"That I do not know," she said. "You must talk to Ridolfo, find out how he knew before anyone else that Marzo was dead."

"I don't think he's likely to confide in Signora du Lac or me," I said. "Will his anger at you ebb now that his brother is gone?"

"It might if I tell him I'd loved him all along. He is stupid enough to believe that."

"I would never ask you to do that."

"It might be amusing," she said, her eyes brightening. "There are things about him I miss. But I could not let his mother see what I am doing. She would be angry."

Rightly so, I thought. "Where does Ridolfo work?"

"Not in Florence. He is a tanner in Santa Croce sull'Arno, halfway to Pisa."

"How far away is that?" Cécile asked.

Lena shrugged. "Thirty miles or so? Far enough that he has a room there."

"Yet he was in Florence the day his brother died?" I asked. "Was that unusual?"

"Not entirely. As I said, he is lazy and does whatever he can to avoid work."

"Was he home when my husband broke the news about Marzo's death?"

"Yes, but I believe Signore Hargreaves told him downstairs when Ridolfo answered the door. What do we do now? Will you talk to him? Or should I pretend to like him again?"

"I will approach him," I said. "I don't want you to put yourself in an awkward situation."

"If you change your mind, leave word for me at Dante's cenotaph.

You can slip an envelope under the arm of the sculpture of the lady weeping. I will check every day—and you should do the same, in case I need to contact you."

"I assure you, that won't be necessary—"

She interrupted. "But it would be thrilling, would it not, passing secret messages?" She smiled again and lowered her voice. "I must go now. There's no need to escort me. I wanted to speak to you away from the family and pretended to cry so that Signora Spichio would ask you to take me home."

"You really must let us escort you—"

She was gone before I could finish my sentence.

Nonplussed, Cécile and I tried to go after her, but she had disappeared from the church. We stopped in front of Dante's monument to gather our thoughts. The poet was exiled from Florence after supporting the wrong side—that is, the losing side—in the strife between the White and Black Guelfs in the early fourteenth century. He adopted Ravenna as his home, died and was buried there, never returning to his beloved Florence. Despite attempts in the seventeenth century to return his mortal remains to the city of his birth, Ravenna refused. Why should Florence have the poet in death, when she banned him in life? Nonetheless, in the nineteenth century, the city commissioned sculptor Stefano Ricci to make a cenotaph for the poet, even if it was to sit forever empty in the church. In a way, it was a long overdue apology from the city.

There was a spot perfect for hiding a note behind the arm of the mourning woman sculpted draping herself over the tomb. I mention this only as an observation, having had no intention of communicating with Lena in such a fashion.

Cécile turned away from the monument before I did. "The girl was clearly upset after she and Ridolfo argued," she said. "Her eyes were nearly swollen shut from crying. Yet now she acts as if she is unaffected."

"I hardly know what to make of her," I said. "She's grieving, that much is evident. Why, then, this bizarre suggestion to pretend to rekindle her old romance with Ridolfo?"

"Maybe she does believe he murdered Marzo."

"All the more reason to keep away from him. I've no idea what she's playing at, but if it is true that Ridolfo knew Marzo was dead before Colin informed the family, there's something odd going on. We know the fall didn't kill him. Colin let as much slip when we found the body."

"If Ridolfo is as lazy as Lena claims, she's right that he wouldn't have dragged his brother's body to the top of a roof," Cécile said.

"I agree. But maybe he knows the actual cause of Marzo's death." I wanted to hear from Colin how Ridolfo had reacted upon hearing about the accident. Had he seemed surprised? If so, was it due to the news itself or to the story being presented, a story he knew to be false?

"What now?"

"Now, Cécile, we play tourist, so that we can convince Darius we're doing nothing else. I want to see Giotto's frescoes of the life of St. Francis."

"I thought you were going to leave flowers on Machiavelli's tomb."

"I would if I had any," I said. "As it is, Niccolò will have to make do with only my prayers."

When we returned to the palazzo late in the afternoon, the gentlemen were waiting for us in the Sala dei Pappagalli. After finishing our exploration of Santa Croce, we had meandered through the shops in the piazza, where I bought a dozen wooden trays—*sezzatini*—carefully painted and decorated with gilt in the manner traditional to Florence since the fourteenth century. Colin's eyebrows rose almost to his hairline when I made a show of opening the parcels. He was not used to me being so enthusiastic about shopping.

"Each one is a unique design," I said. "A husband and wife run the shop and do the painting themselves. It's too marvelous. Just the sort of thing the Medici might have had in their own palazzo. I do hope you don't think twelve is too many, darling, but I couldn't resist."

"Not too many at all," Colin said. I might be laying it on too thick. He looked as if he were having trouble keeping from laughing. Fortunately, Darius did not know me well enough to recognize my purchases as out of character.

"What about you, Cécile?" Darius asked. "Did you manage to resist the siren call of Florentine trays?"

"I did, monsieur. Much as I would like to discuss the details of our day, I'm afraid I must retreat to dress for dinner. I've invited a guest to join us." She excused herself and went upstairs. I wanted desperately to talk to Colin privately, but wasn't sure this was the right time to give him a *longing look.* Surely that would be better when Darius wouldn't be left alone. In the end, I didn't need to decide. Tessa came into the room with a telegram for Colin, who, upon opening it and reading, told me he needed a moment alone with his colleague and stood up to leave the room.

"Don't go," I said. "I haven't had a chance to work on my graffiti project today. This is the perfect opportunity."

I had noticed writing on the wall in the second floor dining room that morning at breakfast, so, after collecting my notebook and pencil from our bedroom, I copied and translated it. The year 1494 appeared twice, and there was a message about charity or alms being dispensed. Another fragment mentioned someone being scourged. There were other dates, parts of phrases, and several names. Just above the floor on a small wall near the door leading to the neighboring *studiolo,* I spotted a sentence written in Latin, the handwriting a match for that I'd found on the first floor landing:

> *quo magis in dubiis hominem spectare periclis / convenit adversisque in rebus noscere qui sit; / nam verae voces tum demum pectore ab imo / eliciuntur et eripitur persona manet res.*
>
> Watch a man in times of adversity to discover what kind of man he is; for then at last words of truth are drawn from the depths of his heart, and the mask is torn off.

I wondered if this, like the Latin sentence I'd seen on the landing, was from Lucretius, and regretted not yet having a copy of *De Rerum Natura* in my possession. I copied the remaining graffiti in the room, sketched a diagram to indicate where it was located, and then rang for Tessa to help me dress for dinner. By the time I returned downstairs, Cécile was already in the Sale Madornale with Signore Tazzera.

"Colin will join us shortly," I said. "He had just arrived to change when I was leaving our room." The timing, unfortunately, had meant we'd had little time to speak privately. I'd asked him what happened to his face—the bruise looked even worse now—and he gave me the same story Darius had about too much drink and would-be thieves seizing on this vulnerability. There had to be more to it, but nothing he would admit.

Signore Tazzera poured a glass of prosecco for me, from the supply he'd sent Cécile. "Your friend is very kind to pretend to like my gift," he said. "I know she would prefer champagne."

I accepted the beverage and thanked him. "I think your prosecco is delightful, but then I—unlike either Cécile or my husband, who brings whisky wherever he goes—enjoy indulging in local delicacies when I travel. Which is why we shall have limoncello after dinner."

"No port?" Darius said, entering the room. "Colin will be shocked."

"He knows my habits too well to be even slightly surprised."

Cécile introduced him to her friend, and Darius welcomed the new acquaintance with boundless warmth. "I have the greatest respect for your profession, Signore Tazzera. My family ought to have a comprehensive library, and did, until my grandfather, the most notoriously eccentric of my ancestors, drew the erroneous conclusion that his wife, who died of consumption, had contracted the disease from a copy of *Les Liaisons dangereuses*. He had forbidden her to read the book, although at the time made no mention of the threat of disease. Convinced it had led to her demise, he burned all four volumes. His friends pointed out the inanity of what he'd done, chiding him for believing one title among thousands could have caused her illness. Rather than back down from his position, he ordered the entire contents of his library taken outside and consigned to the flames. His very own bonfire of the vanities. My father did his best to refill the empty shelves, but these things take a great deal of time. Since inheriting, I, too, have made an effort, but am not in a position to get everything I'd like. As a result, I've spent a great deal of time in the Reading Room of the British Library and owe more of my education to that magical place than I do Cambridge."

"I wonder, signore, which your grandfather feared more: consumption or the ideas in Laclos's novel," Signore Tazzera said.

"There's little doubt in my mind," Darius replied. "I say, this wine is excellent. I'm indebted to you bringing it for us and to the ever-charming Cécile, who is good enough to share it with us."

"Do not delude yourself, sir," the librarian said. "She is grateful to have others drink it so that it disappears more quickly and she can return to champagne."

"You see why I like the man, Kallista," Cécile said. "He is sensible and realistic."

"I had no idea you were drawn to either," Colin said, grinning as he joined us. "Emily, before I forget, I've contacted Hatchards about your Lucretius, but it will likely take a week to arrive."

"You will read *De Rerum Natura,* Lady Emily?" Signore Tazzera asked. "*Splendido!* It is a wonderful work. How is your research into the history of this palazzo coming along?"

"Quite well, thank you. I uncovered a story of hidden treasure stashed away in this house. It seems inconceivable, but multiple sources make similar claims."

"Hidden treasure?" Darius asked. "Now that's something about which I can get excited. What is it? Gold bullion?"

"Florins, more likely," I said, "but I've found no description of what was hidden. The first mention was in a sixteenth-century history of the city, so whatever the treasure may be, it dates at least to then."

"I think it's a hoard of jewelry," Cécile said. "Imagine a young girl, forced to marry an ogre twice her age. After the wedding, when she realizes she cannot bear to live with him, she squirrels away the only things she has of value: jewelry. And then she waits for the right moment to make her escape."

"With her lover, I hope," Darius said. "Please let her have a lover."

"*Mais oui,* monsieur. Naturally she has a lover. But before they can flee—"

"To Siena," Signore Tazzera said. "It is a beautiful place."

"Siena, then," Cécile said. "The poor girl falls ill—"

"With consumption caught from the pages of a sensational novel," I said, laughing. "She dies without ever seeing her love again."

"Thus, leaving the jewels still hidden in the walls of the house," Darius said. "I like this story very much. Except for the consumption bit. Couldn't you let them run off?"

"Not if I want the jewelry to still be here for me to find," Cécile said.

"You can't really think there is treasure hidden in the house," Darius said, tugging at his shirt cuffs.

"It is not rational, monsieur, but some things are best left to intuition. Mine tells me there is something here waiting to be found. While Kallista busies herself with graffiti, I shall start a search. I do like to have a project of my own."

"It would be my infinite pleasure to assist you," Signore Tazzera said, giving a little bow. They would make a formidable team, but I was not convinced either of them was looking for a treasure hunt.

Florence,
1480

14

I did not know what to expect when I entered Santa Trinita the following week. I felt off-balance, unsure of myself. My voice was timid in confession, but Father Cambio did not seem to notice. We started our usual walk around the nave in silence, and I found myself lacking the confidence to start any sort of conversation. Finally, the priest spoke.

"So, Mina, tell me what you think of Dante's limbo."

Relief nearly knocked me to my knees. I had been unreasonably terrified that he would send me away again. In an instant, all of my worries and doubts and confusion evaporated. I smiled. "I recognized it."

"How so?"

"Not the details, of course, but the idea of a place that isn't painful or awful, but neither is it joyful."

"Like your world?"

"In many ways, yes," I said. "I make no attempt to claim my own small life worthy of the attentions of a poet like Dante, but I have very little influence on my circumstances. I want for nothing and shouldn't complain. I don't mean to do so now. It's merely an observation."

"An observation, I hope, that encourages you to seek comfort in Our Lord."

What else would one expect a priest to say? Even so, his response was more than a little disappointing. "Yes, I suppose. But what do you make of those brilliant minds from the past stuck for eternity in limbo? Homer and Socrates, Ovid and Virgil—virtuous men, all of them. I find it deeply troubling. They're excluded from heaven because they lived in the wrong time? What sort of just God would treat his creations so?"

Father Cambio looked around and bent close to whisper to me. "This sort of discussion is better continued somewhere more private. Come." He led me out of the main part of the church and into a small room off the cloisters. "God is just. By giving us free will, he allows us to choose actions that keep us from heaven."

"The ancients did not know the teachings of Jesus," I said. "They had no opportunity to be saved. How is that fair? More importantly, how is it not terrifying? The greatest thinkers in history, excluded from eternal joy, all because they didn't subscribe to a religion not yet invented."

"Our faith is not invented, Mina."

"I don't mean to suggest it is, but I find great solace in the study of humanism and reject vehemently the notion that it cannot help us attain bliss in the afterlife. Do not Augustine and Aquinas rely on secular reasoning to explain religion? Should not God reward the men who taught them—and us—to think logically? If nothing else, he could have at least put limbo on the edge of heaven, not hell. It hardly seems fair."

"You must remember, Mina, Dante is not writing theology. His poem is not doctrine."

"Don't you find it a more exciting catalyst for contemplating theology than other works?" I asked. "He writes in a way that grabs our souls. The beauty of his language stimulates us to consider more deeply, to care more passionately—"

"I fear you're veering away from religion," Father Cambio said.

The room in which we were now sitting—on carved beechwood chairs—was sparsely furnished. The walls were undecorated, but the ribs of the vaulted ceiling were painted with black stripes. The priest had left the heavy wooden door open.

"Must we always talk about religion?" I asked.

He laughed. "No, I suppose not."

"I have not told you what struck me the most about *Inferno*," I said.

"The lines written above the gate, *lasciate ogne speranza, voi ch'intrate.* Abandon hope, ye who enter here. That's the crux of everything, is it not? What do we have without hope? Even the worst days are made more bearable because of it." I was thinking about how awful I'd felt when I couldn't talk to Father Cambio. Yes, I'd been distraught, but somewhere, buried in the recesses of my mind, I had hope that our conversations would resume. "What could be worse than its absence?"

"Being separated from God, Mina."

"You will always turn it back to that, won't you?"

"How could I resist? Your cheeks color when your ire's up, and that occurs whenever I guide our conversation to religion."

I could feel them burning now, and my heart was racing. Our eyes met and at once a fiery sensation consumed me. I knew it was wrong, but all I wanted was to kiss him. It was a shameful urge, one I would have to admit to during my next confession. Looking at him, I believed he wanted it, too, but he did not move toward me. Instead, he rose from his chair and covered his face with his hands.

"We cannot act on this, Mina."

My heart pounded even faster than before. He did feel what I did. His choice to use the word *we* was the greatest gift I'd ever received. He knew we, together, were something. "We need not act," I said. "Knowing you return my affection is enough to satisfy me eternally."

"No blasphemy, not now. Only God can bring eternal satisfaction."

"I don't care. Let me be like Augustine: good, just not yet."

He rubbed his eyes and dropped his hands from his face. "You are a dangerous creature. I never expected this sort of temptation."

"Nor did I. It only started when you refused to see me. Not seeing you stirred in me emotions I'd never before experienced. I thought I could ignore them, but that no longer seems possible." I'd never had any intention ignoring them, but I didn't want him to know that, terrified it might spur him to cast me aside. Everything had changed in the minutes since we'd entered this room, and I never wanted to go back to the way it was before.

"You don't know what you're saying."

"I know what I feel."

"You must control it, or I will not be able to hear your confessions any longer."

I could hardly breathe. "You can't mean that."

"I do, Mina. I have to. We must wrest these thoughts from our minds. If we cannot muster the strength to do so, we can never meet again. These urges do not come from the Lord."

I stood up, my legs shaking. "I will go, then, and return next week for confession. I promise to master this temptation before then."

Florence, 1903

15

Darius and Signore Tazzera left the house together after dinner, and Cécile retired to her room shortly thereafter. Colin and I followed suit. I still had not become accustomed to the layout of the house, with its cold landings open to the sky. It made the contrasting warmth of the rooms all the cozier, and there is something to be said for getting a blast of fresh air, even if it's chilly, before retiring for the night.

"I'm rather disappointed that I had no need to shoot you a longing look tonight," I said, brushing my hair after putting on my nightgown, a filmy concoction of the finest lawn and Venetian lace. "I was rather looking forward to it."

"If you do it with the same amount of subtlety you applied to the account of your shopping this afternoon, Darius will have no doubt that you're up to something that has nothing to do with amorous intentions."

"I admit to getting carried away," I said.

"Your unguarded enthusiasm is one of the things I love best about you." He came up behind me, bent over, and wrapped his arms around my shoulders. I turned my head and he kissed me, but I pushed him away.

"No distractions, not yet." Finished with my hair, I sat on our bed while he unfastened the studs from his dress shirt, removed the garment, and flung it over a chair. "I called on the Spichios this morning," I said and took him moment by moment through my day. "What was your impression of Ridolfo when you met him?"

"Much the same as yours. He's a lout."

"Did he appear surprised when you told him about Marzo?"

"Shocked, I'd say, but I couldn't tell you whether that was due to learning his brother was dead or because he knew my information was not the whole truth. What do you make of Lena?"

I sighed. "She's utterly confusing. She was so upset at the apartment, but made a complete turnaround when we were in Santa Croce. I don't doubt that she loved Marzo—"

"Why?" Colin asked.

"Why don't I doubt that she loved him?"

"Yes. What evidence convinced you of that?"

I considered the question. "Her eyes. They were red and swollen. She could have pretended to cry, but not with that result. Yes, her mood changed after we left the Spichios, but maybe she was relieved to be away from his family. She mentioned that Marzo's mother wouldn't share a recipe with her until after the wedding, which suggests she didn't entirely trust her former future daughter-in-law. Ridolfo lashed out at Lena for not wanting to live with the family. Many Italian girls expect to move into their husbands' family home. It's unusual to do otherwise, yet Lena was insisting upon just that. Whatever her issues with his family, she still wanted to marry him, which is more evidence both that she loved him and that her grief is real."

"You're good at this, Emily," he said, his smile warm. "Anything else?"

"Her suggestion that we communicate by leaving letters hidden at Dante's cenotaph gives insight into her personality. Perhaps she likes adventure. Perhaps she doesn't take things as seriously as she ought."

"Perhaps she has reason to believe that open correspondence with you on the subject of her fiancé's death could prove dangerous."

His response took me by surprise. He rarely embraced such extreme explanations. "Do you believe that to be the case?" I asked.

"It's certainly possible, but I can't say with any confidence it's a reasonable theory. Lena might crave excitement, but that doesn't preclude her from being in danger, even if she's unaware of it. Now let's talk about Ridolfo."

"I know far less about him," I said, "and much of what I do is based on assertions from Lena, whom we have no reason to trust as reliable when it comes to him. She calls him lazy now, but she was romantically involved with him in the past and claims they parted ways when she saw the depths of his lack of ambition."

"Wouldn't she be inclined, even if she was not aware of it, to paint him in a bad light to justify throwing him over for his brother?" Colin asked. "It's not generally considered appropriate to go from one sibling to the next."

"Quite, although Lena can't be more than twenty years old. If she was involved with Ridolfo as an infatuated young teenager, it might not matter so much."

"Agreed."

"Is any of this helpful?" I asked.

"Having more information is always helpful, although I'm still of the mind that Marzo's death has solely to do with his work for the British."

"Even if he were killed directly as a result of his work, his assassin—I feel that's a more fitting term in the current circumstances than murderer—might have planned his crime based on details from Marzo's life, to throw suspicion in another direction."

"An assassin wouldn't bother," Colin said. "He'd do the job quickly and efficiently with an eye on nothing beyond avoiding getting caught. It's difficult to prove culpability after the fact when a killer has no connection to his victim."

"Wouldn't they have a professional connection?"

"Yes, but only in the most tenuous way. If I needed someone eliminated, I would discuss it with my superiors, who would, in turn, decide how to deal with it. They would not ask me to handle the task myself, but rather assign it to a person otherwise unrelated to the situation."

I cringed, never before having considered that my husband might—even peripherally—be involved in an assassination. For the first time, I didn't want more details about his work. Still, something niggled at me. "I understand the point, but surely there are circumstances in your line of work that require immediate action by an agent already on the scene.

In that case, isn't it conceivable that Marzo's life, connections, routine could prove illuminating?"

"It is not impossible."

"Then I shall continue my work and tell you everything."

"I appreciate your candor and am sorry I can't share with you what I've learned," he said.

"At this moment, I'm not sure that troubles me."

"You're not? That shocks me to my core. Do I know you at all?" he asked, his dark eyes sparkling. "I shall have to undertake a careful examination of every inch of your person, to make sure you're not an imposter posing as my wife."

"I suppose your doing so is critical to the empire?" I asked. He nodded, brushed my hair away from the back of my neck, and kissed me. Who was I to stand in the way of such a noble cause?

The next morning, Cécile and I went to the Uffizi Gallery. It's difficult to imagine Florence without this famous Mannerist structure, but it did not yet exist in the days of Cosimo de' Medici—il Vecchio—or his grandson, Lorenzo the Magnificent. Built in the sixteenth century by renowned architect Giorgio Vasari to serve as offices for the city's government, it is now one of the most important art museums in the world. My friend and I both wanted to see the collection, but also needed a place where we could not be overheard while discussing our investigation. In this regard, the limited privacy of a public space was preferable to the house. I was not confident we could trust Tessa.

"Do you think we are being followed?" Cécile asked, glancing back over her shoulder.

"I can't imagine anyone would be interested in following us," I said. "It's not as if we've uncovered sensitive information or have special insight into Marzo's death."

"I've been reading Monsieur Le Queux's book, the one you abandoned and left in the Sala dei Pappagalli. It's quite intriguing. I especially liked the bit where he discusses how the days of British supremacy are coming to an end. He says, *The English have endeavored to rule the world far too long. They must be suppressed, and the Powers have already agreed that the time has come to crush this nation of swaggering idiots.*"

"I believe it was an enemy agent making that claim," I said. "It hardly reflects Mr. Le Queux's own views."

"I say it only to tease you, Kallista. You know I don't despise the English. At least not all of them."

"Your magnanimity is laudable," I said, accepting her teasing in good humor.

"The book leads me to believe that if we're entangled in the work of spies, we have every right to expect to be followed. Preferably by a dashing sort of agent."

"Is there any other kind?"

"*Oui,* if Marzo Spichio was one."

"Don't be unkind to the dead, Cécile."

She shrugged but made no reply.

Inside the museum, we climbed the stairs to the gallery on the second floor, pausing briefly in front of Botticelli's *Birth of Venus.* We then sat on a bench in the corridor near windows that offered sweeping views of the city, the Arno in one direction and the Duomo in the other.

"Because Lena did not allow us to accompany her home, we don't know where she lives," I said. "I want to speak to Ridolfo. We need to learn more about him, and he can tell us where to find Lena."

"Will he still be in Florence?" Cécile asked. "He works outside the city."

"If Lena's characterization of his laziness can be even half believed, I doubt he'd return to the tannery until after his brother's funeral. I had a message for him delivered to the family apartment this morning, asking him to meet us here at eleven." I glanced at my watch. "He's nearly a quarter of an hour late, so it may be that my deductions are nothing but useless drivel."

"He does not strike me as a man who knows his way around a museum. As such, it is sensible to expect tardiness."

Cécile was correct. At twenty past the hour, Ridolfo Spichio sauntered toward us, more interested in ogling the fashionable ladies in the gallery than in showing even a passing concern for art. But he had come, and for that, I was grateful. I thanked him and explained that I'd wanted us to be able to speak freely, without causing his mother further upset.

"I'm curious," I said. "Why did Lena insist on living away from your family?"

"She is a girl who likes to put on airs, who thinks she is too good to live like a peasant. Which is insulting, as my family has never been peasants. She wants to believe she belongs in a palazzo."

"Surely she knew Marzo couldn't afford a house like that," I said.

"She was willing to modify her desires, at least to some degree."

"It must have hurt your mother," Cécile said. "She, after all, still lives with her own mother-in-law."

"Lena thinks she's better than everyone, which is why my mother didn't care what the girl wanted to do. But she didn't like the idea of losing Marzo. Now, though, she's lost him in a far worse way."

"She still has you," I said, "and I imagine she needs you now more than ever."

He snorted. "Unfortunate for me. My work is not in Florence. I cannot move back in with her, and I shouldn't have to."

"I didn't mean to suggest you should. Tell me about your work."

"I'm a tanner. It would not interest you."

"Florentine leather is the most beautiful in the world," Cécile said. "Why would that not interest us?"

"Have you smelled many animal hides, signora? You would not find it pleasant."

Cécile bristled. "I do not equate pleasant with interesting."

"Why am I here?" he asked. "I know it's not to talk about tanneries."

"We want to know more about your brother," I said. "I feel awful about his death and wish I had known him better."

"You told me he was kind. That is what Marzo was good at—making people believe whatever he wanted them to about him. If you lived with him, you would know he was not so kind. He was selfish, more concerned with his fiancée's whims than his mother. He never even feigned the slightest interest in me."

"I'm sure he cared," I said.

"You're wrong on that count. Did you know Lena was engaged to me? Six weeks before the wedding she met my brother. Two days later, she told me she could not marry me."

This was a markedly different version of the story than Lena had told us. "How long were you engaged?" I asked.

"Four months."

"In all that time she never met your family?"

"She met my mother and my nonna. I kept her away from Marzo because I knew he would steal her from me."

"How did you know that?" I asked.

"Because whenever he saw something he wanted, he did whatever was necessary to get it. Lena is beautiful. Any man would want her. It came as no surprise to me when he took her."

"How long after she called off your wedding did she agree to marry Marzo?" Cécile asked.

"Nine days. Nine. I was humiliated."

Cécile frowned. "How long ago did this happen?"

"A year ago."

"I'm sorry," I said. "No one deserves to be treated in such a callous manner, particularly by his own brother."

"What does it matter now?" He balled his hands into tight fists.

"Were you surprised to learn of his death?" I asked.

"Only because it was an accident. Given the way he treats others, I would have thought it more likely he'd be murdered."

"Who would you have suspected?" Cécile asked.

"Who cares? No one had the nerve to do it. But I suppose I can take comfort in knowing that he's gone and can't hurt anyone else."

"You didn't kill him when he stole your fiancée," I said. "Is there someone else who has a stronger motive for wanting him dead than that?"

"Are you suggesting I murdered my brother?"

"No, of course not. His death was an accident." I needed to tread with care. "I just wondered what he'd done to people unrelated to him, given the appalling manner in which he treated you."

"That was his business, and now that he's dead, it's no one's. I'm sorry to throw water on your rosy view of poor Marzo, but the truth is that you should rejoice at not having known him better."

With that, he turned away and stormed back toward the stairs, taking no notice of any of the ladies he passed. His mood had changed completely. I almost let him go before remembering that I needed to know where Lena lived. I leapt to my feet and ran after him.

"Wait, please, Ridolfo," I called. He stopped, glowering at me. "I know it's not appropriate at the moment, but I should like to let Lena know what I think of the way she so callously cast you aside. She did not allow Signora du Lac and me to take her home yesterday, so I do not know how to reach her. Can you tell me where to find her house?"

"Cross Ponte Santa Trinita and go to the Piazza Santo Spirito. Look for a shop there that sells leather accessories. Her father owns it. That is all I have to say to you, signora. Please leave my family alone. We have enough trouble without you looking for more."

Florence, 1480

16

To claim that I had mastered my temptation before I again saw Father Cambio would be a lie worthy of the worst circle of Dante's hell, had he reserved it for those driven by lust rather than treachery. I was convinced I'd tried valiantly, but as I ponder my actions now, so many years later, I recognize my effort as barely even half-hearted. At the time, though, I could not have behaved any differently. I had no desire to. The delicious longing I felt for him was the most exciting experience of my life. It consumed me.

And it focused me. Everything I did was carefully crafted to ensure I could see him again, a strange course of action, given that the only occasions on which I was kept from him had stemmed from his own choice. But I did not recognize that in those heady days.

After confession the next week, we did not take a turn around the nave of the church, instead going directly to the room off the cloisters. Father Cambio had left there his copy of *Inferno.* He directed me to sit down and started to read aloud from it, Canto V, the tragic story of Francesca da Rimini. A high-spirited girl, she was forced to marry a man both deformed and cruel. But Francesca knew nothing of his character, not at first. The wedding took place between her and a proxy: her husband's kind and handsome brother, Paolo. No one, however, told her he was a proxy, and she fell in love with him at once.

Theirs was a love that could not be denied. Together, they read the story of another pair of doomed lovers, Lancelot and Guinevere. As noble as that other couple, Francesca and Paolo did their best to resist temptation, but when they reached the part in the book where the knight, at last, kissed his fair lady, they were overcome.

Quando leggemmo il disïato riso
esser basciato da cotanto amante,
questi, che mai da me non fia diviso,
la bocca mi basciò tutto tremante.
Galeotto fu 'l libro e chi lo scrisse:
quel giorno più non vi leggemmo avante.
When as we read of the much-longed-for smile
Being by such a noble lover kissed,
This one, who ne'er from me shall be divided,
Kissed me upon the mouth all palpitating.
Galeotto was the book and he who wrote it.
That day no farther did we read therein.

That day, we, too, read no further. Like Lancelot, my love came to me and kissed my lips, whispering that I must no longer think of him as Father Cambio but as my own Giacomo. He tasted of wine, sweet and tart. From that moment, everything changed.

Florence, 1903

17

The walk Cécile and I took to the Piazza Santo Spirito was my first excursion into the Oltrarno, the other side of the Arno. The Ponte Santa Trinita's elegant arches spanned the river, offering an incomparable view of Florence's most famous bridge, the Ponte Vecchio. The first structure on the site was Roman, dating to 994, but the current Ponte Vecchio had been constructed in 1345, a flood having destroyed its predecessor. Medieval shops lined it on both sides. Atop the buildings on the east runs an enclosed corridor designed by Vasari in the sixteenth century to make it possible for the Medici to travel from the town hall, Palazzo della Signoria, to their ducal home at Palazzo Pitti, across the river, without having to encounter the public.

After crossing the bridge, we turned toward Santo Spirito, quickly locating Lena's father's leather shop when we reached the piazza. Inside, gleaming wooden counters displayed a stunning collection of handbags, valises, wallets, book covers, portfolios, and more. The leather was indisputably of the finest quality, but adding to its inherent beauty was the method used to decorate it. Florence is famous for its colorful marbled paper. Here, a similar technique was used to stunning effect on leather, giving exquisite detail to the pieces. A boy who looked to be no more than fifteen popped his head out from a door in the back.

"Can I help you?" he asked.

"We're looking for the shop's owner," I said.

"I can fetch him for you if you'll wait." I thanked him and he disappeared behind the door. We could hear his footsteps clattering up the stairs, and a few minutes later a middle-aged man with gleaming raven hair—not yet marred by a single streak of silver—greeted us.

"I am Signore Bastieri," he said. "Are you looking for something in particular?"

"I didn't realize what a pressing need I have for a new bag until I saw your exquisite stock," Cécile said. "It's unlike anything else I've ever seen." She picked up a buttery tan chatelaine bag, its strap decorated with marbling the colors of sunset.

"Your compliments are most appreciated," he said. "If you prefer something made to your specific needs, I can design it for you, using whatever style and colors you like."

"I am overwhelmed, monsieur," she said, "and suspect we are going to require a long, long meeting to discuss what I want. I'm going to keep you busily at work for months."

He smiled. "I am at your service, signora."

"I'm afraid before we can start, however, my friend needs to speak to you about something else," Cécile said, nodding toward me.

"I'm looking for your daughter, Lena."

His eyes narrowed. "What has she done?"

"Nothing so far as I know," I said. "I was acquainted with her fiancé and met her yesterday at the Spichios' apartment. Do you know where I might find her?"

His countenance darkened, turning somber. "She is upstairs in our own apartment, but she is most distraught, signora. Losing Marzo is a blow from which I fear she may not recover. I wish her mother were still alive to comfort her, but we lost her when Lena was only three."

"I am more sorry than I can say. Would it be possible to see her?" I asked. "She expressed a desire that we keep in touch."

"Of course," he said.

"You go without me, Kallista," Cécile said. "I should like to speak with Monsieur Bastieri about ordering a number of pieces."

I followed him into his workshop. In contrast to the beautifully spare displays in the front, the backroom was a jumble, full of stacks of soft leather and gleaming paint. We ducked into a narrow stairway, climbing until we reached a door that, when opened, led directly into a large, bright, sitting room. The furniture was modest but well-built and in good condition. Most interesting to me was a bookshelf full of leather-bound volumes.

"They're beautiful," I said, pulling down a copy of Dante. "Did you make the covers?"

"I am no bookbinder. A friend from my guild does them for me," Signore Bastieri said.

Lena emerged from what I assumed was the kitchen, her face smudged with flour. "Don't start him talking about the guild. He won't stop."

"You should be proud that I'm a consul." There was no censure in his voice, either because he was used to her needling or because he indulged her. "If you need me, I'll be downstairs."

"It's quite an honor to hold an office in a guild," I said after he was gone.

"The consuls are chosen at random, their names pulled from an urn," Lena said. "They only serve a few months. It's nothing to cause excitement."

"The Furriers and Skinners are a powerful guild, are they not?"

"The last in precedence of *Le Arti Maggiori,*" she said.

"Which are the Greater Guilds of Florence, the most influential in the city."

She rolled her eyes. "I ought not be so critical, but I find guild business immensely boring. My father is a respected member, likely to someday be *provveditore* or even *consigliere,* but I doubt you came here to discuss guilds. Would you like coffee?"

"No, thank you, don't go to any trouble. I've come to see how you're doing."

"If you wanted to see me, you should have left a message at Dante's monument to arrange a meeting," Lena said. "How did you find me?"

"It wasn't so difficult," I said. "I prefer face-to-face conversation over notes left on monuments whenever possible."

She raised one delicate eyebrow. "Why are you here? I don't mean to call into question your sincerity, but it seems strange that you would hunt down someone you hardly know on the pretense of caring about my well-being."

"Ridolfo Spichio told me some rather confusing things," I said. "Things that contradicted your account of the relationship the two of you shared."

"Ridolfo is a liar," she said. "I would not have guessed you would fall for his ludicrous inventions."

"I didn't say I believed him. Were the two of you engaged to marry?"

She blew out a long breath, frustration on her face. "Of course he would dredge that up. You must understand, Lady Emily, that I was very young when I first knew Ridolfo. He may not look it now, but he has the potential to be extremely attractive. He is tall and has good hair. His eyes are dark and intriguing. Before he let himself go in that tannery, he was a man worthy of consideration."

"How old were you when you met?" I asked.

"Eighteen."

Not young enough to excuse her behavior. "How old are you now?"

"A lady should never ask that question."

"You're not so old that it's necessary to blanche when it's asked."

She sighed. "I'm twenty."

"How did you meet?"

"I was in the Mercato Centrale, shopping. He and a group of friends were there, loitering. They started to follow me, singing songs they made up as they went, praising my beauty. It was flattering. I enjoyed the attention. The next evening, he serenaded me, standing in front of the shop until I opened the window and begged him to stop."

"Why did you want him to stop? You just said the attention was flattering."

"I didn't really want him to stop, but everyone knows there's no more effective way to keep a boy interested than to pretend you don't want him. That was my plan. It worked."

"You drew him in enough to get him to propose."

"Yes. I didn't love him, but I adored the game of making him want me. It was exciting. When he proposed, I didn't think he meant it, not really. I still don't. It was just that he'd tried everything else to win me. By then, I was so enchanted by the prospect of starting my own life that I said yes before I gave any real thought to what I was doing. It didn't take long for me to see I could never have what I wanted with him. As I told you, he is lazy and unambitious."

"So after you met his brother, you waited barely more than a week before you threw over your fiancé for Marzo, whose ambition made him more desirable?"

"You make it sound worse than it was. Yes, Ridolfo and I were engaged, more or less, but there was never a firm plan for a wedding. Beyond that, I'd known Marzo for ages."

"That's not how Ridolfo tells it," I said.

"Ridolfo knows nothing about it. When I first met Marzo—long before I ever knew Ridolfo—he never showed the slightest interest in me. My father had hired him to do some repairs to the shop. The front window was leaking. I liked him the moment I saw him, but it was clear I had no effect on him."

"His indifference made you want him more?"

"Yes. He taught me that lesson well."

"So you deployed the same tactic on his brother, thinking it would wound Marzo?"

She folded her arms across her chest. "It is not as if I had some grand scheme for revenge. It wasn't like that at all. I didn't know at first Ridolfo and Marzo were brothers."

"Were there specific plans for a wedding?"

"La smetti di rompere le scatole?"

I didn't recognize the expression, so couldn't respond.

She glared at me. "Will you please stop aggravating me? I did not intend for things to turn out as badly as they did. Why does it matter now, anyway? Marzo is dead and my only chance of happiness with him."

"So you did love him?" I asked.

"From the moment I first saw him."

"Why did you lie to me when we discussed this before?"

"I don't know," she said. "I was caught off guard, although I should have expected Ridolfo would tar me in any way he could."

"Why do you care what he tells me about you?"

"I wasn't lying when I said that Ridolfo knew Marzo was dead before your husband informed the family. Wouldn't you be cautious, even deceptive, when a murderer might be on the loose?"

"I don't see how your deception would have any bearing on your safety. You claimed it was impossible that Ridolfo would kill his brother. Has something happened to change your mind?"

"He's a violent man, Ridolfo. I don't believe he murdered his brother, but he very well might use Marzo's death as an excuse to come after me."

"When have you seen him behave violently?" I asked. She certainly hadn't mentioned it in our previous conversation.

"The day I ended our engagement," she said. "The bruises faded long ago, so I can't show them to you."

"I'm sorry." I paused, not sure what to believe. She had lied to me about so many things, how could I ascertain when—or if—she was telling the truth? "Given that, how could you bear to suggest, as you did, that you'd pretend to care about him again to get information?"

"I don't know. It might be worth it, not only if it led to the discovery of who killed Marzo but also for the satisfaction of seeing Ridolfo's heart broken."

"It would not be worth it if he hurt you again."

"I'm too smart to let that happen. Not anymore."

"Regardless, there's no need for you to resort to such measures. The best thing for you to do is grieve your loss and forget all about Ridolfo."

"I will consider your advice, Lady Emily, but in the end I must keep in mind that what is best for you is not necessarily best for me." She crossed to the door and opened it. "If there's nothing further to discuss, you ought to return to the shop."

"Please take care, Lena," I said. "Don't be reckless. If anything happens that unsettles you, contact me at once. Not via Dante's cenotaph but at the palazzo."

"I can promise I will not do that," she said, the haughty tone she'd adopted when suggesting I leave evaporating. "Something's not right about Marzo's death. I may not know what, but he died in your house. I will never go there. If you cannot find me, I hope at least then you will check the poet's monument. That is the only place I will leave a message."

After leaving the Piazza Santo Spirito, Cécile and I did not retrace our steps, instead crossing the river via the Ponte Vecchio. We had decided that each day we would allow ourselves one tourist activity, partly to continue deceiving Darius and partly to satisfy our desire to see Florence.

In the Middle Ages, butcher shops spanned the bridge. The river below made it easy for their owners to get rid of the foul refuse left from their bloody work. In the sixteenth century, Ferdinando I de' Medici, deciding the smell was unseemly, ordered all the shops replaced by more genteel businesses. Specifically, jewelers and goldsmiths. These tradesmen still offer their wares, and Cécile and I browsed through their stores as we crossed the bridge.

The third shop we entered—they were all quite small, their space limited by their location—contained some of the most delicate jewelry I'd ever seen, as well as a handful of items made from florins, the gold coins minted by the Republic of Florence. The proprietor, an elderly man, his spine bent and his knuckles gnarled, explained in flawless English that his family, the di Nardos, had owned the shop from the days of Ferdinando.

"The descendants of the family of the butchers we replaced still harbor animosity, can you imagine? So long after the demise of the Medici, their enemies are still angry. We use the florin in some of our pieces as a nod to the old days, but now make replicas of the coins, as the originals are quite rare. For the rest of our collection, we employ the same techniques used in the Renaissance in order to create jewelry that, while appealing to fashionable ladies like you, would not have looked out of place adorning the wife of Lorenzo il Magnifico," Signore di Nardo said. "I have two sons. The elder is a painter. He designs our pieces. The younger is a goldsmith. He brings his brother's work to life. Did you know that the great Brunelleschi, who put the dome on our cathedral, began as a goldsmith?"

"I did not," Cécile said. "But it should surprise no one that a superior artist would exhibit multitudinous talents."

"The great Alberti said, *A man can do all things if he will.* You know of Alberti?"

"He was one of the most accomplished men of the Renaissance," I said. "A philosopher and architect, I believe."

"There was very little he couldn't do, signora," he said. "We do not have many men like this anymore. It is a tragedy."

"I am curious, monsieur, to learn more about the jewelry of the Renaissance," Cécile said. "Rings, in particular, and other small pieces one could easily hide away."

"Jewelry has long been a form of currency for ladies who are kept from their families' fortunes," he said. "In Florence, a wealthy bride might have received fifteen or twenty rings from members of her husband's family, but, technically, she did not own them. When the time came, she would present them to other girls marrying into the clan."

"So she couldn't keep them?" I asked.

"Not forever, no."

"That rather puts a damper on your idea that we shall find a stash of rings hidden in the palazzo," I said to Cécile.

"Do you expect to find such a treasure?" Signore di Nardo asked, incredulous.

"I hope to," Cécile said. "We know there is something hidden, but we don't know what. I had thought jewelry, as it's small."

"Which palazzo?"

"The Palazzo di Vieri," I said. "I found several references to a treasure that was deliberately concealed in the house."

"*Sì,* signora, its treasure is most famous."

"It is?" I asked, surprised.

"Oh, yes, but I would not try to look for it. Everyone who does ends up dead, in a most unpleasant manner."

Florence, 1480

18

For fourteen weeks, the most glorious passion consumed me. Joy filled every conversation I had, every task I undertook. I saw beauty in everything, was a caring and attentive daughter, a spirited and friendly sister, a generous and indulgent mistress to our servants, Alfia in particular. For without her, I would not have been able to spend so much time with Giacomo.

Fourteen weeks might not seem, empirically, like all that much time, but it was enough for me to give myself wholly to him, body and soul, and enough for him to leave me with an everlasting reminder of the stolen hours during which we clung to each other. Alfia was aware of the problem before I was, having more knowledge of such things than I. First, she noticed that my monthly courses were late. Then, that I was sick in the morning. Neither of which I understood as signals that I was with child. At least, not until she told me.

My mother had never broached the subject. When my courses first began, she left it to Alfia to explain how to contend with the inconvenience. I had almost no insight into the relations between husband and wife. According to my mother, there was no need for me to be burdened with the knowledge of such things until I was on the cusp of marriage. With Giacomo, I had succumbed to every bodily urge, giving little thought to where it might lead. Which is not to say I didn't know I was taking a great risk. I did. But it never occurred to me that it could all happen so quickly.

"You must do something about this at once," Alfia implored me. "Your mother will discover your secret if you wait too long."

"Do what?" I asked. She shrugged, but said nothing. I knew there were women who, for a fee, could eliminate such problems, but I would not consider taking such action. I loved Giacomo. I wanted his child. To describe the fantasies in which I indulged would be mortifying in the extreme. I was sixteen. I never doubted that he loved me, never doubted that, together, we would find a way. First, though, I would have to talk to him. Then we could make a plan.

When I went to confession that week—a ritual that had become charged with a host of inappropriate urges—I told him my sins, finishing, as had become a necessary habit, with those things that happened between us. As always, I struggled. I did not wish to make a bad confession. I was penitent. I tried—how I tried!—to resist letting it happen again, but never was I strong enough to resist when he looked at me, when he touched me. Week after week we swore to each other that we would stop, that we would return to discussing books. No more poetry, though. I suggested Euclid's *Elements,* he a dry collection of the lives of the saints. It was all for naught.

This time, however, after I'd begged for forgiveness and promised to do better, there was one more thing I had to address. My nerves jangled, but with excitement rather than fear. We walked to the little room off the cloisters that I had come to think of as ours, and, once inside, I told him my news, ready to comfort him when he realized he would have to leave the priesthood, but confident that I could help him find equal—if not more—satisfaction in being a husband. The lusty look I'd come to crave seeing in his eyes disappeared, replaced by one harder and colder than stone. Still, I was not scared.

"I know it will cause a terrible scandal, but together, we can face it," I said. "If it becomes too much, we can always leave Florence. Dreadful though that sounds—"

"Signorina, stop." I hardly recognized his voice. All intimacy, all warmth was gone. "I will handle the matter. There will be no scandal. You will come to confession as usual next week. Any alteration in your routine might be noticed. By then, I will have a plan in place."

"Will we—"

He interrupted me again. "Nothing further. Not now. We must not be seen alone together."

He did not touch me, did not offer me a single word of encouragement. Even so, I was more curious than worried, wanting to know the details of the plan he would formulate, never doubting we would have a life together.

Alfia was waiting for me in the nave when I emerged from the cloisters. "Did you tell him?" she asked, waiting until we had left the church.

"I did. He will arrange everything."

"Meaning what?"

"We will be married, of course. What else could it mean?"

She was too kind to introduce me to the truth. Not yet, at any rate. At the time, I saw sadness in her eyes and assumed she feared she would not be invited to join the household Giacomo and I would set up. I told her I would take her with me. She shook her head, but said nothing.

Almost a week later, my mother came to me, a letter in her hand. "Mina, I've received an invitation for you to visit Father Cambio's sister at her villa near Lake Garda. She's a widow now and has always been sickly, he explains, and likes to have a companion, someone amusing and intelligent. He wrote to her about you some weeks ago, and she asks if you would come live with her for the next year. It's a great honor."

My heart was pounding. Lake Garda? Giacomo's sister? I didn't even know he had a sister, but it was a brilliant scheme. We could marry from there, after he'd renounced the priesthood, and present ourselves to my parents as a couple, when it was too late for them to interfere. My mother was watching me, waiting for a reply. Not wanting to show too much excitement, I remained guarded. "I've never been to Lake Garda."

"Signora Cambio married into one of the wealthiest and most influential families in Lombardy. It's likely she will introduce you to many young men who would make suitable husbands."

Indeed, but I was no longer in need of a suitor. I was already all but engaged. I wondered what my mother's reaction would be when she learned of my marriage. I couldn't help but smile. "When will I leave?"

She draped her arm around my shoulder, pulled me close, and patted my hair, like she had when I was a little girl. "This is a marvelous opportunity for you. Your father and I discussed it last night and agreed that you should go. I've already replied to say that you will set off the day after tomorrow. Alfia will accompany you."

I can still recall every detail of that crisp, autumnal day. The bright sun mirrored my mood, and my confidence was unshakable. I knew Giacomo and I would face scathing disapproval, but we could survive that. Love, I believed then, made it possible to survive anything. I desperately wanted to see him, to tell him how heartily I approved of his plan. Ordinarily, I would not be going to confession until the following morning, but my mother would be so busy organizing the details of my trip, she was unlikely to notice if I slipped out for a bit. I couldn't wait any longer to see Giacomo.

I sent for Alfia and told her I needed to go to church.

"Why?" she asked. "What's happening?"

"I'm to go live with Giacomo's sister for the next year and you're to come with me. I never dreamed he would act so quickly! I wonder how soon we'll be married. I don't know what, precisely, he will have to do to leave the priesthood. Speak to the bishop, I suppose, but—"

"It would be best not to go to him right now," Alfia said. "Wait for him to contact you at his sister's."

"Why would you say that?" I asked.

She scrunched her lips and beetled her brows. "This is a delicate situation. Drawing any attention to your connection could put all of your plans in jeopardy."

"Don't be silly. All I'm doing is going to confession, as I do every week. No one will notice if I do it a day early, and even if someone did, I can explain that I was eager to receive one more sacrament in my family's church before going away for such a long time."

Alfia sighed. "I don't think I was ever so young as you."

"What does that mean?"

"Not young, but innocent."

"You're not making any sense."

"I don't think you should go," she said. "It may cause you much pain. Then again, it may be the last . . ." Her voice trailed. She shook her head. "I will do your bidding."

I drew a deep breath as we entered the church, warmth filling me. The lingering aroma of incense smelled like all good things. I searched until I found Giacomo, reading in the garden of the cloisters.

"Forgive me for intruding upon you like this," I said. "My mother told me of the invitation to your sister's. I know I should be more patient and wait for your further instructions, but I had to see you."

"You should not be here," he said angrily, glancing around to make sure there was no one else present and then motioning for me to follow him. We went to our room. "I told you to come for confession as usual. This is not usual."

"My mother tells me I am to leave the day after tomorrow, so tomorrow will be hectic and I might not have been able to come. I couldn't leave Florence without seeing you again."

He closed his eyes, but I thought I saw his face soften. "Yes," he murmured, pulling me to him. "Just once again."

It was the sweetest hour of my life.

Afterward, as I arranged myself, I felt all aglow. "I suppose we won't meet again until we marry. I don't know how I shall wait—"

"Marry? Marry?" He stepped away from me and laughed. "Signorina Portinari, I don't know how you came to the conclusion we would marry. I am a priest. My life is dedicated to God. I can take no wife. My sister will help you see to the baby. Beyond that, we can have no further relationship."

"I know that leaving the priesthood is something not to be taken lightly, but—"

"Why would I leave the priesthood?" he asked. "It is unfortunate that our encounters have left you encumbered, which is why I have offered my sister's assistance, but this has no bearing on my holy orders."

I was reeling, confused, angry, crushed. "We sinned together and must face the consequences together."

"Not together, signorina. Quite separately. If you want me to hear your confession one last time, I will. Otherwise, there is nothing left to be done. I do have another appointment this afternoon, so if you would repent, we should get on with it."

"I am in great need of the sacrament," I said and followed him back into the church. I mumbled half coherently in the confessional, fighting tears. Upon my exit, I nearly collapsed. Alfia rushed from the pew on which she'd been waiting and steadied me.

"I'm sorry, signorina," she said.

"No, Alfia, it will be all right. He just—" I stopped. "I must go back and speak to him again, if only to—"

She steered me around so that I was looking back at the confessional. There, pulling open the door was a young girl, about my age, beautiful and elegant, bright with anticipation in a way wholly inappropriate for one about to ask for absolution from her sins. I recognized the look all too well.

When Alfia went outside, I refused to leave the small, triangular piazza, insisting that we wait until the girl left the church. I marked the time with the bells ringing from the campanile. She did not emerge for nearly two hours, and when she did, she was radiant, just as I used to be.

My heart broke in that instant, never to heal again.

Florence,

1903

19

"Dead in a most unpleasant manner?" I repeated the jeweler's words back to him. "Could you please provide more details?"

"*Sì*, there are at least three stories that spring to mind," Signore di Nardo said. "The first, of course, is that of the lady who hid the treasure in the first place. It is said Savonarola burned her as a heretic, and that his action led to the curse that has held the house in its grip ever since."

"Who was she?" I asked.

"I do not know her name," he said. "But a century or so after her death, a man decided to start opening walls in the palazzo. He'd heard rumors of a treasure hidden away from Savonarola's gangs who marauded through the city seizing anything they considered sinful."

"Jewelry, for example," Cécile said.

"Exactly." Signore di Nardo continued. "Jewelry and any trappings of luxury frowned upon by the little friar and his thugs. No sooner had the gentleman then living in the house breached the first wall than he was stricken with plague. It killed him within a few hours. His son had the wall repaired. No one else in the family fell ill."

"And the third story?" I asked.

"That is the one I know in the most detail. Bartolomeo di Vieri, the last member of the family that built the palazzo, had fallen into a genteel poverty. The Vieris had once been powerful allies of the Medici, but their influence and their fortune were long gone by the time Bartolomeo inherited. He married three times, but none of his wives ever gave him a child. Two died trying, and an illness strangely like the plague that held Florence in its grips during the fifteenth century claimed the third. No doctor could explain how she might have acquired it. We all know how contagious the disease is, yet no one else in the city exhibited any symptoms, only Bartolomeo's poor wife."

"What does this have to do with the treasure?" I asked.

"Because he was teetering toward financial ruin, Bartolomeo started to research the stories about the valuables hidden in his house. He spent much of his life trying to find them, to no avail."

"Yet his wives, not he, were the ones who died," I said. "That seems to argue against a curse."

"No, signora, it does not. The curse is a punishment, meant to deter anyone tempted to seek the treasure. Bartolomeo did not care whether he lived or died. Death would have released him from poverty. But he did care, very deeply, for his wives. The curse struck them down to punish him." He grinned. "Or so they say. I myself do not put much stock in such tales, although they are most entertaining."

"Do you believe there is a treasure hidden in the house?" Cécile asked.

"All old houses hold secrets, do they not? Most are not worth finding."

We spent another quarter of an hour in the shop. I bought a pair of cuff links for Colin. As Cécile and I ducked in and out of the other establishments on the bridge, we asked if their owners knew the stories of the treasure at Palazzo di Vieri; they all did. Each told us a version that varied slightly from the rest, but the essential message was the same: look for the treasure and expect a grisly death.

Colin and Darius roared with delight that evening when, having gathered in the Sala dei Pappagalli after dinner, we recounted for them the tales shared by the jewelers. Neither they nor Cécile was put off searching for the Renaissance treasure by a legendary curse.

"It only spurs me on," Cécile said. "I wonder, Kallista, about the Latin graffiti you've discovered. It could contain a coded message that reveals the location of the treasure."

"I don't see a connection," I said. "We have two quotations from a Roman poet: *The first beginnings of things cannot be distinguished by the eye,* and the advice that

> Watch a man in times of adversity to discover what kind of man he is; for then at last words of truth are drawn from the depths of his heart, and the mask is torn off.

Neither seems like a code."

"*The first beginnings of things cannot be distinguished by the eye,*" Darius said. "How much more clearly could a sentence warn us that at first we won't recognize what we are seeing?"

"You found that one on the landing outside this room, correct?" Colin asked. I nodded. "That is the first place a visitor reaches after passing through the more public areas of the house, which does suggest that it's the initial message being communicated by whoever wrote it. Where are the rest of the Latin sentences?"

"I've only barely made a start finding them," I said.

"It sounds as if it's time to look for more," Darius said. "Don't you have a notebook for the project? Colin, fetch it for her."

"It's in the room on the third floor directly above our bedroom," I said. "I've been using the space as my study."

"I'll get it," Colin said. "Don't start before I return." He dashed from the room. When he came back, with lanterns for each of us as well as my notebook and pencil, he asked where I would like to begin.

"If we are to adopt an organized approach to this project, based on the layout of the house, we ought to start on the ground floor and work our way up," I said. The air having grown chilly since sunset, Cécile and I pulled on wraps, and we clattered down the stairs, along the side of the courtyard, and into the loggia.

During the Middle Ages and the Renaissance, the loggia would have served as a semipublic space. Here, the master of the house might conduct business or hold political meetings, but it could also be used for private family ceremonies, like weddings and funerals. Over the centuries, many homeowners divided loggias, converting the space into shops, either renting them to tenants or using them for their own commercial ventures.

Our loggia, with its vaulted ceiling, showed no signs indicative of how it had been used in the past. We scrutinized every inch of its walls, illuminating their surfaces with our lanterns, finding traces of three frescoes but no graffiti, and so moved into the courtyard. The Vieri family coat of arms was displayed on the walls above the Corinthian columns that defined the space, and carved heads of individuals whose hats identified them as medieval topped the corner pilasters. A rendering of the di Vieri family tree hung near the entrance and a certain amount of faded paint remained on stones of the staircase. Above us, stars twinkled in the sky.

"I don't see any graffiti," Darius said, crouching down to examine one of the walls. He started to rise, but lost his balance and reached out to steady himself. His dinner jacket caught on the wall, tearing the sleeve. "That's bloody inconvenient."

"No cursing in front of the ladies," Colin said, his voice teasing.

I crossed to Darius to inspect the damage. "It doesn't look too bad. Your valet will have no trouble mending it."

"Let's hope so. I've no desire to see my tailor anytime soon." He brushed dust from his suit. "Right. Any graffiti to be found here?"

There was none, so we moved to the storage rooms and then returned to the first floor. We found nothing more until we entered a small room off the Sala dei Pappagalli. As originally built, each floor of the palazzo contained a latrine, one stacked above the next, floor after floor. The countess, after buying the house, had modernized them, a task made easier by the existence of the admittedly primitive plumbing. Humans have a long history of scrawling on the walls of such spaces, as witnessed in the ancient public lavatories in Pompeii.

"What does it say?" Colin asked.

"A single phrase," I replied. "*Who betrayed me?*"

"There's more," Cécile said. "Look here." She pointed to one of the other walls.

I translated as best I could:

Love brings me happiness. I feel sorrow when I'm hurt.
There'll be trouble for whoever tells me they're leaving.
They'll have to be quick or I'll pay them back sooner or later.

"I don't think this has anything to do with the Lucretius quotes," I said. "The handwriting is completely different and it's in the *dialetto toscano,* not Latin." Nonetheless, I recorded it, and its location, in my notebook.

"*Who betrayed me?*" Darius whispered. The light from our lanterns flickered eerily. "Someone was afraid for his life. Someone who could have lived here with whoever wrote the Latin phrases."

"Or could have lived here two hundred years later," Colin said. "We have no way to reliably date any of the graffiti."

"Some include dates," Cécile said.

"Yes, but the mention of a date doesn't prove when it was written," he said.

"I'm not sure it matters," I said. "We're taking quite a leap thinking that the graffiti will lead us to the treasure. It's an enchanting idea, to be sure, but nothing in the sources I've uncovered mentions it. I shall continue my project, recording everything written on every wall in the house; and then, once we have that in its entirety, we can examine the texts and locations and draw a conclusion, one way or another."

Colin nodded. "That's the way to proceed. In the meantime—"

"I'm awfully tired, darling," I said, drawing out each of the words and shooting him what I hoped was a longing look. "Exhausted, even."

He met my eyes and smiled a dreamy half smile. "Are you, my dear girl? We can't have that."

"I hoped you'd say so." I held out my hand to him. "Will you escort me to our room?"

"Of course," he said, "so long as our friends won't scold us for abandoning them."

Cécile shrugged. "Monsieur Hargreaves, none of the thoughts currently racing through my head is suitable for public airing. Go, without delay."

"It was a bit clunky," I said, once we'd reached our bedroom and locked the door behind us, "but more fun than I'd expected, despite the fact that we were standing in a latrine."

"Let's not dwell on that last point," Colin said. He was pulling the pins out of my pompadour, which collapsed, leaving my hair hanging down to my waist. He kissed me, then sighed. "Right. Work first."

"Must we?" I asked. "This subterfuge is more arousing than I'd expected."

"It will only get more so, I promise." He walked away from me and leaned against the wall and then, seeming to remember it was decorated with centuries-old paint, moved to the door. He leaned there, but only for a moment before straightening up and starting to pace. "What do you have to tell me?"

"I spoke to Lena, who revealed herself to have lied quite substantially." I related to him the contents of our conversation.

"So Ridolfo is violent. I can't say that comes as a surprise. I don't have any evidence to lead me to believe he killed his brother, but it's quite possible whoever did kill Marzo is deliberately trying to make us think otherwise."

"Your assassin might be using Ridolfo to throw our suspicions away from him?" I asked.

"Precisely."

"We don't have evidence to tie Ridolfo to the crime, but neither do we have evidence that condemns anyone else."

"I have enough to feel confident Ridolfo is not involved," he said.

"You can't share it."

"No."

"I understand." I studied every detail of his handsome face. "It's not that I don't trust you, or your methods, but I can't agree that we should dismiss Ridolfo's potential involvement." He opened his mouth to reply; I raised my hand to stop him. "I'm not making an attempt to persuade you to share your evidence. I know you can't. At the same time, however, I feel strongly that something in this mess between the brothers and Lena is pertinent."

"Ridolfo was not in Florence at the time of Marzo's death."

"You're certain?"

"I am."

"Lena thought—"

Now it was his turn to stop me. "Like you, I believe she's being deliberately dishonest. Whether that is to hide something she knows or to misdirect us, I can't say, but it would be helpful if you would continue to try to determine what is motivating her."

"I shall keep at it."

"As for this curse . . ." He paused, and I could tell he was no longer in agent-of-the-Crown mode. He peeled off his dinner jacket and fumbled with his cuff links. "Are you making it all up? It would be quite clever if you were. Darius is completely taken with it and hasn't the slightest suspicion that you're investigating Marzo's death."

"I wish I could take credit, but I can't," I said. "The treasure is mentioned in books, and given that all the jewelers on the Ponte Vecchio are familiar with stories of the curse, it's likely a well-known local legend."

"Do you give it any credence?"

I considered the question. "Everyone knows about the bonfire of the vanities and Savonarola's gangs of boys who forced Florentines to give up jewelry, art, books, anything deemed sinful. It's not outrageous to conclude that some citizens of the Republic would have chosen to hide things they considered precious."

"Savonarola was executed little more than a year after the bonfire in question. On the same spot, too, if I recall," Colin said. "Wouldn't whoever hid the treasure have taken it back out afterward?"

"Not if she'd been executed herself, burned under Savonarola's orders."

"I can't claim expertise on the subject, but I don't remember Savonarola burning great swaths of the Florentine population. He did like torture, though. Believed the fear of it was enough to control people. Of course, for that to work, you first must employ the punishment, often enough that the general population becomes afraid. Even so, I'm not convinced it's an effective measure. At any rate, it's possible that your Renaissance lady fled the city, fell ill, died—there are numerous explanations of why she might not have ever removed her treasure from its hiding place."

"And the stories of the curse could have sprung up, as they often do, when people search for explanations of the deaths of loved ones," I said.

"Quite. Regardless, hunting for treasure, though a pleasant diversion, is not going to bring us closer to learning the identity of Marzo's killer. Which is why you're brilliant to focus on it. Or at least appear to. Now, are there any other pressing concerns we need to discuss? If not, I'd like to explore the promises held in that longing look you cast my way when we were in that wretched latrine. Have you any objections?"

Naturally, I did not.

Lake Garda, 1480

20

I had never traveled far beyond Florence, only to my family's villa in the countryside, a short drive from the city, but I hardly noticed the view from the carriage that took me to the villa on the shores of Lake Garda. I'm sure it was beautiful; I did not care. The housekeeper led me to a spacious suite of rooms where Alfia helped me bathe and change into a fresh gown. While she unpacked my belongings, a maid took me to her mistress.

Fabbiana Cambio greeted me in an ornately furnished room off of which was a loggia that overlooked the lake. She bore a shocking resemblance to her brother. They both had the same green eyes, the same dark brown hair, the same elegant posture. But her face was paler and she coughed frequently.

"You poor thing," she said, not even introducing herself. "I will do what I can to make you comfortable here."

"I'm grateful to you, but I'm certain that Giacomo—Father Cambio—I don't know how to address him anymore—"

"It would be best if you found a way to stop thinking about him altogether, Mina. There will never again be a need for you to address him."

"But surely he'll come, he'll want to see—"

"His child?" She pressed her lips together and shook her head, ever so slightly. "He won't. He never does."

"Never?"

"Mina, you are not the first, nor will you be the last. I'm accustomed to my brother's shortcomings, of which there are many. Sometimes I wish the consumption would take me, so he'd no longer have a convenient place to send you girls."

"How many have there been?"

"It doesn't matter. I spoke to your slave. She says the child is expected in the spring. Winter is cold here, and will only get colder, but I prefer it to southern climates, no matter what the doctors tell me. You will be well looked after."

"And then?"

"You will stay through the summer. By then, we will have found you someone to marry. Your parents are unaware of your condition?"

"They suspect nothing." A crushing guilt descended upon me as I said the words.

"Good. That will make things easier."

"I'd rather not marry."

"It's either that or the convent. I promise to choose a man who will be kind to you. You deserve that much. It won't be a brilliant match, but given the circumstances, it is the best anyone can hope for."

"And my baby?"

"We will take it back to Florence, to the Ospedale degli Innocenti. They will take care of the child, see to its education, and put it on a righteous path."

"More righteous than that walked by its parents," I said.

"Don't be too hard on yourself. Giacomo is a beast. Once he chose you, you had very little chance of getting away. I don't know anyone who's managed to do it, but then, I suppose I wouldn't, would I? I will send food to your room so that you don't have to face any more conversation today. Tomorrow, I will show you my gardens, and we will settle into what I hope you find a satisfying routine. All I ask in return is that you try not to weep in my presence. That, I cannot abide."

Fabbiana, as she insisted I call her, proved an amiable companion, although I worried I was not the same for her, despite my having been invited on just that pretense. Every morning, we took a walk, even in bad weather—in defiance of ominous warnings from the doctor who wanted her inside as much as possible—and then made lace until it was time for my hostess's afternoon nap.

Those few hours were among the only ones I had to myself each day. At first, I resented the lack of privacy, but I soon came to realize that I was more content in Fabbiana's company than when I was on my own. Alone, I thought about Giacomo, about our child, about the dreams I'd for us.

Fabbiana insisted that I write to my family regularly, so I composed cheery notes about the mountains and the lake and my ever-increasing skills as a lace maker. As the weeks turned to months, I stopped fantasizing about what might have been with Giacomo and instead grew angry with him. When I fell into bed, though, I still could not help praying that he would come to me, at least to see our child. I told no one these thoughts, not even Alfia, who spent many nights comforting me as I cried in bed.

The new year arrived. Spring was violent, with unforgiving storms lashing down on us, one after another. My pains began late on the day before Easter. The baby, a boy, was born just after midnight on La Pasquetta, Easter Monday. His eyes were dark, not like his father's, but the midwife told me that might change. Not that I would ever know. I called him Diotisalvi and handed him over to Fabbiana as instructed. I would not see him again.

She took him to Florence herself. When she returned, three days later, she pressed into my hand a golden medallion, cut in half, a medal of St. Anthony. "Little Salvi has the other half," she said. "Should he ever try to find you, you'll need this to prove you're his mother."

"Might he try to find me?" I asked.

"It's not likely, Mina," she said. "But it never hurts to make it easier, just in case."

Florence, 1903

21

The next day, I was left alone. Cécile had accepted an invitation from Signore Tazzera to visit a winery in Chianti; Colin and Darius had gone out after consuming an enormous breakfast, saying they wouldn't be back until late afternoon. I decided to finish copying the graffiti on the walls of the house.

Much of it was irrelevant, at least to me. There were names that I did not recognize, dates that had lost their significance over the centuries, comments about measures of hay, and phrases rendered incomprehensible by the erosion of the letters that formed them. There were also four more passages written in Latin:

> *Saepius illa*
> *religio peperit scelerosa atque impia facta.*
> Again and again our foe, religion, has given birth to deeds sinful and unholy.
>
> *Ita res accendent lumina rebus.*
> So clearly will truths kindle light for truths.
>
> *Omnis cum in tenebris praesertim vita laboret.*
> Life is one long struggle in the dark.

Infidi maris insidias virisque dolumque
ut vitare velint, neve ullo tempore credant,
subdola cum ridet placidi pellacia ponti.
Never trust her at any time, when the calm sea shows her false alluring smile.

The first brought Savonarola to mind, guiding me a step closer to accepting that someone may well have hidden valuables to keep them out of the friar's bonfire. The fourth read as ominous. The other two did not immediately strike me as illuminating when it came to my investigations.

Life is one long struggle in the dark. As I contemplated this statement, I thought about Marzo. He certainly wanted money. Ridolfo claimed Lena insisted upon a house of her own, something his brother couldn't afford. Lena did not deny this. What if he knew about the treasure and his death was a result of trying to find it? He could have come to the house at night, mistaken as a burglar by Fredo. Furthermore, Marzo might not be the only one who was searching for it. If he had made progress that became evident to someone else, that someone else could have eliminated his competition.

I'd been working in my study on the third floor and went out to the gallery landing, poking my head over the railing, looking for Fredo, whom I'd seen earlier in the courtyard. He wasn't there now, but I could hear him whistling—a tune by Puccini—so I went downstairs, following the sound, and found him in one of the ground floor storage rooms.

"Fredo, what do you know of the stories of hidden treasure in this house?" I asked.

He grinned. "Oh, signora, we all know those tales, and I can promise you there is not a single person who has lived or worked in this house who has not tried to find whatever it is. But there is nothing. Trust me. I myself have made a thorough examination of every nook, every cranny, every dark space, every room."

"How did the stories start?"

"They go back to the days of that crazy friar who burned art," Fredo said. "Savonarola."

"Why have they persisted for so long when no one has ever found anything?"

"Most people need money, signora, and they all cling to hope, even ridiculous hope."

"What about the curse?" I asked.

He laughed. "There is no curse. If there were, I would be dead many times over. Surely you do not believe in such things?"

"I don't."

"Good, signora. You are safe in this house, even if you look for treasure. I can promise you that."

"The man whose body we found in the courtyard was named Marzo Spichio. Had you ever seen him before? Perhaps doing work on the house?"

"No, he was never here. I do all the maintenance needed. Tessa, Signora Orlandi, and Cook take care of the rest. The countess arranged her household so that it would require only a small staff, one she could trust."

"But she's been dead for more than a decade, and the house has been empty most of the time since then. Surely things have changed."

"I do not think so," Fredo said. "I did not work for her, but my father did. When he retired, I took his place. That is how it often goes here, one relative replacing another. Signora Orlandi is from the old crew, and she chose to hire Tessa, who is the cook's niece. We are all kept on at full pay, even when no one is in residence."

"Tessa is a well-educated young woman," I said. "That seems unusual for someone in her position."

"The countess had no tolerance for ignorance and required an educated staff. Tessa showed promise as a girl, so her schooling was taken care of."

"By the countess?"

"Until her death, after which the estate continued to support her."

"Who took care of the finances before my stepdaughter first came here?"

"For many years, it was handled by the man called Gruber from Vienna."

Mr. Gruber was the solicitor in charge of the countess's estate. It was he who informed Kat of her parentage and managed the assets she inherited from her mother. "And has that changed?" I asked.

"Six months ago your husband stepped in."

"Did he make any changes?"

"None, signora. Things in the Palazzo di Vieri do not often change."

I thanked him and then sought out the rest of the household staff. Signora Orlandi was in the kitchen with the cook. Neither of them told me anything that differed in the slightest from what Fredo had said. That left only Tessa, whom I found in my study, where she was dusting.

"You have asked the others these same questions, yes?" She left her dust cloth on a table and went to the window, looking outside.

"I have," I said.

"My answers will be the same as theirs. This household is run in a manner designed to protect the countess. Now that she is gone, the same standards apply. Nothing has changed, so far as I know."

"Have you searched for treasure in the house?"

"No, signora, you know I would never do that. Am I not the one who warned you that the house stops anyone who does?"

"You did, but I don't believe you give any more credence to the notion of a curse than I do."

"You're correct on that count," she said, "but I can't deny that strange things occur here, like those described by my grandmother."

"What other secrets does the house hold?"

"I wish I knew. Did you speak to the Spichio family?"

"I did."

"What did you learn?"

"Only that they are deeply saddened by their loss."

"That's all? Did you talk to Marzo's fiancée?"

"Yes. She's heartbroken."

All this time, Tessa had stood facing the window. Now, she turned to me. "Is she? I find that hard to swallow, given that she had once loved his brother."

"How do you know that?"

"You're not the only one curious about the dead man in our courtyard," she said. "I am not ignorant, signora. I know that Marzo was murdered and that the police should be investigating the crime. Why are they not? What is so special about this house, and the people who own it, that protects them from lawful inquiry? Should I worry about continuing to work here? If I die in mysterious circumstances, will the true cause of my death be hidden?"

"I would never stand for that," I said, wanting to reassure her, even as I knew I couldn't make her any promises.

"I trust you, signora, although maybe that is foolish. Your husband and his friend . . . I do not know what to make of them. They are not honest."

"My husband is honest."

"Is he? It does not seem so. He is congenial and polite, but that is not the same as honest."

My hackles rose and I wanted to defend Colin, but I reminded myself that she did not know anything about his work. "I know how outrageous it seems to keep the police out of the house, but, unfortunately, that is standard procedure among many well-to-do families. They don't like scandal. It doesn't mean that they aren't talking to the police. I assure you, Marzo's death is being investigated."

"But in private?"

"Yes."

"This, signora, is the sort of thing that leads people to build guillotines. The upper class thinks it can do whatever it wants. It never works out for them well in the long run, not when they start interfering with matters of life and death."

This was not the time to start arguing over historical details. She had skillfully manipulated a change in the direction of our conversation. It was time for me to do some manipulation of my own. "Tessa, please sit down." She did as I asked, taking the seat across from me near the fireplace. "I shall bring you into my confidence, but must insist that you do not share what I tell you with anyone else. Do I have your word?"

"Yes." Her voice was solemn.

"My husband and I have investigated murders going back more than a decade. Initially, my participation stemmed from the death of the gentleman I was married to before Mr. Hargreaves. Everyone told me he had died of natural causes, but I proved that one of his closest friends had murdered him. Since then, Mr. Hargreaves and I have been frequently called upon to assist with criminal inquiries. Time and time again, we have found that we cannot rely on the police."

"Yes, but you are English. In Italy—"

"I have seen this in England, yes, but also France, Russia, Austria, the Ottoman Empire, and more, including Italy. There was a murder in Venice some years back. I identified the culprit. We all want to believe that the police are capable of bringing criminals to justice, and often they are. Sometimes, however, it takes an outside investigator to get the job done."

"Wouldn't it be better to work with the police?" she asked.

"In my experience, I've generally found it is not. When it appears otherwise, I happily collaborate with them. In the meantime, I promise you I will see to it that Marzo's murderer is brought to justice."

"Is there anything I can do to help?"

"I've made a record of all the graffiti in the house, hoping that it might provide a clue as to the treasure supposedly hidden here during the fifteenth century, but nothing stood out. Why don't you take a look and see if you notice something I missed?"

"Searching for this is not a good idea."

"You just told me you don't believe in the curse," I said. "Neither of us does. However, if Marzo thought he could find whatever's hidden, his subsequent actions may have catalyzed someone to attack him. We both know he wasn't working in the house. We don't know why he was killed and his body flung into the courtyard. I'm trying to find anything that connects him to the palazzo."

"So you do not ask me to look for the treasure?"

"No, Signora du Lac is already bent on doing that and there's no reason for two of you to waste your time on what is bound to be a futile task. Instead, I would like you to look at the graffiti. Beyond that, I would welcome anything further you can learn about Marzo."

"That is easy enough," she said. "I will do as you ask."

I gave her my notebook and left her to her work. She insisted on finishing dusting before studying the graffiti. There was nothing for me to do in the house, so I decided to go for a walk. Fresh air always cleared my mind. I set off from the house, heading north, in the general direction of the Archaeology Museum, which stood on the corner across from the Ospedale degli Innocenti, a foundling hospital designed by Brunelleschi decades before he was chosen to build the famous dome atop the city's cathedral. His plan for the portico, supported by Corinthian columns, marked a departure from the old medieval architecture, returning to the perfect proportions of the classical era. At the time, it was so revolutionary, people gathered in the piazza to watch the construction.

As I crossed the street, the sky, which had grown gradually more cloudy as I walked, opened up, pounding the city with a sudden rain. I tugged at the museum's door, but it did not budge. A handwritten note tacked to it announced that the museum was closed, offering no further explanation. Having been seduced by the earlier sun, I had not brought an umbrella with me, and my hat, designed for style, not protection from the elements, did very little to fend off the deluge.

I ran back across the street into the piazza and took shelter under the vaulted ceiling of Brunelleschi's portico. The rain showed no sign of stopping. I considered my options and decided to go to the Mercato Nuovo, where Tessa had learned Marzo's surname. I, too, might find illumination there. And if not, at least an umbrella.

It would have been a sound plan if the market weren't nearly a mile from the Ospedale. I walked as quickly as I could, but it was impossible to avoid getting soaked. As my planned destination was only a few minutes from Kat's palazzo, I decided to return there, dry off, and collect an umbrella. I unlocked the heavy front door, stepped into the loggia, and brushed as much water as I could from my coat before taking off my hat and shaking it as I crossed through the iron gate into the courtyard. There, I heard heated voices coming from above.

"You cannot tell her anything." Signora Orlandi was speaking.

"She is too smart to be easily put off. That was obvious when she asked me about the graffiti this morning. We have got to—"

Fredo interrupted Tessa. "You are not the one to be ordering us around. Let's go back into the kitchen before Cook wonders what we're arguing about. We will meet later, in the usual spot, and formulate a plan."

"What if we can't get her to do what we want?" Tessa asked.

"Should it come to that, I will deal with her." Fredo's voice had taken on a hard edge.

"Let's hope that's unnecessary," Signora Orlandi said.

I stayed where I was until I heard the kitchen door open and close. They were talking about me; I no longer felt safe in the house. Unsettled, I crept silently upstairs and changed out of my wet clothes on my own, not wanting Tessa's help. I rescued my pompadour as best I could, pinned a new hat atop it, pulled on a gabardine coat, and collected an umbrella. Then I slipped out of the house, dismayed, shocked, and more than a little angry at what I'd overheard the staff saying.

I was still upset when I reached the Mercato Nuovo, so took a moment to collect myself. Standing in front of the market's famous fountain—*Il Porcellino,* a wild boar sculpted in bronze—I rubbed his snout and dropped a coin from his mouth to the grate below, ensuring my return to Florence. That done, and my mood slightly improved, I snapped closed my umbrella and stepped into the sixteenth-century covered loggia. I made my way through the stalls slowly, playing the curious shopper, examining the goods offered and buying more than strictly necessary, all the while conversing with the merchants in Italian, gently probing to see who among them had known Marzo.

I was careful not to arouse any suspicion, inquiring in general terms about the man who had died in the tragic accident at a house nearby. All of the merchants had heard about Marzo's death. It was the main topic of gossip, at least according to an elderly couple selling flowers.

"The city is generally quiet," the man said. "This brings some excitement."

"Do not judge my husband for sounding cavalier," his wife said. "We take no pleasure in Marzo's death, but that he would die in an accident was no surprise. He was always careless."

"You knew him?" I asked.

"*Sì*, signora," the man said. "Not well, but he bought flowers from us for his sweetheart, every Tuesday, to bring them to her at noon, right after he left us. I don't know why Tuesdays, but it was a kind gesture."

"You think he was kind," his wife said. "I think he was always apologizing. There was never joy in his eyes when we saw him. And he never chose the flowers himself, always left it to me to decide what he should buy."

"Young men are not as sentimental as you women would like," the man said. "He bought her flowers every week. Can't you be satisfied with that? Why does he have to do more?"

"Now he'll do nothing and the poor girl will be all alone."

"Are you acquainted with her?" I asked. They were not. "You mentioned that he was careless. What made you believe that?"

The man shook his head, but his wife answered. "He was clumsy. I can't count the number of times he knocked over displays."

"It happened often?" I asked.

"Often enough that we girded ourselves when we saw him approaching," the man said. "Not that we held it against him. As I said, he was a kind man."

"Would you say he did it every other time or every third time?"

"There was no regularity to it, signora," he said. "He was clumsy, that's all. Maybe he should have paid better attention, maybe he couldn't help it. Either way, it doesn't matter anymore, does it?"

Three people had lined up behind me, waiting to buy flowers, so I didn't linger. I purchased a bouquet of bright red blossoms and thanked the couple before moving on. I learned nothing new until I reached a booth where three young women proffered a variety of woolen goods. Before I could gently segue from complimenting what they had on offer to inquiring about Marzo, the tallest of the girls, who introduced herself as Vittoria, addressed the subject directly.

"I hear you are asking about Marzo," she said. "Did you know him?"

"A little," I replied. "Did you?"

"More than I would have liked, but at the same time, not as much as I would have liked."

"What do you mean by that?" I asked.

The other two girls started shouting at her, speaking too rapidly for me to follow. She barked at them, then turned back to me. "My sisters never liked him. They aggravate me, but their instincts about him were right. He was trouble. Mind you, I did not know he was engaged to be married when we met."

"You had a relationship with him?"

She shrugged. "Of sorts. He liked to flirt. So do I. I saw no harm in it. He asked if he could call on me, and I said yes. Why not? We would go for walks near my parents' house, but nothing really happened between us. He was funny and kind, handsome enough, but he never wanted anything more than those walks."

Not all flirtations develop into things more serious, but the way she told the story revealed something that went beyond ordinary romantic disappointment. Her tone and the furtive way she kept glancing back to see if her sisters were listening struck me as odd.

"That sort of thing happens often enough," I said.

"It does," Vittoria said. "He gave every appearance of enjoying the time we spent together, but now I think he was using me to get to someone else."

"To make his fiancée jealous?"

"No. To murder our neighbor."

Lake Garda, 1481

22

I can recall almost nothing about the weeks that followed Salvi's birth. I passed them in a haze of sorrow and regret. After a month, Fabbiana stopped indulging my moods and insisted that I return to making lace and taking walks with her. Gradually, the signs that I had carried a child faded from my body, and although I could feel I was different, no observer would have noticed. As spring turned to summer, my hostess started planning my marriage.

I only met Agnolo once before our betrothal. Before she introduced me to him, Fabbiana offered assurances that he was a good man, who would never suspect me of having lost my virtue, let alone that I had given birth to an illegitimate child. I wondered how that could be true, but was in no position to question her. And what did it matter? If he would have me, how could I object? If later he discovered my secret, I would still be his wife.

"He is an excellent choice for many reasons," Fabbiana said, as we waited for him to be brought to the loggia, where we were sitting. "At thirty-three, he is the right age to marry. Much older and one would start to ask questions. He doesn't involve himself much in politics, which keeps this from being a brilliant match for your family, but his fortune is enormous. He deals in silks, the most beautiful to be found in the world. Your trousseau will be the envy of every girl in Florence. His success means he spends most of his time engaged in business, so he will trouble you very little. I've no doubt you will find it a satisfactory arrangement."

I stared across the lake to the mountains, not wanting to look at her. The weather could not have been more favorable: sunny and warm, with a slight breeze, perfectly refreshing. Yet I was sweating as if it were the hottest day of summer. I heard footsteps behind me and knew he had arrived. Following Fabbiana's example, I rose to greet him, but almost keeled over when I saw his face. He was the man who had scowled at me when I was leaving the Medici palazzo with my grandfather, more than a year ago.

If I'd still possessed even an ounce of confidence, it would have fled in that moment. As I did not, seeing him only served to make me feel even smaller and more worthless than I already did. Fabbiana made the introductions; Signore di Vieri showed no sign of recognizing me. We made polite conversation for a quarter of an hour before our hostess excused herself, leaving us alone.

"Fabbiana speaks highly of you," he said. "Your family is well respected. I have no objections to marrying you. I do, however, realize that you may feel different. If that is the case, tell me now. There is no need for explanations or discussion. It's time I married, but I will not have a wife who's taken by force."

His words surprised me, and I could hardly find my voice. I stared down at the floor. "Do I not displease you?"

"Why would you ask that?"

"I saw you last year, when I was leaving the Palazzo Medici with my grandfather. You were waiting to speak to il Magnifico and glared at me in a manner so menacing I've never forgotten it."

"I have a vague memory of seeing a young lady with Signore Portinari. That was you?" He shook his head. "At the time, my thoughts were consumed by an unfortunate business development, one that I'd come to discuss with Lorenzo. I assure you my expression reflected no judgment on you and apologize to have caused you any pain."

How foolish I'd been to assume he'd taken any notice of me! The hurt and vulnerability that had spurred me into Giacomo's arms was no one's fault but my own. "You owe me no apology," I said. "I ought not have misread the situation. It doesn't matter now. Fabbiana told me you are kind. I have no objections."

"Very good. I will speak to your father this week, immediately upon my return to Florence. Regarding your cassoni, is there an artist you favor for the decoration?"

These marriage chests, a gift from him, would contain my trousseau and be carried through the city in our wedding procession as I made my way to my new home, a public display of the wealth and power of both our families. "Botticelli," I said, looking up at him.

He nodded. "Very good. I will see you back in Florence." Another nod, and he walked away.

And that was it. He made no effort to kiss me, to touch me. I was glad.

"Good news, I'm told," Fabbiana said as she stepped back onto the loggia, her arms spread wide. She embraced me. "I am pleased that you can now move on from this unhappy stage of your life."

I was, too, although at the moment I felt more off-balance than happy. It was as if I could hardly recognize the world anymore. Three weeks later, I returned to my father's house, where my ecstatic parents welcomed me, delighted that I was making a good marriage. I had undergone what should have been the most transforming experience of my life—giving birth to a child—but to everyone around me, it was as if nothing had changed. I had managed to escape public ruin, but inside, I was a tangle of despair.

I arrived home on a Saturday and did not go to church with my family the next day, pleading exhaustion after my journey from Lake Garda. In the excitement of making plans for the wedding, my mother did not notice that I skipped confession that week. The following Sunday, however, I could not avoid Mass. I girded myself, not knowing how I would feel when I saw Giacomo, how he would react to seeing me.

Sacrilegious though some might consider it, church was a place where Florentine girls could display their beauty and wealth in the hopes of enticing a well-heeled bachelor. I had no need for this, but I wanted to look my best. Alfia chose the gown I wore. It was the most beautiful one I owned, vermilion silk embroidered with gold. She brushed my hair until it gleamed and I looked like a model of Venus. Alfia understood, without being told, how much I needed to believe I could torment Giacomo. I would never forgive him for what he'd done to me. The only way I could make him suffer was to make him want me, when he could never have me again.

How naïve I was! I held my head high as we walked to our family pew. I met his eyes when he gave me Communion. But there was nothing in them. No reaction, let alone regret, not even a hint of recognition. Nothing that had transpired between us mattered to him. You can't hurt someone who doesn't care.

Which meant I was the only one in pain after Mass that Sunday.

I pleaded a headache when we got home and went straight to my room, where I collapsed on the bed, weeping.

"You must forget him," Alfia said, sitting next to me and gently brushing her hand over my forehead. "He is the worst sort of man and abused you terribly. See him for what he is. Despise him. Only when you've given yourself over to that will you be able to close your heart to him."

"I wish I could expose him," I said. "He's doing this to others and will continue to do so because no one will stand up to him."

"You can't expose him. Doing so would hurt you more than anyone. Your life would be in tatters. His would hardly change."

"Can I have him murdered?" I asked.

"That's the first encouraging thing you've said in months." Alfia smiled. "If I ever encounter a wandering assassin, I shall send him directly to you."

Florence, 1903

23

"Marzo murdered your neighbor?" I asked.

"I believe so," Vittoria said. She shouted something to her sisters and then came around the side of the booth to stand close to me, continuing in a low whisper. "I am not some innocent fool who believes every man who flirts with me might be interested in marriage. When Marzo and I went for walks, we always followed the same path, starting from my parents' house, going through the Piazza Santa Maria Novella, and then up past the railway station and around in an unremarkable loop."

"Not a route you would expect a young man with romantic inclinations to suggest?"

"Not at all. Wouldn't you prefer a stroll along the Arno?" She glanced over her shoulder at her sisters and then, satisfied that they weren't about to harass her, continued. "When we made our way back toward my home, instead of going the most direct way, he would always have us turn into the street immediately before the one on which I live. We would walk to the end, turn around, and then he would take me home."

"The street dead-ends?"

"Yes, so why go down it?"

"He may have wanted to prolong his time with you," I suggested.

"Nothing in the rest of his behavior made me think so," she said. "It's not as if he were bringing me to a secluded corner to steal a kiss. I didn't think much of it at the time. Then, not long before Marzo died, a man called Signore di Taro was murdered in his house in that little street. We never again went that way."

"Marzo may not have wanted to take you past the site of a grisly crime."

"If so, he never mentioned it. Everyone was talking about the murder, but he showed no interest in it whatsoever. When I brought it up, he only shrugged and said that we all eventually die."

"A callous reaction, certainly, but it doesn't mean he killed the man," I said.

"I know, signora, and I wish I had something more concrete to support my belief. I swear to you, Marzo was involved. We walked out together once more after that, and then he never called on me again. Soon thereafter he, too, was dead. I know in my heart there is a connection, even if I can't prove it. I tell you all this only to warn you. Marzo was not the man he appeared to be. Asking questions about him could prove dangerous. There are many things about him that did not quite make sense. Now I must return to work. I wish you good health and safety."

"Wait!" I called to her as she stepped back to her booth. "What is the name of the street where Signore di Taro lived?"

"It's better that you don't know." She set about helping a customer and wouldn't so much as look at me again. Recognizing that continuing to press her was unlikely to garner a result, I continued to make my way through the market, but gleaned no further information about Marzo.

My task was complete, but I had no intention of returning to the house yet. Instead, I marched straight to the Piazza Vittorio Emanuele II and into the lobby of the Savoy Hotel, which had opened twenty years earlier and was still lauded as providing the most modern accommodations in Florence. A bit of Britain on the Continent, for the unadventurous traveler who required that sort of thing. I penned a message to Colin, asking him to meet me at the first possible moment, and had the concierge arrange delivery to the Palazzo di Vieri. Then, knowing it would be some time until my husband returned home to receive it, I settled into a comfortable spot in the lobby, ordered a pot of tea, and regretted that I did not have a book to occupy me while I waited.

In the ensuing hours, I went over everything I'd learned pertaining to Marzo and his death, so that by the time Colin arrived, I would be able to present him with a measured overview.

"My dear girl, are you all right?" I had seen him enter the lobby and saunter over to me as if we made a habit of meeting in hotels. The concern in his voice was at odds with his deliberately casual demeanor.

"I am," I said, "but I thought it best not to return to the house without first speaking to you privately. I'm sorry if I alarmed you."

He sat next to me on the settee, ordered a whisky from the waiter who appeared almost the minute he arrived, and listened without taking his eyes from mine as I recounted for him all that had happened. When I finished, he nodded. "You were right to err on the side of caution. I find it hard to believe that the household staff pose a threat, but we shall have to take what you heard very seriously. I suspect it's nothing more than them wanting to find this wretched treasure, but I will speak to them and get to the bottom of it. I can promise you that everyone working in the house has been carefully vetted. The entire—"

"Yes, I know. The entire household was set up to protect the countess, and no systematic changes have been made since her death. I don't doubt that she knew how to address outside threats, but in the ensuing years, those threats may have changed."

"That's entirely possible," Colin said, "especially given that Darius and I are working from the palazzo."

"I want to think more about what Vittoria and the couple at the market told me. Forgive me if that means I'm treading into forbidden territory. Marzo demonstrated odd patterns of behavior. He bought flowers every Tuesday, but only sometimes knocked over a display, often enough that it was noticed. I'm wondering if his clumsiness was deliberate, meant to send a signal to someone. His regular pattern of appearing in the market at noonish once a week would seem innocuous, unremarkable. But to someone watching, the occasional deviation in his actions could have a specific meaning."

"You're quite right," Colin said. "It's a variation—admittedly an unnecessarily complicated one—of a common enough technique for signaling a message."

"Could Darius shed light on it?"

"He may be able to. Marzo was his contact, not mine. I can tell you it was not how he communicated with Darius. They used a different method."

We both fell silent as the waiter brought Colin's whisky. Once he'd gone, I continued. "I see a resemblance of sorts in the walks he took with Vittoria. They followed the same route each time, changing only after she brought up the murder. He may have been trying to establish a regular habit of being seen on the dead man's street. Once he'd killed Signore di Taro, he had no further need either for Vittoria or the walks."

Colin frowned. "That's more of a stretch. First, we have not established any connection between Marzo and di Taro. Second, it would be careless to stop the walks so quickly after the crime. Better to keep taking them until more time had passed."

"Perhaps he'd intended to do so, but being murdered prevented him," I said. "I agree we need more evidence, but it taxes credulity to suggest that coincidence led him to walk out with Vittoria, who lived so conveniently near the victim, particularly as Marzo did not actively pursue the relationship in any meaningful way. She did not strike me as the sort of girl who expects every man she meets to fall madly in love with her. He was engaged to Lena. Why would he start a flirtation with someone else but make no move to so much as kiss her?"

"He could have been hoping to find a friend."

"I do hope you're being facetious," I said.

"I am." He drained his whisky, returned the glass to the table in front of us, and drummed his fingers on the wood. "Your observations about Marzo's behavior are insightful, Emily. Good work. We should return to the house. I told Darius I was going to collect you after you'd had tea here at the hotel."

"Does he think me too fragile to make the five-minute walk on my own?"

"No, of course not. I told him you'd been ambushed by an unwelcome acquaintance we'd made on the train and needed my help extricating yourself from the threat of a dinner invitation."

"How complicated your life is," I said.

"My dear, no loving husband would leave his wife under obligation to the dreadful Baroness von Hohensteinbauergrunewald."

"The Baroness von Hohensteinbauergrunewald?" I beetled my brow. "Why is that name familiar?"

"Five years ago, when we were searching for Estella Lamar in Paris, you and Cécile stumbled upon the name in a hotel registry. The Meurice, I believe. The baroness had nothing to do with the case, but Cécile described to me a rather hilarious account of the lady's adventures in Egypt. There was some sort of archaeological controversy. The surname was so outlandish I could not help but remember it. I've long hoped for the opportunity to use it."

When we reached the house, Colin went straight to the top floor to talk to the staff, leaving me to find Darius in the Sala dei Pappagalli, reading. He leapt to his feet when I entered the room.

"What a lot of rot this is," he said, waving the book. "Please tell me it's not yours."

It was my volume of William Le Queux's stories. "I abandoned it soon after our arrival, but Cécile picked it up. She's finding it rather diverting."

"I suppose that's what fiction's meant to do," he said. "In this case, I object, however. Le Queux isn't interested in entertaining his readers. He's trying to stir up fear among the British people."

"I don't think anyone takes him that seriously."

"Forgive me. I have a tendency to outrage when I feel the citizens of the empire are being misled. How did you get on with the Baroness von Hohensteinbauergrunewald?"

"I'm surprised you can recall her name."

"I met her once, nearly ten years ago, while hiking in the Bavarian Alps."

"The baroness is an outdoorswoman?" I asked.

"Heavens, no. I was with friends from university, one of whom was acquainted with her family. Their estate was near the village we used as our base to access the mountains. She invited all of us to a positively appalling garden party, where she served the worst tea I have ever tasted and droned on about her collection of Egyptian antiquities. She was quite taken with me. It was appalling."

"It sounds it," I said. "Fortunately Colin bustled me out before she could invite me to dinner."

"Well, I shall be giving the Savoy a wide berth as long as she's there," he said.

"No need, Darius," Colin said as he entered the room and crossed to the end table upon which he'd placed the bottle of whisky he'd brought from home. "She's leaving on a late train tonight, headed for Venice, I believe."

"Heaven help La Serenissima," Darius said. "Pour me a glass, will you?"

"If I'd known that before I sent my message, I wouldn't have begged to be rescued," I said, smiling at Colin. "One dinner would not have been too much to bear."

"Oh, Emily, I assure you it would," Darius said. "Not even the promise of her imminently having to leave for the station would have been enough to get you through the meal. Tedious doesn't begin to describe her. You owe your husband a great debt."

"I shall keep that in mind." I met Colin's eyes and felt my cheeks color. "I'm off to dress for dinner and shall see you both shortly." I knew he would want to talk to Darius privately about what the servants had said. Before I reached our bedroom, I heard Cécile coming into the house. I waited until she had started up the stairs and then hailed her from the gallery landing. Together, we went to my study, where I updated her on the events of the day.

"*Mon dieu,* I would not have suspected anything of that sort from Tessa," she said. "I had a lengthy conversation with her last night. Her only secret is *un petit copain* called Giotto. Madame Orlandi knows his family and disapproves, so Tessa meets him away from the house."

"What about the treasure? Did she say anything about it?"

"She confided that all of the servants have searched for it at one point or another, but that no one has found anything. She insisted that if any of them had, they would not have kept it for themselves but reported it to us or Kat or the countess, I suppose, when she was still alive."

"Did you believe her?"

"I did, but not in the way you mean. I don't think anyone has hunted for it in years."

"Yet so many people have mentioned it to us," I said.

"Yes, but most of them only after we've asked. Something was hidden here, long ago. Maybe it still exists, maybe it doesn't, but regardless, it makes for good stories, like those told by the jewelers on the Ponte Vecchio. But to suggest that its existence matters now to anyone but us? I'm not convinced."

"The servants were definitely discussing it in a context that involved me. If they mean to distract us with it, what are they distracting us from?"

"This terrible business with Marzo, I imagine. Kallista, I know how hard you are trying to respect the boundaries of Monsieur Hargreaves's work. We are both aware that the murder has something to do with what he does for the Crown. I suspect your husband has asked Tessa and the others to encourage our interest in this little mystery so that we will apply ourselves to finding treasure and leave Marzo's death to them."

Could he be playing a more manipulative game than I knew? I didn't think so. We were being honest with each other, even if that meant him being straight about admitting that he couldn't tell me anything. "He wouldn't rely on servants to do that. He's been very clear with me and I've told him we accept the limitations of his work and won't interfere."

"He will not have believed you, not unless you put up a very strong fight before capitulating."

"He believes me."

"Kallista, the man is no fool. He knows we are investigating. About that, there can be no doubt. He could never be persuaded that you would abandon a murder investigation in favor of a treasure hunt likely to turn up nothing."

She was correct, of course, but I couldn't tell her that he not only knew exactly what we were doing but also that I was keeping him abreast of all our discoveries. It seemed ridiculous to hide it from her, but I had promised him I would and had to trust that he had reason to believe such subterfuge essential. I hated the deception, just as he had warned me I would. A dull pain ached in my abdomen.

"Let's not worry about what he thinks or doesn't," I said. "How was your time in Chianti?"

"Kallista, I did not go to Chianti. If I had, I would not have arrived back here in time for dinner." She sighed. "Renzo and I spent the day together, but we did not leave Florence. I invented the excursion to the winery so that neither Monsieur Hargreaves nor Monsieur Benton-Smith would know the more intimate nature of my plans. If they hadn't been at the breakfast table, I would have never felt the need for such a fiction."

"Colin wouldn't have judged you, and Darius is far too polite to have commented. He would have pretended not to hear."

"I am in complete agreement," she said. "I've become so accustomed to leading them both astray in order to make them think we've abandoned our investigation that I find myself firmly in the habit of lying to them. It's rather appalling how easily it happened."

I knew all too well what she meant. "Let's hope we don't have to carry on in this manner much longer."

Barking at the door told us that Caesar and Brutus had taken note of their mistress's return. I let them in and they raced to Cécile, who scooped them up and deposited them into her lap. "Many of the details of my day are irrelevant to our purposes, although I will tell you that Renzo's home has a roof terrace with an incomparable view of the city," she said. "We shared a bottle of champagne—a delicate attention that did not go unnoticed—there this afternoon. He is intrigued by the possibility of the treasure and has done further research into it, digging through a cache of letters dating to the days of Savonarola's control of Florence. They aren't specifically connected to records or histories of this house, so he did not bring them to you when we were in the library.

But now, knowing more, he thinks it could be advantageous to expand the search for other sources that might be of use. One of these letters—written by a silk merchant to one of his colleagues—mentions that there is a way to keep things safe."

"Things?" I asked.

"Unfortunately there is nothing more specific as to the nature of the items. However, the author of the letter was an avid collector of art, who expressed concerns that Savonarola's supporters would force him to destroy many of the paintings he owned. Those are the things that could have been kept safe here in this house."

"Paintings, not jewelry." I pondered the idea. "Or paintings and jewelry. The palazzo might have been a haven for anything to which Savonarola objected."

"That is just what Renzo deduced," Cécile said. "Many things could have been hidden here, but, alas, he believes that if that were the case, they all would have been returned to their owners after the friar's execution."

"Colin came to a similar conclusion. Does this mean you no longer give credence to the idea that there is any remaining treasure to be found?"

"Far from it." She removed a small, folded paper from her reticule. "This all but proves there's something yet to find."

Florence, 1481

24

I will forever be grateful to Fabbiana for finding me Agnolo, not because he proved a decent husband—which he did—but because marrying him made it possible for me to think about Salvi. In my parents' house, I was in constant fear of my secret being discovered, but by the second day of my marriage, I realized that had all changed.

The wedding had been like any other that united two wealthy Florentine families. I wore a gown made from the finest silk in the world, the color of a robin's egg and embroidered with gold thread. The impressive procession—the highlight of which was the magnificent cassoni Botticelli had decorated with scenes from classical mythology—left in awe those gathered on the sides of the city streets to watch. Or so my brothers told me. I went through the motions of the day feeling numb. I hardly tasted the food at our banquet. I felt nothing when Alfia helped me out of my gown and into a filmy nightdress, just as I felt nothing when my husband came to me. Had I managed to summon the energy to consider the details of our encounter, I would have been dumbfounded. How could the same actions result in sensations so entirely different? When Giacomo touched me, every nerve in my body sang. Agnolo's touch I hardly noticed.

The night before, my mother sat down with me to speak to me about marriage. Not the practical requirements of running a household; those she had drummed into my head for years. Now, she could no longer avoid discussing the more private aspects of the relationship between husband and wife. I had to bite back the reply I wanted to give when she admonished me to submit quietly and expect nothing. The act of love, she explained, was much enjoyed by the man, but nothing to a woman. Past experience had taught me otherwise.

My husband showed me she was not altogether wrong. It was not that he was unkind or insensitive, only that he awakened in me no passion, and, so far as I could tell, I awakened none in him, either. He seemed satisfied enough and I was content to think on it no further.

As Fabbiana had predicted, we spent little time together. He made a point of sitting with me every morning before he started work, but our conversation was largely limited to pleasant banalities. We frequently had guests at dinner, which kept me from having to talk to him. I do not wish to insult him. As I have already said, he was never unkind, not in any way, nor was he uneducated or uninteresting. He was perfectly adequate, but I knew I would never love him.

While he worked, I ran our household, a task I tackled with efficiency and found I enjoyed very much. The servants respected me and Agnolo appreciated me. Still, I was not happy. Alfia, whom my parents had sent to my new home after my marriage, was the only one who knew of my private pain.

I kept with me all the time the half of the golden St. Anthony medal Fabbiana had given me after she took Salvi to the Ospedale degli Innocenti. I wore it on a thin golden chain that I looped through a buttonhole in my petticoat, safely hidden away. I could not risk anyone seeing it; it was well known that charms of this sort were used as *segni,* marks of recognition for abandoned children. Once, Alfia and I walked past the Ospedale, but I found it too difficult to be so close to my baby and yet unable to see him. I never went again.

Every night, I included little Salvi in my prayers. Every night, I grieved the loss of him. In my parents' house, the servants would have alerted my mother to my tears. In my own home, I could cry when I needed to. As the weeks turned into months and the months to years, my tears came less frequently. Never, though, did a day pass without me regretting having given away my son.

Alfia said a new baby would lessen my pain. She might have been right, but I was never to know. Three times Agnolo got me with child, but I carried none of them beyond a few months. I never doubted these losses were punishment meted out to me for having sinned so terribly. Why would God give me a child now? I did not deserve one. In the sixth year of our marriage, having abandoned hope that I would ever give him an heir, my husband brought a little girl, Bianca, into our household. Before introducing her, he came to me, alone, and explained that she was his daughter with his mistress. Her mother had died from malaria. Bia, as he called the child, had nowhere else to go. Would I welcome her into our family?

I felt no outrage at his betrayal. I understood that many men kept mistresses. If anything, I was grateful he had found affection and satisfaction elsewhere; I would never be able to give him, either. My heart was too dead for that. And though it was shameful, I hoped he would find another mistress. I appreciated him asking if I would accept little Bia, rather than commanding I did. I said yes, of course, and almost at once, I found our house felt less empty.

Florence, 1903

25

Cécile had a letter that proved there was still treasure hidden in this house? She passed me a single page, yellow with age and folded into thirds. A red wax blob with the impression of a shield bearing a coat of arms had once sealed it. It was written in the old *dialetto toscano,* penned in a beautiful hand, but left unsigned.

"You can probably read it with little trouble," Cécile said. "But Renzo provided a translation as well." She handed me a second sheet, this one gleaming white, its words in English:

> 8 May 1496
>
> Signore,
>
> I have made all the arrangements you requested. No one will ever suspect the passage is there, let alone be able to locate it. I agree to meet you as your letter described.

"I'm not sure how this proves anything," I said.

"I did not understand either at first. Then Renzo explained." Cécile pointed to the seal. "The coat of arms depicted here did not belong to any family in Florence in the year the letter was written. On the top is a bat, which means watchfulness. The arrow below it means readiness. The odd-looking spiked object at the bottom is a caltrap, which is an emblem of warning. Renzo believes the arms were adopted by a group, not a family, and given the date of the letter, 1496, when Florence was firmly in Savonarola's grip, he hypothesizes that the group opposed the friar."

"I adore the idea in theory," I said, "but I still don't see how any of his conclusions are based on solid evidence. Furthermore, nothing about the letter connects it to this house."

"It was among other documents pertaining to the Vieri family. This man must have been a member of the Arrabbiati, the faction in Florence who opposed Savonarola and called his supporters the Piagnoni—the Snivelers—because they wept and wailed when listening to their leader preach."

"You propose that he hired someone to make alterations in the house that would enable him and his compatriots to hide precious object from Savonarola's gangs?"

"*Oui,* precisely."

"Do we even know that he was a member of the family?"

"Maybe he was a servant, the steward even. He could have acted without the knowledge of the family."

"Then why did this letter wind up where it did?" I sighed. "It is a seductive idea, but we still lack proof."

Cécile raised an eyebrow. "There is a second letter." She handed it to me. Like the first, it was yellowed with age, bore the same seal, and appeared to have been written by the same hand, this time in Latin:

Saepius illa
religio peperit scelerosa atque impia facta.

I read the words aloud, translating. "*Again and again our foe, religion, has given birth to deeds sinful and unholy.*"

"You recognize it?" Cécile asked.

"I do." The text was identical to one of the passages from Lucretius I had found in the Great Hall on the second floor of the house.

"Is that proof enough?"

"It certainly changes things," I said. "Does it prove a treasure was hidden here? Perhaps not, but it is strong enough evidence that I wouldn't object to mounting a serious search."

"Even in the midst of a murder investigation?"

"Did you not tell me we ladies are more than capable of applying ourselves to multiple tasks simultaneously?"

She left the letters with me and retreated to her room to dress for dinner, Caesar and Brutus trailing at her heels. I went down to my bedroom and rang for Tessa, wishing I could avoid her until I knew what Colin had learned when he confronted the staff about what I'd overheard. Ladies' evening wear, however, required assistance, so I would do my best to pretend nothing had happened.

I watched as she walked into the room, carrying my notebook. She showed no sign of even the slightest discomfort, which led me to believe that either she was not party to any plan that might harm me or that she was eminently skilled in the art of deception. The latter seemed unlikely for a maid, unless her employment here was part of a larger scheme, possibly one organized by an agent of the Crown, i.e., my husband. If that were the case, I ought to be able to trust her, or at least feel confident that she would not lead me into harm's way.

"Did you enjoy your tea at the Savoy, signora?" she asked as she started to assist me with the gown I wished to wear.

"More or less," I said.

"A pile of parcels containing your purchases was delivered from the Mercato Nuovo. It's a marvelous place to shop, is it not?"

"Yes. I thought the flowers would look nice in the dining room." I was chafing, not interested in continuing this mundane conversation. "Did you have a chance to look at the graffiti?"

"I did. It's quite interesting, but I don't see how it applies to the fabled treasure. The text doesn't seem related at all. At first, I thought the locations might be significant, but I couldn't figure out how." Finished tightening my corset and fastening the buttons on the back of my dress, she opened the notebook to the page on which I had drawn a floor plan of the house and marked the locations of each graffito. "The Great Hall on the second floor is the only room in the house that has two Latin passages. I plotted the line between them to see if it crossed an obvious spot where something could have been hidden, but a line doesn't really give that."

"No," I said. "We'd need more points to form an *X*. It was a good idea, though."

"*Grazie,* signora. I then used all four of the phrases on the second floor and drew lines to connect them. They intersect over a bit of the courtyard just below the first floor landing." She showed me on the floor plan. "But if they are meant to direct us to a specific place, how do the other two, both on the first floor, fit in?"

I studied the floor plan. "If one includes all the locations, regardless of floor, the lines cross in the same place. Did you look at the spot on the floor?"

"I did not, signora. I thought you would want to do that yourself."

"What about the non-Latin graffiti?" I asked. "Could any of them be used in conjunction with the Latin as an anchor of sorts, to point us to another location?"

"I don't believe the rest of the graffiti has any relation to the Latin. It probably wasn't even written by someone of the same generation."

"A valid point, particularly as we have no way to prove what was written when. We're choosing to accept that the Latin dates from the days of Savonarola but cannot come to any reasonable conclusion as to what else was on the walls at the time. Did anything strike you as noteworthy among the non-Latin graffiti?"

"I'm afraid not," she said. "Although I find it inconceivable that people were writing on the walls of a rich man's house."

"These houses, as first built, were more than simple family dwellings. Business was conducted in them. Even the Medici met with clients in their palazzo."

"And someone waiting and waiting to speak to whoever was in charge might grow bored and start scribbling. It is strange, but I suppose I understand. If there's nothing else to discuss, I should start on your hair or you'll be late to dinner."

Once my toilette was complete, I returned to the Sala dei Pappagalli, where Colin and Darius were standing in front of the fireplace, whisky glasses in hand, heads bent close in quiet conversation. I could see that Darius's jacket was mended, but the work badly done. He needed a better valet. As I approached, they stepped apart and greeted me. I'd brought my notebook down, and showed them the lines Tessa had plotted.

"It's an interesting idea," Darius said, "even if the evidence is tenuous at best. All the same, I'll admit I'm more than a little tempted to excavate the spot in the courtyard."

"Don't even consider it," Colin said. "I've led Kat to believe we're here on a pleasant holiday and don't want her to think anything is amiss. We're not going to start digging up anything."

"Surely she knows about the break-ins?" I asked.

"I saw no reason to worry her."

This did not seem wise to me, but I was not about to tell him how to best deal with his daughter. Fortunately, Cécile joined us just then, eager to show them the letters, so there was no more discussion of Kat. As they read, both gentlemen lit up, invigorated.

"We've been too quick to dismiss the possibility that the treasure is still here. I'm beginning to believe there's a real possibility of finding something," Darius said.

"Intriguing though the letters are, they offer no proof that the treasure—if it ever existed—remains hidden," Colin said. "The house might have been ready and the passages impossible to find, but neither means anything was placed in them. Furthermore, *passages* are a far cry from a pit dug in the courtyard, so I'd abandon any thoughts of looking there."

"You throw too much cold water, Monsieur Hargreaves. Let me have my fun," Cécile said. "I am more convinced than ever that I am the one who will, at last, uncover the famous treasure of the Palazzo di Vieri. Unless the servants, who know the house better than any of us, get there first."

"The servants have better things to do than waste their time on a hopeless business," Colin said.

"Do they?" Darius asked. "I'd far prefer hunting for something that might bring me a fortune to scrubbing floors."

"Anyone would," I said. "Even in the face of terrible odds."

"The staff here are dedicated to their work," Colin said. "I'm certain they'll leave the treasure hunting to you, Cécile."

She narrowed her eyes and stared at him. "Are you, monsieur? I wonder how you can be so confident. It is not that I doubt you. I'm your staunchest supporter."

"For that, madame, I am most humbly grateful." He gave her a little bow.

"I shall leave it to you to make sure the servants stay out of it," she said.

"You might change your mind about that, Cécile," Darius said. "Fredo could be quite useful when it comes to digging up floors and opening walls."

"We are not doing either," Colin said. "This is my daughter's house. I won't see it destroyed."

"Monsieur, I would never destroy it," Cécile said. "Only poke and prod it a bit. We will repair anything we disturb. So far as your daughter is concerned, she'll never know we were here."

"Unless we do find the treasure," I said. "Then we shall have to give it to her."

"*Bien sûr,*" Cécile said.

I hadn't heard her enter the room, but suddenly Tessa stepped forward and announced dinner. I wondered how much of our conversation she had overheard.

Later that evening, Colin did his best to assure me that the conversation I'd heard the staff having was innocuous.

"They each, separately, recounted the same story," he said. "They admit to having mounted a search for the treasure and to being concerned that you and Cécile would find it before them."

"So they intended to steal it?"

"No, that was never part of their plan. They assumed that if they discovered it, they would be given some sort of reward, but if you found it, they would get nothing."

"And Fredo's statement that he would *deal with me*? What did that mean?" I asked.

"That if worst came to worst, he would come forward and ask you to leave the search to them."

"That makes no sense whatsoever."

"It's clumsy at best," Colin said. "However, I can assure you that none of them means you the slightest harm. Before being hired, each underwent extensive investigation into their backgrounds. They are paid a salary considerably higher than their peers in other households. There's more, but I can't share it. I do hope you will trust me when I say I am confident in my assessment of the situation. They pose no danger whatsoever."

Colin had—more often than I would like—exhibited a tendency to overreact at the slightest suggestion I might be in danger, taking what I felt to be excessive protective measures. I had no reason to believe he wouldn't do the same now. I trusted him, but I didn't believe that the servants were being entirely candid. Something about the robberies could have proved to them the treasure did exist and could be found. If that were the case, they hadn't told us everything they knew, and I did not share my husband's confidence that they would alert us should they locate it. If the treasure was, in fact, what he'd discussed with them. I wouldn't be surprised to learn that they knew far more about Colin's work than I did, or that they were more like colleagues than servants. To me, that seemed a more reasonable explanation than any other for the uneasiness I felt around them.

The following morning, Colin and Darius breakfasted more quickly than usual, leaving me alone in the dining room, where, while Cécile finished her repast, I studied the map of Florence in my Baedeker's.

"Can I help you find something, signora?" Tessa asked as she came in to clear the gentlemen's plates.

"I'm looking for a small, dead-end street," I said.

She peered over my shoulder at the map. "A specific street?"

"Yes, but I don't know its name only that it's near Santa Maria Novella."

"Is it the street you seek or a specific building on it?"

"A house, but I don't know . . ." I hesitated. She knew I was investigating Marzo's death, but did I want to tell her that I was also interested in another murder? Did it matter? "Have you have heard about a murder that occurred in Florence not long before Marzo died?"

"Oh, yes," she said. "A Signore di Taro, killed in his home. Shot twice in the head."

"*Mon dieu,* Tessa, how do you come to know such brutal details?" Cécile asked.

"It was in the newspaper. Everyone knows. A boy heard the shots and tried to report them, but no one believed him. The body was not discovered for two days. It was a hideous scene."

"Two days? Why so long?" Cécile asked.

"The signore's wife died some years back," Tessa said. "They had no children and he lived alone."

"It is his house that I'm looking for," I said.

"Why? Is his murder connected to Marzo's?" Tessa asked.

"I suspect they were both killed by the same man," I said. This was a lie. Although Colin had not shared with me any details about the cause of Marzo's death, I had seen the body. He had not been shot. More likely, his killer had bashed in the back of his head, as that sort of injury would fit better with him being flung off the roof. Nothing in the methods of the two crimes suggested a single killer; and, if Vittoria was correct, it was possible Marzo had murdered di Taro. "Do you know where Signore di Taro lived?"

"I do." Referring to my map, she showed me how to get there. I thanked her and Cécile and I set off, heading north to the Piazza Santa Maria Novella and then along the Via della Scala, pausing briefly to look in the windows of the Officina Profumo-Farmaceutica di Santa Maria Novella. The Dominican friars of Santa Maria Novella cultivated a garden in the nearby monastery to provide raw materials—generally herbal—for a variety of medicinal cures. The friars founded the Profumo-Farmaceutica in 1212, but didn't sell their wares to the public until 1381, when they offered their rose water as a means of warding off the Black Death that devastated Florence in waves throughout the fourteenth and fifteenth centuries. They still sell their rose water, and I had every intention of popping in to buy some after we'd finished our work for the day. One can never be too careful about keeping the plague at bay.

From there, the walk to Signore di Taro's street was short, and within a few minutes we'd arrived in front of the nondescript edifice in which he had lived. I couldn't imagine why Marzo would have brought Vittoria here again and again. The street was wholly unremarkable.

"What now, Kallista?" Cécile asked. "We're not going to be able to get into his apartment."

"No," I said, "but we can talk to his neighbors. If we're fortunate, we may even be able to locate the boy who heard the gunshots."

I never much enjoyed this part of my work: knocking on the doors of strangers. Generally, once I apologized for disturbing them and explained my purpose, things became easier. Many people who find themselves within touching distance of a horrible crime welcome the opportunity to discuss it, enjoying their proximity to notoriety, but that was not the case today. No one among the four other families who lived in Signore di Taro's building would speak to us. They all claimed not to have known the dead man. We tried the residents of the other apartments in the street, but met the same resistance, so turned our attention instead to the shopkeepers on the main road.

We started at a small greengrocer, then a butcher, places I thought it likely Signore di Taro would have regularly patronized. He did shop in both, but neither the owners nor the clerks knew him in the slightest. They claimed he never bothered to make conversation. We'd made our way nearly a quarter of a mile down the street before we finally found a clockmaker who admitted to having known him.

"He was not from Florence," he said. "He came in here with an old Viennese clock that needed repair. Seemed a pleasant enough fellow and he appreciated the work I did for him. He stopped in once in a while to chat and to see what I was making, but I can't claim to know much about him. We were not close."

"Where was he from?" I asked.

..ıl village somewhere in the Dolomites," he said. "I don't know ... than that."

"Had he lived here long?"

The clockmaker shrugged. "I never asked."

"Was he employed?"

"He wasn't a gentleman, if that's what you mean. He had money, so I assume he worked, but I don't know where or doing what."

"Did you notice anything unusual in the neighborhood on the day he died?" I asked.

"No," he said, "and it's an odd question coming from a fashionable lady. What interest can you have in such a ghastly crime?"

"It's such a shock to find ourselves in a place where something so awful happened," I said. "What was it like to actually be here that day?"

"It was no different from any other day," he said. "I had no idea that anything was amiss. No one did, not until the body was found."

"Who found it?" Cécile asked.

"The man who lives across the hall from him. The smell, you see . . ." He swallowed hard.

"It must have been dreadful," I said. "I understand a boy claims to have heard the gunshots."

"Carlo claims many things. I wouldn't put stock in most of them."

"Does he live nearby?" Cécile asked.

"I don't know precisely," the clockmaker said. "He hangs around the piazza with his friends. They're all of them useless."

"How old is he?" I asked.

"Twelve, maybe thirteen."

"Poor thing," Cécile said. "If he is telling the truth, it was a ghastly thing to hear, but if he invented the story, that's even more ghastly." She shuddered, paused, and then smiled. "You have beautiful things here, signore. Do you ship to Paris?"

When we left the shop half an hour later, Cécile had bought three carriage clocks and arranged to have them delivered to her house. "Investigating murders is more expensive than I thought," she said as we walked back to the piazza.

"You didn't have to buy something."

"He was helpful and I felt we owed him something for taking up his time." She shrugged. "They are lovely clocks. I ought to be able to find somewhere to put them. If not, I'll have to give you one for Christmas."

The stunning marble façade of Santa Maria Novella, designed by Leon Battista Alberti in the fifteenth century, rose from the north end of the piazza. We immediately spotted a group of motley-looking boys clustered in front of the Loggia di Santo Paolo, across from the church. They stared as we approached them.

"I'm looking for Carlo," I said.

"I'm Carlo." He was leaning against a column. "Who are you?"

"I'm Lady Emily Hargreaves. This is my friend Signora du Lac. Could we speak somewhere more private?"

The boys laughed. "What can you possibly want with him?" one of them asked.

Carlo shushed them. "Will you get me something to eat?"

"Of course," I said. "There's a café over there that looks quite nice."

The boys howled as Carlo walked away with us, but I couldn't tell if they meant to taunt or praise him. Either way, he looked happy enough, a wide grin on his face. We took seats around a tiny table in the café. Cécile ordered coffee, I asked for tea, and Carlo requested an enormous piece of focaccia laden with prosciutto and a glass of lemonade.

"What do you want with me?" he asked.

"We've been told you heard gunshots the day Signore di Taro was murdered," I said. "Is that true?"

"Of course it's true, even if no one believes me. I don't much care. The police are useless. I didn't bother to prove to them that I'm telling the truth."

"How could you prove it?" I asked.

"I have the gun that killed him."

Florence, 1489

26

Agnolo, Bia, and I made an odd little family. We made no attempt to pretend I was the child's mother. No one would have believed it, even if the girl hadn't already been six when she came to live with us. Her dark hair and eyes were nothing like mine or her father's. Agnolo doted on her. Watching him with his daughter revealed he had a deep capacity for love. I was glad he had someone upon whom to bestow it.

Our marriage was not unhappy, but it brought me no joy. As the years passed, I felt more content, and, eventually, I suspect, I might have come to love my husband, but I was never to know. He died during a minor outbreak of the plague when Bia was eight years old. In his will, he had arranged for me to take possession of the house and settled upon me a fortune that, combined with my dowry, left me a wealthy woman. I was still young and could have married again, but had no desire to do so. I told my family this was because Bia would have nowhere to go. Children from a first marriage were rarely welcomed into a second husband's home. They stayed with their father's family. Illegitimate offspring would be even less welcome. Agnolo had only one surviving brother, who lived in Rome. I'd grown fond of the girl and didn't want to send her away. At first, my parents objected, insisting her uncle would take good care of her, but I managed to convince them that I wanted her with me and had no interest in another husband. In the end, they acquiesced, but they never knew why I cared so deeply about her. She was the same age as my Salvi, born thirteen days after him. In those first months we were on our own, we circled each other suspiciously. She grieved her father while I faced a ghost from my past.

I had not seen Giacomo since my marriage. My husband and I attended Mass in the cathedral, Santa Maria di Fiori, and I swore I would never again set foot in Santa Trinita. The longer I went without seeing him, the more I began to realize that even the strongest feelings fade when one is separated from the object of them. I thought about him less frequently than before and when he did come into my head, it conjured no lingering fondness or desire. I despised him. For a while, at least. Eventually, I came to the place Alfia had promised I would eventually reach: a place where I felt nothing for him, no more sadness or grief or even a remnant of the slightest twinge of love. I'd come to terms with that awful part of my past and no longer let it haunt me.

Until he came to my house.

Agnolo's death was so recent that my servants would not have let any other visitor in to see me except my family, but who would deny a priest the opportunity to console one of his former parishioners? A maid brought him to my favorite room in the house, one decorated with wall paintings of parrots and trees, a place that had always felt to me like a sanctuary from the world.

He looked very much as I remembered him, but with more lines around his eyes. Much though I hate to give him any compliment, they made him more handsome. His intrusion should have angered me, but instead it brought me the greatest pleasure I'd known since our final encounter in that little room off the cloisters in Santa Trinita. Not because I still loved him, but because as he stood there in front of me, close enough that I could have touched him, I realized that even his presence caused in me no stirring of emotion.

"I am most sorry for your loss, Signora Portinari." His manner was formal, but he looked deep into my eyes as he spoke.

"I appreciate your condolences, Father Cambio," I said. "Truly, though, there was no need for you to come. I have all the spiritual support I need."

"I have missed you, Mina. You are as beautiful as ever. I don't know how I let you slip away from me."

"I had nothing to do with it. You pushed me away."

"You must forgive me for that," he said. "I was weak, so very weak." He stepped closer; I backed away.

"There is nothing to forgive. What happened years ago no longer matters. You should not have come here."

"I never dared hope there would be a time when I could come to you again. Your husband's death, though tragic, shows how the Lord opens doors for us just as others are closed. When I heard the news, I was compelled to seek you out."

"Why? Are you now willing to leave the priesthood? Is that what the Lord compels you to do? So that you can marry me? So that you can find the child—a son—I gave away?" As I said the words, I could hardly fathom that I'd ever hoped for any of it.

"A son, was it?" he asked, coming closer again. I could feel his breath on my cheek. "Fabbiana would not tell me. She was very cruel to me when it came to you."

"She's too good for you," I said. "She told me everything. About the other girls, the other babies."

"They were never like you, Mina." He reached out and touched my hair. "Did you name him?"

If he had asked any other question I would have stormed out of the room, but he was the only other person on earth who shared my connection to the boy. I wanted to tell him our child's name, wanted to speak it aloud. "Diotisalvi."

"A beautiful name."

I glared at him. "It means *God save you*. Having been abandoned to grow up in an orphanage, he will need all the help our Savior can provide."

"Do not be hard on yourself, Mina. There was nothing else we could do." Now he was touching my cheek. The sensation of his hand against my skin almost brought me to my knees. My body, betraying me, burned hotter than any fire. My breath came hard and ragged. "I knew you missed me, too," he said.

"I don't miss you."

"You should not lie to a priest, Mina. I see how your cheeks color. I should hear your confession and then we can proceed as we used to."

"No," I said, and stepped away from him.

"There's nothing to fear," he said. "It's safe for us now. Your husband has not long been dead, so even if I were to get you with child again, everyone would assume Agnolo was the father. We can take our pleasure for the next few weeks—a month, even—without having to worry."

"Take our pleasure?" I spat the words. "You disgust me."

He took no notice of my venom. He smiled that lazy half smile I used to love. "I know you want me."

"You observe signs of the most primitive sort of attraction, a physical response beyond my control. But I am no longer the girl you seduced years ago. I remember the punishment Dante meted out to sinners damned for their lust. I will not be battered with endless winds like them. I don't accept that desire is something we cannot control."

"It's obvious that you want me, Mina. You're flushed. Your eyes are bright. Your lips are parted in that way that always told me exactly what to do. Attraction like that between us is something no one can control."

I hated my body in that moment, for he was right. Partly, at least. I did want him. I ached for the pleasure we had shared, but I knew I could control my body. "God gave us free will. I am not bound to act upon a passing desire, no matter how strong it is. Before, I succumbed, unaware of my strength. Before, I loved you so much that I thought I was powerless in the face of such emotion. I could deny you nothing. Now, though, I see my actions for what they were: an abdication of the responsibility that comes with free will. Never again will I allow you to seduce and abuse me."

"You don't know what you say." He stepped forward again. This time, I did, too. Stepped forward, raised my hand, and with a strength I did not know I possessed, I struck him, hard enough that his cheek blazed red, hard enough that one of my rings cut a thin line across his face. He looked at me in disbelief. "You are crazed with grief. Sit down, I will hear your confession."

"You will leave my house. Now. And never return."

"You don't mean that. You don't know what you want you—" I raised my hand again. He stepped back. "You will regret this."

"My only regret is that I did not recognize the depths of your evil sooner."

"You cannot speak to me like that, Mina. You—"

I turned away from him and left the room, slamming the door behind me, my heart pounding. A maid, standing on the gallery landing asked if I needed assistance.

"Inform all the servants that they must never again let Father Cambio into this house. No matter what he says, no matter what he claims, no matter how many times he comes. His presence is hateful to me and this house is closed to him forever."

She nodded and started to walk away, presumably to do as I asked, but then she turned around and opened the door to the Sala dei Pappagalli. "My mistress would have you leave," she said. "Will you go quietly or shall I summon someone to encourage you?"

The priest stormed out of the room, pausing to turn around and look at me when he reached the top of the stairs. He said nothing, but his expression told me I now had a powerful enemy. Blood trickled from the slash on his face. I shook my head. Never had woman been faced with a less worthy adversary.

Florence, 1903

27

When Carlo told us he was in possession of the gun that killed Signore di Taro, Cécile gasped. My own reaction was more guarded. Could we trust the boy? Even if he produced the weapon, could we prove it was the one used in the murder?

"How do you know it's the same gun?" I asked, speaking quietly so as not to alarm the other patrons of the café.

"What other gun would have been flung to the ground just behind the building shortly after the murder?" He looked defiant.

"Tell me exactly what happened."

"I was milling around that morning, minding my own business. Didn't have much of anything to do, so I just let myself wander. I turned into Signore di Taro's street for no reason in particular. Because it was there, I suppose. I walked up and down twice and was halfway back up again when I heard the shots. Two of them, one right after the other."

"Could you tell where they were coming from?" I asked.

"Not exactly, no," he said. "The sound bounced around a bit. But I figure it must have been from a front room in one of the buildings. Otherwise, how could I have heard them? Probably wouldn't have noticed anything if the windows hadn't been open."

"How do you know the windows were open?"

He shrugged. "If they weren't, the sound wouldn't have been bouncing around, would it?"

It was a keen observation. "Did you look to see which buildings had open windows?"

"I can't say I did." He shifted uncomfortably in his chair. "Truth is, I was a bit scared, but I won't admit that to anyone ever again, all right? So don't go telling my friends."

"I wouldn't dream of it," I said. "It's perfectly natural to be frightened in such a situation. What did you do next?"

"I ran as fast as I could to the main street, and once I got there, didn't stop for more than a mile. Then, when I did, I thought maybe I should try to see what had happened, so I went back. This time, though, I went into the alley that runs behind those houses."

"Why did you do that?"

"I was afraid that whoever fired the shots might be coming out the front door, since they were fired from the front, at least that's what I thought. If he knew what I heard, he might decide to shoot me, too, mightn't he?"

"The situation certainly called for an abundance of caution," Cécile said.

The boy nodded. "Exactly, signora. There was no one else in the alley, not even a cat. It was completely empty. I crept along, keeping quiet. And then I saw it."

"The gun?" I asked.

"Yes. It was right there on the ground. Must have been flung out a window."

"So you picked it up?"

"I did."

"I understand that you tried to report what you'd heard," I said. "Did you go to the police?"

"Well, I saw one of them right after I left the alley, which seemed like a sign, telling me what to do, so I went up to him and said what I'd seen. He didn't believe me and said that making up stories could land me in jail."

"Didn't you show him the gun?" I asked. "Surely that would have helped persuade him you were telling the truth."

"No, he only would've taken it away from me."

"What did you do with it?"

"I've got a place where I hide things. It's there."

I needed to tread carefully. Colin should examine the weapon, and it seemed more plausible that I could persuade the boy to allow that than to get him to agree to speak to the police again. If I first suggested the latter, I might be able to bring him around to the former. "Now would be a good time to bring it to the police. They won't doubt you so readily, given that they know Signore di Taro was murdered."

"I'm not going back to the police. If I tell them that it's the gun that killed him, they might decide I was the one who did it."

"I can't believe they'd think you're a murderer," Cécile said.

"I've got a reputation, signora," he said, sounding rather proud. "So they might indeed think I'm a ruthless killer."

Between his short stature, skinny build, and the incomprehensible odds that he could have managed to acquire a gun in ordinary circumstances, this seemed beyond unlikely to me. That said, if the gun truly was in his possession, he had managed to acquire it. The police might not accept the story that he found it discarded in an alley.

"Tell me again how you came to be in Signore di Taro's poky little street," I said. "Why would you be there of all places?"

"Like I told you, I was just wandering around with no aim."

"I don't believe you, Carlo." I motioned for our waiter and ordered the boy another lemonade.

"There's nothing more to tell. I guess I liked the look of it."

"Why?" I pressed.

"I don't know."

"I think you do." I sat back and waited for the waiter to return with the fresh lemonade. Carlo stared at me, then at the full glass, then back at me. "You might as well drink it," I said.

He took a large gulp. "All right. I don't want anyone else to know, but there's a girl." His cheeks flushed vermilion.

"My dear boy, there is always a girl," Cécile said. "You need not be embarrassed. "Does she return your affection?"

"I don't even know her name. I saw her walking out of a butcher shop, carrying a package. I followed her, just so I could see where she lives, thinking if I did, maybe I could figure out a way to bump into her again. She's very pretty."

"Where does she live?" I asked.

"She went into the building directly across from Signore di Taro. I walked back and forth, hoping she might come out again, but she didn't, so I'm confident that is where she lives."

"Have you seen her again since?" Cécile asked.

"No, and I'm not sure I want to anymore," he said. "Doesn't seem like a good sign, finding a girl you think you like only to wind up hearing a murder instead of meeting her."

Carlo put a great stock in signs.

"I agree it wasn't the best start," Cécile said. "There are many, many pretty girls in Florence. She is not the last one you'll see."

"I suppose so." He sounded dispirited.

"Carlo, I'm sorry about all of this," I said. "A boy your age shouldn't have to worry about murders interfering with meeting a pretty girl. It would be best if you put this all behind you, starting with letting go of the gun."

"I don't want the police to have it."

"I understand that." I paused, just for a moment, trying to construct an argument he might accept. "Is it possible that everything surrounding your finding of the gun was a sign? You might well have decided not to go into the alley, or not to go back to the vicinity of the murder at all, yet you were compelled to, weren't you? So you found the gun, just as you were meant to. It's quite a coincidence that you ran into a policeman immediately thereafter. Just as you were meant to. Perhaps his unwillingness to believe your story should serve as a sign that you were supposed to confide in someone else, someone who would believe and protect you."

"And you think that someone is you?" he asked.

"I do, along with Signora du Lac. Would you trust us to take care of the gun for you? My husband knows a great deal about weapons. He might be able to learn something from examining it that could lead us to the man who killed Signore di Taro."

"He could do that?"

"It's worth a try. You do want the murderer to be caught, don't you?"

"Yes." He chewed on the inside of his cheek. "It does seem a bit like a sign, signora. What are the odds that the two of you wound up talking to me when you were wondering about the murder? You're sure your husband won't tell the police about me?"

"I can promise you he won't." He had no intention of ever telling the police anything in conjunction with this case.

"All right," he said. "But I don't want you to know where my hiding place is."

"Is it nearby?" Cécile asked.

"I'm not telling you that." He crossed his arms. "I appreciate your kindness in feeding me and all, but that doesn't make me indebted to you forever. You know the Ponte Vecchio, right? All tourists do. I'll bring it to you there, at midnight."

"Midnight?" I raised an eyebrow and did my best not to smile. Young Carlo had a flair for the dramatic. "I shall be asleep at midnight. How about now? Signora du Lac and I can wait here while you collect the gun." Cécile looked at me, concern writ on her face. I had no intention of letting him out of our sight, but I couldn't tell that to my friend without the boy also hearing it, and that might scare him off.

"No, I do not like this plan," Cécile said. "Carlo, I am coming with you. Do not argue, I am implacable."

"I won't let anyone see my hiding place." Just as I'd feared, he looked ready to bolt. However, I'd underestimated Cécile.

"You will let me see it," she said, her voice calm and commanding. "In return, I will give you five gold sovereigns."

"Gold?" His eyes widened.

"Yes. That should make sharing your hiding place with me more palatable."

The boy squinted as he looked at her. "I think you might be crazy, signora."

"That is very likely," Cécile said, "but it has never concerned me."

"What about her?" He motioned to me.

"She will come behind us, keeping enough distance to be able to make sure no one is following. That way, you won't have to worry about anyone else discovering your secret. The integrity of the hiding place will remain intact."

He considered her words and then nodded. "I suppose that would be all right. Are you sure she can tell if someone's following us?"

"Quite sure," I said. "I've been specially trained in the art."

He pursed his lips, nodded, and then spoke. "I guess finding the gun and you finding me really was all meant to happen. I'll do as you ask."

I hung back while he led Cécile to his hiding place, which was in a narrow passageway running between two houses about a quarter of a mile from the site of the murder. No one followed us. I waited at the end, just by the main street, watching as Carlo tugged a loose stone from the wall of the building on the west side and pulled the gun out from behind it. He gave it to Cécile, who removed the remaining cartridges before slipping the revolver into her reticule. Carlo returned the stone, making sure it was not even slightly out of place.

"Thank you, Carlo," I said when they came back to me. "You've done the right thing."

"When do I get my gold sovereigns?" he asked. Cécile produced them from her bag and handed them to him. "Thank you, signora, it's a pleasure doing business with you. May I go now?"

"First I need to know how to reach you again should it become necessary," I said.

"Why would it be necessary?" he asked, blanching.

"I assumed you would want to know the outcome of our investigation," I said. "It's nothing to cause you concern." That seemed to satisfy him. He told us his full name and address, thanked Cécile, and skipped away. I turned to my friend. "Do you make a habit of carrying gold coins with you?"

She shrugged. "I find them useful in a variety of situations."

"You unloaded that gun with remarkable speed."

"As I said, I'm an excellent shot, Kallista."

Darius did not dine with us that evening, so there was no need for me to deploy a longing look to let Colin know I needed to slip off alone with him. Cécile took for granted that any well-matched couple would wish to retire early and always encouraged such behavior. Colin took me in his arms the moment we entered the narrow corridor outside our room, pushed me against the wall, and kissed me until I was left almost delirious. Then, to my dismay, he released me, stepped away as if nothing had happened, opened the door, and ushered me into the chamber.

"I do hope that was a prelude," I said, tugging the bodice of my gown back into place and smoothing my hair.

"Count on it, my dear. I know we must discuss the case before we succumb to further distraction, but I wanted to put you on notice. Further distraction is coming."

A delicious warmth coursed through my body, but I ignored it. "I've had a rather productive day." I retrieved the gun, which I'd stashed in a fifteenth-century wooden chest decorated with scenes from mythology that looked like they could have been painted by Botticelli, and handed it to him.

"Where on earth did you get this?"

I told him about our encounter with Carlo. "He's convinced it was used to kill Signore di Taro."

"This is most well done, Emily. I confess I did not put much stock in your decision to make queries about his murder, but you may be onto something," he said, examining the weapon. "It's a Nagant M1895 revolver, used as a side arm by the Russian army. Was di Taro Russian?"

"No, he came from a village in the Dolomites. Does it matter, though? Surely his killer would have brought his own gun."

"Quite," he said. "Two shots to the head in rapid succession suggest a person experienced in eliminating those who need eliminating. If he and his killer were both Russian, it might have be easier to find the connection."

"A non-Russian could have a Russian gun, couldn't he?"

"Yes, but . . ." He sighed. "This wretched situation becomes exponentially more complicated every time I blink. If the Russians are involved . . ."

I waited, but he did not continue. "As in the Russian government?" He nodded. "Aren't we friends with Russia?"

"I'm afraid it's not that simple," he said.

"Few things are. Do you think Marzo killed Signore di Taro?" I asked.

"Darius has no knowledge of any connection between them. He wasn't aware of di Taro's murder until I told him about it. If Marzo was involved, why would he use a Russian weapon?"

"In order to make it clear there was no British involvement in the crime? After all, he does—did—work for the British in some sort of mysterious capacity."

"True," he said, "but we would never have had him use a Russian revolver, even unofficially. Furthermore, he was not an assassin. Do you know anything about Signore di Taro?"

"Sadly little. No one except a man who repaired a Viennese clock for him would talk to us. He didn't know him well."

"I shall see what I can learn."

"I shall regret never being able to hear about it."

"I'm sorry, Emily," he said and ran his hand through his tousled curls.

"I wasn't looking for an apology."

"Weren't you?"

"No. I was merely trying to give you the opportunity to apply yourself to distracting me from wondering whatever it is you might or might not learn."

"Is that so?" He put the revolver down on the table between the two chairs where we were sitting. "Is there anything else we need to discuss before I take the task in hand?"

"Nothing about either murder, but watching Carlo remove the gun from his hiding place made me think we should search for loose stones in this palazzo. Our Renaissance friend may have adopted a similar strategy when it came to securing his own treasure."

"We could leave that to Cécile and Signore Tazzera," he said. "They're fascinated by the treasure, but I'm more enticed by other things."

"Are you?" I asked, the delicious warmth returning to my body.

He knelt in front of my chair, gripped my legs, and pulled me closer to him. "Far more enticed."

Florence,

1491

28

After Giacomo came to my house, exploding the remaining shards of my peace, I lived in fear that he would try to see me again, not because I worried I might find his lewd advances irresistible, but because further angering him could push him to expose my secret or find some other way to ruin me. As weeks went by without hearing from him, I started to feel a slim hope. Perhaps he would heed my words and leave me alone. I prayed it would be so, and, so far as I could tell, it appeared the Lord was listening.

That first year of my widowhood shaped the rest of my life. Some of the choices I made met with criticism. I kept to myself, alienated the few friends I had, and saw my family only rarely. I was grieving a husband who had treated me with kindness, but I was also giving careful thought to what I wanted as I entered this new stage. What mattered to me? What did I value? What kind of world did I want Bia to inhabit? I considered my own childhood, the best parts of which were the times spent with my grandfather. Now, as an adult, I pulled him closer.

I hosted dinners for him and his humanist friends. I studied Neoplatonism and argued with them about it. After my experience with Giacomo, I had stayed away from books. Now, at last, I returned to them. I went back to my Greek and Latin, until I had mastered both languages. I patronized artists whose ideas—and ideals—mirrored my own. I was wealthy enough to never need worry about money, but not so outrageously rich that anyone paid much attention to me.

I saw to it that Bia was educated in the manner of a Medici heir, under the tutelage of some of the most brilliant minds of our time. Her natural curiosity bore no bounds. My grandfather claimed he saw me in her.

"Sometimes she gets a glint in her eyes that is identical to yours," he said as we sat in the Sala dei Pappagalli after he had dined with us. It was late, and Bia long ago sent to bed.

"If so, it's nothing but coincidence. She's not mine and cannot have inherited any trait from me," I said.

"She is yours in all the ways that matter and you will eventually be unable to deny how many traits you share. Not everything about us is defined by our physicality. Our environment shapes us as well, maybe even more. It is a credit to you that you accepted her so readily, and a credit to her that she, from the beginning, allowed you to mother her."

"What choice did either of us have?" I asked.

He laughed. "You are in possession of a brilliant mind, Mina, but I see you have not lost all of your girlish naïveté, despite now being six and twenty. Many ladies in your place would not have welcomed the child of their husband's mistress into their home. And many such children would have resented their father's wife, given that their own mothers were relegated to a far lower position in society."

"I suppose so, but why bother? What would it accomplish save to make everyone miserable? Bia is a delight. I've always been grateful for her. She adored her father, and he deserved to be loved like that."

"Indeed. He was a good man and you were a good wife to him."

I could see in the way he was looking at me that he knew I'd never adored Agnolo, but I could also see that he did not judge me for it. Passionate love was something no reasonable person expected from marriage. "As good a wife as I could be."

"Plenty good enough," he said. "I did not come here to discuss marriage, however. I want to talk to you about something else, Mina. My books. My personal library is large, too large for many houses. When I die, I want you to have it, but I do not require that you keep every book."

"I should sooner cut off my hand than get rid of a book."

"You are a good girl and I believe you, but there may be times in the future when you feel differently. I have drawn up a list of the volumes in my collection that are the most important. Not because they are necessarily rare or beautiful, but because of the ideas found in them. You know that I spent much of my youth hunting through monastic libraries in search of ancient works long forgotten. It was a thrilling pursuit, dangerous at times, and illuminating. But not everyone, even in this enlightened city of ours, sees value in what the ancients wrote. The Church often finds threats in such things."

"The friar at San Marco certainly does. I've heard him preach."

"Savonarola is a dangerous man," he said. "He stirs up fear."

"Fortunately, not many take his words to heart," I said.

"Not yet, at least. My friend Lorenzo will not rule Florence forever. He is mortal like the rest of us. Piero, his heir, is a fine soldier, but I fear he has not inherited his father's head for politics. If he cannot maintain control of the city, who knows what will happen? In times of crisis, any populace is far more vulnerable than usual to religious extremism."

"This is not Savonarola's first time in Florence," I said. "He was here years ago and garnered so little support that he left."

"It is a different time now. I do not mean to frighten you, only to implore you to promise me that these important books don't get lost again. I remember so well the first time I read *De Rerum Natura,* written by that brilliant Epicurean, Lucretius. Poggio Bracciolini, a dear friend of mine who died before you were born, found the manuscript somewhere in Germany. You have read it, Mina, and know the power of the ideas it contains. It teaches us not to fear death."

"And denies the possibility of an afterlife," I said. "The Church would never condone the notion, but neither has it forbidden us to read and discuss the book. Many great theologians study the ancients. It informs their own work."

"Imagine if Poggio hadn't uncovered the manuscript. Imagine if we had no knowledge of Lucretius, no Aristotle, no Cicero. What would it mean for our great thinkers today to have no grounding in those ideas? As I said, I do not want to scare you, Mina. I consider you the heir to my ideas. Your father has never shown much interest in them, nor do your brothers. You alone understand and respond to them in the way I had once hoped they would. As a result, you will be the one responsible for guarding my legacy. I do not know what Florence will face in the future, only that there are bound to be as many disasters as there are triumphs. I would like to know that you will do whatever is necessary to ensure that these books will never be forgotten. Remember the words of Lucretius: *Sic volvenda aetas commutat tempora rerum. / Quod fuit in pretio, fit nullo denique honore.* So rolling time changes the seasons of things. What was of value, becomes in turn of no worth."

"I will make sure that never happens, at least not in Florence. It is an honor to be entrusted with so noble a task," I said. "I will do as you ask."

"I know you will. There is one other thing. Do you remember this cameo, the one Lorenzo gave me long ago?" He pulled it out of his pocket and handed it to me.

"I do," I said. "Minerva in profile, expertly carved."

"Before I die, I will give this to a man I trust above all others. He is honest and good. Should you ever come under threat because of what I have asked you to do, he will help you. He will identify himself by showing you the cameo."

"What is his name?"

"You don't need to know that, not now. If you did, you might unknowingly put him at risk by mentioning it or by finding yourself startled should you happen to meet him."

"But I won't be able to reach him if I do need him."

"Never fear, he will find you." He rose, offered me his hand, and I stood with him. He embraced me. "You are the brightest light of my old age, Mina. Remember that, always."

I walked him through the loggia and watched as he set off back to his own house, wondering how much longer I would have him in my life. The natural order demanded that he die before me, but what consolation was natural order? Losing him would gut me. His death, whenever it came, would lay bare for me the true depths of grief.

Florence, 1903

29

Colin was gone when I rose the next morning, off to meet Darius somewhere. He'd left a letter he'd written to Kat, with room on the last page for me to add greetings. It read like a lighthearted travelogue. I scrawled a message at the bottom, thanking her for letting us use her house, but did not expand on her father's fiction that everything was fine. She might forgive him for misleading her, but I was unlikely to receive the same treatment. I left it on a tray to go out with the afternoon post and collected the envelopes that had already been delivered. The day was unusually warm, so I decided to have my tea and toast in the open air of the roof terrace, with its sweeping views of the city. A missive from the boys had arrived, and I was reading it, laughing despite myself at Henry's account of having tricked his brothers into joining him on a snipe hunt.

> As your own dear friend Mrs. Michaels was the source of my information about this novel American tradition, I know you will not scold me for what I've done. The snipe is not real, Mama, so there was no danger that any of us would get shot.

The image of three armed (and preternaturally articulate) seven-year-olds would have terrified me if I'd not first read the other letter contained in the envelope, written by the gamekeeper at Anglemore Park, our estate in Derbyshire. He explained that the young master had asked for his help and that he'd agreed, thinking it was wiser to have the expedition supervised than not. He'd made sure the shotguns weren't loaded and accompanied the boys on their trek across our land. Cook, he added, consoled them afterward with their favorite pudding.

Henry's version of the events was decidedly more colorful. Richard, always the most likely of the three to believe any sort of legend, exhibited excitement unmatched by Tom, but he had been disappointed by his inability to find any information on the snipe in our library.

> He considered it a great failing of our collection, never once suspecting the absence was due not to oversight but to the snipe not existing in real life. He wanted to send a wire to Papa before we set out, asking for books to be ordered. I stopped this foolishness not to spare my brother embarrassment but because if Papa replied fast enough it might have ruined the hunt. Please take note of my honesty in making this confession to less-than-gentlemanly motives. Tom proved an excellent tracker, following signs of an animal that turned out to be one of Papa's foxhounds (I am certain it was Iphitos, but Richard wrongly insists it was Pollux. You shouldn't believe him—he does not know the dogs so well as I). Both of them were angry when I told them they were hunting an imaginary animal but if they are man enough to acknowledge the truth, they will admit they enjoyed the excursion, even if I might be accused of laughing rather too much when I revealed I'd duped them. I expect to be in disgrace when you return home. I ask only that you remember I did not go so far as Americans do. They leave their victims alone all night, still trying to find a snipe. I told my brothers the truth once Richard's loud attempts at calling the beast started to get on my nerves.

"What is so amusing?" Cécile asked, dropping onto the chair next to mine. She'd slept even later than I, yet still appeared fatigued. Her eyes were puffy, but her skin glowed.

"Henry has played a rather successful prank on his brothers," I said. "I'm glad to have learned about it while away, so I can laugh openly instead of having to look stern. Did you sleep well?"

"Henry is a dear boy and I'd appreciate your not mentioning how dreadful I look," she said. "I was up late."

"Doing what?" I wondered if she'd gone out with Signore Tazzera after Colin and I retired. It would explain the glow.

"Nothing that concerns you." She poured herself a cup of coffee. "What did Monsieur Hargreaves have to say about the gun?"

"Very little beyond its being Russian," I said.

"Russian?" She frowned. "Is that significant?"

"Marzo works for the British, reporting to Darius. I don't know how that could connect to Russia, but Vittoria's story compels me to think there is something—was something—between Marzo and Signore di Taro. We've seen the dead man's street. Why would Marzo have randomly decided to include it on his walks with the girl?"

"Maybe like Carlo, he was inspired by a pretty face."

"The description certainly applies to Vittoria, but Marzo showed little interest in her. He was using her as an excuse to be in the neighborhood."

"And the street was not a place one would go to without a specific purpose," Cécile said. "I wonder . . . do you think Lena knows about Vittoria?"

"I can't imagine she does."

"Marzo made no attempt to even kiss Vittoria, but he must have wanted something from her, and I agree that something was an excuse to be near Signore di Taro's house. If he was seen frequently in the vicinity for a period of time before the murder, it would be far less likely that anyone would take notice of him on the day of the crime," Cécile said. "Given that we have no reason to suspect there was anything romantic between him and Vittoria, he might well have told Lena what he was doing."

I folded Henry's letter and slipped it back into its envelope. "Colin said that the manner of Signore di Taro's murder suggests assassination.

Marzo needed money to afford the house Lena wanted. Perhaps in the course of his work for the British, he came across an underground network of odious individuals who offer murder for hire and decided to work for them in an effort to earn something on the side."

"An underground network of odious individuals who offer murder for hire?" Cécile asked. I braced myself for her reply, but she did not heap scorn upon me as I'd expected. "This, Kallista, sounds most promising. We all know there are evil men who lurk in the shadows, bidding others to do their dirty deeds. I've read enough of Monsieur Le Queux's book to know spies and those who work with them come into contact with this sort of person more than an ordinary man."

"I admit it's something of a ludicrous theory, but it may have some merit. Let's talk to Lena."

We walked directly to her father's shop in the Oltrarno, but she was not there, and Signore Bastieri had no idea where she'd gone.

"Marzo's funeral was yesterday," he explained. "As you can imagine, she was terribly upset. I struggled to get her home afterward. She could hardly walk. A foreign gentleman offered his carriage and I was glad to accept. When I woke up this morning, she was gone."

"Who was the gentleman?" I asked.

"I don't know his name. It was difficult to understand his accent, which was quite heavy. It appeared that he'd been at the funeral, too, so I saw no harm in accepting his kindness. I didn't have much time to think about it, as I was afraid Lena was on the verge of collapse."

"What did he look like?"

"He was wearing a top hat and a scarf. I remember his hair was on the dark side and he had a large moustache. Not too old, not too young."

"Did he accompany you in the carriage?"

"No, Lady Emily, he did not. He said his home was not far away and, as he could see we needed the carriage more than he, he would happily leave it to us and walk."

"He lives in Florence?" I asked.

"I assume so," Signore Bastieri said. "He said home, not hotel, and has a carriage here."

"Did you recognize his accent?"

"It was foreign, but I couldn't tell you from where. Does it matter?"

"Could it have been Russian?"

"It might have been. It sounded vaguely Eastern."

It wasn't firm confirmation, but better than nothing. "Did Lena receive any messages after you got home?"

"No," her father said, "but something came for her this morning. She left the envelope on the kitchen table. I will get it for you."

He disappeared upstairs and returned with an envelope that was perfectly ordinary in every way but one: it had been sealed with wax, stamped with an impression of a coat of arms bearing a bat, an arrow, and a caltrap. What could this mean? Had Lena been searching for the treasure hidden in our house? And, if so, had she angered someone else who also sought it?

"*Mon dieu,*" Cécile said.

"Is this something bad?" Signore Bastieri asked. "Should I be worried?"

"I wouldn't say it's necessarily bad, but as to whether you should worry . . ." I looked at him and saw the concern in his eyes. I had to tell him the truth. "I'm afraid I would be worried."

"I will summon the police and ask them to start a search for her."

"She hasn't been gone long enough for them to believe she's missing, and it is entirely possible she decided to go for a walk or to the market or something else wholly innocuous. Signora du Lac and I will see what we can find out. Lena told me if she ever needed to contact me, she would leave a note at Dante's cenotaph in Santa Croce."

Her father gave a sad smile. "That sounds like her, always looking for adventure. May I come with you?"

"There's no need," I said. "Better that you stay here in case she comes home. I'll keep you abreast of any and all developments."

"I would appreciate that."

I wished I could do more to reassure him. "My husband has a great deal of experience locating missing persons. I can promise you he will do everything in his power to help find your daughter."

"*Grazie,* signora," he said.

We left the shop and walked to the river, following it to the Ponte alle Grazie, which would take us across the Arno near Santa Croce. "Do you really think something bad may have happened to Lena?" Cécile asked.

"Let us not forget that the original reason Colin wanted to come to Florence was because Kat's house had twice been burgled," I said. "Marzo wanted money, and the house may have something of value hidden in it. He might have been killed for trying to find it."

"And Lena could have known what he was doing," Cécile said.

"Marzo's connection to the house keeps niggling at me. It belongs to Kat, not Colin, and Marzo works with Darius, not my husband."

"The legend of the treasure is known throughout the city. His interest in it needn't have stemmed from anything to do with his work."

"True. But if the household staff is involved in Crown business, which I suspect they are, Marzo may have been a frequent visitor to the house long before we ever arrived in Florence."

"It would be much simpler for us to figure out what is going on if Monsieur Hargreaves would take us into his confidence," Cécile said. "Surely he knows we can both be trusted."

"Of course he does," I said, "but it's not always for him to decide whom he can tell what. There's a man above him whom I believe supervises it all. He's called Sir John Burman. I overheard him and Colin talking about the situation in Florence before we came here. He's a decent, honorable man whose role is to protect the empire and all her citizens. I've never heard a word spoken against him and am confident that Colin would not follow his direction if he had even the slightest doubt as to his character."

"I should like to meet this Sir John and explain to him that his goals would be met with far greater speed if he would let you and me help. I could persuade him."

"I have infinite faith in your ability to persuade, but Sir John would never succumb to any such temptation. He is a man of unshakable principle."

"That leaves us with you," Cécile said. "Surely you could tempt Monsieur Hargreaves into telling us more. In exchange, you could give him timely updates of our own investigation instead of making him wait until we've solved the crime."

A stab of guilt pierced my abdomen. If only she knew my proposal for just such an arrangement had resulted in my agreeing to give information without receiving anything in return. "It would be wrong of me to entice him to act against his principles."

Cécile narrowed her eyes and remained silent for the rest of the walk to Santa Croce. Colin had been right. Deceiving her was exacting a heavy price from me.

Inside the church, we went straight to Dante's monument. Reaching the spot on it that Lena had chosen as her ersatz postbox proved a challenge. Santa Croce, as usual, was crowded with tourists and their guides. I would not be able to hide what I was doing from all of them. Better, I decided, to abandon discretion entirely.

I let out a loud sob, threw my arm across my face, and spoke loudly. *"Oh lasso, / quanti dolci pensier, quanto disio / menò costoro al doloroso passo!"* There is no greater sorrow / Than to be mindful of the happy time / In misery, and that thy Teacher knows. "There can be nothing but sorrow for us, Great Poet, to know that we shall never have a new poem from you."

I stepped forward and onto the bottom of the cenotaph. I had to get up higher, and gripped the wreath held by the sculpted mourner, but could tell it would not support my weight. As destroying Florence's monument to her favorite son was unlikely to be met with favor, I looked for something I could use to boost myself up to the top of the next level of the sculpture, the rectangle upon which the empty sarcophagus sat. I put my arm around the waist of the female figure, got one foot onto the base, and heaved myself up. Then, as quickly as possible, I felt around beneath her arm and found an envelope. I grabbed it, shoved it into my jacket, and then tugged at my hat, removing one of the flowers decorating it. This, with great flourish, I placed on the top of the stone sarcophagus.

"You will never be forgotten, Dante Alighieri!" I wished I could remember another quote from *The Divine Comedy*, but, alas, I'd already used the only one I'd memorized. I leapt down from the monument. A herd of tourists had gathered to watch my antics, and a docent was approaching, a stern look on his face. Before he could scold me, I looped my arm through Cécile's and dragged her out of the church, loudly reciting *Oh lasso, / quanti dolci pensier, quanto disio / menò costoro al doloroso passo* over and over until we escaped back into the piazza.

"That was quite a display, Kallista," Cécile said. "Although a broader knowledge of Dante would have made it more impressive."

"I entirely agree, but as I did find a message, we succeeded despite my limitations." We stopped beneath the statue of Dante in the center of the piazza and I opened the envelope. The paper inside was covered in a girlish scrawl:

> Meet me in the Cappelle Medicee today, as soon as you read this note. I will wait there for you, however long it takes, in a secret room reached through a trapdoor in the Sagrestia Nuova. Be careful not to be followed. There is grave danger.

"Good heavens," I said. "She really did expect us to check every day. It's fortunate we went to see her father."

"For all we know, she left this for us days ago, and obviously, given she went to Marzo's funeral, didn't remain indefinitely in the Medici Chapel," Cécile said. "As for her warning of danger, even her father admits that she longs for adventure. This may be nothing more than a game to her."

I was not convinced.

We raced to the Duomo, skirted around the Baptistry of San Giovanni, and turned into the Piazza San Lorenzo. Inside the church, I inquired as to where we would find the New Sacristy and was informed that it had a separate entrance, in the Piazza Madonna. Fortunately, this was only a couple hundred feet away, so within moments, we entered the chapel Michelangelo constructed to house the Medici dead. The artist never completed his work on the space, and to this day, the most famous member of the family, Lorenzo the Magnificent, remains interred beneath the floor, with no spectacular monument to mark his resting place. Ironically, the only tombs Michelangelo finished belong to the least interesting of the Medici.

Today, though, there was no time for musing about the Medici; we were searching for a trapdoor. The chapel's brightly colored marble floor revealed nothing, and I thought it unlikely that there was anything beneath it other than tombs. We turned our attention to the small rooms that came off the chapel and in one of them, beneath a well-worn rug, was a trapdoor.

"How did Lena know this was here?" I mused.

"The girl is clearly in possession of hidden depths," Cécile said.

As the vestry was not of much interest to tourists, we had the room to ourselves. I tugged at the ring on the door, which opened with remarkable ease to reveal a set of narrow stone stairs. I pulled out the candle and matches I always kept in my reticule—one never knows when one might need to illuminate a dark space—lit the candle, and started down the steps, Cécile following immediately behind.

At the bottom was a small room, slightly more than twenty feet long, but only about six and a half feet wide, its walls covered with charcoal sketches. Lena had indeed come here to wait for us, but we'd arrived too late. She was there, on the floor, lying in a dark pool of blood.

Florence, 1491

30

A mood of profound morbidity clung to me for weeks after my grandfather told me I would inherit his books. Every time a servant brought me a message, I feared it would contain news of his passing, even though he had never suffered from ill-health. Eventually, reminding myself that we have no control over death, I managed to push aside my gloomy preoccupation and, soon thereafter, accompanied him to the villa of one of his friends, outside Florence. The owner, Giovanni Tornabuoni, a banker, was hosting a hunt on his grounds. I had no interest in sport, but Nonno wanted me to come regardless, insisting I would find much to enjoy from the company of the other guests.

"You haven't hunted for years," I said.

"I'm too old for it. I will sit with the other ancient men and argue about life while you have your fun."

"*Fun* is not the word I would choose."

"Try to have a more positive outlook, Mina," he said. "You might find you like *la caccia*. Even if it's not to your taste, it's an opportunity to make a few friends. You can't spend all your time with old men."

"I don't spend all my time with old men. I do have Bia, too, you know."

"Children and octogenarians ought not be your primary sources of companionship."

When we arrived at the villa, the guests were already gathering outside the house. Introductions were made, and I had to admit it was a lively group, everyone well educated and urbane, but I would have little chance to get to know any of them until after we'd returned from the hunt. I was, at best, an adequate horsewoman, so there was no way I would be able to simultaneously converse and keep up with the others. Not wanting to disappoint my grandfather, I tried to look cheerful as one of our host's grooms helped me onto my mount. A pack of tan and white pointers—Bracci, a fine hunting breed—gathered in the front of the assembled riders and we set off into the woods. I lagged behind almost at once, and before the group had downed their first boar, I'd fallen off my horse when he jumped over the trunk of a fallen tree. The steed, better trained than I, noticed the absence of my weight and stopped. Even if I could manage to get back on top of him without assistance, I had no chance of finding, let alone catching up to, the other hunters. If he had an inclination to return to his barn, I might be able to make my way back to the villa.

I was trying to remember any stories of horses making their way home on their own when I heard the sound of snapping branches and snorting, followed by a squeal of some sort, all of which presumably came from a boar. As a hunting novice, I had been given a small cudgel to carry, rather than a spear or anything likely to be of use against a wild beast. No one had expected I would face any creature on my own, and, to be fair, no weapon of any sort would have made much of a difference. I knew how to wield none of them.

My heart was racing as a boar came into sight. His head was enormous as were the tusks jutting from the sides of his jaw, which he was popping, making his saliva foam. I was half a step from the trunk of a tree. Without stopping to think, I reached for its lowest branch and started to climb. The boar lunged forward, reaching the tree before I'd made it very high. My limbs were shaking and I wasn't sure I could keep myself from falling. If I did fall, one of two things would happen: Either I would land directly on his head and somehow that would incapacitate him, or I would come crashing down and incapacitate myself, which would make it all the easier for the beast to eat me.

Do boars eat ladies? I wasn't sure. If they did, it couldn't be pleasant.

Lucretius was right when he said we had nothing to fear from death. It would come as a relief, particularly if one met it at the hands—tusks?—of a wild boar. I started to laugh. What else could I do in such a ridiculous situation?

Then, all at once, the boar dropped, a spear piercing its side. A man stepped forward, dagger in hand, checked that the beast was dead—he was—and then looked up at me.

"Were you laughing?" he asked.

"Yes, I'm sorry, I was," I said. "Absurd, I know."

He held his arms up and told me to let myself fall into them. I did as ordered, and he caught me with no apparent effort. "I noticed you were having trouble keeping up with the group and then realized you'd disappeared, so I thought I ought to backtrack and try to find you. Are you hurt?"

"I fell off my horse but injured nothing aside from the overly lofty opinion I hold of myself."

"Climbing the tree was clever," he said, carrying me away from the boar's corpse and setting me down.

"I didn't think the cudgel would prove an adequate weapon. At least not in my hands."

"Most likely not in anyone's." He whistled and my horse came to him. He tied the reins around a tree. "We'll leave him here while we get mine, which is nearby. We'll walk to get him. You might want another moment or two to settle before you ride." He held out his gloved hand. I took it. It was warm and made me feel safe.

We'd soon collected his horse and returned to the small clearing where mine stood patiently waiting. Once my rescuer was persuaded I was suffering from no meaningful injury, he strung a rope through the boar's rear legs, just above his hooves, flung one end over a sturdy tree branch, and pulled until the animal was hanging above the ground. Then, he made an incision with his dagger and removed the gory mass of the beast's innards from his body.

"It's not pretty, I know, but I hate to waste the meat." When the blood had finished draining, he brought my horse over to the tree, lowered the carcass, and draped it over the steed's back, using more rope to secure it. He tied another length around his horse's neck and then knotted the other end around my horse's tail. That done, he helped me onto his horse and finally, in a swift, fluid motion, leapt onto it behind me, and we set off for the villa.

He kept one arm around my waist to steady me. I needed the assistance, but the gesture felt oddly intimate. "I'm mortified, sir, but after all you've done for me, I owe you the truth. I can't remember your name."

He laughed. "Cristofano Corsini. Do not feel bad. In your state, after nearly being attacked by a vicious boar, I would not be able to recall my own name, let alone that of someone I've only just met. You are Mina Portinari. I have long admired your grandfather."

"You know him?" I asked.

"Only from a distance. I see him at the occasional dinner but am not fortunate enough to count myself among his friends. Tell me something. Why were you laughing when I found you?"

"I was in a tree trying to escape unwelcome attention from a boar. The situation was so inane, what else was there to do? *Nil igitur mors est ad nos neque pertinet hilum, / quandoquidem natura animi mortalis habetur.*"

"*Therefore death to us / Is nothing, nor concerns us in the least, / Since nature of mind is mortal evermore.* That must be Lucretius."

"You're an educated man."

"I'm a Florentine. Would a badly educated man be tolerated in our city?" I couldn't see his face, but it felt as if he were smiling. "Did your grandfather teach you Latin?"

"He did, but I also studied with my brothers and their tutors."

"I believe il Magnifico's mother did the same with her daughters. A wise decision, I always thought. Who wants a dolt for a wife?"

My whole body tensed. Much as I was enjoying our conversation, I was not looking for a husband. Then I realized I had no idea whether Signore Corsini was already married. "So you chose an educated wife?"

"I will, eventually," he said, "but see no need to rush, so if you want me to propose, I'm afraid you're destined for disappointment."

"Signore Corsini, a proposal is the last thing I would ever want, from you or anyone else."

"I'm most relieved. It's a dangerous business, rescuing ladies and them expecting you to marry them."

"You've nothing to fear from me on that count," I said. "But I am curious. How many ladies have you rescued?"

We had reached the villa. He stopped the horses, dismounted, and helped me down. "You're my first, but I've heard stories."

I hadn't taken much notice of his appearance until then. He wasn't all that handsome. His nose was a bit long and his mouth a bit thin. His eyes, hazel, were unremarkable, but something about them drew me to him. They danced. He called for a groom to tend to the horses and see to the boar and then led me inside. The maid who greeted us looked shocked and bustled me off for a bath. I hadn't realized just how filthy I was.

My dress, streaked with mud and ripped in several places, was deemed unwearable. A substitute was produced, borrowed from our hostess. The others had not yet returned when I made my way back downstairs, where I found Signore Corsini with my grandfather and his friends in the loggia. Their conversation fell silent as I approached, and I was quiet, too, struck dumb by a fresco on the wall behind the table around which they sat. It was obviously painted by Botticelli and depicted the Three Graces with Venus, who was handing a gift—flowers, but I knew they represented more—to a lady. The face of the middle Grace, who stood immediately to the left of the goddess, was mine, taken from the sketch the artist had done of me on that night so long ago, when I'd dined at the Medici palazzo.

"Have you recovered from your adventure, Mina?" my grandfather asked, beckoning me to join them. I did as he wished, but could hardly tear my eyes from the fresco. The Graces and Venus looked so much lighter and nimbler than the mortal. Would her stiff form alter and bend once she took the flowers from the goddess? Would she welcome into her world lofty ideas and beauty?

The men were all staring at me. I realized I hadn't replied. "I have, thank you," I said. "I owe a great debt to Signore Corsini."

"As do I," my grandfather said.

"Neither of you owes me a thing," my rescuer said. "The swooning compliments I'll be getting from ladies for months after they hear of my feats will be more than enough." He smiled at me, then tilted his head and squinted, looking as if he were seeing me for the first time. He turned to the fresco, then back to me. The other men paid no further attention, returning to their discussion, something about Alcibiades, but Signore Corsini continued to stare at me.

"A muse of Botticelli's. What a lucky man I am to have rescued you."

I looked at him, alarmed.

"Fear not," he said. "I've no romantic designs on you. I've long been an admirer of the artist, and now he will be indebted to me for saving you. He may even agree to paint the chapel in my palazzo."

Florence, 1903

31

The light from my candle made the grisly scene of Lena's death all the more eerie, its flickering flame mirrored in the dark, pooled blood. "Go back upstairs," I said to Cécile. "Find the police. We'll need Colin as well."

"Monsieur Hargreaves did not want the police involved," my friend said.

"It would be impossible to keep this from them, given where the poor girl died. I've no idea where Colin is at the moment, but we can't let her body stay down here indefinitely." The cloying smell of blood in the small space almost made me retch. I wanted nothing more than to return upstairs, run outside, and breathe fresh air. "Leave an urgent message for him at the house and fetch the police."

"What about Signore Bastieri? He needs to know his daughter is dead."

"I wouldn't want him to see her here, like this, would you? We will inform him as soon as she's been taken to the morgue and cleaned up."

Cécile nodded. "You are right that he should not see this. I will do as you ask, but, Kallista, you cannot stay down here alone."

"I'm not the one in danger from being alone. She was." Hot tears stung my eyes. "I should have taken her more seriously."

"Now is not the time for lamentation and regret," Cécile said and gave my arm a little squeeze. "We had no reason to suspect something like this would happen."

I nodded, but couldn't find my voice to reply. She squeezed my arm again and set off to do as I'd asked. The room felt even closer with her gone, the smell more oppressive, but I forced myself to examine the scene. Lena lay on her back, her head turned to one side. She had faced her attacker and would have had nowhere to run, no way to flee. The narrow stairs could easily be blocked by an ordinary-sized man.

A single gash in the left side of her neck had severed her jugular. I wondered if she had raised her right hand in an attempt to protect herself from the knife. Regardless, she could never have changed the outcome. A man capable of causing such a wound with a single strike was no amateur. He knew how to kill.

I forced myself to kneel next to her so that I could search the contents of her coat pockets. She had left the envelope behind at her father's, but not the message within. If she'd brought it with her to the Sagrestia Nuova, she no longer had it. There was nothing in any of her pockets. I gently tilted her so that I could see if there was anything under her body—her reticule, at least—but again found nothing. Her murderer must have taken all her personal effects.

I rose to my feet, wobbling a bit, and inspected the cell-like room. Its ceiling was arched, surprising for a space so small. Why had the architect given a tiny cellar such a beautiful detail? I stepped closer to the walls to better see the charcoal drawings that covered them. Many of them were figures of men, life-sized, the rest sketches of parts of buildings. The style was so reminiscent of Michelangelo that I wondered if he had used the room while working in the chapel above. I studied every mark, hoping to find something that might provide a clue as to why Lena had come here. Graffiti, like that in the palazzo, or a symbol from the coat of arms on the seal, but there were only the drawings, which, no matter how I tried to bend it around in my head, I couldn't connect to anything to do with Lena or Marzo.

I'd scrutinized every inch of the room. There was nothing left to do, so I removed my jacket, draped it over Lena, and sat next to her on the floor. One of her hands remained uncovered. It looked so small, so fragile. I touched it and had never felt anything so cold.

"I'm sorry," I whispered. "You did not deserve to die like this."

I know not how much time passed before clattering footsteps above alerted me to the arrival of the police. They ordered me out of the room and had no interest in hearing anything I had to say about the victim. The most senior officer, recognizing that I had no intention of going away gently, took me by the arm, steered me to the steps, and prodded me up them.

"Signora, I apologize most sincerely that you had the misfortune to witness such a dreadful scene," he said. Cécile was standing nearby, tapping the tip of her parasol on the stone floor and scowling. "It is only natural that you would become hysterical. Don't try to speak. You'll only upset yourself more. We have the matter in hand and require nothing further from you."

"Do you know the victim's name?" I asked. "Do you know where she lived? Do you know why she came here?"

"These are all questions we will answer in good time," he said. "There is no need to let it further trouble you." He started back toward the steps. I called after him.

"Her name is Lena Bastieri. She lives above her father's leather shop in the Piazza Santo Spirito."

He paused and turned around.

"I assure you, signore, I am anything but hysterical," I continued. "I don't know why she decided to come here, or even how she knew about the trapdoor, but she came of her own volition and asked my friend and me to meet her."

"When did she ask you to meet her?" he asked.

"She left us a note, but we don't know precisely when," Cécile said.

"Do you have the note here, with you?"

"No," Cécile said. "I didn't see any need to keep it and threw it away after I read it. It's not as if her message was complicated. It was perfectly straightforward: meet me in the little room beneath the Medici Chapel."

"I did not know this room existed," the policeman said. "How did she?"

"That, inspector—are you an inspector?—I do not know," Cécile said. "I assumed it was common knowledge. Now, if you've nothing further to ask of us, I'd like to take my friend back to the house at which we are staying. She is not hysterical, but she is very upset."

"I'm perfectly fine—"

Cécile did not let me finish. "Should you require our assistance, you may reach us at the Palazzo di Vieri." With that, she pulled me out of the vestry, silencing me when I started to object. Only when we were back outside, standing in the sunshine streaming through the piazza, did she let me speak.

"You've quite a flair for lying to the police," I said.

"I did not think it wise to give the police any details Monsieur Hargreaves would not want them to know, and I certainly was not going to give him the opportunity to seize Lena's message to us."

"They need to investigate the murder."

"*Oui,* but if Lena's death is connected to Marzo's, we both know they will not have access to the sensitive information necessary to find the killer."

"Only Colin and Darius have that." As I said their names, I saw the gentlemen striding toward us. As they drew closer, Colin rushed forward, looking alarmed.

"Emily, my dear girl, are you all right?"

I was more than a little disheveled, my jacket gone, my hands and clothes streaked with blood. "As well as can be expected. The police are inside."

"We'll take care of them," he said. "You two go back to the house. We'll follow as soon as possible."

Part of me wanted to see how he planned to deal with the police, but I did not have it in me to protest. All I wanted was a hot bath and the privacy it provided to break down and cry.

Colin could see I was not well. "Will you give us a moment?" he asked, nodding at Darius, who immediately took Cécile by the arm and stepped away.

"How did you arrive here so quickly?" I asked. "I didn't expect you to receive the message Cécile left until this evening."

"I didn't get the message. We heard about the murder from another source, and after your speculations about di Taro, I didn't think we should dismiss any other suspicious death as unconnected to our investigation."

"I shan't bother to ask the identity of your source."

He frowned. "I'm worried about you. Let me take you to the palazzo and get you settled. Darius can handle this."

"No, that's not necessary, although the offer's much appreciated," I said. "I'm feeling awful because I should have done more for Lena. I didn't take her seriously and thought she was playing games. And now it's too late—"

"Lena?" Colin asked. "It's Lena who's dead?"

"I thought you knew."

"Only that a body had been discovered in the Medici Chapel. I'm escorting you and Cécile and will brook no argument." He waved Darius over. "This is not some random murder. Lena Bastieri is the victim. I'll take the ladies back to the house and return as quickly as possible. In the meantime, do whatever you can to keep the police from making too much of a mess of things."

"Right." Darius nodded. "Do we know how long she's been dead?"

"She was cold when Cécile and I found her," I said.

"I'm sorry, Emily. I wish there were words that could soothe you," he said. "Instead, I can only promise to find the wretch who did this to her and make sure he can never hurt anyone else again."

"Thank you, Darius." I can't say his words were a comfort, but I knew he and Colin would do everything possible to set things right. Whether that meant I would ever know what happened remained to be seen. I had been doing my best not to let Colin's need for secrecy aggravate me. I knew his motives were noble, but inside, I was fuming. What in theory sounds reasonable and measured does not always prove so in reality. As upset as I was about Lena, my pain was minuscule compared to that felt by Signora Spichio, who lost her son. She had accepted Colin's story about him falling from the roof. She would never know the truth about his death. How could a just world require such deception?

By the time Colin left Cécile and me at the palazzo, I had decided I would stand for nothing short of knowing the whole truth, regardless of the consequences.

I paced in our bedroom while Tessa filled the copper tub in the bathroom with steaming water and dismissed her before I sank into it. The heat released my pent-up emotions, and I sobbed as I scrubbed the blood from my hands. Not long after my tears were exhausted, the maid poked her head through the doorway.

"I'm sorry to disturb you, signora," she said. "I'm not sure what—that is, your clothes . . ." She was holding the blood-streaked walking suit—minus its jacket—I'd been wearing.

"The stains won't come out," I said. "Don't bother to try. It's best that we get rid of it. I couldn't wear it again even if it were clean."

"*Sì*, signora." She was still standing in the doorway.

"Is there something else?" I asked.

"Signora, what happened? Is it true Marzo's fiancée is dead?"

"She is," I said.

Tessa gasped and went so pale I was afraid she might faint.

"You didn't know her, did you?"

"No, only stories about her, like what I told you about her and Marzo's brother."

"Come all the way into the room and shut the door," I said. "It's time we had a frank conversation. I have taken you into my confidence and given you the opportunity to participate in my investigation. In return, you have deceived me from the beginning, first, by pretending not to speak English."

"Signora, no, I do not lie to you."

"I overheard your conversation with Signora Orlandi and Fredo about the treasure and me. My husband spoke to you all about it, and was reassured by whatever you told him. I, however, was not, and can only conclude that you are not trustworthy."

"I should never have told you I was not interested in the treasure. I—"

"I don't care about the treasure right now," I said. "Did you know Lena?"

Tears streamed down her face. "No—"

"Then why are you crying?"

"No one should die so young."

Not wanting to continue this discussion in the bath, I rose from the tub and grabbed a towel. "Of course not, but it happens every day. I've had enough of your lies and misdirection. How well did you know Lena?"

Tessa gulped and looked at the floor. "I grew up not far from her father's shop," she said. "So, yes, I knew her, but we were not close. Acquaintances at best."

"You didn't like her."

"No, I didn't. She was one of those girls who knew how to use her beauty to get anything she wanted. Our upbringings were similar, yet I work as a maid while she was going to marry and have a house of her own."

"You resented her for that?"

"Yes."

"Soon after my arrival here, I asked you to find out what you could about Marzo. Why didn't you tell me you knew Lena?"

"I don't know."

"That's not an acceptable answer, Tessa," I said. I pulled on my dressing gown and tossed aside the towel. "Marzo is dead. Lena is dead. There is another girl connected to Marzo. Should I be fearful of her safety?"

"Another girl?" She'd stopped crying and wiped her face with the back of her hand. "That can't be. Marzo adored Lena."

"So why was he walking out with someone else?"

"How would I know?"

"When I asked you to find out what you could about Marzo, you went to the Mercato Nuovo," I said. "There, you learned his Christian name, but not much else. I went there, too, and discovered considerably more."

"I was trying not to draw attention to what I was doing," Tessa said. "I thought you wanted me to be discreet."

"You told me Marzo's death was the subject of gossip, yet no one in the market mentioned to you that he'd been seeing the daughter of a wool merchant who works there? I would have thought that would have been much discussed. Why did you withhold information from me then, and why do you continue to do so now?"

She stared at the floor.

"Tessa, I liked you the moment we met, but if I cannot trust you . . ." I let my voice trail, hoping the silent threat would provoke her to open up to me. When it appeared my ruse hadn't worked, I walked past her into the bedroom, picked up the tea gown she'd laid out for me on the bed, and started to dress.

"I can help you, signora," she said, following me.

"I don't need help with a tea gown. I need help with Lena." I pointed to the chairs in front of the fireplace. "Sit down and tell me everything."

She sat and clasped her hands together, hard. Her knuckles were white. She bit her lower lip. She knitted her eyebrows together. Finally, she looked at me. "Lena wasn't the first girl with plans to marry Marzo. I was engaged to him before they met."

Florence, 1492

32

After Signore Corsini rescued me, he became a frequent visitor to my house. I liked him. We shared the same taste in poetry, preferring Dante to Petrarch, and considered Greek a superior language to Latin. We read the entire *Decameron* aloud to each other. We argued about Plato's dialogues. But never once did our relationship stray beyond the bounds of friendship.

It was Signore Corsini who brought me the sad news of Lorenzo il Magnifico's death, and we mourned together, raising a glass to the great man.

"Florence will no longer be what it was."

His words reminded me of that conversation I'd had long ago with my grandfather, on the night he asked me to promise to keep his books safe. He hadn't believed Piero, Lorenzo's heir, would ever live up to his father's legacy.

Six weeks later, I summoned Signore Corsini to my house. My grandfather had died in the night. Again, we grieved together. Again, we raised a glass.

"I knew he could not live forever, but at the same time, I never truly believed he would die," I said.

"That's because the little girl he adored is still somewhere inside you. She would have considered him invincible."

"You're insightful, Signore Corsini—"

"You must stop addressing me so formally. We've known each other for more than a year and spend so much time together my mother is convinced I plan to marry you. My father, on the other hand, is convinced you're my mistress. Surely that means you can call me Cristofano."

"She thinks you plan to marry me?" My jaw went slack with horror.

He laughed. "You're not offended at the suggestion you're my mistress, only that someone suspects you'll become my wife."

"I'll never be either to any man. You know that."

"I do, Mina."

Our eyes met. It was the first time he'd addressed me by my Christian name. He'd always followed my lead, never wanting more than I, content to adopt the formality I'd imposed on our friendship.

"That comforts me greatly, Cristofano." His name felt awkward on my lips.

He looked away from me and changed the subject. "Where is Bia today? I expected her to race to greet me when I arrived."

"Her nurse took her to see the lions in the Piazza della Signoria. She was very upset when I told her about Nonno."

"He doted on her."

"He had already started to teach her Latin," I said. "I'm sorry she won't have the pleasure of learning more from him."

"As am I. He was a good man. Did she go willingly to see the lions?"

I smiled. "You know her too well. She protested, insisting that, at eleven, she is too old to find consolation in such distractions. I told her she could watch them being fed and all her objections faded in an instant."

"I suspected as much."

"You're good to her."

"She makes it easy."

Bia loved Signore Corsini fiercely. It was a different love than she'd had for her father, more guarded and more possessive. When he'd first met her, he brought a chess set as a gift and taught her how to play, even though everyone else told her she was too young. She appreciated the attention, and from that day, considered him hers.

"Not many men would bother with her."

"You wouldn't tolerate me coming around if I didn't."

"I wouldn't tolerate you coming around if I thought you were using her to impress me."

He took my hands. "Happy though I always am to banter with you, I'm not doing much to console you. The loss of Signore Portinari is a blow to all of Florence, but for you it is not just intellectual. I know what he meant to you. Is there anything I can do to ease your pain?"

"Having you here is more than enough," I said. "He's left me his library. I knew he planned to. We spoke about it long ago. He trusted me to keep it safe. It seemed such an odd thing to me at the time, but Savonarola had started preaching here again, and his fire and brimstone never made a favorable impression on Nonno."

"Nor me," Cristofano said. "He's only grown more powerful since Lorenzo's death."

"He's saying that we're approaching the end of times, that we're facing tribulations of epic proportion."

"More terrifying than his prophecies is the reaction of the citizens of our city. Many of them are starting to believe him."

"Lorenzo has not been dead long," I said. "Piero is mourning his father at the same time he's learning to rule. Periods of transition are always unsettling. Once Piero proves he's capable—"

"Lorenzo did what he could to prepare him, but it may be that Piero is not capable." He frowned. "I have great concerns about what he will do to Florence. But we are not meant to be discussing politics, not today of all days. Instead we should read aloud from Lucretius. He was your grandfather's favorite, and his ideas are potently applicable in the present circumstances."

"Nonno always regretted that it was Poggio, not him, who discovered the manuscript," I said. "Did you know he copied it out himself, so that he'd have it, even before Poggio managed to acquire a personal copy of his own?"

"I did not."

"I don't think there's anything I will ever treasure more than that volume of Lucretius, written in his own hand. What a gift to be given."

"You don't have it here, do you?" he asked.

"No."

"Bring me your own copy, then. I will read to you."

I did as he asked and listened as he read:

Denique si vocem rerum natura repente
mittat et hoc alicui nostrum sic increpet ipsa:
"quid tibi tanto operest, mortalis, quod nimis aegris
luctibus indulges? quid mortem congemis ac fles?
nam si grata fuit tibi vita ante acta priorque
et non omnia pertusum congesta quasi in vas
commoda perfluxere atque ingrata interiere;
cur non ut plenus vitae conviva recedis
aequo animoque capis securam, stulte, quietem?"

Once more, if Nature
Should of a sudden send a voice abroad,
And her own self inveigh against us so:
"Mortal, what hast thou of such grave concern
That thou indulgest in too sickly plaints?
Why this bemoaning and beweeping death?
For if thy life aforetime and behind
To thee was grateful, and not all thy good
Was heaped as in sieve to flow away
And perish unavailingly, why not,
Even like a banqueter, depart the halls,
Laden with life? why not with mind content
Take now, thou fool, thy unafflicted rest?"

He closed the book. "There is some comfort in that, I hope."

"How can I feel regret to know that he rests now, forever without pain or want or need?"

"Seek solace in the poet's words, but they don't mean that you're not allowed to be sad, Mina. I know how much you will miss him."

When I went to bed that night, I could not sleep. I cried and cried, consumed with loss. I was thinking about my grandfather, but then my thoughts turned to Salvi. He would be eleven now, and I would not recognize him if I saw him. Was he still in Florence? The loss of Nonno was something over which I had no control. Painful though it was, it fell neatly within the bounds of the natural order of things. Losing my son was altogether different. I had chosen that loss, chosen it because I was too young and too cowardly to face my sins. My grandfather was free from the suffering that comes with life, but Salvi was not. He would never experience the daily luxuries I took for granted. Instead of becoming a successful merchant, like my father, he would be apprenticed to a tradesman. He would never study humanism, never know the delights of art. His life would be defined by backbreaking work that might never bring him a decent living.

I sat up in bed and dried my eyes.

If Salvi showed an aptitude for art, in any form, he might not be destined for a miserable existence. Had not Brunelleschi himself apprenticed as a goldsmith and worked in that trade until he became one of the greatest architects of our age? Florence was not a city that required inherited wealth. Yes, it helped, no one anywhere in any century could deny that universal truth, but here a man was judged first on his merits. He could study with a famous painter or sculptor.

Did he like art? Was he drawn to it? If I could find out, I could ask Botticelli to teach him. He would not judge me for taking an interest in an orphan.

I sank back against my pillow. It was nothing but fantasy. I would never be able to find Salvi unless I used my half of the St. Anthony charm to identify us both. I was no longer so young as when I'd given him up, but I was just as cowardly, still unwilling to face the shame that would come from acknowledging my greatest sin.

Florence, 1903

33

"You were engaged to Marzo?" I asked. Tessa was shaking. I poured a small glass of whisky from the decanter Colin kept in our room and pressed it into her hand. "Sip this. It will help calm you."

She downed it in a single gulp. "My father is a shoemaker. He hired Marzo to make some repairs when our roof started to leak during a rainy spring."

Lena had met him in similar circumstances, only her father had a leaky window rather than roof. Marzo's work as a handyman certainly helped him make an impression on the girls. "How did you come to be engaged?"

"I was only ten years old then, so that didn't happen for a long while. At the time, I thought him dangerously handsome. I greeted him at the door each day he came to work, and fetched him water when he was thirsty. When he was finished—he was with us for only a week or so—I did not see him again for eight years, but I clung to his memory. I compared every young man I met to him. He allowed me to adopt an impossible standard that no one else could ever meet. That should have kept me safe from a broken heart."

"So you were eighteen when you renewed the acquaintance," I said. "What happened?"

"I ran into him in the Piazza Santa Croce. Literally. I'd been doing errands for my mother and was carrying a load of parcels. I was more worried about keeping them balanced than watching where I was going. I smacked straight into him. The parcels went flying. He helped pick them up and carried them home for me. He hadn't recognized me, but I knew him the moment I saw his face. I told him as much, and he was flattered that I remembered him. We started going for walks, my mother cooked for him, and before long everyone assumed we would get married. Me, especially."

"And Marzo?" I asked.

"He never wanted to talk about the future," she said. "We would take walks every week, going all the way to the Piazzale Michelangelo. There, with Florence below us, he would kiss me. It was frightfully romantic."

"When did he propose?"

"He never did, not precisely, but we had an understanding. At least I thought we did. I wouldn't carry on like that with a man unless I believed he was going to marry me."

"Did his attentions, shall we say, go beyond kissing?"

"A bit," she said, blushing furiously.

I would not press her further on the subject. "What brought the relationship to an end?"

"It was no one thing. Gradually, he called on me less frequently. We were both busy working, so at first I took it in stride, thinking he'd have more time at the end of his next job. I got very good at making excuses for him. Then he stopped coming around at all. I left messages at his mother's house, but he never replied. When he got engaged to Lena, I heard it from neighborhood gossip. I suppose he found her more worthy than I."

"Did you ever talk to Lena about Marzo?"

"No. We were never friends."

"When was the last time you saw her?"

A flash of concern crossed her face. "Why do you ask?"

"I'm trying to piece together as much as I can about her final days," I said. "The fuller a picture I have, the more likely I am to figure out who killed her."

She nodded. "I saw her at Marzo's funeral. She sat in the front with his mother. I stayed in the back, not sure if I had the right to have come at all. When the family processed out behind his coffin, she looked at me, but I don't think she remembered who I was. We grew up in the same neighborhood, but our lives were very different. I'm not the sort of person she would befriend."

"Did you speak to her afterward?"

"No. When I left the church, her father was helping her into a carriage. She was very upset, signora. Couldn't stop crying. I guess she did love Marzo, more than I thought."

I sighed. "You will forgive me, Tessa, if I struggle to accept everything you say at face value. You've lied to me so many times."

"I know and I'm ashamed of it. I'm sorry."

"Did you see the owner of the carriage?"

"There was a gentleman standing with her and her father, but he had his back to me. I never saw his face."

"Can you recall anything about his appearance?"

"Not really. They were at quite a distance from me and I only saw him from the back. All I can tell you is that he had a scarf around his neck. Green. I remember because it made me wonder if such a bright color was appropriate for a funeral."

"Were there any markings on the carriage?"

"No, it was plain black." She fidgeted in her seat. "Can I bring you tea or something, signora? I feel so awful about everything. I want to make it up to you. I want to prove that I can be trusted."

Bringing tea would not begin to put her on the road to regaining my trust, but I appreciated that she wanted to try. I accepted her offer, but told her to bring it to the Salle dei Pappagalli, where Cécile had planned to wait for me until I'd finished with my bath. There was no point interrogating Tessa more just now. Having heard her story, I was more inclined to believe it than not, but it had many gaping holes. It also gave her a strong motive for wanting Marzo dead. Jealously is a powerful emotion.

"*Mon dieu,* Kallista, you can't think that wisp of a maid could have flung Marzo off a rooftop. How would she have got him up there?"

"With the assistance of an accomplice," I said.

"I will never believe that someone who looks as if she stepped out of Botticelli's *Birth of Venus* could commit a brutal murder."

"Venus herself was hardly an innocent. I'm sure Vulcan had little good to say about her."

"A cuckolded husband is unlikely to prove a source of reliable information," Cécile said. "Regardless, what do we do now?"

"We have to tell Signore Bastieri what happened to his daughter."

I hated delivering news of violent death. Right now, Lena's father was probably in his shop, helping a customer or in the backroom, constructing another magnificent piece out of his perfectly tanned and beautifully decorated leather. He was no doubt worried about his daughter, but in vague terms, never suspecting something so brutal could have happened to her. His life would forever be changed after today.

I was wrong about him being in his shop. We saw him standing outside in front of it as we crossed the Piazza Santo Spirito. As we approached, his face crumpled. He knew without being told his daughter was dead. We took him inside through the shop and upstairs to his home, where I made him a cup of tea, the English panacea for all problems. Knowing Signore Bastieri would be unlikely to have any on hand, I'd brought a small packet from the palazzo.

"Where is she now?" he asked. "I want to see her."

"The police will let you know when she's ready," I said. Enough time had passed that she'd likely already been moved to the morgue.

"They won't keep me from her?"

"No, they'll need you to formally identify her. I'm sorry."

"Who did this to her?"

"I swear to you, Signore Bastieri, I will find that out," I said.

"How can I help?"

"There's no need for you to—"

"No, Lady Emily, it is necessary. I cannot sit here idle while the man who drained my beautiful daughter of her life walks around our city, free. I will find him and I will deal with him."

Now was not the proper moment to discuss the moral ambiguity of vigilante justice. Better that I give him something else on which to focus. "There are many things you can do, starting with showing us her room. Something in it might provide a clue as to who attacked her."

Aside from her wedding dress, hanging in a wardrobe never to be worn, Lena possessed very little that shed light on her life. She had no books, no letters, and no diary. I still had in my reticule the envelope she had left in the kitchen. I pulled it out and asked her father if he recognized the coat of arms on the wax seal.

He examined it closely before answering. "It is familiar, but I don't know why. Is it one of the arms frescoed onto the battlements of the Palazzo Vecchio?"

"I haven't the slightest idea," I said. "What do they represent? Families who were involved in the city government?"

"No, they are all things significant to Florence: her citizens and their factions; the cross of John the Baptist, her patron; famous events in her history."

"Let's go see if we can find this one among the others," I said. I doubted it would be there, but appreciated his need to feel like he was doing something. Purposeful activity might keep his mind from scratching itself raw.

The palazzo, built in the late thirteenth century, had served as the seat of Florence's government for centuries, and was still the city's town hall. It had been constructed on the site of the home of the Uberti family, which was razed after they were exiled for backing the Ghibellines rather than the Guelphs in a long-running struggle for control of the government. For decades, the rubble of their home had been left as a makeshift monument to the Guelphs' triumph, cleared only to make way for the Palazzo Vecchio. Until 1873, Michelangelo's *David* was displayed in front of the entrance, but it was now in the Accademia museum, safe from the elements after more than three centuries of exposure.

We stood in the piazza, staring up at the coats of arms that circled the battlements of the palazzo's tower. The detail was easier to make out than I had expected, but that meant that it only took us a short while to determine that the arms for which we searched were not among them.

I was struggling to think of something else I could ask Signore Bastieri to do to assist our investigation when he offered a suggestion of his own.

"There are arms on many buildings in Florence," he said. "I will make a study of them until I find the one we seek."

He was proposing a Herculean task, one I was not confident would ever produce a favorable result. But if it was what he wanted, I would neither stop nor frustrate him, but could only hope the activity would prove a balm to his sorrows.

"The poor man," Colin said, after we'd retreated to our bedroom that evening. "He's unlikely to uncover anything of use, but you are right that he needs to feel he is doing something productive."

"There is a chance, slim though it may be, that he will find the arms," I said. "I think it more likely that we can track down the possibly Russian gentleman who loaned his carriage so Lena did not have to walk home from the funeral."

"I'll start inquiries in the morning. The evidence that he's Russian is flimsy, though."

"I agree, but given that the gun used to kill Signore di Taro is Russian, wouldn't it be prudent to see if we can get a list of Russians who live in Florence? Surely it's not a large community."

"The consulate might be able to assist. I'll see what I can do."

"Leave that to Cécile and me," I said. "It's just the sort of thing we're good at."

"Heaven help the consul."

"Have you any thoughts as to who else might have killed Lena?"

"I know how upset her death has made you," he said. "And that, no doubt, you have made sweeping—and well-intentioned—promises to her father about bringing her killer to justice."

"Don't try to convince me that he can't ever know what really happened."

"At the moment, I can't make any sweeping promises of my own," he said. "I will, however, do my best to bring him closure and peace."

"What does that mean?"

"He will have a satisfactory explanation."

"But not the truth?"

"That, Emily, remains to be seen."

"Don't expect me to be so easily satisfied," I said.

He met my eyes. "I wouldn't dream of it, and I shan't stand in your way."

"You won't enlighten me, either."

He was still holding my gaze. "I shan't stand in your way."

"I may resort to underhanded means in an effort to find out what you know."

"I shan't stand in your way."

He took my hand and looked at the floor, conflict written on his handsome face. Never had I less envied him his work.

Florence, 1495

34

I could not have imagined how Florence would change in the years that followed Lorenzo de' Medici's death. Savonarola's sermons drummed fear into the population. He preached about Noah's ark, comparing those who did not heed his warnings with the unfortunate souls who taunted Noah. The ark's door would soon be closed and locked, he said, and anyone living a life of sin would drown in the coming flood. Penance was the only hope.

Lorenzo's son and heir, Piero, as incompetent and immoral as my grandfather had feared, had turned his back on our city's long-standing alliance with France in favor of one with Naples. Savonarola claimed a new Charlemagne was coming, and when France invaded Italy, few were willing to dismiss his prophecies any longer. Piero, trying in vain to emulate his father, went to confront his enemy's king, Charles VIII. Despite not having the authority to do so, he ceded land to the French: six of our territories, including Pisa. When he returned home, he was refused entrance to the Palazzo Vecchio. The city no longer wanted his rule; the people flung mud at him. He fled, ending the Medici's long control of Florence, and never again saw the city of his birth.

The King of France rode through our gates on 17 November 1494 and paraded his army through the city. Soon, he'd negotiated peace and promised not to destroy Florence. We would have Pisa returned to our control, among a few other concessions, but in exchange, we were to pay the king 120,000 gold florins. Savonarola's new Charlemagne was no friend to us.

The Medici gone, the friar at last had the opportunity to seize power and return the city to republican government. He wrote a new constitution. He encouraged Charles VIII to start a crusade to the Holy Land. He preached that God had allowed the rule of the Medici tyrants as punishment for our citizens' sins. Now, he said, we'd entered a new era. Florence must change its very character and become a city of God.

Many people listened. They believed him. Had he not, after all, prophesized the French invasion? They accepted his claim that God communicated directly through him, that he had been divinely chosen. He had personally spoken to Charles VIII, imploring him not to sack Florence. Did we not, then, owe him everything?

The tone of the friar's sermons shifted. He promised that God was singling Florence out for greatness. With Christ as its invisible king, it would become a second Jerusalem, and like the Jews freed from captivity, the Florentines must build a new temple. No longer should we revere the ancient texts that had spurred our city to become a center of art and learning; only virtue mattered now. Savonarola rejected the humanists' notion that one could come closer to God through Neoplatonism. He stated clearly that Cicero and Aristotle could not help us know the Lord.

The leaders of Florence had long been learned men, poets and scholars. Were we to reject this tradition? Savonarola insisted he was returning us to the old days of the Republic, before the Medici had corrupted the city. We would be free again. Florence, he promised, would be *richer, more glorious, more powerful than ever.* Who did not long for that?

Florentines knew factions caused chaos. In Dante's day, the Ghibellines had fought the Guelphs. Later, the Pazzi attacked the Medici, their conspiracy culminating with the bloody assassination of Lorenzo il Magnifico's brother in the cathedral. Now we would be divided again, this time into the Piagnoni and the Arrabbiati, the former Savonarola's supporters, the latter those who rejected him.

We had all read Dante, memorized his words. He had illuminated the punishments of hell. Who, then, would choose damnation, if following Savonarola could lead to salvation? Never before in the history of Florence had the fate of our mortal souls been brought into political discussion. What more powerful motivator could any leader have?

Florence had led the world in the rediscovery of ancient ideas. These ideas had, in turn, ignited a golden age, when artists and poets, architects and men of science showed us the limitless possibilities of human achievement. Brunelleschi built his dome, insisting it could be done even before he knew how. Botticelli brought pagan mythology to life, inextricably connecting it to contemporary Florence. Petrarch taught us how to reconcile ancient ideas with Christian beliefs.

None of it could have happened without men like my grandfather, who rescued from monastic libraries the manuscripts full of the ideas that had sparked it all. He had warned me such ideas could come under threat. Savonarola had catalyzed his worries, and the friar was far more powerful now than he'd been then. What would Nonno do, when the humanist values of Florence looked more fragile than I would have ever thought possible? I had promised him I would save his books, but had always understood this meant more than just preserving paper and ink. The ideas were what mattered.

And so, I embarked upon a project, a project that must be kept quiet. First, I hired a printer to make copies of the most important books in grandfather's collections, the books he had named as such on a list: Cicero's letters, the works of Aristotle, Lucretius's *De Rerum Natura,* and more. The books, however, would only be the start. There was much, much more to be done.

Florence, 1903

35

Cécile and I went to the Russian consulate the next morning, finalizing our strategy en route, so that by the time the consul agreed to see us, we were more than ready for him. My friend took the lead.

"Monsieur, one of your countryman has done a dear friend of mine a great service," she said. "Her fiancé was killed in a terrible accident, and she would have collapsed outside the church following his funeral had not a Russian gentleman offered his carriage to take her home."

"I would expect nothing less from a Russian," the consul said. "We are a noble people."

"The trouble is," Cécile continued, "she now finds herself in a rather embarrassing situation. She doesn't know the gentleman's name, and hence, is unable to write to thank him for his kind service. We were hoping that you might be able to point us in the right direction. Do you keep a list of Russians in Florence? I always register with the French consulate when I travel."

"We do, but I'm afraid I can't give it out."

"Of course not," I said. "We completely understand the need for discretion. Would it be possible, however, for you to take a look at it and let us know the names of any likely candidates for our anonymous Samaritan? It would be someone in a position to have a carriage."

"Or someone who had happened to hire one that day," the consul said. "I'm afraid what you ask is impossible. The information I have is not all that detailed, just names and where each individual is staying while here."

"Oh, but that's quite enough, sir," I said. "We know the date of the funeral, and we know the gentleman was staying in a house, not a hotel. Surely that narrows it down."

"It would, to some degree," he admitted.

"Please, monsieur, I beg you to help our poor friend. Having suffered so devastating a loss, thanking this gentleman would allow her the comfort that comes from social niceties," Cécile said. "It seems a small thing, I know, but to her, it will mean much more. It will give her something positive to act upon, and that is what she needs more than anything right now."

"I will see what I can do. Tell me the date of the funeral and then come back in an hour. That will give me time to check if anyone registered matches your criteria. I cannot tell you where, precisely, they are staying, but the names will give you something, at least."

"We are indebted to you," she said. *"Я очень благодарен."*

His eyes lit up. "You speak Russian?"

"Not much," Cécile said. "The Princess Mariya Alekseyevna Bolkonskaya is a dear friend. She's taught me a bit."

An enormous grin split his face. "You are a friend of Masha's? Why did you not tell me that first? Of course I will help you. Together, we will find the gentleman you seek."

When we returned as instructed, the consul greeted us at the door himself and gave us a list that included six names and complete addresses. "If I can offer any further help, do let me know," he said. "I am at your service." He kissed Cécile's hand, nodded at me, and waved as we set off.

"Mentioning Masha was a stroke of genius," I said. "You timed it perfectly."

"I knew waiting until we'd finished the meeting would lead to the most desirous outcome," Cécile said. "It made him feel guilty for not having been more helpful from the beginning, which is why he overcompensated by providing the addresses. I'm finding that I have quite an affinity for this sort of work. Perhaps I should speak to Monsieur Hargreaves about having the Palace hire me."

"You'd be bored in three days flat."

We stopped in a café, where we plotted the locations of each of the six houses on my map. Aside from one in the Oltrarno near the Palazzo Pitti, they were all in the city's historic center, not far from the Duomo. Proceeding with caution was essential. It was quite likely that the man whom we sought had killed Lena, Marzo, and Signore di Taro.

"Do you think we should have Monsieur Hargreaves and Monsieur Benton-Smith accompany us?" Cécile asked.

"We'll do better on our own," I said. "Showing up unannounced with gentlemen in tow looks more suspicious than a pair of ladies calling to offer thanks. Our strategy worked perfectly on the consul and we should employ it now as well."

"A violent criminal is unlikely to know Masha or even recognize her name."

"We know for a fact she was friends with at least one murderer." Almost four years ago, while Cécile and I were visiting St. Petersburg, a charming Russian prince, Vasilii Ruslanovich Guryanov, hired me to investigate the death of his mistress, the greatest ballerina of her generation, Irina Semenova Nemetseva. The identity of the murderer shocked us all.

"That man would have fooled anyone," Cécile said.

"My point is that a well-heeled Russian traveler, murderer or not, may well move in the same social circles as Masha."

Cécile shrugged but did not look convinced.

We started with the house in Oltrarno, and by three o'clock had made the acquaintance of every gentleman on the consul's list. Half of them we dismissed the moment we set eyes on them, as their white hair and advanced age did not meet the description Signore Bastieri and Tessa had given of the man with the carriage. The others each seemed promising in their own way, but none admitted to having assisted Lena, nor could offer any suggestions as to any fellow countrymen who might have. They all were acquainted with Masha.

"We've been naïve," I said. "A Russian assassin wouldn't register with the consulate."

"Nor would the consul divulge the identity of someone skulking about undercover," Cécile said.

"The consul probably wouldn't even be aware of the presence of such a person." I frowned. "No wonder Colin was so willing to let us pursue this angle."

"What now?" Cécile asked.

"We play tourist, just for an hour or two. I need to let my thoughts percolate and do that best when my brain thinks I'm otherwise occupied."

We went to the Palazzo Vecchio, where we wandered through the enormous Salone dei Cinquecento—the Hall of the Five Hundred—built on the order of Savonarola in the late fifteenth century. The friar, having helped create the environment that led to the ousting of the Medici, had longed to return Florence to Republican glory. With the Medici gone, he finally had his chance. He established a Great Council of five hundred men and needed a space in the palazzo that could hold them all. After Savonarola's downfall, the room was enlarged again, with Michelangelo and Leonardo da Vinci hired to decorate the walls, but neither artist completed their work.

My brain would not quiet. I couldn't master my thoughts, which remained disjointed and confused. I half snapped into focus when Cécile and I entered the La Sala delle Carte Geografiche, a wood-paneled room whose walls hid cupboard doors, behind which jewelry, scientific instruments, and a variety of other precious items had been stored over the centuries. Fifty-four maps decorated them, each depicting the known world at the time of Cosimo I's rule. Beneath the wooden-coffered ceiling stood a huge globe in the dead center of the room. Hovering next to it was a young man working as a docent, who introduced himself as Frosino.

"Ladies, please, may I show you something very special?" he asked, bowing as he spoke. "There is a chamber accessed from a hidden door, just over here, behind one of the maps. Would you like to see?"

"Most definitely," I said. We followed him through the door into a small room.

"Bianca Cappello, a courtesan, was the mistress of Francesco de' Medici. Someone conveniently murdered her husband. Two years later, Francesco's father, Cosimo I, died, and Francesco became grand duke. This gave him the power to do what he'd long wanted: move his mistress into the palazzo. Four years later, his wife died, and he secretly married Bianca, but the Florentines never accepted her as their duchess. They used to sing *The Tuscan Grand Duke has married a whore / Who was a Venetian noble before*. This little room was her private space. She could look through that window to watch, unobserved, everything happening in the Sala dei Cinquecento."

"Was their marriage happy?" Cécile said.

"I believe they did care deeply for each other," the docent said, "although it did not end well. They died one day apart, after both falling hideously and simultaneously ill. Many suspect they were poisoned by enemies."

"How ghastly," I said. "Was it common for secret passages to be built in palazzi?" I asked.

"Common enough," Frosino said. "There was much fighting in Florence before the days of the Medici. Violent factions loyal to powerful rival families frequently caused chaos. Those families wanted to be able to come and go from their houses without being seen. Some even had tunnels dug so that they did not have to walk in the street."

"Do those tunnels still exist?"

"I very much doubt it, signora," he said. "Such things were not necessary once the violence stopped. They were probably filled in long ago."

"What caused the violence to stop?" Cécile asked.

"The merchants eventually convinced the city that it was bad for business. The oldest palazzi originally had tall towers for defense, but they were ordered to be taken down so that the government, not individual families controlled Florence."

"But the Medici controlled the city after that," I said. "They were an individual family."

Frosino made a dismissive gesture. "We Florentines have never much minded having to reconcile contradictory facts. There were remnants of the old republican democracy, even under the Medici."

I was still mulling over the existence of those long-forgot tunnels after we'd thanked Frosino for his tour and walked back to Kat's palazzo. Upon reaching front door, I did not immediately go inside but instead stepped into the narrow alley that ran along the side of the house.

"If you're hoping to find a secret door, don't bother," Cécile said. "In addition to inspecting every inch of the inside of the house, I've done the same to the exterior. There's nothing to see but the old service entrance the countess had blocked up."

"There could be hidden passages inside that we've missed. Do you think Signore Tazzera could find the architect's original designs?"

"I've no doubt he could, if they still exist, but surely they would not include anything meant to be secret. If the Vieri family wanted to hide something in their house during the time of Savonarola, they could have added a passageway or little room at that point."

"Such a project would have been risky," I said. "The builders might have talked. Better to conceal a treasure somewhere extant."

"Are we back to looking for the treasure? What about Lena?"

"I'm frustrated, Cécile. If her death has something to do with the treasure, we've a chance at finding her murderer, but if it's connected to Colin and Darius's work . . ."

"We've no hope at all."

"Quite."

"*Non,*" Cécile said. "I refuse to accept this. From the beginning, we've known we would not have access to certain resources and information available to Monsieur Hargreaves. That has not changed. We've always believed we could find something from Marzo's life that would point us to his killer, even if only by discovering how an assassin may have intended to misdirect anyone investigating."

"Thank you." I squeezed my friend's hand. "I ought not lose faith. Marzo went to the Mercato Nuovo every Tuesday to buy flowers. Sometimes, in the course of doing so, he knocked over a display, often enough that the florists noticed. I'm convinced this was a deliberate signal to someone." I was about to say that I'd talked to Colin about it, and knew Marzo was not using it to contact Darius, but stopped myself in time.

"It is a rather clunky method, is it not? Monsieur Le Queux's spies are far more subtle," Cécile said. "This makes me suspect it is something Marzo came up with himself."

"He wanted money. Darius might not be the only person to whom he was supplying information."

"Have we even the slightest insight into the nature of the information Marzo supplied?"

"Broadly speaking, I assume it's something politically sensitive coming from Britain's enemies, perhaps to do with their military or strategy or—"

"How would someone like Marzo gain access to anything of that ilk?" Cécile asked. "It's not as if he could have waltzed into a gentlemen's club and eavesdropped on other members as they lunched."

"No, he couldn't. It may be that he was simply a messenger."

"Unless he was a master of disguise," she said. Her eyes sparkled, and I knew she was about to embark on a flight of fancy. Her voice grew dramatic. "To those who knew him in Florence, he was an ordinary laborer, but those who saw him in Berlin or Moscow encountered someone entirely different: a gentleman educated at the Sorbonne, who developed a passion for adventure after joining friends on an ill-conceived expedition to ski across Greenland."

"Ski across Greenland?" I raised an eyebrow.

"The frostbite he suffered put him off cold weather, but did not dissuade him from looking for more civilized forms of excitement. He became a spy, effortlessly moving between worlds, making contacts in every world capital."

"A mercenary spy, willing to do anything for anyone, so long as the payoff was sufficient."

"Precisely," Cécile said.

"I will never believe he tried to ski across Greenland, though the image is more than a little amusing."

She shrugged. "The details are not important. It is the essence of the man that matters."

I would never believe Marzo sophisticated enough to have become a master of disguise, but then again, maybe it was wrong to completely dismiss Cécile's outlandish theories. A good spy, after all, should be able to deceive everyone around him. Still, I doubted very much Marzo had been leading a complicated double life. More likely, he was selling his information to more than one party, and that deception, once discovered, was enough to get him killed.

Florence, 1495

36

After Piero de' Medici—Piero the Unfortunate, as he came to be known—fled Florence, a mob ransacked the family's palazzo, wreaking havoc on what was arguably the most important private art collection in our city, if not the world. It included Donatello's *David,* a putto sculpted by Praxiteles, paintings of Fra Angelico and Jan van Eyck, and countless other precious items. I never learned the precise details of what happened, only that some pieces were damaged, some stolen, and others destroyed.

I cannot claim that Savonarola directed the looters, but he certainly encouraged their behavior, although he was careful to maintain the appearance of being above the city's increasingly divided factions. He said we must end the rule of the elite, rejecting the notion that the old, powerful families should control the government. Few people publicly objected to him closing the city's brothels, but he also enacted brutal policies welcomed only by the most extreme religious zealots. He expanded the use of torture. He wanted us to fear him, and fear him we did. Anyone guilty of blasphemy had his tongue cut out. Gangs of boys—thugs called Bands of Hope—roamed the streets, harassing anyone whose appearance did not reflect the friar's values. I saw them stop in the street a lady whose dress they considered too luxurious. They stripped her bare and then continued on their way, going door to door, demanding people surrender *sinful possessions.*

What was sinful? Dice. Playing cards. Cosmetics. Mirrors. Jewelry.

Anything that encouraged vanity. But also art, if it was not sufficiently religious, and books whose ideas did not mesh with Savonarola's principles.

"Which, broadly speaking, is any book a thinking person would like to read," Cristofano said, pacing in front of me. He was with me on the roof of the house, where I liked to sit on sunny days, following the example of Venetian ladies who'd discovered the secret to lightening one's tresses to the most desirable shade of pale blond. I'd purchased a hat without a crown, through which I pulled my hair, wetting it with a sponge soaked in a watery potion. It worked well enough, enhancing my natural color, while the hat protected my face from getting burned. "Not just the ancients, mind you, but anything popular as well. No more Boccaccio. *The Decameron* is sinful."

"Delightfully sinful, I'd say."

"There's nothing amusing in any of this, Mina. What are we to do? Sit back and let this deranged man destroy the culture of learning and the open exchange of ideas that has so long defined our city?"

"No, we can't do that. I'm doing my bit. You know I've had copies of books printed and I'm now tutoring Bia's friends, teaching them Latin and Greek, exposing them to humanist ideas. They will be armed with knowledge that, when they are adults, will help them prevent more men like Savonarola from gaining power."

"He must be exposed as a charlatan."

"I don't like him any more than you, but I do think he's sincere."

"Which makes him all the more dangerous," Cristofano said. "He appeals to the masses, those who felt excluded by the elite, but what is he actually doing for them? The city is on the verge of bankruptcy. He cares about nothing beyond his quest to reform the church. We were wise to have banned the clergy from our government and will regret having allowed him in."

"What can be done to stop him?" I asked.

"I wish I knew."

"I have my grandfather's books, and I shall never give them up, no matter how many times his Bands of Hope come to my door."

"You can hide away as many copies as you like, Mina, but what good will that do in the end? If they can't be read and discussed, they are as lost to us as they were before men like your grandfather rescued them from dusty monastic libraries."

"It's better than losing them altogether."

He dropped onto the chair next to mine. "I'm sorry. You're right, of course. Preserving them is essential. It complements what you're doing with Bia and her friends."

"Savonarola is one man. He cannot hold power forever, and whoever comes next won't be such a zealot. So long as we can outlast him, we will see Florence once again blossom as a cradle of ideas." I watched him as he stood and started to pace back and forth along the roof. "You're very agitated today. Is it more than politics?"

He sighed. "It is. My father wants me to marry. I suppose I can't avoid it forever. He's identified a potential bride and is negotiating with her family."

This was unexpected. "Who is she?"

"Maddalena Bandini. Do you know her?"

I shook my head. "You know how little I socialize with ladies."

"She's beautiful. Wealthy. Cultured. Intelligent. It could be worse."

"So you will agree to the marriage?"

"I can't fight it forever."

My stomach clenched. I did not like the idea of a married Cristofano.

"Have you nothing to say?" he asked, frustrated.

"How would you have me respond?" I struggled to keep my voice from shaking. "It's not for me to tell you what to do."

"You're closer to me than anyone," he said. "I trust you absolutely and value your companionship above all. I know your aversion to marrying again, but can you honestly tell me you have never considered a life with me? I'm confident we could find much pleasure in each other."

My skin prickled. I knew all too well the dangers of that sort of pleasure. I looked out across the city, not wanting to see his face. I thought about how the intimacy Giacomo and I had shared changed everything between us in an instant. "I've never sought that from you."

"Which doesn't preclude you from considering it now."

"Is this a roundabout way of asking me to marry you? If so, I must beg you to stop."

"Am I so repulsive?"

"Nothing about you is repulsive," I said. "The problem is me. I have secrets that I can never share. Secrets that you could never accept, that would destroy everything between us. They stem from things that happened in my past, things about which I will never be able to speak. They would change forever how you see me and make it impossible for you to hold me in any esteem." Since Agnolo's death, I had taken to wearing my half of the St. Anthony medal around my neck, tucked behind my bodice. Right now it felt as if it were searing my skin.

"Nothing could ever do that, Mina."

"If you can't respect my judgment on the matter, how could you ever trust me as your wife?"

"Will you at least consider my offer before rejecting me? Surely I deserve at least that."

He was deserving of that much and more, but I saw no kindness in pretending I might change my mind. False hope did not offer solace. I said nothing.

"I must marry," he said, rising from his chair. "Your refusal means I might as well accept my father's decision and ally myself to Maddalena. Doing so will change our friendship forever. Wouldn't you rather—"

"I would rather that nothing change."

"The world does not work that way." He stood in front of me, blocking the sun, and pulled me to my feet. I did not look up at him until he took me by the chin and forced me to do so. "I would make you a good husband and Bia a good stepfather. Mina, please, you're making this far more complicated than it needs to be. We can—"

"There's nothing more to be said. I'm very sorry, but I will never marry again."

He closed his eyes, drew in a deep breath, and held it before releasing the air. I thought he was going to speak again, but he did not. Instead, he opened his eyes and met mine, standing immobile, staring at me. He shook his head, turned on his heel, and walked away.

My heart broke a thousand times as I watched him go, but not for a moment was I tempted to call him back. I would never have another friend so dear, but I'd survived before without him, and I would do so again. He would never be able to understand the guilt I felt at having abandoned Salvi. I had no right to the kind of happiness he was offering and would never deserve it. And that burden, I had to carry alone.

Florence, 1903

37

Cécile's flight of fancy in imagining Marzo's life as a master of disguise was an amusing absurdity, but it did raise an interesting point. He might well have been selling his information to someone other than Darius. I told Colin as much that evening after dinner, when we'd retired to our room.

"I quite agree the theory has merit," he said. "It was one of the first things Darius and I considered, which is why we have done everything possible to investigate it. Ultimately, we found no evidence whatsoever."

"Is that so surprising?" I asked. "Surely he would have taken measures to ensure his duplicity wouldn't be exposed."

"And if he had done so successfully, he wouldn't have been murdered." Colin frowned. "I wish I could tell you more. I will share this much: we have determined that whoever killed him did so to stop him from giving the British sensitive information about Germany."

"Do you know the nature of the information?"

"I do."

"So what now?"

"It's unlikely we will ever know the identity of the assassin," he said. "At this point, however, it doesn't matter. We know the Germans gave the order and we will adapt our own work accordingly."

"Why the Germans? How did they come into this? And what about Lena?" I asked. "Are we to believe her death is unrelated?"

"Not at all."

I waited for him to say more, but he didn't. "And the Russian connection?"

"There is no Russian connection. The Germans also killed Signore di Taro."

"How can you be so sure about all this?"

"I cannot tell you that."

"What about the coat of arms? Is it a coincidence that it appeared on the envelope Lena received the morning of her murder?"

"No. The Germans, knowing she and Marzo had been searching for the infamous treasure, exploited it to lure her to the Medici Chapel."

"What evidence do we have that they were searching for the treasure?" I asked. He did not answer. "Why would the Germans kill Signore di Taro?"

"That had nothing to do with Lena or Marzo."

"I can't believe that. Was it because he was the one supplying Marzo's information?" I asked, trying to swallow my frustration. "I understand that you can't share details with me, but are you satisfied with the conclusions you've drawn?"

He sat down. "No, Emily, I'm not. The evidence gives us an ironclad explanation of everything that has happened. Too ironclad, if you ask me. I've never seen anything so perfectly tied up."

"What about the fact that we now know Tessa was in love with Marzo? She has a powerful motive for murder. If she killed him and Lena, shouldn't she be punished?"

"She didn't kill either of them."

"What does Darius think?"

"He agrees, but there's nothing more to be done. The Crown is satisfied."

"Does that happen often, them telling you to stop before you're satisfied?"

"Sometimes," he said. "Not even I, Emily, am fully informed about all aspects of every operation."

"Could the Crown have wanted Marzo dead? Go back to our earlier meritorious theory, when we suspected him of double-dealing. Surely the Crown wouldn't have tolerated that. Would they have ordered him killed to stop someone else from getting the information he was supplying?"

"It's entirely possible."

"And if they did?"

"They would only take that sort of action if it were absolutely necessary."

"And might they then send in two of their best and most trusted agents to conduct the investigation? I would. Who would doubt the conclusions of two such agents, even if they were based on the evidence supplied by the Crown? The matter would be closed forever."

"Yes."

"Does that not outrage you?"

"No, Emily, it doesn't. This is not something into which they would have entered lightly. I trust the judgment of the men for whom I work. If I didn't, I could not do my job."

"All men are fallible," I said.

"Indeed, but in this case, I see no reason to doubt the decisions from above. I know that will not satisfy your own curiosity, but it is all I can offer."

He might be able to rationalize unsatisfactory conclusions, but I could not, not when I wasn't privy to any of the evidence. Still, it would not help to prod him further. Better to let him think I would let it all go. "I suppose I knew from the start I was unlikely to know how things were resolved, but that doesn't mean I have to like it."

"No, it doesn't." He touched my cheek. "Are you willing to step away?"

"Do I have a choice?"

"You always have a choice."

I did not want to lie to him, but in the circumstances, what better course of action was there for me? "I will step away, unless something comes to light that compels me to do otherwise." Not a lie. Not precisely.

"What will you tell Cécile?"

"The truth. The matter is settled, even if in ways we can never know. She won't like it any more than I, but what else can we do?"

"Thank you," he said.

"Please don't thank me."

He studied my face and I could see in his eyes that he knew I had no intention of doing what I'd just promised. "Emily—"

"Don't," I said. "A lady can't share all of her secrets, even with a beloved husband. Best that we find some way to distract ourselves. Isn't that your general prescription in such circumstances?"

"I'm beginning to have a great appreciation for the restraint you show when I am obliged to keep information from you."

I balked. "Restraint? Restraint? I've never been accused of such an abominable thing."

"I was being facetious, my dear. About the restraint, not the admiration I have for how you contend with what I force you to tolerate."

"I do appreciate that," I said, "and hope you are capable of reacting with more grace and patience than I am wont to do."

"It's unlikely I can, so you ought to start with that distraction now." He kissed my neck.

"You're the one being distracting."

He pulled away. "I'll stop and leave it all to you."

I came down to breakfast before Cécile and waited, rather impatiently, for her to emerge from her morning ablutions. When she did, I explained that Colin and Darius had finished their investigation and wanted us to do the same. She was no more inclined to abandon our work than I, and rejected outright the notion that the Germans had killed Marzo and Lena.

"Not to mention Signore di Taro," she said. "I refuse to accept such absurd conclusions with no evidence."

"I quite agree. But is it any more likely that the Crown ordered their deaths?"

"I shouldn't think so."

"Nor do I. The coat of arms is a clue we can't ignore, and it's one that points us back to the treasure. Someone connected to the murders is looking for it, of that I am convinced." I pressed my lips together. "I have not been entirely honest about all of this with you, Cécile. I told Colin from the beginning that we were investigating. He supported that, but only so long as I kept him abreast of everything we discovered, which I've done. He didn't want you to know and I agreed to his terms. I'm sorry I deceived you."

She shrugged. "Kallista, I never for one moment doubted that you were telling him everything. He is far too handsome to resist."

"Can you forgive me?"

"There is nothing to forgive. I have told you many times that we all have the need for secrets. I will never share all of mine and would expect nothing else from you. A little mystery is not a bad thing, but I do expect you to tell me whatever it is you managed to get out of him. I suspect he is little better at resisting your charms than you are at resisting his."

There was sadly little to reveal, but I went through the case for her, detailing every discussion I'd had with Colin about it. Before we could decide how to proceed, the gentlemen entered the room, both in a jovial mood.

"Now that this sad business is behind us, it's time we make the most of Florence," Darius said. "Have you two been to the Accademia yet? We could go this afternoon. You can't leave the city without seeing Michelangelo's *David*."

"*Non,* monsieur," Cécile said. "I find myself unable to enjoy the delights of Florence when this sad business, as you call it, is resolved in a manner thoroughly unsatisfactory to me."

"Cécile, I—"

She interrupted Colin. "I am not interested in any explanation that does not include the name of the vile murderer who has caused so much chaos and grief. As you cannot share that with us, I would prefer to spend the day here, reading. Monsieur Le Queux's fictional spies are far more satisfying than the two of you real ones."

"Cécile, we're not spies," Darius said.

"Style yourselves however you like," she said. "I will eventually forgive you both your shortcomings, but not today. That's how it is with us ladies. We may have to accept the limitations of what your work allows you to share with us, but that does not mean we can't punish you, at least a little, for excluding us. Now, can you please find it in your hearts to leave us in peace? Go to the museum. Gaze upon *David*." She looked at Colin, and I could see her resolve wavering. She wanted to compare him to the statue.

"Or don't gaze upon *David*," I said. "Why not travel farther afield? Take a drive in the countryside. Cécile may want to stay here and read, but I'd prefer a long walk through the city. A long walk during which I don't have to worry that I'll run into you."

"We're quite thoroughly in disgrace, Hargreaves," Darius said. "It's best we flee. I don't fancy the countryside, however. Let's climb to the top of Brunelleschi's dome instead."

"I'm game," Colin said. He came around the table and gave me a quick kiss. "If you won't let things lie, at least promise me you will be careful," he whispered.

"You need not worry," I murmured against his neck. "We've no plan to do anything today. I'm not even sure where we would start. Tomorrow, however . . ."

He kissed my cheek, reassured by my words, and looked up as Tessa entered, announcing that Signore Bastieri was at the door. I had not rejected my suspicions of her, regardless of what Colin had said about her not being guilty. She couldn't have carried Marzo to the roof, and I doubted she had the skill with a knife to have killed Lena with a single blow, but she might very well have been working with someone else. Someone trained as an assassin, either by the Germans or the Crown. Someone who wanted the treasure, for I was still convinced there was a connection between the murders and whatever had been hidden in the house during the Renaissance.

I told the maid to let in Signore Bastieri, whom I introduced to the gentlemen. He looked a mess, his hair unkempt, his face drawn and pale. I doubted he'd eaten in days, so I encouraged him to fill his plate with food from the sideboard. He did so, but only half-heartedly, and explained why he'd come.

"I've found that coat of arms on six buildings," he said.

"So many?" I asked. "Surely that's unusual."

"Not necessarily," he said. "Wealthy families might own more than one house, or maybe their supporters displayed the arms to show their loyalty."

"What arms are these?" Darius asked.

"The ones that were on the letter my daughter received the morning she was killed," Signore Bastieri said. "I'm convinced they will lead us to her killer, and the treasure you seek, Lady Emily. With luck, we will have it in our hands today."

I flashed a frantic look at my husband and nodded toward the door, hoping he would understand that I wanted him to leave rather than to choose this moment to give whatever pathetic explanation he and Darius had agreed to share with the grieving father.

"I'm so very sorry for your loss, signore," Colin said. "When this sort of awful thing happens, we cannot help but yearn for an explanation that provides solace. Sometimes, though, there is none."

"What are you saying?" Signore Bastieri said. "Do you know who killed Lena, or are you telling me that we will never catch the murderer?"

"We're close to unmasking him, Signore Bastieri," Darius said. "Very close. My colleague is only trying to save you from disappointment. I am familiar with the arms to which you refer, and was myself excited about the prospect of them leading us to the killer, but they are nothing more than a deliberate misdirection, leading away from the man responsible for your daughter's death."

"How can you know this?" Signore Bastieri asked.

"Because we followed the same trail," Darius said. "It caused us to lose valuable time."

"But you are close to catching him?"

"We are. In fact, it is likely we will have firm information for you later today," he said. "If you'll excuse us, the sooner we get to it, the sooner we'll have answers for you."

I hated the false hope we were giving the poor man.

"Thank you for your work, all of you," Signore Bastieri said. "I know it will not bring her back, but if this man is brought to justice, it will give me a little peace."

"We will do everything in our power to see that happens," Colin said.

If only that were true.

When they were gone, I turned to our guest, who had hardly touched the food on his plate. "I believe it's significant that you found the arms on so many buildings. It may not lead to the murderer, but I am certain it will provide a fuller explanation for what happened to Lena. To explain, I should share with you some Latin graffiti from the walls of this house." I pulled out my notebook and went through it with him and then showed him the letter that Signore Tazzera had found with the coat of arms on it. This proved an adequate distraction. He finally started to eat. His eggs had long gone cold, so I rang for fresh ones and poured him another coffee.

"I will show you my map now," he said, as he accepted the steaming cup. "I have marked the houses on which I found the arms." He pulled it out of his jacket pocket and passed it to me. The pattern was identical to the locations of the graffiti I'd found in our palazzo. Two of the houses were on this side of the river, the rest across the Arno, mirroring the two graffiti on our first floor and four on the second.

"This is remarkable," I said. "If we—"

A piercing scream interrupted me. We raced from the dining room and saw Tessa on the gallery landing below, just outside Cécile's bedroom.

"Please come quickly," she shouted. "We need a doctor."

"Find Fredo and have him go after Mr. Hargreaves and Mr. Benton-Smith," I called down to her. "They went to the cathedral, to climb up the dome."

"I can't do that, signora," Tessa said, tears streaming down her face. "It's Fredo who's hurt."

"I will find your husband and Signore Benton-Smith," Signore Bastieri said. "They are no doubt still at the Duomo." He ran out of the house while Cécile and I went to Tessa, who was shaking uncontrollably.

"You stay here with her," I said to my friend. "I'll see what we can do for Fredo." The bedroom was dark, the shutters closed. I switched on the light and saw Fredo lying on the bed, his head at an impossible angle. Someone had snapped his neck. No doctor could help him. I closed his eyes and went back to Cécile and Tessa, who had been joined by Cook and Signora Orlandi.

I shook my head. "He's dead," I said. "I'm more sorry than I can say. This is a terrible loss. We need tea. Lots of it. I'll go brew it and bring it to the Sala dei Pappagalli."

Much as I wanted to give them space to grieve, I knew it was crucial to question them about everything that had happened that morning as soon as possible, before they could no longer recall the events with clarity. When I rejoined them, tea tray in hand, Cécile already had the situation under control. Tessa was no longer crying, Signora Orlandi looked furious, and the cook was finishing a detailed narrative of her day.

"And that is all I have to tell," she said. "I saw nothing unusual, heard nothing unusual, until Tessa screamed. But I was in the kitchen from the moment I arrived at the house."

"What time was that?" Cécile asked.

"Before five o'clock. The sun was not yet up."

"And you, Signora Orlandi?" I asked, pouring the tea.

"I am always here by six. The front door was locked, as usual, and I let myself in with my key. I spoke to Fredo briefly—he was in one of the storage rooms on the ground floor—and then went straight to the kitchen, where Cook had a coffee ready for me. It was like any other morning. I drank the coffee and then began an inventory of the supplies in the pantry. When that was done, I checked on Tessa, who had already lit the fires and was cleaning the Sale Madornale on the first floor. The day was perfectly ordinary until Tessa screamed."

"When did you arrive?" I asked Tessa.

"A little before Signora Orlandi," she said. "As the others have already told you, everything was the same as usual until I came into Signora du Lac's room to clean. That's when I found Fredo."

"Was the door to the house locked when you got here?" I asked.

"*Sì*, it always is. I came in, locked it behind me, and got straight to work."

"I know it seems useless, but I need you to tell me every single thing you did," I said. "You may have heard or seen something that didn't seem significant at the time."

She did as I asked, going into astonishing detail, but nothing stood out as pertinent.

"I can't help but notice you are all skilled at recounting details," I said. "That seems an unlikely characteristic of most household staffs."

"The countess relied on us to do more than run her house and had us trained accordingly," Signora Orlandi said. "I am not at liberty to discuss the minutiae of our duties. Suffice it to say we are all capable of keeping the palazzo secure."

Not secure enough, given Fredo's murder, but I was not about to draw attention to their shortcomings. When Signore Bastieri returned with Colin and Darius, I had him stay with Cécile and the servants while I took the gentlemen to Fredo.

"This is Kat's room, when she's here, isn't it?" Darius asked. "She won't be best pleased when she hears about this. Wicked stepmother allows murder to occur in her stepdaughter's bed?"

"I hardly think it's time to make light of the situation," I said.

"Of course not. Forgive me," he said. "It's an occupational hazard, I'm afraid. I see so much violence I'd go mad if I couldn't joke about it."

"We may as well drop all pretense," I said. "Given that people are still being murdered, it's obvious your investigation was terminated prematurely. As it's unlikely Fredo was engaged in some sort of international espionage, we need to consider the possibility that all of these deaths are connected to something going on in this house."

"The treasure," Darius said.

"What did Signore Bastieri discover about the coats of arms?" Colin asked.

"They are on buildings laid out in an identical pattern to the Lucretius graffiti I found."

"Does that tell you where the treasure is?" Darius asked.

"I haven't had time to consider the possibility," I said.

"It very well might," Colin said. "And if so, we need to find it before the murderer does."

"We could use it to flush him out," Darius said.

"Don't think for one second that Cécile and I will tolerate being excluded any longer," I said. "I'm quite fed up with the parameters of your work."

"At this point, we're not in a position to reject any help we can get," Darius said. "Let's send for Signore Tazzera. He knows the most about the history of the house, the treasure, and all those sorts of things. He and Cécile can focus on that. Emily, I want you to have Signore Bastieri take you to the buildings with the arms on them. You may notice something about them he didn't. Colin and I will deal with Fredo's body and then search his lodgings. He may have learned something about the treasure that drew the attention of the murderer."

I crossed my arms and raised an eyebrow. "Just like that, you both abandon your theories about sensitive information and the good of the empire and instead accept that all of these deaths stem from a treasure hunt?" I asked.

"If our theories had been correct, Fredo wouldn't be dead," Colin said. "The only thing that matters now is doing whatever is necessary to stop this man before he kills again."

Florence, 1496

38

I expected life without Cristofano's friendship to be sadly empty, but I had not anticipated just how violently Bia would react. At first, she questioned why he no longer came to see us. Then, she wrote to him. Not finding his reply satisfactory, she went to his house. When she returned, her face streaked with tears, she lashed out at me.

"You've destroyed everything," she said. "I despise you. I wish you'd died instead of my father. I wish I were old enough to be married so I didn't have to live with you."

That was a year ago. She was fifteen now—almost old enough to be a bride—and although her anger at me had cooled, we were no longer so happy as we used to be. Fear of reprisal from Savonarola had led the parents of her friends to forbid me to tutor their children. It was too dangerous. The little friar still held Florence in his grip, and his Bands of Hope continued to terrorize our citizens.

Three times they had come to my house, demanding objects to burn in the next bonfire. The first time I slammed the door on them. The second time, they were more threatening. I gave them a handful of jewelry and two mirrors, hoping that would pacify them. The third time, they came inside, knocking me over when I tried to stop them. They took close to a dozen books, six paintings, a bust carved in Greece during the fourth century BC, and two cases full of valuable jewelry, one mine, one Bia's.

I was furious. Furious and terrified.

Having anticipated that they would want books, I had prepared accordingly. The ones on the shelves in my library were not the originals from my grandfather. Those, I had hidden away. I hadn't, however, thought they would object so vehemently to our art and jewelry.

I remembered Cristofano's words, when he'd said that simply saving the books wasn't enough. If we weren't free to discuss them, they were as good as lost. Florence was more than books. It was an entire culture, one full of art and beauty. It all had to be preserved. The looting of the Medici palazzo had only been the beginning. What would be left of our world if more was destroyed?

I did not have many friends, but the few I did had spectacular collections of art, far superior to mine. I called on them, one at a time, pleading with them to ensure these great works would be kept from Savonarola's thugs. Most of them thought I was overreacting, but even those who didn't hesitated to take action. They were afraid they'd get caught. Afraid of being tortured.

Cristofano had married Maddalena Bandini two months after that awful conversation on my roof. I had not seen him again. Now, though, I needed him. He would understand. He would be able to help me find a way to save the essence of Florence.

Because we had been so close for so long and then our friendship had ended abruptly before his wedding, most people assumed we had been lovers. I heard the gossip, and knew that Maddalena herself believed this. She'd made a show of saying that I would never be welcome in her house, so calling unannounced did not seem a good strategy. Instead, I sent Cristofano a note, asking him to meet me somewhere we could speak privately, wherever he wanted.

He did not reply for four days. I had started to despair. At last, a message came. He would meet me in the Duomo tomorrow at noon, near Michelino's painting of Dante. His words were impersonal, businesslike. It wounded me, even though I had no right to expect anything else.

Nervous and on edge, I went early, arriving a quarter of an hour before the appointed time. He was already standing in front of the painting when I arrived. I stood back and watched him, remembering the day we had met, how I had observed, when we returned from the disastrous hunt, that he was not handsome. I realized now how wrong I'd been. His beauty came not from his features but from his manner, his intelligence, his confidence, his wit. I remained there, staring at him from a distance, until the church's bells struck noon. He heard my footsteps as I approached and turned around.

"I did not expect to hear from you again, Signora Portinari," he said. He was looking at me, but showed no sign of seeing me, not in any way that mattered. "It's funny, in all the years of our friendship, I never gave your name much consideration, but after that day on your roof, when everything changed, it occurred to me that you share a surname with Dante's Beatrice. I should have anticipated unrequited love."

"I'm so sorry," I said, feeling tears welling in my eyes. "I—"

He shook his head. "Don't apologize, signora. None of that matters anymore. I shouldn't have mentioned it. Why did you want to see me?"

I told him about the Bands of Hope, about their seizing things from my house, about the fears I had, and asked for his help.

"I can't help you," he said. "First, it's too dangerous. Second, it's wholly inappropriate. Renewing our acquaintance would hurt my wife."

Our acquaintance? How could he be so dismissive of the friendship we had shared? I knew I deserved his scorn, but I had hoped that some ember of kindness remained. I was wrong.

"I should not have written to you," I said. "I'm sorry to have disturbed your domestic tranquility. Forgive me."

I turned away and walked across the nave, thinking he would follow. He did not. When I looked back, he was gone. I sank to my knees and wept. How different it would be if I had married him. Together, we could have worked against Savonarola and saved countless treasures. Instead, I had ruined my own happiness and left art and books to be wantonly destroyed.

"Signora, don't cry."

Someone was standing above me, his voice soft.

"Please leave me alone," I said.

"I would be remiss to do so."

He crouched beside me, and I saw he wore the robes of a Dominican, Savonarola's order. This made me cry harder. Had he heard what I'd told Cristofano? Was I about to be dragged off to a prison?

"I understand why you are upset."

He had heard. I was doomed.

"I was speaking without thinking," I said. "I—"

"No more, not here." He helped me to my feet and led me to a narrow staircase, the one the workers who built the cathedral's dome had used during its construction, saying nothing further until he'd closed the door behind us. "No one comes here. It is a safe place. I heard your words and share your fears. I know better than most how dangerous Savonarola is. I came to Florence as a young man, drawn to her community of scholars. Not all friars believe God wants us to destroy art."

I still didn't trust him. "I'm angry at losing jewelry that had sentimental value. My mother gave it to me and a Band of Hope took it. I overreacted."

"This isn't about jewelry," he said. "We both know that. I believe you know Sandro Botticelli?"

His question caught me off guard. "I do. What has that to do with anything?"

"Savonarola has all but convinced him to destroy his paintings that have pagan themes."

"He wouldn't do that."

"Have you seen him recently? He's like most of the rest of Florence: scared. He'll do whatever the friar tells him to."

"I will never believe that."

"Will your beliefs on the subject matter in the slightest when he starts burning his paintings?"

"Who are you?" I asked.

"Friar Baldo Cipriano."

"I'm scared of what Savonarola is doing to this city," I said.

"As am I. I belong to a group of like-minded individuals. Together, we are trying to save as much as possible from the friar's bonfires. We gather what we can and hide it in a place that is safe."

"Do you have much?"

"Not so much as we would like," he said. "People are not eager to part with their possessions. Not because they fear they won't eventually be returned, but because they're afraid of what they will suffer if they are exposed."

"So how do you convince them?"

"We don't."

"Then how do you . . ." I stared at him. "You steal?"

"There is no other way. We can discuss the morality of the issue at some other time. A lady like you has better access to the homes of the wealthy than we do. Will you help us?"

"I can't steal—"

"You won't need to. We're quite capable of handling that ourselves. What we can't do, however, is ascertain where the best pieces—and the most vulnerable—are kept. Who owns what? Where is it displayed? Are there books as well? Ancient sculpture? Cameos? Other objects that should be kept from flames? All we'd want from you is information, information you can gain from a perfectly ordinary routine. Visit your friends. Report what you see."

For a moment, I worried that I was treading on dangerous ground. He was taking a great risk being so open with me. I could denounce him to Savonarola. Unless his openness was a feint, designed to trick me into condemning myself.

"Our meeting is no coincidence, Signora Portinari," he said. "I knew your grandfather. He spoke of you often. I met you once, at a hunting party. You were thrown from your horse. I was one of the friends with whom he was sitting in the loggia when you returned. I recognized your face in the fresco Botticelli painted there. He modeled one of the Three Graces on you. I have hesitated to seek you out, but things are so bad now I had no choice. I didn't come to your palazzo or write to you because I did not want to risk anyone else in your household learning of a connection between us. I've watched you for weeks, hoping for an opportunity to talk. That you came here, to the Duomo, today, seemed prescient. Savonarola is not doing God's work. We are."

"I want to trust you," I said.

He pulled something out of his robe and passed it to me. "Your grandfather gave me this before he died."

I recognized the object. It was the sardonyx cameo showing the goddess Minerva in profile that Lorenzo il Magnifico had given to my grandfather the evening we dined with him in his palazzo. The evening I had first seen Agnolo and thought he despised me. The evening that left me feeling so vulnerable I had welcomed Giacomo's advances when I should have resisted them.

I'd seen the cameo only once since then, when Nonno showed it to me the night he asked me to keep his books safe. He'd told me he planned to give it to someone more trustworthy than any man he had met, someone who could help me if I ever found myself in trouble. And he'd promised that I would never have to seek him out; he would find me if I was in need.

"I will do anything you want," I said. "Where do we start?"

Florence, 1903

39

Signore Bastieri blossomed with renewed purpose when I told him what Colin and Darius wanted us to do. We waited until Signore Tazzera arrived, bringing with him a large box of documents. Once he and Cécile were settled at a table and starting to go through them, we left and went to each of the houses he'd identified on the map. I noticed nothing unusual about them.

When we reached the final one, in the Oltrarno, I leaned against the wall of the palazzo across the street from it. "The pattern of their locations is the same as that of the graffiti in our house, but what does it mean? Obviously, the arms couldn't have been carved on the houses without the owners noticing. They don't represent a family, and we know they date from the time of Savonarola. I think they were put on these buildings to signal membership in a group opposed to him."

"But would their presence on the houses not have been noticed by his supporters?"

"They are much smaller than most others," I said, "and etched into single stones. It's easy to miss them. They're far more discreet than, say, the emblems on the Palazzo Medici, which protrude from the façade. Or like that one, there." I pointed to a house across the street upon which an enormous coat of arms was displayed.

"Yes, these arms are more subtle," he said. "I think you are right, signora, that they were meant to send a message to the members of a secret organization. This is very good."

I was less enthusiastic, for while the revelation might have proved helpful if it were the fifteenth century and we were looking for a haven from Savonarola's henchmen, it did not bring us closer to finding either the treasure or the murderer. Or did it?

Many people had searched for the treasure in the Palazzo di Vieri over the centuries, yet no one had found it. What if it had never been there? The house could have been the center of an anti-Savonarola group, but its members may have chosen somewhere else to hold whatever precious items they wanted to hide from him. The letter that Signore Tazzera had found mentioned a passage, but we'd located no such thing. Maybe it was a tunnel that led away from the house. I needed to clear my mind. Too many thoughts were racing in too many directions.

"Signore Bastieri, tell me again about the man who lent you his carriage after Marzo's funeral. Do you remember him wearing a scarf?" Tessa had mentioned a scarf.

"Yes, it was green. A paisley pattern. I noticed the design because the color scheme was similar to something I use in my own work."

"Did he say anything at all that gave you an idea as to where his house was?"

"No, he did not, but as he walked home from the church, it couldn't have been too far away."

Florence was small enough that the distance being walkable told me very little. Why had he bothered with a carriage if the walk was so easy? "Was it raining the day of the funeral?" I asked.

"No, it was sunny and bright."

I was convinced he had brought the carriage because he wanted to be able to get Lena into it, so he could eliminate her, just as he had Marzo. Perhaps he hadn't expected her father to be with her, and had to adapt his plan, finding another opportunity to kill her.

Colin had not balked when I suggested the man might be Russian, and he had readily agreed that Cécile and I should be the ones to go to the consulate in an attempt to identify him. What did he and Darius know about this man? They would never tell me, not even now; and although it was disgracefully underhanded, an idea began to take hold of me.

Darius's rooms were in the Oltrarno, in the same building in which the Brownings had lived, across from the Pitti Palace. I had not questioned his intention to stay on his own rather than with us in the palazzo. A bachelor is in need of a certain amount of privacy, particularly a bachelor whose sensitive work might include documents his partner's wife could not be allowed to see. Colin wouldn't have been able to hide anything from me in the palazzo, but that would be of no concern if they kept everything at Darius's. I hesitated. I couldn't let Signore Bastieri know that my husband and his friend were agents of the Crown, and anything I found in Darius's rooms would require explanation.

"Signore, I need you to return to the palazzo. Search every inch of the cellar for evidence of old tunnels or passageways. While you do that, I'm going to revisit each of the buildings with our coats of arms. I'm certain I'm missing something."

"I don't like to leave you alone, signora," he said, frowning.

"I'll be perfectly safe. No one's going to snatch me off the street in broad daylight."

"I don't like it."

"It will be fine."

"It's not worth the risk," he said. There was so much pain in his eyes, I couldn't bring myself to cause him more worry.

"All right, we'll go back to the house together. I'm not sure looking at the arms again is a productive use of time. On the way, I need to pop in and leave a message for a friend who lives nearby. It will only take a moment." When we reached Darius's building, I asked Signore Bastieri to wait for me outside. "Make sure no one is following us."

Unsure of where, specifically, Darius's rooms were, I climbed the interior stairs in the courtyard up one flight and knocked on the first door on the landing. I told the woman who answered that I had just arrived from England to visit my brother.

"He won't be home at the moment, but do you know if there's a concierge or someone who might be able to let me in?" I asked. "I hate to wait in the corridor for hours."

"Go two doors down the hall. The landlord lives there. He will help you."

Fortunately, the man did not doubt my story. He took me up to the third floor and unlocked the door. "Signore Benton-Smith will be happy to see you, I am sure," he said. "He rarely has visitors and often looks lonely, so very lonely. I did not even know he had a sister."

"Our family is not so close as I would like," I said. "I've come here to try to change that."

He nodded. "*Bene.* There is nothing more important than family. If you need anything else, you know where to find me." He went back downstairs and I stepped into Darius's rooms.

His accommodations were shockingly small: a poky sitting room and a minuscule bedroom. The space was clean but had little else to recommend it. Now I understood why his dinner jacket was so badly mended. He couldn't afford a valet, let alone a tailor. I felt a prickle of guilt, knowing he would be embarrassed that I had seen how he was living.

An empty bookshelf, two threadbare chairs, and an unsteady table stood in the sitting room. There were no letters, no papers, nothing personal. The bedroom contained a narrow bed and a table with a lamp. I found a battered valise shoved under the bed. It was locked, but a hairpin made a fine substitute for its key. It was empty. I felt along its lining, looking for anything that might be hidden, but to no avail.

All that was left was the wardrobe. A row of shirts and two perfectly pressed suits—their pockets empty—hung from its bar, two pairs of shoes below. On the top shelf was a sponge bag and shaving kit, along with a hat box. Inside the latter was an elegant top hat with a green paisley scarf tucked into it.

My heart was racing. I returned the hat and scarf to the box and took it with me, glad that Signore Bastieri was waiting for me downstairs. "Do you recognize this?" I showed him the scarf.

"*Sì, sì,* it looks like the one worn by the man who lent us his carriage.

You have found him! I must thank him—" He stopped. "How did you get it? You were not leaving a message for a friend, were you?"

"No," I admitted, "but this was the last thing I expected to find. We need to go back to the palazzo."

"What does this mean?"

"I think the man with the carriage killed Lena," I said.

"Who is he?"

I swallowed hard. It had to be Darius, unless he and Colin had tracked down the man and taken his scarf. But why would they have done that? "I can't prove anything yet," I said. "You will know the instant I can."

"Tell me his name."

"Not until I'm sure. I don't want to give you false hope."

He accepted this.

Cécile and Signore Tazzera were in the dining room at the palazzo when we arrived, poring over a heap of documents that covered nearly the entire surface of the table.

"So far, we have nothing concrete," the librarian said. "These are all to do with people arrested when Savonarola controlled Florence. We are looking for any prisoner who has a connection to this house."

"Can I help?" Signore Bastieri said.

"Please," Cécile replied. "I do not read Italian so well as I speak it."

"Might I have a word with you, Cécile?" I asked. We stepped out of the room as Signore Bastieri took a seat.

"What's going on, Kallista?"

I showed her the hat box and its contents. "I found this in Darius's rooms. Signore Bastieri identified it as the one worn by the man at Marzo's funeral who lent his carriage to Lena and her father. It's exactly as Tessa described it."

She beetled her brows. "*Mon dieu*. What does this mean?"

"Darius is living like a pauper," I said. "His lodgings are appalling, not at all what I would expect for someone who has five estates in England and a hunting lodge in Scotland."

"Didn't he come here from his family's villa in Lake Garda?"

"Yes, I forgot about that. So why is he living in a space that a girl working as a maid would find barely acceptable?"

"He wouldn't be the first gentleman to have run through his inheritance," Cécile said.

"Let's go up to my study. If Colin and Darius return, I don't want them to find us with this." We stopped in the kitchen on the way. The cook was stirring something on the stove—I'd told her she should take the rest of the day off, but she insisted that cooking was the only distraction that soothed her—while Signora Orlandi and Tessa were sitting at the table. I asked Tessa to come with us.

Once in my study, I showed her the scarf. She blanched and clutched her throat. "It's his. The man from the funeral. I didn't see his face, but I remember that scarf. Where did you find it? Do you think he had something to do with the murders?"

"We do," I said.

She crossed herself. "He will deserve the punishment he gets in the seventh circle of hell, where he'll spend eternity in a river of boiling blood."

It was easy to forget how seriously the Florentines took Dante. Here, his work was still a living, breathing entity, part of everyday life. "Have the gentlemen been back to the house?" I asked.

"No, signora," she said.

"Very good. Return to your colleagues, and, please, don't any of you try to work. You must give yourselves time to grieve."

"I cannot do as you ask." The expression on her face, grim and determined, told me she would not be deterred. "Fredo was my friend. I will not stand by while his killer continues his spree. You've already figured out that I have more specialized training than the average maid. Let me help you."

"All right." There was no time to argue, and she might prove useful. "I think we must assume Darius is our murderer," I said. "He's bankrupt, or nearly so. All the things we suspected Marzo of doing for money could be true of Darius instead. His work gives him access to sensitive data, data that he could sell for a fortune."

"But he is an Englishman," Cécile said, "and surely not the sort of person who would turn traitor."

"I wouldn't have thought so, but can you offer another explanation? Think back to this morning. We were all convinced the investigation was over. The gentlemen were planning an excursion, but Signore Bastieri's arrival delayed their departure. What did he tell us?"

"That he found the coat of arms on buildings."

"Colin and Darius left," I said. "An hour or so later, you discovered Fredo, Tessa."

"Surely Monsieur Benton-Smith could not have murdered him without drawing the attention of Monsieur Hargreaves."

"If he is responsible for all the murders, he is a cunning assassin, capable of deceiving even Colin, who would never have suspected his colleague of slipping off to do something so vile. We can figure out the details later; but for now we must assume that Signore Bastieri's revelations spurred Darius to kill again. Why? So far as we can tell, the location of the arms didn't reveal anything telling. What are we missing?"

"If he needs money, Signore Benton-Smith would want the treasure," Tessa said, "and he'd have to make sure no one finds it before him."

"He directed Signore Bastieri and me to go back and look at each of the houses that bear the coat of arms," I said. "That tells me something about them made him fear exposure."

"If he had not sent you out to the houses, what would you have done?" Cécile asked.

"I would have looked at the graffiti again, not my translations, but the originals. It had to have been placed deliberately to mimic the pattern of the buildings, which had already been built by Savonarola's time. There must be something hidden in it."

"Then let us find out what it is," Tessa said.

We started on the landing, with the first graffito I'd found, collecting Signore Tazzera and Signore Bastieri en route. I scrutinized the words, but they provided no illumination. Signore Tazzera stood next to me, using a magnifying glass.

"There's nothing strange about it at all," he said. "Whoever wrote it possessed a fine hand and scored a horizontal line on the wall to ensure his work would be straight. That suggests that the writer was likely a copyist or a scribe. Few others would have such beautiful handwriting, and a scribe would be in the habit of ruling a page before writing on it."

"I don't see the line," I said, leaning closer. The librarian gave me his glass. Peering through it, I could just make it out, a faint line scraped into the plaster. "Ah . . . yes . . . I can spot it now. And there's something else."

The text read *Quod nequeunt oculis rerum primordia cerni*. Below the line under each of the *C*s were two impossibly small dots that looked like they'd been made by pricking the plaster with the sharp point of a knife.

I went into the Sale Madornale and applied the magnifying glass to its graffito, the others following me. There, below the line, were dots under each of ten letter *A*s. From there, we examined the rest, and found dots corresponding with one *L*, two *O*s, seven *U*s, and four *P*s. I wrote the letters in my notebook.

"The layout may tell us how to decode the message," Cécile said. "What are the addresses of the buildings? Put them in numerical order and we will know the order of the letters."

"There are twenty-six marked letters," Signore Tazzera said. "Could that be significant?"

"I think we're making things overcomplicated," I said and turned my notebook toward them to reveal the word I'd made from the letters. "*CUPOLA*."

"Whatever they hid, they put it in the dome of the cathedral," Tessa said.

"Time for us to find it," Signore Tazzera said.

"I'll grab my coat and meet you downstairs," I said.

The day was too warm to merit a coat, but I wanted one nonetheless, to conceal the revolver Cécile and I had taken from Carlo. I loaded the weapon and slipped it into the right-hand pocket, hoping I would have no cause to use it.

Florence, 1496

40

That year, it rained nearly every day for eleven months. The crops meant to feed the city destroyed, we knew we would face famine. Close on its heels, as always, would come the plague. None of this made me despondent, however, for at last I had a purpose. I'd become more social in the nine months since Friar Baldo pulled me up from my knees in the nave of our great cathedral. I renewed old friendships and made new ones, all in order to identify objects that must be saved from Savonarola's bonfires.

I enjoyed it more than I thought I would. While I would never move in the lofty intellectual circles enjoyed by my grandfather, the Florentines rarely disappointed when it came to conversation. Once again, I found myself happily discussing Neoplatonism, even if it could not be done quite so openly as it had in the past. Twice I saw Cristofano at gatherings. The first time, we did not speak, but I could feel his eyes following me as I made my rounds of the guests. The second time, I encountered him on the wide marble stairway leading up to the party on the piano nobile. He was leaving as I arrived. There was no one else around. He stopped, took my hand, and brushed his lips over it.

"Mina," he said, his eyes burning bright.

I could not find my voice to reply. He smiled at me and continued on his way down the steps. Doubtless I was a fool even to hope, but I took it as a sign that someday, perhaps, we would rekindle our friendship.

As the months passed, Savonarola's grip on the city began to ever so slightly crack as the damage wreaked by his policies began to come clear. Nonetheless, those who were not his devoted followers still lived in fear of the torture meted out indiscriminately by his government. Rumors began to fly about the rain, that it was a sign from God that the little friar was not doing the Lord's work. Everyone was uneasy.

This should have made my job simpler, but it didn't. I'd always shown great interest in my friends' art, but now I had to curb my enthusiasm. As Friar Baldo and his colleagues stole more and more pieces, everyone began talking about the thefts. One day, a cousin of mine pointed out that her cassoni and two ancient sculptures had disappeared from her house soon after I'd dined with her and was rhapsodizing about the pieces. She mentioned it at a party, and several others chimed in, saying that I had commented on possessions of theirs shortly before they'd been burgled. They were teasing, but I began to worry that they might suspect I had something to do with the crimes. After all, many of the stolen items were things I had earlier begged them to hide away so that they'd be out of Savonarola's reach. How long until someone made the connection?

These concerns had been eating at me, so I cannot claim surprise when, at a dinner party, the host jokingly suggested that I was paying off my friends' servants to remove and bring to me everything I'd not long ago asked them to put in safe storage. He didn't mention Savonarola by name, but everyone knew what he meant.

I'd been on edge all night. Father Cambio was a guest as well, seated diagonally across from me at the table. From the moment I saw him, it was evident that he had not forgiven me for what I'd done the last time we met. The cut on his face caused by my ring had healed years ago, but it had left an invisible scar. Or rather, a scar visible only to me. There was no mistaking the hatred in his eyes.

"I would not have thought you a heretic, Signora Portinari," he said. Everyone fell silent. This was not an accusation anyone should make in jest.

"I'm no heretic." I met his stare.

"You are if you want to divert sinful objects from the fires in which they belong. The corruption in our Holy Church runs deep, signora. Only Savonarola can reform these evils. You should not stand in his way."

"She's so petite" our host said, trying to change the direction of the conversation. "Not big enough even to block the friar, as short as he is." Everyone laughed and started to discuss the feud in which Savonarola was engaged with the pope. Father Cambio continued to glare at me with venom in his eyes.

The next day, a group of boys appeared at my door. One of Savonarola's Bands of Hope. Their leader, who could not have been more than fifteen, demanded to see me.

"We are here to cleanse this house," he said. "You have been given opportunities to do this yourself voluntarily, but we have learned that you kept back many objects that continue to lead you to sin."

"You are not welcome here," I said.

He shoved me aside, slamming me into the wall. "That is not for you to decide."

He said many things after that. I remember none of them. The only thing that mattered to me was the golden half medal of St. Anthony hanging around his neck. This boy, this thug, was my son. He looked like me, with golden hair and light eyes, and might have grown up like me, too, educated and erudite, had I not abandoned him. I no longer tried to stop them from coming into the house, nor did I stand in their way when they looted my possessions. Everything precious was hidden safely away, but even if it weren't, I'm not sure I could have fought to save any of it. Not then. Not when I saw what my son had become. I had destroyed his life, leaving him vulnerable to men like Savonarola. I wanted to tell him who I was, to show him the other half of the medal he wore, but I was too cowardly. I shrank away and said nothing.

The next day, I met with Friar Baldo in a vestry of the Cappelle Medicee. "We have just finished arranging to use this passageway," he said, pushing a large wardrobe along the wall, revealing a trapdoor below it. He pulled it open and led me down a narrow set of steps into a small room that was stuffed full with items stolen to save them from Savonarola.

"So much," I said, astonished by the quantity.

"Our work will have a significant impact," he said. "But that is not what you wanted to discuss with me, is it?"

"No," I said. I told him what had happened at the party, sparing no detail about Father Cambio's threats. I told him that I'd then been visited by a Band of Hope, but made no mention of my relationship to the boys' leader.

"You must be more careful," he said. "You've provided us with information on nearly every fashionable house in the city. Now it is time for you to step back."

"Even if I do, I'm afraid Father Cambio will still come after me."

"Why does he despise you so much?"

I looked into his eyes. "Do the details matter?"

"I suppose they don't, though I am curious," he said.

"Suffice it to say that he will do anything in his power to hurt me. If I'd known he'd been invited to that dinner, I never would have gone. I hoped he'd forgot about me, but now . . ."

"Would you consider leaving Florence?"

"Never. It is my home."

"Petrarch and Dante both survived exile," he said.

"There's nowhere I could go."

"Then the only way to keep you safe is to make the Piagnoni believe you are one of them. Renounce your friends and take up with a new set. You can say that the Band of Hope changed your way of thinking and that you now support Savonarola."

"Is that necessary?" I asked.

"It's the only way to stay safe if you insist on remaining in the city."

And so I followed his advice. I told my friends that after the Band of Hope looted my house, I'd had a vision, and that I now knew we were all on the wrong path. Only Savonarola could lead us to salvation. It was not yet too late for us to repent.

My newfound zeal was off-putting to everyone, especially Bia, who knew how much I'd always despised the friar.

"I don't believe this conversion," she said. "It's absurd. What game are you playing at? It was bad enough when you ruined everything with Signore Corsini, but now, just when you've let us reclaim some semblance of an interesting life, you throw it away. Do you have an aversion to happiness?"

"Of course not," I said. "I—"

"I think you do," she said. "And I know why."

She lunged forward and tugged the thin gold chain around my neck, pulling the charm that dangled from it out from my bodice. I strained to grab it back, but she clasped it in her hand and held it high above her head, out of my reach.

"You don't know what you're doing," I said.

"Who was your lover and why wouldn't he marry you? Did my father know what you'd done? No wonder you never had a child of your own. You were left barren as punishment for your sins."

"It wasn't like that." But I was lying. She had it exactly right.

"Did my father know?"

"No."

"I suppose that's a slim consolation." She flung the necklace at me and then stormed out of the room.

I hadn't noticed Alfia was there, standing in the shadows, until she stepped forward and enveloped me in an embrace. I wept and wept, wondering how one mistake could so completely destroy a person's life.

Florence, 1903

41

I desperately wished I had some way to surreptitiously contact Colin. Much as I was loath to expose Darius—if my conclusions proved erroneous, his reputation would be irrevocably ruined—I saw no other viable option. Tessa and Cécile already knew, so when we met the others in the loggia, I told Signore Tazzera and Signore Bastieri what I had deduced about the crimes, and asked them to go to Fredo's lodgings.

"If you find Colin and Darius still there, you must get them to return to the palazzo at once," I said. "Don't let either of them know we believe Darius is the murderer. If he feels threatened, he may lash out, and we know all too well how dangerous he is. Tell them I twisted my ankle and you had to bring me home."

"Should we arrange to have the police waiting at the house?" Signore Tazzera asked. "If there's no one to arrest him, he'll be no less dangerous here than at Fredo's."

"Yes, that's exactly what I was thinking," I said. It was the best strategy for a good outcome, even if it is was an outcome Colin would have liked to avoid.

"What if they are not at Fredo's?" Signore Bastieri asked. "Where else should we look?"

"I'm afraid I don't know." If Darius had killed Fredo because he feared exposure, would he now feel safe? Or was he hatching another plan to ensure he would never take the blame for his actions? If that was the case—and I strongly suspected it was—I had no idea where he would go next.

"Do not worry, signora," Signore Bastieri said. "We will track them down. Two well-heeled gentlemen can't have made their way through a neighborhood like Fredo's without drawing a certain amount of attention."

"Cécile, you and Emily will wait for us here, yes?" Signore Tazzera asked.

"No," I said. "We're going to the Duomo to see if we can find the treasure in the cupola."

"Can't that wait until this other business is finished?" he asked.

"Not if we want to make sure Darius doesn't get to it first. If he does, he'll have the resources to flee and never pay for what he's done."

Signore Bastieri shook his head, his eyes narrowed. "It is not worth the risk. My Lena is dead. Catching him will not change that. If any of you is injured—or, heaven forbid, killed—trying to stop him, I will never forgive myself."

"Whatever happens, none of this is your fault," Tessa said.

"She's correct," I said. "Furthermore, we have no reason to believe he knows to look in the dome," I said. "To learn what we have, he'd have to come here first and study the graffiti. If we're here when he arrives, and it's before the police have come, that could be dangerous."

"There are always many tourists in the Duomo," Tessa said. "We will be in no danger there."

Signore Bastieri nodded. "That is true. We will come for you after we've handed Signore Benton-Smith over to the police."

We all left the house together, separating only when we'd reached the end of the street. Signore Tazzera took four steps away from us before turning around, dashing back, and kissing Cécile.

"Be careful," he told her, and then ran to catch up with Signore Bastieri. My friend said nothing, but the slightest smile curled her lips.

The Duomo was only a short walk from the palazzo. We went inside and headed straight for the narrow stone steps that would take us to the top of the cupola. We climbed and climbed, the stairway becoming increasingly narrow the higher we got.

"Four hundred and sixty-three steps," Tessa said. "Let's hope the treasure isn't at the very top."

We didn't rush. Instead, we took our time, inspecting the walls around us for any sign that we were on the right track. I almost missed the first: a bat, just like that on the top of the coat of arms, carved into the riser of a winder step. Around it, I found no sign of a hiding place. We continued on, encouraged. Tessa found a second sign—an arrow—carved into the riser of another winder step. Again, I could see nowhere to hide anything. Would a caltrap, the third sign from the coat of arms, mark the spot?

We climbed higher, until the stairs briefly flattened. A short corridor took us back into the interior of the cathedral, opening onto a walkway that ran around the base of the dome, just beneath Giorgio Vasari's enormous fresco of *The Last Judgement*. The artist died before he'd finished the work, which took Federico Zuccaro five more years to complete. Centuries of soot and grime now darkened it, but from where we stood, that only made Vasari's hell appear more ominous. We paused to catch our breath and were so distracted by the painting above that I almost didn't notice two figures on the other side of the whispering gallery: Colin and Darius. The expression on my husband's face made it clear they were arguing.

"Let's creep around slowly, approaching them so that we come up behind Darius," I said. "He won't be able to see us unless he turns around." We had made it no more than ten yards when Cécile stopped.

"I can't go on, Kallista," Cécile said. "The height is giving me vertigo. I feel like I'm spinning." The cathedral's altar was nearly two hundred feet below us.

"I'll take her back if you'd like," Tessa said. "It makes better sense for only one of us to go. Much more discreet."

"You're right," I said. "Thank you."

She took Cécile's hand and they hugged the wall as they made their way to the doorway. I continued on. Colin spotted me when I was about thirty yards away. He fixed his eyes on Darius and made a subtle gesture with one hand, signaling me to go back.

Something about the walls of domes makes them excellent conductors of sound. In any other sort of space, I would not have been able to hear their conversation, but here, even though they kept their voices low, every word was clear. I crept forward, only far enough that I was firmly out of Darius's line of sight. I pressed my back against the wall and listened.

"You should have asked for help," Colin was saying. "I could have—"

"I couldn't risk asking you for anything," Darius said. "You still don't understand the danger, do you? We are headed for a disastrous confrontation with Germany, one that can only be stopped by making victory impossible for either side. If two enemies have the same weapons and the same capabilities, they will have to face the reality that neither can win and find some other, less destructive way, to live in the world together."

"You are betraying your country," Colin said.

"It is the only way to save it."

"You needn't have killed Lena."

"But you don't object to my eliminating Marzo?" Darius laughed softly. "He was useful to us for a long time, but then he started demanding more money. More than Britain would pay, and more than I had to give. I've spent every penny of my inheritance funding this venture. That's how important it is to me. I may be bankrupt, but it's worth it to serve my cause. He was nothing but a mercenary."

"Most men like him are."

"Which makes them expendable," Darius said. "The house next door to yours has an attic window that opens onto your roof. I had Marzo meet me in that attic. I would have done nothing more than cut ties with him if he hadn't made overtures to the Russians, but he did, so I killed him. The next day, when you arrived in Florence, I dragged his body over to your roof and tied it with a rope I'd frayed so that he'd fall into the courtyard only after I had joined you at the house. It was a bit complicated, I suppose, but I've always had a flair for the dramatic. At any rate, Marzo had to be eliminated. He was going to give the Russians, who could pay what he wanted, the information from the Germans instead of me."

"Which would have hurt Britain. I understand that completely. But you were giving the Germans details of our own military secrets. That undermines the empire."

"Not if you want the empire to survive. Can't you see, Hargreaves? We need to know everything the Germans are doing and they need to know everything we do. That's the only way forward, unless you want carnage. You haven't been in combat. I have. I saw the horrors first-hand at Colenso in the Second Boer War. Men mowed down, endless casualties."

"Colenso was a disaster," Colin said. "No one can argue otherwise, but that only proves we need a matchless military to defend our interests. Had we been better prepared, we wouldn't have suffered such terrible losses in the Boer Wars. Our tactics were dated and wholly unsuitable. We must keep ahead of our enemies."

"Keeping ahead is exactly what leads to war. Would we have fought in Africa if we'd known we couldn't win? No. Think how many lives would have been spared."

"We could have won if we were better prepared."

"We will never agree on any of this," Darius said.

"Then tell me why you killed Lena."

"Your oh-so-clever wife figured out that di Taro's death was related to Marzo. Emily didn't know he worked for the Russians or that Marzo was going to give him the information I needed, but she exposed the connection. Lena might have known that Marzo had gone to the Russians looking for money and I couldn't trust her to keep her mouth shut if she did. I would have dealt with her after the funeral if her father hadn't been with her. As it was, I had to wait."

"How did you make the connection with di Taro?"

"Once I determined Marzo to be unreliable, I started following him. He communicated with di Taro using a florist's booth at the Mercato Nuovo. He went there once a week at the same time. If he needed to meet with his Russian contact—di Taro was not Italian—he would knock over a canister of flowers. They would rendezvous that evening near di Taro's house."

"On the nights that Marzo took Vittoria for walks."

"Yes. One cannot accuse him of mastering the art of subtlety. Your wife figured it out with little effort. I should have realized long ago he was more dangerous than useful."

"So you killed di Taro, using a Russian revolver."

"I thought it a nice bit of irony. Brought down by his own people, so to speak."

"The gun was designed by a Belgian," Colin said.

"But for the Russians."

"And the coat of arms on the message you sent Lena?"

"I knew it would distract Emily," Darius said. "I didn't want her tangled up in this."

They stood silent for a moment, staring at each other.

"I never meant to get you caught up in all this, either, but now that you are, you know I can't let you walk away. There's too much at stake."

"I shouldn't think a self-described pacifist would want more blood on his hands. You needn't have killed Fredo. It was an extreme measure."

"Perhaps, but it was him or Emily. She and Bastieri were getting close to finding the treasure. He announced as much when he came to the house this morning. I knew I had to act quickly."

"Bastieri doesn't know where the treasure is, nor does Emily."

"It won't be long before they find it," Darius said. "I'm the one who needs the money it will bring. Marzo taught me as much. It will fill my currently empty coffers and I'll be able to pay for more reliable informants. I'm sorry Fredo is dead. I liked him, but I had to do something to stop your wife."

"When we were on our way to the Duomo after breakfast, you stopped and told me you'd left your wallet in your rooms. You asked me to wait while you ran back to fetch it," Colin said. "Instead, you went to the palazzo and snapped Fredo's neck. And then, after we learned of his death—or, rather, I learned of his death—and were searching his lodgings, you found a coded message, supposedly dropped by his assassin. We easily deciphered it—too easily—and determined the man had a meeting here, in the Duomo. You wrote that message, didn't you?"

"Days ago," Darius said. "I kept it with me in case I was not able to bring you here in a less underhanded manner. I couldn't make the code too difficult or I wouldn't have been able to get you here quickly, should doing so become necessary."

"Which it did."

"Yes. I'd hoped we could come to the cathedral and have this conversation without any more drama, which is why this morning I suggested that we climb the dome."

"Why are you so bent on us being here?"

"That will become clear. Look, Hargreaves, I apologize for exploiting your trust. I only killed Fredo to keep your wife safe. His death will distract her from hunting for treasure, which means I won't have to force the issue. It may not have been the most elegant way to solve the problem, but I thought you would prefer it to my killing her."

I saw Colin draw a deep breath. "You've made a right mess of it all, but I can talk to Burman, explain your troubles. Financial pressures have made many a man crack, and—"

"You still don't understand, do you?" Darius took three steps toward him and stopped. "I will do whatever is necessary to continue my work. I will stop the next war from ever coming. Sadly, in order for me to do so, someone else must take the blame for what I've done, and that someone is you. You're the only other person involved enough to have pulled it off, so I lured you here. It was I who broke into the palazzo, knowing you would come to investigate. Once you were here, I could eliminate Marzo and pin his death on you."

"No one will believe I killed him," Colin said.

"Only if you're here to defend yourself. Dying in the service of one's country happens in our line of work. I'm afraid there's no way I can avoid destroying your reputation. Everyone will believe you betrayed Britain. That may not seem fair, but sacrifices must be made to ensure the human race isn't condemned to a state of perpetual war. I will tell

Emily that you regretted what you'd done, that you confessed everything and were sincerely repentant. She will accept that suicide was the only honorable action in the circumstances. I thought the Duomo a suitable place for you to end it all, in full view of the public. The details of what happens will never be questioned."

Colin remained immobile, but I could see he was braced for a fight, a fight I could not stand by and watch. I pulled the revolver out of my pocket, aimed, and fired. The bullet went wildly astray from my target, hitting Vasari's fresco instead of Darius, but the noise—and the direction from which it came—startled him. He spun around to face me, just as Colin lunged for him, knocking him off-balance. Darius had a gun of his own, and raised it at me. Colin's fist crashed into his jaw and sent him careening over the railing. With a sickening splat, he plunged onto the floor in front of the altar, his limbs at awkward angles, blood streaming from his head.

Screams echoed through the cathedral, not for the first time in its history. It was here, after all, that the Pazzi and their allies attacked Lorenzo and Giuliano de' Medici, killing the latter and leaving the former bloodied but more powerful than ever. Cécile stuck close to the wall, but managed to overcome her vertigo enough to follow Tessa, who ran toward me the moment I'd fired the gun. Gingerly, Cécile peered over the railing, looking down at Darius. "You really must learn how to shoot, Kallista. Your aim is atrocious. A single shot to the head would have finished the matter more neatly."

"I should have fired," Tessa said.

"You have a gun?"

"I do, but I doubt I could have made the shot."

"You ought to have given it to me," Cécile said. "I could have with no difficulty."

"It would have made a terrible mess of Vasari's fresco," Colin said, coming to stand with us. "The bullet hole is bad enough."

"A valid point, Monsieur Hargreaves, a valid point."

Tessa ran down the stairs ahead of us. When we caught up to her, she was standing over Darius's body, her hands on her hips, shouting invectives. The police, whom a tourist had summoned from the piazza outside, were behind her. She spat on the corpse, told us she was going back to the palazzo to update Cook and Signora Orlandi, and stalked out of the church. Only once she had gone did the police step forward. Colin introduced himself and told them what had happened. They accepted his explanation without question.

"It's rather embarrassing, really," he said. "We've been friends for years. I had no idea he'd taken a fancy to my wife and certainly never thought he was the sort of bloke who would react violently when she rejected him. I didn't think he'd go over the railing, but I had to get the gun away from him before he could shoot again." He handed the Russian gun over to the police. He had Darius's, too, tucked away in his jacket. I had no idea how he'd managed to come into possession of it. "I'd be most appreciative if we could keep this incident as quiet as possible. Gossip is so hard on the ladies."

The police didn't question what he said and reassured me that I need not make any sort of statement. I did not object, as my husband's words had left me too stunned to speak. They said it was obvious what had happened and agreed that the less said about it, the better. Colin promised to pay for the repair of the damaged fresco and the cleaning of the blood-spattered floor. They thanked him and told us we were free to go.

Cécile arched her eyebrows as Colin offered each of us an arm. "Truly, Monsieur Hargreaves, you are a remarkable man. Is there no one who won't bend to your will?"

Florence, 1497

42

By the turn of the new year, I had alienated all of my friends. Even Bia now believed me to be an ardent follower of Savonarola. Only one person doubted my sincerity: Father Cambio. He came to my house frequently, but my servants, always loyal, turned him away again and again.

Friar Baldo and his friends continued to remove and preserve art, books, and other objects from Florentine palazzi, but I did not see them anymore. I kept a safe distance so that none of us would be exposed. Only once did I engage in risky behavior, going late at night to the Cappelle Medicee and climbing down the narrow stairs to the little room where we kept our trove. I'd brought with me my grandfather's handwritten copy of Lucretius, the most precious thing I owned. I left it with everything else we'd saved and added it to the meticulous inventory Friar Baldo kept. I looked through the long list and saw that several things from Cristofano's household were included, one a sketch by Botticelli, depicting the Three Graces. I wondered if it were the study the artist had used for the fresco in the Tornabuoni family villa, where Cristofano and I had met, so long ago. If so, how had he come to possess it, and why had he wanted an image of me?

Regret and sorrow pierced me. I could not sleep when I returned home. I paced for hours and then wrote a letter to Cristofano, apologizing for the way I'd treated him and telling him that I was now, at last, ready to tell him my secret. In the morning, I gave it to Alfia to deliver, telling her to give it to no one but him. I dozed for a while after she returned. He'd sent no reply.

Sometime in the early afternoon, I dragged myself out of bed and got dressed. Bia had gone to see a friend, so I would be free from her scorn for a few hours at least. I sat in the Sala dei Pappagalli with a book on my lap, but could not focus enough to read. I stared at the parrots painted on the walls, half in a trance.

Which is probably why I didn't react quickly when Father Cambio came through the door and closed it behind him. The bleeding knuckles on his right hand told me how he'd got past my servants.

"It is time for us to reconcile," he said, coming toward me.

I stood up and backed away. "There will never again be anything between us."

"I don't agree," he said and held up a sheaf of papers. "You recognize these, yes?"

I nodded. It was Friar Baldo's inventory.

"I've had you followed for months, Mina," he said. "I wanted to see what you were doing. No one who's seen you delight in the pleasures of passion could believe you follow Savonarola. I knew you to be a wanton trollop, but I never suspected you'd steal from your friends. What do you intend to do with your bounty? Move to the countryside and fill a villa?"

"That was never—"

He waved me off. "Don't bother. The questions were rhetorical. I don't care what you do with any of it. I do, however, care very much about the power your actions have bestowed upon me. I don't support Savonarola any more than you do. We are similar creatures, Mina. We both know what it takes to survive. But if I were to expose what you're doing—to the little friar, to your friends—your life would be destroyed. I always thought it was our son who would enable me to do what I wish to do to you, but you've given me a far greater gift. Now I can take what I want without having even to invoke his name. I'm not a monster; I have no desire to cause him any embarrassment or discomfort. Not that I suppose he ever would have suffered, even if I had publicly named him. For all we know, he's long gone from Florence. How old would he be now? Fifteen?"

I did not answer. I stepped back again and felt the wall behind me. He laughed.

"This is a game we never before played, you pretending to want to get away from me. It's more arousing than I would have thought. I've always preferred a willing partner, but you, Mina, you have always tempted me like none of the others." He lunged forward, gripped my neck with his hands, and pressed me hard against the wall. "Struggle as much as you want. Nothing will stop me from taking my pleasure."

I could hardly breathe, let alone scream. I kicked at his legs. He flung me onto the floor and pinned me there with the weight of his body. I stopped moving and let my knees fall open, wanting to lull him into a sense of security. He responded exactly as I expected he would, raising himself slightly and pulling up his cassock. I grabbed him where I knew it would wound him the most, dug in my nails, and twisted.

He shrieked and leapt to his feet, shaking his head. "You will pay for that, Mina."

"I don't agree." Cristofano was standing in the doorway. "She's obviously in no need of my help, but if you think I won't have a go at you all the same, you've never met a man."

"This is not what you think," Father Cambio said. "She is the worst sort of slattern, although I suppose you know that as well as I. You were suspiciously close friends for quite a while, weren't you? I'm certain you took full advantage—"

Cristofano silenced him with a blow to the jaw that sent four of the priest's teeth skidding across the floor, but that did not deter my adversary. He struggled to his knees. I grabbed a heavy marble bust of Venus from the table and brought it down on the back of his head. He slumped down and did not move.

"Is he dead?" I asked.

Cristofano felt for a pulse. "Yes, and I can't say I'm sorry. Are you hurt?"

"No," I said. "Thank you for rescuing me, again."

"There's no need for thanks. You had the matter well in hand and were in no need of rescue."

"Did you come because you read my letter?"

"I did."

"I shouldn't have rejected your proposal." A sob caught in my throat. Some mistakes can never be corrected.

"It seems like that happened in another lifetime, to another man." He did not meet my eyes. "What are we going to do about the dead priest on your floor?"

"I don't suppose we could convince anyone he died of the plague?"

Cristofano gave me a wry smile. "No, but I can testify that you acted only to defend yourself."

"No one will believe he attacked me," I said. "He's a well-respected priest."

"Why did he hate you so much?"

Tears started to fall down my cheeks. "Because I loved him once."

"That was your secret," he said.

"Along with this." I removed the half charm hanging around my neck and handed it to him."

"You have a child."

I nodded.

"A son or a daughter?" he asked.

"A son. Salvi."

"Good name." He passed the necklace back to me. "And that is why you wouldn't marry me?"

"It is."

He shook his head and closed his eyes. "So foolish, Mina, so very foolish. Why would I have cared? It would have changed nothing."

"I didn't believe that. I couldn't."

"Then you were right to reject me," he said. "I would never want a wife who had so little faith in her husband."

For a moment, I let myself imagine that I'd married Cristofano. That we'd found Salvi and brought him into our home, saving him from the grip of Savonarola. But what is the point of indulging in fantasy? "I have made so many mistakes."

"I feel sorry for you, Mina. You should have had more faith in yourself, in me, and in those around you. Not everyone is like Father Cambio."

True to his word, Cristofano testified that the priest's death was a direct result of him having attacked me. I would not be punished, not officially, at least. I wrote a letter to Fabbiana, telling her what had happened, but it was returned to me, undelivered. She had succumbed to the consumption that had so long tormented her.

Plague swept through Florence, as it had done at least once a decade for the past hundred years. This time, I caught it. Friar Baldo, further proving his courage, prayed over me when I was sick, showing no concern for his own safety. During those days, when I slipped in and out of consciousness, Savonarola staged his largest bonfire—art, books, musical instruments, and more, piled fifteen feet high, all to be consigned to the flames. Rumor had it that Botticelli flung some of his paintings into it, but I will never believe those stories. I took much comfort in the knowledge that I had helped spare so many precious things from the flames. I'd made a mess of so much of my life, but at least in this, I had succeeded in doing some good.

I survived the plague, but just barely. My illness brought Bia back to me. During my long recovery, after it was clear I was out of danger, I told her my story, sparing no detail, and she better accepted my flaws after hearing it.

The next year, the city finally turned on Savonarola. Famine and plague had eroded his support. A Franciscan friar challenged him to a trial by ordeal, in which two men, one representing the Franciscans, the other the Dominicans, would walk through fire. Whoever survived—if either could—would be accepted as favored by God. Savonarola agreed, but on the day in question, spent so long arguing and negotiating that before the trial could start, the skies opened and doused the flames. At last, the citizens of Florence began to believe that God had abandoned Savonarola.

Soon thereafter, he was arrested, tried as a heretic, and executed, burned on the same spot in the Piazza della Signoria where he'd held his largest bonfire. Now it was his turn. I went to the piazza that day, not to see the spectacle but because I thought Salvi might be there. He was not. I never saw him again.

Not that I didn't try. Six months later, I went to the Ospedale degli Innocenti and showed them my *segni.* He'd been apprenticed to a leather worker but left his position to follow Savonarola. After the friar's demise, he'd fled, to where, no one could tell me. Abandoning him was a mistake I would never be able to correct. I mourned him and prayed that he would find happiness somewhere.

Eventually, the world righted itself. Art and culture flourished. The Medici returned to rule Florence. I became part of a small social circle, comprised mainly of obscure intellectuals and artists. Bia married one of them. Botticelli decorated her cassoni, just as he had mine. She gave her husband seven children.

I did not see Cristofano for a dozen or so years after Savonarola's execution. He came to me on a sunny day a month after Maddalena died. I was sitting on the roof of my house, my damp hair pulled through a crownless hat. I started to speak, but he silenced me, pacing for nearly an hour. Finally, he fell to his knees, buried his head in my lap, and wept. And then, we were friends again. It was almost as if the intervening years had never happened. A week later, he told me he knew better than to propose to me a second time. We both laughed, but I realized that if he had, I would have accepted. Not that it mattered. What more could I want than his friendship, ever steady?

From that day, I kept no secrets from him. I told him what I'd done to help Friar Baldo. We decided to write the story of that tumultuous time in Florence and hide it somewhere safe, so that no matter what the centuries brought, it would be secure, waiting to be found. I copied it into the margins of my grandfather's Lucretius. Cristofano hired a stone mason to alter three steps in the stairs that climbed to the top of Brunelleschi's dome so that we could hide mementos of those days. In one, we placed the inventory of everything spared from the bonfires of the vanities. In another, Cristofano put two sketches, both given to him by Botticelli. The artist, as I'd suspected, had used the first when he was working on the fresco of *Venus and the Three Graces* on the wall of the villa where we'd first met. The second was the drawing he had made of me that night so long ago in the Palazzo Medici. Within the final altered step, we put Nonno's copy of Lucretius.

My grandfather's most precious book would be safe, but not lost. To ensure this, we left a code, embedded in quotes from *De Rerum Natura* written on the walls of my palazzo, placed carefully to mimic the locations of the houses of Florentines who had refused to stand by and let Savonarola destroy their cultural legacy. The houses are marked with a coat of arms bearing a bat, an arrow, and a caltrap, the design conceived by Friar Baldo. Cristofano and I adopted those same symbols to serve as signposts to our hidden treasure, carving them into those three altered steps in the Duomo, where they wait to be found by some future book hunter.

Florence, 1903

43

Colin's statement to the police distressed me, but at least Signore Bastieri would know who had killed his daughter. He and Signore Tazzera arrived at the cathedral not long after the police. When they hadn't found the gentlemen at Fredo's rooms, they came in search of Cécile and me. I explained what had happened, omitting—at my husband's insistence—all references to war and espionage.

"This will bring me some peace," he said. "I am glad her mother did not live to see this, and I am glad that no one else will be hurt by this terrible man. I will return home now. I hope you and your friends find the treasure but have no interest in doing so myself. Whatever it is will prove insignificant compared to the lives we have lost."

I could not argue with that.

Cécile and I retreated to a far corner of the nave.

"I did not suspect Monsieur Benton-Smith," she said. "He was so affable, so charming. The very embodiment of an English gentleman."

"It kept us from seeing the truth. We should have noticed he had financial difficulties. His clothes showed signs of wear and he told us he couldn't manage to get the books he wanted for his library. I assumed it was because the volumes were rare, not that he couldn't afford them."

"A spy in dire financial straits is always a danger," Cécile said. "Monsieur Le Queux has taught me that. The Germans agents who are working in Britain are motivated solely by money."

"Mr. Le Queux writes fiction," I said.

Cécile shrugged. "That does not preclude it from being true."

"Darius wasn't motivated by money, not in that way," I said. "He only wanted it so that he could fund his scheme, not for himself."

Colin and Signore Tazzera, who had been chatting quietly, came over to us.

"I don't want to press you ladies in these awful circumstances, but do you think it would be wrong for us to finish the search you began of the cupola?" Colin asked. "There's no need for you to accompany—"

"We won't be left behind," I said.

Once again, we mounted the stone stairs and climbed up and up, past the carved symbols of the bat and the arrow, the stairway growing narrower as we went. The walls shifted from stone to brick, laid in a herringbone pattern. Just below the top, I spotted a caltrap, identical to the one on the coat of arms, carved into the riser of a winder step. We inspected the walls around it for any variations in the appearance of the mortar or the bricks, but could find nothing to merit further scrutiny.

"I'd hoped the hiding place would be in this final location," Cécile said.

"We're missing something," I said. "It wouldn't have made sense to violate the walls. Doing so could bring the whole dome crashing down. Maybe the treasure is hidden in the stairs themselves."

I crouched down. Unlike those above and below, which appeared to be made from single stones, on this step, a thin line of mortar was visible at the top of the riser, just beneath the tread. Colin handed me his pocketknife, which I used to dig it out. Then, with his help, we tugged the tread loose, revealing a wooden box.

"It's small," Cécile said. "I was right all along—the treasure is jewelry."

"It's not *that* small," I said. "It could contain any number of things."

"Including jewelry," Signore Tazzera said.

We heard footsteps approaching. "You might as well open it." It was the policeman who had come after Cécile and I found Lena's body.

"You've secured permission?" Colin asked.

"*Sì*, signore, so long as you are willing to pay for the repair to return the step to its original state."

"Of course," my husband said and handed the box to me.

I opened it. Inside was a pristine copy of Lucretius's *De Rerum Natura*, the text written in a hand strikingly similar to that of the Latin graffiti in our palazzo.

"That's it?" Cécile asked. "No jewelry? No gold florins?"

"This is . . ." Signore Tazzera reached for the book, a look of rapturous reverence on his face. "I have never seen its match. I wonder if Poggio himself made the copy. The handwriting is very like his. Although, not quite . . ."

Cécile turned to me. "I am glad he, at least, is pleased."

"There are two other steps," I said.

This gave her hope. We went down to the one marked with the arrow. It, too, contained a slim box. Inside were two sketches: one, the face of a beautiful young lady, the other showing four women facing a fifth, handing her flowers. One of the women had a face identical to that in the other drawing.

"It is very like a Botticelli fresco that's in the Louvre," Cécile said. "*Venus and the Three Graces Presenting Gifts to a Young Woman.* These must be the artist's studies for the piece." She gently touched the paper. "To imagine Botticelli himself holding these, a pencil in his hand . . ." Her voice trailed.

"As good as jewelry?" I asked.

"Better," she replied.

The final step, marked with a bat, had in it a tube rather than a box, and we were abuzz with excitement. Would it contain carefully rolled canvases? Paintings saved from Savonarola's bonfire of the vanities?

It did not.

Inside was a rolled-up sheaf of papers, an inventory of sorts, with three columns, the first listing objects; the second, names; and the third, dates, all in the second half of 1498.

"Savonarola was executed on the twenty-third of May that year," Signore Tazzera said. "We were right. Someone was hiding things from him. After his death, they could be returned to their owners."

I was reading over his shoulder. "Many of these are far too large to fit in a hollow step."

"They must have put them somewhere else," Colin said.

"Are there dates associated with every single item?" I asked.

"There are," Signore Tazzera said. "Dates that are likely to record when each item was returned to its owner. My guess is that the treasure is no more."

"Are the book and the sketches included?" I asked.

He skimmed through the list and nodded. "The book was owned by Mina Portinari and returned to her three days after Savonarola's death. The sketches belonged to Cristofano Corsini. He got them back on the sixth of November 1498."

So why did they wind up hidden again?

The police agreed to let us take what we'd found back to the palazzo for further examination. We would, of course, return it all to the authorities. The book and the inventory would go to the Laurentian Library, the sketches to the Uffizi.

I didn't read Latin well enough to understand Lucretius, but when we got home, I paged through the book, wondering about the life of the man who had copied it. Was he a scribe? A book hunter? A scholar?

I turned another page and saw that someone had covered every inch of the margins with writing, in pencil, not ink. Then, I recognized one of the passages on the page:

quod nequeunt oculis rerum primordia cerni
The first beginnings of things cannot be distinguished by the eye.

It was the first Latin graffito I had found in the house. I called Signore Tazzera over, so that he could translate the marginalia, which was written in the *dialetto toscano.*

"This is remarkable," he said. "It tells the story of Teo Portinari, a book hunter and a close friend of Lorenzo de' Medici. His granddaughter, Mina—"

"She owned this book," I said.

"*Sì*. She wrote the words in the margin. Remind me, what are the other quotes in your graffiti?"

I brought him my notebook. Over the course of the next several hours, he located each of them in the volume of Lucretius and translated the marginalia on the corresponding pages. When he was done, we had a complete account of the group—led by a friar called Baldo, assisted by Mina and others—that had stolen objects in order to save them from Savonarola.

"He must be the man who received the letter that talks about the passage being ready. I don't suppose we have any way to find out where that passage was."

"Even if we did, it would be empty now," Colin said. "They returned everything to the rightful owners."

"We think they did, but still, I'd like to see it," I said. I looked down at the book on the table, gently touching Mina's penciled words. Her handwriting was very like her grandfather's. What a life she must have led! Did she socialize with the Medici? Was she, too, friends with the great Lorenzo? No doubt she'd had courage and power, otherwise she wouldn't have been able to accomplish what she did. I imagined she was much lauded after it all came out, when the Florentines no longer lived in fear of Savonarola. "Did she live in this house, do you think?"

"I should be able to find that out easily enough," Signore Tazzera said. "My guess is that she was the wife of whichever member of the Vieri family owned the house at the time."

"She might be wholly unrelated to this house," Colin said.

"The story of the treasure was always connected to this house," I said. "That must stem from her involvement. It was she, after all, who recorded what happened."

He had the answer for us the next morning. Mina Portinari had married Agnolo di Vieri in 1481.

"I remember reading about him," I said, "that first day we met you, when Cécile and I came to the library. He was a silk merchant, spectacularly rich, but stayed in his medieval family home instead of building something more fashionable. Just the sort of man you'd expect to support his wife's quest to save art and books."

"It's a nice thought, Emily," Colin said. "It is, however, based entirely—"

"On speculation and intuition," I said. "Quite. Still, I'd like to think it's the truth."

"It's entirely possible Signore di Vieri had nothing to do with his wife's interests. Or that he would have stopped her if he'd known what she was doing," Colin said. "You're giving in to your love of the romantic, my dear. The past is rarely what we want it to be."

"True words, Monsieur Hargreaves," Cécile said. "Delighted though I am by the Botticelli sketches, I would have liked there to be some jewelry, too. I will learn to live with the disappointment."

Colin and I set off for London a week later. Cécile stayed behind with Signore Tazzera, but I knew she would not keep away from Paris for long. When we arrived in Park Lane, the boys were there, waiting for us. For once, it was Richard, not Henry, who greeted us in an outlandish costume.

"What's this, old chap?" Colin asked, crouching next to him in the entry hall and tugging at the velvet cap on his head.

"We're playing Renaissance," he said, his voice solemn. "My role is that of a gentleman of Florence. I haven't settled on my name just yet, but I'm a confidant of Lorenzo de' Medici."

"It's very boring, Papa," Henry said. "I refuse to take part."

"I'm meant to be an artist," Tom said. That explained the paint smudges on his face and hands.

"That was the only fun bit," Henry said. "Painting Tom."

Nanny rounded up the boys, telling them it was time for their tea. Colin retreated upstairs to change out of his traveling clothes, and I retired to the library, wondering if I should give the work of Mr. Le Queux another chance. I'd left my copy of his short stories with Cécile, but pulled from the shelf one of his novels, *The Great War in England in 1897,* a riveting account of a fictional invasion of Britain by the French and Russians. Well, not quite riveting. Once again, Mr. Le Queux put me to sleep, and once again I awoke to familiar voices.

"Don't be hard on yourself," Sir John Burman was saying. "I would never have thought Benton-Smith capable of betraying his country. He was one of us."

"He was an ideologue," Colin said. "He truly believed that what he was doing was best for the British people. I can't condone his actions, but neither can I condemn his motives."

"You're more principled than most, Hargreaves. I admire that. It was good work you did."

"I just hope it's all settled now."

"You say you found the plans for the dreadnought in his hat?" Sir John asked.

"Underneath the lining. We've no reason to believe he got a copy to the Germans."

"Thank heavens for that."

A small voice piped up. "What's a dreadnought?" I had been wondering the same thing.

"Henry, where are you?" Colin's voice was stern. I heard shuffling and then the dragging steps of a small boy. "How many times have you been told that eavesdropping is not an honorable practice?"

"I'm sorry, Papa. I was already under your desk when you came in. I use it as my submarine, you see. It's much more fun than playing Renaissance. I didn't know you had a visitor until the two of you started talking, and given the nature of your conversation, decided it would be in my best interest to remain unseen."

"You won't repeat a word of what you heard, will you?" Sir John asked. "Doing so could cause great trouble for our king and our empire."

"Of course not, sir," Henry said, solemn and serious.

"That's a good lad. I'll rely on you. Handle this well, and I may ask for your help in the future." There was a brief pause. I suspected Henry was shaking Sir John's hand. "I'll leave you to it, Hargreaves. Again, well done."

I heard him cross the room and leave, shutting the door behind him.

"We are not finished discussing this, Henry," Colin said. "I'm most disappointed in your behavior. You should have made your presence known the moment Sir John and I entered the library."

"I'm truly sorry, Papa. Well, not *truly* but most definitely *sorry.* I can't be too repentant, can I, when my admittedly bad behavior resulted in learning so many fascinating things? I have loads of questions about your work. It seems like you might be a decent candidate to join the crew of my submarine—"

He stopped talking at the sound of the door being flung open. The click of heels on the floor told me a woman had entered.

"Well, Father, I heard you'd returned from Florence," Kat said. "Tessa has informed me that it wasn't the pleasant holiday you'd led me to believe. Am I correct to understand that your wife allowed someone to be murdered in my bed?"

Eavesdropping might not be an honorable practice, but I was not about to make my presence known.

ACKNOWLEDGMENTS

Myriad thanks to . . .

Charles Spicer, my editor, a constant joy to work with.

My wonderful team at Minotaur: Sarah Grill, Andy Martin, Sarah Melnyk, Danielle Prielipp, David Rostein, and David Stanford Burr.

Anne Hawkins, Tom Robinson, and Annie Kronenberg: nobody does it better.

My brilliant son, Alexander Tyska, for his extensive knowledge of Lucretius.

Brett Battles, Rob Browne, Bill Cameron, Christina Chen, Jon Clinch, Jamie Freveletti, Chris Gortner, Jane Grant, Nick Hawkins, Robert Hicks, Elizabeth Letts, Lara Matthys, Carrie Medders, Robbie Milonas, Erica Ruth Neubauer, Missy Rightley, Renee Rosen, and Lauren Willig. Love you all.

My wonderful friends and neighbors at Fish Creek Ranch, who have been tirelessly supportive: Bill and Linda Biles, Bill and Claudia Cordes, John and Susie Davis, Rob Mason, Mike Parrie, and Larry and Carol Wiles.

My lovely stepdaughters Katie and Jess. Special thanks to Katie for teaching me what it feels like to feed a giraffe.

My parents.

Andrew, my everything.

AUTHOR'S NOTE

Immersing myself in the rich culture and history of Florence while writing this book was an absolute delight. I love learning how cities have changed over the centuries. Mina might have shopped in the Mercato Vecchio, site of the old Roman forum, but in Emily's day the space had become the Piazza Vittorio Emanuele II. Today, it's the Piazza della Repubblica. It's hard to imagine the city without the Uffizi Galleries, but they weren't constructed until the sixteenth century and never a part of Lorenzo de' Medici's Florence. It would have been at the top of Emily's list of places to visit; but in her time, Botticelli's *Primavera* was not yet housed in the museum. The famous statue of Dante that now stands on the steps of the church at Santa Croce was originally in the center of the piazza, where Emily sees it.

Agnolo bringing his illegitimate daughter into his household was inspired by Cosimo I, who did just that with his own daughter after his mistress died.

Women in Renaissance Florence did not take their husbands' names, which is why Mina and her compatriots retain their own surnames throughout the book.

The significance of the manuscripts found by Renaissance book hunters is profound. I highly recommend that all book lovers read Stephen Greenblatt's magnificent *The Swerve: How the World Became Modern* to learn more about these extraordinary men.

Emily finds Lena's body in a hidden room in the Medici Chapel. The room does exist but was not discovered until 1975, when Paolo Dal Poggetto, then director of the museum, moved a wardrobe and found a trapdoor. The walls are covered with 180 sketches, 97 of which are thought to be the work of Michelangelo. Dal Poggetto speculates that the artist may have spent two months hiding in the space when the Florentine Republic fell in 1530 and was under threat of attack by papal forces.

Signore Bastieri's shop is based on one of my favorites in Florence, Cuoiofficine. It's run by two brothers, Timothy and Tommaso Sabatini, who apply the seventeenth-century art of marbling paper to perfectly tanned Tuscan leather. Their work is exquisite (as you can see if you visit either the store or their website).

Emily's story is set in 1903, when relations between Great Britain and Germany were already on the decline that would lead to World War I. The British public was being bombarded by stories of possible invasion and German spies hiding in the countryside. In January 1900, the *Daily Mail* claimed that "Every German officer has his own little bit of England marked off." Books and stories like those written by William Le Queux fueled what became known as spy fever. Although after the war it became clear there had been virtually no spies in Britain—and certainly no effective ones—the paranoia of the prewar years catalyzed the formation of intelligence services in both countries. One of the great triumphs of the period was that Britain developed its famous dreadnought battleship without the Germans so much as suspecting what their enemy was doing. Berlin, already too aware of Britain's naval superiority, was taken completely by surprise when its enemy launched the dreadnought in 1906, rendering every other battleship in the world obsolete. During the development of the design, Colin and his colleagues would not have wanted to see the plans fall into German hands.

Darius Benton-Smith is loosely based on Kim Philby, arguably the greatest spy in history. Most secret agents are motivated by money, but Philby was a firm ideologue, believing from his days at Oxford that communism would benefit the British people. His astonishing story is brilliantly told in Ben Macintyre's *A Spy Among Friends: Kim Philby and the Great Betrayal.* Finally, Colin's superior, Sir John Burman, is named in honor of John Mortensen Burman, longtime supporter of the Albany County Library in Laramie, Wyoming. He is missed by friends, family, and colleagues every single day.

BIBLIOGRAPHY

Ajmar, Marta, Flora Dennis, and Elizabeth Miller. *At Home in Renaissance Italy.* London: V&A Publications, 2006.

Albala, Ken. *The Banquet: Dining in the Great Courts of Late Renaissance Europe.* 2007. Reprint, Chicago: University of Illinois Press, 2017.

Alighieri, Dante. *The Divine Comedy of Dante Alighieri.* Translated by John D. Sinclair. 1939. Rev. ed., New York: Oxford University Press, 1961.

Bracciolini, Poggio, and Nicolaus de Niccolis. *Two Renaissance Book Hunters: The Letters of Poggius Bracciolini to Nicolaus de Niccolis.* Translated with notes by Phyllis Walter Goodhart Gordan. New York: Columbia University Press, 1974.

Brown, Alison. *The Return of Lucretius to Renaissance Florence.* Cambridge, MA: Harvard University Press, 2010.

Cavini, Daniela. *Behind the Medici Men: The Ladies.* Firenze: Mauro Pagliai, 2018.

Crum, Roger J., and John T. Paoletti, eds. *Renaissance Florence: A Social History.* New York: Cambridge University Press, 2006.

Cutts, Simon. *The Translated Latrine Inscriptions of the Palazzo Davanzati.* Clonmel, Ireland: Coracle Books, 2015.

French, David. "Spy Fever in Britain, 1900–1915." *Historical Journal* 21, no. 2 (June 1978): 355–70, www.jstor.org/stable/2638264; accessed July 17, 2019.

Gaston, Robert W., and Louis A. Waldman, eds. *San Lorenzo: A Florentine Church*. Cambridge, MA: Harvard University Press, 2017.

Gavitt, Philip. *Charity and Children in Renaissance Florence: The Ospedale degli Innocenti, 1410–1536*. Ann Arbor: University of Michigan Press, 1990.

Greenblatt, Stephen. *The Swerve: How the World Became Modern*. New York: W. W. Norton, 2011.

Hibbert, Christopher. *Florence: The Biography of a City*. New York: W. W. Norton, 1993.

Hollingsworth, Mary. *The Family Medici: The Hidden History of the Medici Dynasty*. New York: Pegasus Books, 2018.

Klapisch-Zuber, Christiane. *Women, Family, and Ritual in Renaissance Italy*. Translated by Lydia G. Cochrane. Chicago: University of Chicago Press, 1985.

Lee, Alexander. *The Ugly Renaissance: Sex, Greed, Violence and Depravity in an Age of Beauty*. 2013. Reprint, New York: Doubleday Anchor, 2015.

Levy, Allison. *House of Secrets: The Many Lives of a Florentine Palazzo*. London: I. B. Tauris, 2019.

Lewis, R. W. B. *The City of Florence: Historical Vistas and Personal Sightings*. New York: Farrar, Straus and Giroux, 1995.

Lucas-Dubreton, J. *Daily Life in Florence in the Time of the Medici*. New York: Macmillan, 1961.

Lucretius. *On the Nature of Things*. Translated by W. H. D. Rouse, revised by Martin F. Smith. 1924. Rev. ed., Cambridge, MA: Harvard University Press, 1992.

Macintyre, Ben. *A Spy Among Friends: Kim Philby and the Great Betrayal*. 2014. Reprint, New York: Broadway Books, 2015.

Philby, Kim. *My Silent War: The Autobiography of a Spy*. 1968. Reprint, New York: Modern Library, 2002.

Pisani, Rosanna Caterina Proto. *Palazzo Davanzati: A House of Medieval Florence*. Edited by Maria Grazia Vaccari. Firenze; Milano: Giunti, 2011.

Servadio, Gaia. *Renaissance Woman*. London: I. B. Tauris, 2016.

Stafford, David A. T. "Spies and Gentlemen: The Birth of the British Spy Novel, 1893–1914." *Victorian Studies* 24, no. 4 (Summer 1981): 489–509, www.jstor.org/stable/3827226, accessed July 17, 2019.

Staikos, Konstantinos. *The Great Libraries: From Antiquity to the Renaissance*. New Castle, DE: Oak Knoll Press; London: British Library, 2000.

Staley, John Edgcumbe. *The Guilds of Florence*. London: Methuen, 1906.

Stapleford, Richard, ed. and trans. *Lorenzo de' Medici at Home: The Inventory of the Palazzo Medici in 1492*. University Park: Pennsylvania State University Press, 2013.

Strathern, Paul. *The Medici: Godfathers of the Renaissance*. London: Jonathan Cape, 2003.

———. *The Medici: Power, Money, and Ambition in the Italian Renaissance*. 2016. Reprint, New York: Pegasus Books, 2017.

Todorow, Maria Fossi, ed. *Palazzo Davanzati*. Firenze: Becocci, 1979.

Trexler, Richard C. *Public Life in Renaissance Florence*. 1980. Reprint, Ithaca, NY: Cornell University Press, 1996.

Welch, Evelyn S. *Art and Society in Italy: 1350–1500*. New York: Oxford University Press, 1997.

Witthoft, Brucia. "Marriage Rituals and Marriage Chests in Quattrocento Florence." *Artibus et Historiae* 3, no. 5 (1982): 43–59, www.jstor.org/stable/1483143; accessed October 10, 2019.